KISSES, FAMILY & HOPE

A SMALL TOWN LATER-IN-LIFE MYSTERY ROMANCE

HOPE & HEARTS FROM SWAN HARBOR
BOOK 4

SOPHIE BARTOW

CONTENTS

The book is dedicated to ...
My street team;
The Wall-Giennie Wicks-Delaney,
Connector Inspector- Linda Hagerty
Reactor Inspector-Jami Fenton
Plot Catcher- Barbara Berry
Sign Crew- Kate Semenyuk

The Clean-up crew: Cindy, Laura, Kim, Maggie, and Sylvia, whose feedback was valuable.
And my family, who are still waiting for me to clean the house.

Two Hearts Press
An imprint of LLIPSS, INC.
Copyright © 2020 by Sophie Bartow

Regular Print Hardback: 978-1-965510-24-7
Regular Paperback: ISBN: 978-1-965510-07-0
Large Print Paperback: 978-1-965510-10-0
Large Print Hardback: 978-1-965510-11-7

Cover Design by Kate Semenyuk

*Inspiration began
when a lost girl fell for a lost boy.*

Without hope there would be no happy endings.

FROM DARKNESS INTO LOVE

KITTENS, PUPPIES & LOVE

BROTHERS, HOPE & HEARTS

KISSES, FAMILY & HOPE

A TREE, MISTLETOE & A SUNSET

HOPE, HEARTS & FOREVER

THE MEMORY OF LOVE

THE INNOCENCE OF LOVE

THE FORGIVENESS OF LOVE

THE POWER OF LOVE

THE CHRISTMAS LOVE SONG

THE KISS OF LOVE

THE LESSONS OF LOVE

THE HEART OF LOVE

THE JOURNEY TO LOVE

Bonus Hope & Hearts

CYGNETS & DREAMS

Hope & Hearts Historical Novellas

GUIDED BY LIGHT - 1952

GUIDED BY HEART - 1964

GUIDED BY LOVE - 1969

WELCOME TO SWAN HARBOR- 1979

FINDING HER LOST HEART- 1983/1990

GUIDED BY A KISS - 1995

SOME RESIDENTS OF SWAN HARBOR

Sally Miller Patterson: Owner of Sally's Diner, the place to see and be seen in Swan Harbor. Sally is married to **Daniel Patterson.**

Danny Patterson: Married to Sally and the head of neurology at Swan Harbor General Hospital. Their story is told in **Welcome to Swan Harbor**

Hayden Patterson: His parents were killed when he was eleven and he became a ward of Sally and Danny. He is a college student at Swan Harbor University majoring in Computer Science.

Mary Hunter: The Psychiatrist at Swan Harbor General Hospital. Married to **Clint Hunter** and mother to sons, **Cameron** and **Grayson.**

Clint Hunter: Owner of Hunter Construction, (HCI). Married to Mary Hunter.

Grayson Hunter: Engineer at Hunter Construction and married to **Sadie Martin Hunter.** Their story is told in **The Memory of Love.**

Sadie Martin Hunter: The office manager of Swan Harbor Veterinary Hospital and an accountant. Married to **Grayson Hunter**.

Dylan Prince: The Sheriff of Swan Harbor and married to **Molly Barnes Prince**. He is the brother of Jessie and the late James and son of the late Ruth and Robert. Their story is told in **The Innocence of Love.**

Molly Barnes Prince: She teaches first grade at Swan Harbor Elementary School and is married to **Dylan Prince**.

Killian Reade: Investigator for the Swan Harbor Sheriff's Department. Brother to **Liam Reade** and son of **Finley Reade** who lives in New York. Engaged to **Emma Foster**. Their story is told in **Kittens, Puppies & Love**

Emma Foster: The Veterinarian and owner of Swan Harbor Veterinary Hospital. Daughter of **Ava King** and **Peter Foster** and engaged to **Killian Reade**.

Liam Reade: Chief Paramedic and works for the Swan Harbor Fire Department. Engaged to **Elsa Winters**. Their story is told in **Brothers, Hope & Hearts**.

Elsa Winters: She is a pediatrician with a private practice in Swan Harbor. Engaged to **Liam Reade** and is best friends with **Emma Foster.**

Finley Reade: Owns a real estate business in New York City. Father of **Liam** and **Killian**. His story is told in **Kisses, Family & Hope.**

Ava King: Philanthropist and businesswoman for King Industries. Mother of **Emma Foster**.

Rusty Langley: He is an investigator for the Swan Harbor Sheriff's Department and partner of **Killian Reade**. He is married to **Rene Langley.** Their story is told in **The Power of Love**.

Rene Langley: She is the mayor of Swan Harbor, married to **Rusty,** and the mother of **Roland**.

Captain Jack: Retired Naval officer and local legend of Swan Harbor who gives out sage advice to the locals of the town. Owner of Captain Jack's Fine Dining, located at the newly renovated pier in an old Spanish galleon. (The Journey to Love - May 2024)

Welcome to Swan Harbor

A Haven of Hope for Lost Hearts.

ONE

New York City
October 29
4:00 p.m.

AVA KING SMILED AT CONSTANCE HAWKINS, THE WOMAN TO WHOM she'd just handed a two-hundred fifty-thousand-dollar check.

"Congratulations, Connie. Is there anything else you need?"

Connie had been staring at the check with wide eyes, but the question had her glancing up. "N-No," she stuttered, her tears flowing freely. "I-I just don't know what to say."

"You say thank you." Ava pushed down the rush she got every time she was able to help someone's dream come true.

"Thank you," Connie sighed gratefully. "When my husband died, I just never ..."

Ava blinked several times as Connie's story never failed to bring a lump to her throat.

"We all deserve a chance to make our dreams come true," she whispered. "Your last child just graduated from high school, and now it's your turn. Have you always wanted to own your own business?"

Connie's face took on a far-away look. "Frank and I had such plans. He was going to stay with the police force for twenty-five years, and then we wanted to open *Connie's Cupcakes*. But ...."

Her chin quivered, and Ava wanted to reach out and hug her.

"But Frank was killed in a senseless accident a week before he was going to retire."

"That's right," Connie agreed tearfully. "But now, thanks to you, I can open the business in his memory."

"I'm glad I could help." Ava closed Connie's folder and slipped it into the Louis Vuitton shopper's bag she carried in lieu of a briefcase. "If there's nothing else, I'll get out of your way. Be sure and let me know about the grand opening."

"I will, Ava." Connie walked with her to the door. "Thank you, again."

"You're very welcome. Bye now."

Ava stepped from the building onto Seventh Avenue and glanced up. The sky was blue, the temperature was moderate, and she had the rest of the day to do nothing.

It had been nine months since her health scare had sent her on a new journey. One that took her out of her position as the CEO and president of her family's multi-million-dollar corporation. And into a world that allowed her to use the skills she'd developed as a businesswoman and share them with others.

Ava was trying to learn to enjoy life and take it one day at a time. Growing up, she'd felt like Rapunzel. A princess trapped within the walls of a tightly run castle, who'd heard from a young age her dreams didn't matter. What mattered was learning how to behave as a King. Which meant the woman inside had been shoved into a corner, where she'd laid dormant for almost thirty years.

Then, in the blink of an eye, a broken blood vessel had been followed by a miracle drug, and Ava King was given a second chance. Since she'd made peace with her grown daughter, she was trying to create the life she wanted to live.

She wanted balance.

Work.

Family.

Love.

And her very own Flynn Ryder.

There's ...

His name circled ...

Stop!

Ava shut down her thoughts and turned toward Central Park. She'd just crossed 40th Street when that awareness she felt whenever he was near skated across her skin. Her pulse raced and fear had her darting into the doorway of the nearest glass building.

She took a deep breath, working to get her nerves under control, and peered around the wall. The sidewalks were crowded, and she didn't see him anywhere, but she knew he was there. She could *feel* him. He was near. So near, the tiny nerve endings on the surface of her skin came alive. Then his unique smell surrounded her.

"Who are you hiding from?" Finn Reade's low baritone, with the sexy British accent, whispered in her ear.

Her heart stopped, she forgot to breathe, and her mouth dried.

Ava whipped around, but with her back to the glass window she was trapped.

You're a King. She could hear her late father's words.

Stand tall.

Look them in the eye.

Don't let them see you sweat.

"What did you say?" she retorted in her clipped executive voice.

Finn's black eyes glittered, and Ava fought not to get lost in them.

"I said." His voice grew huskier. "Who are you hiding from?"

"Me? No one. Why do you ask?"

"So, it's normal for you to hide in doorways and peer around the wall?" A corner of his mouth ticked up into a sexy grin, and he straightened as if to say, 'Caught you'.

"I wasn't hiding." She fumbled in her pocket for her phone. "I just took a call."

"Right," he responded, tongue-in-cheek.

"Really. Now, if you'll excuse me. I should go. It was nice to see you again."

She moved from the doorway and let the other pedestrians carry her away. With every step, she relinquished a little more of her corporate persona weight.

It seemed heavier every time she had to bring it out. Especially in situations where she was in jeopardy of losing control. Then, it was there ... handy ... comfortable.

"Are you late for an appointment?"

His voice sent a zip up her spine. How had he snuck up on her?

"No," she responded, in what she hoped was a nonchalant manner. "Why do you ask?"

"Good."

He slipped his arm around her waist and led her into Central Park.

Ava wasn't used to people trying to push her around, and side-stepped out of the flow of traffic, then turned fiery eyes on Finn.

"What are you doing?"

FINN CURSED HIS NEED TO PUSH, BUT SHE'D TWISTED HIM IN KNOTS since the first time he'd had the pleasure of looking into her beautiful face.

"Forgive me," he tempered his response, giving her a flirty smile. "You said you don't have an appointment, right?"

The longer she stared at him with those crystal-clear blue eyes of hers, the more he had to work to stand still.

"Right," she finally answered.

"And it's a beautiful day, right?" he tossed another question at her, hoping she'd let down her guard.

"Right."

Finn fought the smile that threatened to break free at the way she stretched out the word. Almost as if she knew all was not as it seemed, but couldn't quite figure out what was going on.

"And you never did buy that apartment in the City, right?"

Ava narrowed her eyes. "Just spit it out, Finn."

"Have you ever been to the Central Park Zoo?" he asked, his heart racing. "Or ridden on the carousel?"

He could swear her eyes lit up, but she quickly dropped her head, and when she glanced back at him, her expression was banked.

"You want to take me to the zoo?"

"Yes."

Ava crammed her hands in her pockets and studied her foot as she slowly toed the ground.

His heart raced, wondering what was going through her head. He made million-dollar deals on a regular basis, but he was more nervous waiting for her to answer.

"Why?" she asked, so softly he almost didn't hear her.

"Why not?" His flippant reply was out before he could call it back. But the gentle arch of her right brow had him amending his answer. "I've always wanted to go."

"You never took Liam and Killian when they were young?"

A corner of his mouth curved at the thought. "No. Claire wasn't a fan of being outdoors." He was quiet for a minute. "How about you? Did you take Emma?"

A sad expression flitted across her face before she quietly admitted, "I missed out on so much when Emma was young."

"And was the zoo one of them?"

Ava nodded, prompting Finn to push, "So will you ... go to the zoo with me?"

The twinkle in her eyes appeared first, and Finn's heart rate slowed.

"Yes," she conceded. "But just the zoo."

"Just the zoo?" he asked innocently. "I should forget the carousel?"

Her grin was impish. "We'll see," she tossed over her shoulder on her way toward the zoo entrance.

As he walked next to her, he kept trying to label what he was feeling. He was happy, but it was so much more. Had he experienced it before? Maybe ... but then again, maybe not.

Once they entered the zoo, Finn found his greatest pleasure wasn't in looking at the animals. It was in watching Ava and the myriad of expressions that crossed her face.

"What are you thinking?" he finally asked as she stared at the brown bears.

A melancholy smile crossed her face. "About the book *Goldilocks and the Three Bears*."

"The children's book?"

"Yes. Most of the time, Emma's nanny, Johanna, read to her before bed. Then one night," her voice took on a dreamy quality, as if what she was saying had brought her great joy. "I was home early, and Johanna was sick."

"So, you read to Emma?"

"Yes. Looking back on it, I realize I didn't appreciate it as much as I should have …"

"Isn't that how many things are in life?" Finn murmured. "Not knowing how precious they are … until they're over?"

"Point," Ava agreed with a sigh.

"And so that night, you read *Goldilocks and the Three Bears* to Emma?" he circled back to his initial question.

"I did," Ava laughed. "I remember thinking she liked the story because she was comparing herself to Goldilocks. But boy, was I surprised."

"By?"

"Emma wanted to make sure I knew the bears used in the story were *Ursus arctos* and not *Ursus americanus.* Then she proceeded to list the similarities and differences between the two."

"*Ursus arctos.*" Finn pointed to a sign with the scientific name written on it. "Grizzly Bear."

"Very good, Mr. Reade," Ava nodded, leading the way toward the seal pool. "Even at the age of four, Emma loved animals, something I never could understand.

"You didn't have animals growing up?"

"My father was allergic. How about you?"

"A stray cat here and there," he remembered with a smile. "Except that was before …" His voice faded, unsure if he was comfortable sharing his past.

"Before?"

Her blue eyes pinned him with a look that made him feel she was pulling things out of his memory he hadn't thought about in years.

"When I was a kid."

His comment succeeded in moving the conversation from places he wasn't ready for it to travel. When she changed the topic, he breathed a sigh of relief and let her ramble. There was something endearing about it, but he couldn't put his finger on why he found it so.

Maybe it was because most of the time, she didn't share with him. They'd been as close as any two people could be, on more than one occasion. Yet, he didn't know how she liked her coffee or if she ate breakfast.

"... Liam and Elsa?" he heard her say, when he tuned back in. But he was helpless with what she'd asked.

"What?"

"You weren't listening to me, were you?" She slanted a side-eyed look at him. "Was I that boring?"

❧

WHAT ARE YOU DOING? AVA SCOLDED HERSELF. *YOU AREN'T supposed to be flirting.*

I was just being friendly.

Sounded like flirting.

The look in Finn's eyes stopped her thoughts. There was a banked fire in them, as if he wanted nothing more than to drag her into the bushes and have his way with her. And damn if that wasn't what ....

Stop!

She slammed the door on those thoughts because they just got her into trouble.

"Never mind," she waved away the question. "It wasn't any big deal. I'd better, ugh ... go. Yes. I'd better go."

Finn grabbed her hand and gave her a lopsided grin. "I'm sorry. You could never be boring."

The warmth of her hand in his short-circuited her brain for a second. "No? You should hear me in a business meeting."

He chuckled. "I was just enjoying watching you. You sparkled."

"Wait a second," she giggled. "I thought you were supposed to be from England. You sound like you kissed the Blarney Stone."

"I only speak the truth." His voice dropped an octave. "You're very beautiful."

Ava had been told she was beautiful many times, and she always blew off the comments with a witty comeback. With Finn, though, she was at a loss. He wasn't supposed to charm her out of her panties so easily.

"I—"

He laid his finger over her lips. "Say thank you."

"Thank you," she forced out through a mouth that felt like cotton. "But I need—"

"To ride the carousel with me." He led her from the zoo and toward the playground.

The entire time she followed, she kept asking herself, *Why?* What was it about him that touched that spot deep inside that had lain dormant for so long?

Was it his looks? He was lean, just under six feet, with dark hair and eyes and sexy dimples in his cheeks. An amazing dresser, and very easy to look at. But it was more. There was something about him that compelled her. Like his pheromones were calling to hers, and when he was near, she wanted.

Except that was not her!

Finn bought them tickets for the ride and led them along the path. "Have you decided which color carousel horse you'd like to ride?"

"I get to choose?"

He grinned. "Sure, but once it stops, and it's our turn, it's every man for himself. If someone else gets it, well ..."

"I do like the white one." She pointed at a large steed on the edge as it passed by them. "That black one is nice too. So is the grey one. I don't know."

As the merry-go-round slid to a stop, Finn cupped her elbow and held on while she stepped onto the platform. "Ava, love, take your pick."

No, you can't ride the carousel, Ava, Leo King snapped. There are too many germs.

Which had been her father's excuse for everything she'd wanted to do. He'd worried she'd end up with pneumonia, just like her mother.

Ava spotted a large white horse to her left and before she could think better, took off toward it. She was an adult and didn't want to run, but that horse was meant to be hers.

"Got it," she laughed, reaching it just ahead of Finn.

"Let me help."

His hands closed around her hips when she placed her foot in the stirrup. He was so close, his heat wrapped around her and she fought the desire to lean back against him.

"I've got it," she told him breathlessly, pushing up and slipping her leg over. "You'd better grab your own horse or you're going to miss out."

"I can't climb on with you?" he teased.

She rolled her eyes and pointed at the horse next to her. "He's waiting for you."

"Bossy."

"You haven't seen anything yet," was out of her mouth before she could stop it.

You're still flirting.

She knew that, but couldn't make herself care.

The carousel sped up, pulling her heart-rate along with it. It was exhilarating, and as the scenery around became a blur, she had the most uncontrollable urge to giggle.

She glanced at Finn, and she could almost swear he was feeling the same things. How was it she was already imagining she could read his mind?

When the ride slowed to a stop, she didn't immediately dismount, hesitant to lose the feeling of euphoria inside.

"Ava?" Finn was waiting next to her horse, sending her a confused look. "Are you alright?"

Their eyes locked and almost against her will, she slipped off the horse and into his arms. That invisible thread pulling her toward him was tightening, and with his full bottom lip within reach, it would be so easy to ....

Then the laughter of a little girl burst the bubble surrounding them.

"That was fun." She forced herself to step back, putting both physical and emotional distance between them. "Thank you."

"You're very welcome."

He held her hand as she stepped off the carousel and led her a few steps away. Ava opened her mouth to say she needed to leave, when he once again waylaid the conversation.

"You were saying you'd like a hot dog with chili and cheese, right?" Finn led her toward the nearest vendor.

Ava's mouth watered and, as if it had been her plan all along, she found herself sitting on a bench eating a messy hot dog.

"Do you make a habit of this?"

"What?"

He took a bite and a piece of chili lay on his lip, waiting for him to lick it off. Ava found she couldn't look away as he chewed and swallowed. His tongue peeked out and swept across his bottom lip, leaving behind a spec.

Don't even think ....

But she was too far gone, and as soon as he'd swallowed, she wiped her thumb across his mouth.

"Chili?" Ava held her thumb up for his inspection before sticking it in her mouth to lick off the spice. Finn's eyes flared, and a ruddy hue appeared on his high cheekbones.

"I'm not usually such a messy eater."

"Good thing I was here then, wasn't it?"

"A very good thing," he agreed huskily.

She finished her hot dog and stood to toss the wrap in the trash, and yet again—he hijacked her plans.

"A carriage ride?" Ava sent him a pointed look. "You're doing this on purpose, aren't you?"

Instead of frightening her, his sexy smile sent a chill of anticipation up her spine.

"Doing what?" he dimpled. "Showing you a good time?"

She was prevented from saying anything until they were in the carriage, and on their way around the park.

"What makes you think I'm having a good time?" she tossed out, instead of directing him back to her original question.

Finn grinned, and Ava had the strangest desire to run her finger along the deep groove in his cheeks.

"I told you earlier," he murmured softly. "You're sparkling."

She leaned back in the carriage and fought the grin that threatened.

"It's probably just sweat."

"Hardly."

Finn straightened in the seat, aligning his thigh with hers. Her quick intake of air assured him she was affected by his nearness, but she wasn't willing to jump in with both feet.

"Do you feel like Cinderella?" He indicated their carriage that resembled a pumpkin.

"If you think of me as Cinderella," she gently chided. "You need to bone up on your princesses."

"So, not Cinderella?" He studied her closely. "Snow White?"

The carriage rolled to a stop, and he helped her down, wishing he could convince her to spend more time with him.

"I've always had an affinity for Rapunzel," she admitted when they resumed walking.

"Rapunzel?" He frowned. "Which one was she?"

"The one trapped in the tower until she was rescued." She hesitated, and Finn held his breath, hoping she would continue. "At least that was how I felt as a child. My father was very over-protective."

"And were you the dutiful daughter?"

Ava laughed. "Until I was a teenager, and then I was quite the defiant daughter. And every time I screwed up, dad cleaned up the mess and tucked me back inside."

The little bit of insight was giving him a picture of a young Ava King he'd not expected.

"Did you ever stop running away?"

She slanted a smile in his direction. "It's one reason why I've left the running of King Industries to others. I'm looking for that balance."

The entire time she'd been talking, he'd followed her into her hotel and onto the elevator. He'd waited for her to tell him goodbye, but as they exited the elevator onto her hotel floor, he had hope that maybe some day ....

"What does balance look like?" Finn stepped into her space, forcing her to tip her chin slightly. "Is there room in there for ... us?"

Ava's gaze dropped to his lips before bouncing back to his eyes. "You know how I ..."

"No, love, I don't," he reminded her. "There is something there. You feel it when we're together. It's why we've made love—"

"Had sex," she interrupted.

"No," he pushed a little harder. "If it were just sex, you wouldn't be so scared. What's going on up here?" Finn gently brushed his fingers over her temple. "Why won't you let me in?"

When she relaxed her face against his palm and closed her eyes, he fought the need to touch his lips to hers.

"I won't deny there's something between us," she acknowledged. "But I can't risk it. I've finally got the relationship I've always wanted with Emma. Plus, she's engaged to your son. I can't risk putting both of those in jeopardy."

"But—"

"Thank you for today. Goodnight."

Before he could say more, she opened the door and slipped inside the room.

Finn took a deep breath, pushed away from the wall, and began the walk home. Except his thoughts kept traveling back to Ava's comment about feeling like Rapunzel. She might have broken free of the tower that was King Industries, but the woman was still trapped. He just needed to figure out how to rescue her and show her he was worth the risk.

TWO

New York City
October 30
1:00 a.m.

As the credits began to roll on the modern-day adaptation of Rapunzel, Finn shut down his computer. He'd been curious about Ava comparing herself to the princess, and after watching the movie, he could see some similarities between the two.

Both Rapunzel and Ava had been raised in very rigid situations — their dreams and desires buried. Both longed for a life beyond those walls. The differences between the two came after their rescue. One had surrounded herself with both family and the man who loved her. Whereas the other felt, if she grabbed hold of one, it would jeopardize the other.

What would Ava think if she knew there were also similarities between the Flynn Ryder in the movie and himself? Would she be surprised?

He glanced at the silver coin that was habitually rolling across his knuckles. A memento of just how far he'd come in the last thirty-five years. And just like the man in the movie, Finley Reade had reinvented himself for love ... more than once. But each time he'd thought he was close to having it all, something beyond his control would snatch his happiness.

Somehow, he'd always managed to land on his feet, growing and gaining more than he had the time before. Until Claire. When she'd left him, he'd become a shell of a man, spending most of his time arseholed. Until a recurring dream woke him, giving him the push to change once again.

It had taken him a while to get there, but finally, he was in a good place. He had two grown sons who were set in careers they both loved. His successful real estate business was in the heart of Manhattan. A penthouse apartment on the Upper East Side belonged to him, as did a home in the suburbs.

He'd thought he had everything a man could want. Except he was alone.

For the longest time, it hadn't bothered him. If he'd wanted a date, he could find one. But after meeting Ava, he'd finally realized he was looking for the one to fill the empty space inside.

When he'd met her, it had been under circumstances that, if they'd taken the time to talk, would have been laughable. Because it had happened when his son, Killian, was on a journey to find himself. That journey had been *because* he'd wanted to be worthy of a woman's love. That woman was Emma, Ava's daughter.

The first time they'd met, talking had been the last thing on their minds. Their chemistry had been tangible, and all he'd wanted was to see how she'd look without the royal blue jumpsuit she'd been wearing.

January 1

While Finn waited for his client in the building's lobby on E. 63rd Street, he tried to picture what she looked like. They'd spoken on the phone twice, and both times, she didn't mince words, almost to the point of rudeness. Except there was an underlying something that sparked curiosity.

Was she short or tall? Heavy or thin? Did she have light hair or dark? Was she ...?

"Finley Reade?"

He turned toward the familiar voice, with a ready greeting on his lips. After just one look, everything he wanted to say flew from his head.

Glossy black hair, alabaster skin, and eyes that were so blue they took his breath. 'Perfect', whispered through his mind. She was perfect.

"You are Finley Reade, aren't you?" she repeated impatiently.

Finn gave himself a mental shake. "Forgive me. Yes, I'm Finn Reade. You must be Ava King."

"Tell me about the apartment."

Her no-nonsense, let's get down to business attitude had his lips threatening to break into a smile.

"It's two-bedroom, two bathrooms," he began, leading her toward the elevator for their ride to the fifteenth floor.

She asked questions, each meant to gain the maximum amount of information in the most succinct way possible. So much so that by the time they'd stepped off the elevator, he had a good appreciation for her mind and not just her looks.

Ava King moved with purpose, but her movements were graceful. Her scent was spicy, with a hint of mystery. And when she talked, he had a hard time looking away from her ruby red lips.

He led her through the apartment and with each step, their movements took on a dance-like quality. Circling around each other, waiting, wondering who would make the first move.

A touch here, a brush there, seduction and foreplay working hand in hand.

"It comes furnished, right?"

The way she was running her hand back and forth along the comforter had Finn's body tightening.

"That can be discussed," he murmured, his feet unerringly moving toward her.

"Good," she purred.

HIS DREAMS HAD COME TRUE WHEN SHE'D ENDED UP IN HIS ARMS. And he'd discovered the woman under the designer clothes was just as perfect as he'd imagined. Then hours later when he'd woken, and she'd been gone, he'd felt used, hurt, and annoyed with himself for crossing that line with a client. He'd then spent months unsuccessfully trying to get her out of his mind.

Except fate had stepped in when he'd arrived in Swan Harbor for Killian and Emma's engagement party, and she'd walked back into his life. Even though she'd behaved nothing like the woman he'd met on New Year's Day, the connection between them had been just as strong.

During the party, they'd spent the evening dancing around each other. With their choreography so in sync, each movement had become foreplay for the act to come. The anticipation climbing higher and higher, until they'd returned to the hotel.

He'd given up on her, and opened the balcony doors to enjoy a nightcap when a knock on his hotel room sent his heart racing. When she'd stepped inside and into his arms, it was as if they were long-time lovers and not strangers.

Once again, though, she'd slipped out in the early hours of the morning, leaving his arms empty and his mind confused.

Upon returning to New York, his goal was to get her out of his mind. But fate intervened. She'd swirled around inside his brain, playing havoc with his sleep and concentration. When he saw her at Liam's engagement party, the upper hand had again belonged to her. They'd spent hours between the sheets and when she'd walked out, she'd taken all his rational thoughts.

It had been then he'd met Captain Jack, Swan Harbor's resident eccentric, who'd told him to listen to his heart. Although he was familiar with that concept, he'd always been the one forced to change. If he wanted a future with the lovely Ms. King, would that be necessary again? Or was it possible, this time someone might change for him?

New York City
October 30
8:00 a.m.

AVA ROLLED OVER AND REACHED FOR HER PHONE, ONLY BECAUSE the ringtone told her it was her daughter.

"Hello."

"Mom?" Emma's unusually chipper voice came across the line. "Did I wake you?"

"Yes, but that's okay. I need to get up, anyway."

"Are you feeling okay?"

"I'm fine," Ava hurried to assure her. "Just didn't sleep well." Primarily because Finn Reade had starred in her dreams all night – but that wasn't something Emma needed to know. "Why are you so chipper this early?"

Emma giggled. "An emergency surgery, too much coffee, and sugar from Paula's cinnamon buns. I'll probably crash later."

Which was one thing Ava remembered about Emma's childhood. She'd fill up on sugar and then suddenly crash.

"Not that I mind," Ava decided to ask before Emma got side-tracked telling some animal story, "but did you call for a specific reason?"

"Right." Emma's voice faded, and she could be heard giving instructions to someone before returning. "You're still coming to Swan Harbor tomorrow, right?"

Ava hummed in agreement, her sleep-deprived brain sorting through her schedule. "I have an early afternoon flight. Why?"

"Do you need to a ride from the airport?"

"No. I reserved a car, since I'm staying a few weeks."

"About that," Emma began hesitantly, "why is it you're staying so long?"

"I thought I told you," Ava pulled out her excuse, "I'm going to help Becca with her business proposal."

Which was only partially true. Her daughter didn't have to know the main reason had to do with Peter Foster, Emma's father. She hadn't seen him in thirteen years and knew that he'd changed, but that didn't mean she trusted him not to cause problems.

At one time, she'd been madly in love with him, and thought he was going to be her Flynn Ryder. But, as she'd told Emma, he'd turned out to be the Gothel in her story. And while she'd tried to put that part of her life behind her, the feelings that went along with the memories weren't as easy to forget.

Especially when her instant, all-consuming attraction for Finn Reade reminded her of her blind love for Peter. And that had ended badly.

She'd buried herself in work, and her relationship with Emma had practically disappeared. All that had changed after her health scare. Emma was happy, and they were working on becoming friends as well as mother and daughter. She wouldn't jeopardize that for anything.

"You're sure about that?" Emma asked again. "It has nothing to do with dad coming to Swan Harbor?"

"With Peter coming to Swan Harbor?" Ava echoed, working to twist the language as to not outright lie. "Why would that matter?"

Emma was quiet for several minutes, and Ava knew she was trying to decide if she wanted to pursue the topic. "No reason."

Except there was a tone in her voice that said she was nervous about seeing her father again. And that was the reason Ava had arranged her schedule to spend the holidays in Swan Harbor.

"Besides," Ava reminded Emma, "while you refuse to set a wedding date, Liam and Elsa haven't. And with Patty ..."

Since Elsa's mother had been diagnosed with Alzheimer's, Ava had offered to help plan her wedding. She wasn't sure how it was going to work, but ...

"Very subtle," Emma laughed. "It's nice you offered."

"It will give me practice for yours," Ava muttered tongue-in-cheek.

"Soon," Emma promised.

"Are you sure about that?" Ava asked before thinking about how it would sound.

"Mom! Why would you ask that?"

Ava wanted to bite her tongue, but now that it was out there, she pushed forward.

"You're not getting cold feet because of your father and me, are you?"

Again, Emma was quiet for so long, Ava almost jumped in to apologize.

"Mom," Emma sighed. "I'll admit happily-ever-after wasn't something I ever considered until I fell for Killian. And sometimes, the thought of marriage is terrifying. But then I see how great Dylan and Molly are, or see how Rupert and Lois are even after fifty years, and I want that. Except lately, I've not been thinking of it as a happy ending."

"No? What do you mean?"

"Finn said something about it being a happy beginning. And you know, I kind of like that."

"The first day of the rest of your life," Ava murmured.

"That's exactly what I said," Emma laughed. "I guess I know where Killian's romantic side came from."

"Finn?" Ava barely squeaked out, hoping Emma didn't pick up on the breathless way she'd said his name.

"Yes, Finn." His name hung in the air for a few beats. "Speaking of him, you never told me what he said that made you mad at Elsa's engagement party."

Ava's heart raced at the thought of how she'd felt in his arms as they'd danced. And when he'd started seducing her with his words and voice, she'd wanted ....

"Just a silly misunderstanding," she lied, hoping Emma would drop it. "But I'm looking forward to planning your wedding."

"And what about you, Mom?" Emma moved the conversation away from setting a wedding date. "Have you found your Flynn Ryder yet?"

Who needs a Flynn when they have a Finn?

"My what?"

Emma chuckled, obviously seeing through her. "Who knows? You'll be here for a while. Maybe one of the Swan Harbor men will catch your attention. I know Tate thinks ..."

"Oh, hush," Ava forced out. "I'm perfectly fine without a Flynn Ryder."

"I know that, but Swan Harbor has a way of making you listen to your heart."

"Right," Ava tried to blow off the comment. But thankfully, the man she wanted wasn't going to be in Swan Harbor. If he was, temptation might prove to be too great, and she didn't want anything to jeopardize Emma's happiness.

"Trust me, mom," Emma reiterated. "When your heart speaks, it's best to listen."

"I'll remember that, but don't worry. My heart is safe." Except whether she was assuring her daughter or herself, she didn't know. "I need to get ready. Was there anything else?"

"Actually," Emma hummed, "any chance you could bring me some cannoli from my favorite Italian Bakery? Molly was craving and I sort of ..."

"Bragged about Mike's," Ava guessed.

"Maybe, just a little."

"I'll see what I can do."

"Okay, that's it. See you tomorrow."

"Bye."

After disconnecting the call, Ava couldn't stop the happiness bubbling up inside her. She might not take a chance on her feelings for Finn, but that didn't mean her life wasn't better now than ever before.

What if?

Except she refused to allow those thoughts to form. Right now, Emma was her priority. It wasn't time for her to have it all.

***

New York City
October 30

5:00 p.m.

Finn strolled into his office after his last showing, his thoughts already filtering through everything he needed to go over with Kim before he could leave.

"That's good to hear, Mrs. Connor." Kim rolled her eyes as he shut the door behind him. "Yes. I've written everything down."

"Mail?" Finn mouthed, while the person on the other end was talking.

"On your desk," Kim mouthed back.

He nodded, and after grabbing a cup a coffee, slid into his desk chair, and leaned back. It had been a long day on too little sleep, and now that he'd stopped, the fatigue was catching up with him.

"You look tired." Kim tossed the notes from Mrs. Connor on his desk. "Late night?

"No." Finn forced his eyes open. "Didn't sleep much."

"Anything I can do?"

Finn groaned. "I wish." He waved his hand over the pile of mail on his desk. "There's much to be done before I leave."

Kim studied him, but Finn knew she wouldn't be able to pick up anything in his expression. He was too good at hiding his thoughts.

"If you're sure."

"I am. How's Ross?" he asked, knowing it would get her off topic of why he was tired.

"He's good." The dreamy smile that appeared when she spoke of Ross blossomed on her face. "We're going to the Catskills for the weekend."

"Sounds wonderful," he murmured, thinking how nice it would be if Ava would go away with him. "I'll let Liam know his matchmaking abilities are still spot on."

She laughed. "It took your son long enough to realize how he felt about Elsa. But his matchmaking skills *are* quite good."

"That they are," Finn agreed. He glanced at the pile of messages on his desk. "Let me take care of these, and then I'll let you know what needs to be done while I'm gone."

"Sounds good."

As soon as she'd left, he sorted through his messages and returned a few phone calls. While he was listening to a rundown from Owen, one of his younger agents, he casually sorted the mail on his desk.

A white linen envelope caught his attention, and something about it caused his radar to fire. As soon as he'd gotten rid of Owen, he grabbed a pen and flipped it over to see only his name, but no return address.

"Bloody hell."

Then he stopped, and something had him carefully examining his desk. His computer had been moved, pushed to the left a little more than normal. The cup he kept his pencils and pens in was closer to the edge than it had been. And the pile of folders he'd reviewed earlier in the day had been rearranged.

"Kim!" He rushed into the other room. "Who's been in my office?"

"What?" She looked up from where she'd been typing out a contract. "Someone was in your office?"

"Yes," he snapped impatiently, even knowing he must sound like a nutter. But after the situation with Santora, he'd realized you could never be too careful.

"Uh-uh," she frowned. "Since your meeting with the young realtors this morning, just the cleaning guy."

Finn tilted his head in concentration. "Do they usually come in the early afternoon?"

"N-N-No," she stammered.

"Call and find out who was in today." But when he noticed the stricken look on her face, he softened, "Please."

"Sure, Finn."

While she was making the call, he went back into his office and looked over the entire space.

He was anal about his belongings being where he'd left them. So much so, he could tell the pictures on the bookshelf had been rearranged. A pile of reports had been switched with a pile of flyers, and two of his marketing books had been moved.

"Finn?" Kim stepped into his office and by the look on her face, he knew he wouldn't like what she had to say.

"What did you find out?"

She winced. "Housekeeping said no one's been on our floor yet."

"Bloody hell!"

"Yeah," she agreed. "Do I need to call the police?"

Should he call Killian's old captain? Or Killian?

What if he was wrong, though? What if he was just tired and imagining things had been moved?

Do you really believe that?

"No." He touched Kim's shoulder apologetically. "Nothing was taken that I can tell. Did you see the person you thought was housekeeping?"

"In passing," she told him, "They were coming in as I was leaving for lunch. Male, twenty something."

"And when you didn't recognize them, nothing seemed out of place?"

Kim arched a brow as if to say, *Really*? "Housekeeping changes staff like I change shoes, Finn."

"Right. Alright, thanks." He took a deep breath. "I'm sorry, but I'm just a little jumpy after everything with the man from Killian's past."

While she didn't know the entire story, she'd heard pieces of it from Liam.

"I get that. Let me know if I need to do anything."

"I will."

He sat again and picked up the linen envelope with Finley Reade written on the outside. There was a single piece of paper inside, made of the same linen, and folded a single time. Finn slowly unfolded the paper. In block letters, he read,

WHERE IS IT? WE KNOW YOU HAVE IT.

"What the bloody hell?" He tugged the ever-present silver coin from his pocket and sent it rolling back and forth over his knuckles.

THREE

Swan Harbor Zoo
October 31
1:00 p.m.

Emma sat on the bench in Swan Harbor Zoo's small aviary and watched Jonesy, the white swan she was trying to save. She'd tried to tell Captain Jack avian medicine wasn't her area, but he'd insisted the bird needed her. Except she'd been at a loss for what to do.

Elsa said she thought Jonesy was losing hope, and while Emma had scoffed at the thought of a swan having hope, she hadn't been able to come up with anything else.

Then when September moved into October and the temperatures dropped, and Jonesy didn't leave, she'd begun to worry. That's when she'd reached out for help to an organization that specialized in saving wild birds.

They'd captured Jonesy and moved him to the aviary in the zoo where another mute swan lived. Her hope had been a 'friend' and a special diet would help his demeanor. Except so far, she'd seen little progress.

The door to the aviary bounced shut and when she looked over her shoulder, she had to hold in the groan.

"Captain Jack," she greeted the older man, who seemed to be Jonesy's biggest champion. "What brings you out this way?"

He studied her carefully. "Sadie told me where you were. I was hoping you had good news from those bird doctors."

Emma held up the report she'd been reading. "No answers," she admitted. "Jonesy has no parasites, hasn't been poisoned by chemicals, and all his blood work came back normal."

"So, it is his hope." Captain Jack came forward slowly and sat next to her. "I was afraid of that."

There was a part of Emma that wanted to laugh at the older man's affinity with the swan, but the other side of her felt bad. And even though she couldn't figure out where he was going with his comment, she couldn't stop her question.

"His hope?"

Captain Jack sent her a side-eye look that had her fighting to stay still.

"Think about it." He went back to watching Jonesy. "Swan Harbor was founded over three-hundred-years ago."

"Okay," Emma began hesitantly. "But what does that have to do with Jonesy?"

"What's our motto? Swan Harbor is a haven—"

"—Of hope for lost hearts," Emma finished. "So, you're saying …?"

"Swans are symbols of purity, beauty, grace, and love. Some say when they're around, they help your communication with other people. Some say they're a sign of marital fidelity. And others say they combine the elements of air and water and embody eternal life. And what is the first step to forever?"

"Hope," Emma murmured, struggling to connect all sides of herself.

She was an animal doctor and wanted to believe she could help the sick. However, she was also a woman in love. One who'd changed the way she thought about things since moving to Swan Harbor.

Except, she was a realist, and believing the hope of a town could be connected to a wild bird was … well … ridiculous.

"That's right." He beamed happily, and she knew it was because he thought he'd gotten through to her.

Emma took a deep breath, not wanting to hurt him, but scientifically, it was ….

"Let's say," she offered, striving to maintain a neutral voice, "there's something to what you're saying. How do you return *hope* to a swan?"

He shrugged as if it was no big deal. "We find the key to set us free."

"Okay." Emma stretched out the word, her mind going in multiple directions. "I guess I'd want to know where we look for the key, and what we do in the meantime."

A look of intense concentration crossed his face. "As for where we look for the key, I can't tell you. I've been searching for it since I was a boy. But in the meantime, Swan Harbor needs more hope. It's the only way we'll survive."

Emma's phone buzzed and, with relief, she pulled it from her pocket. "I'm sorry, Captain Jack. While this has been an enlightening conversation, I have an emergency. We'll talk later."

"Okay, dear."

But as she left him behind, she could hear him talking to Jonesy, and the thought, *'Kooky old man'*, floated through her head.

Is it any different from you talking to Millicent, or Trudi, or Nina?

Which was true, so maybe she'd cut him some slack for talking to the bird. As for everything else, well ....

Portland Airport
October 31
2:00 p.m.

AVA STOOD AT THE LOST LUGGAGE COUNTER AND OBSERVED THE young woman who was looking for the missing suitcases. She was around Emma's age, very pregnant, and obviously uncomfortable. And while it wasn't the first time her own unplanned pregnancy had crossed her mind, the feelings this time seemed to be more raw ... closer to the surface than ever. Why was that?

Was it that Peter had reached out to Emma and would visit soon? Or was it because the out-of-control way Finn made her feel reminded her of that time in her life?

"Here's what I found out." The young woman set the claim stubs on the counter and pointed to the notes she'd taken. "Your luggage is on the way to Portland ... Oregon."

"My luggage is on the way to Oregon?" Ava echoed, fighting the annoyance inside. "So now what?"

The young woman winced and rubbed her back. "Once it gets to Portland, they'll re-tag it and ..." Then her voice died and a panicked expression crossed her face.

"Are you okay?" Ava asked, looking around for someone to help.

"My water just broke," the young woman whispered.

"Oh, wow." Ava felt her eyes widen in shock and stepped behind the counter to support the woman's weight. "Is there someone to call?"

"I'll do it," the younger woman panted. "Just help me sit."

Ava guided her to a chair about three feet away, and pushed the phone toward her. "Here," she glanced at the girl's name badge, "Rachel. Tell me what extension to dial."

"2 5 ..." Rachel panted, wrapping her hands around her contracting stomach.

Feels like you're being turned inside out, Ava remembered.

"7 6," Rachel continued once the contraction subsided. "Hello," she began when someone answered. Then another pain hit, and the phone fell out of her hands.

Ava grabbed the receiver just before it clattered to the floor. "Hi, this is Ava King," she introduced herself, taking charge of the situation. "I'm in lost luggage with Rachel, and she's in labor."

"In labor?" the male on the other end repeated. "How can she be in labor? She's not due for another month."

"Excuse me," Ava snapped. "I'll let you ask the infant when it's here. Apparently, she—"

"He," corrected Rachel.

"Apparently, he has other plans."

"Alright," Rachel's supervisor gave a long-suffering sigh, "I'll call medical."

"Gee thanks," Ava murmured when he'd hung up.

"He's a jerk, isn't he?" Rachel grunted.

"That's being nice." Ava squatted in front of her. "What can I do?"

Before she could be given any instructions, Rachel groaned and grabbed her hand. "Tell me it's going to be okay. It's too early."

Ava searched for a way to comfort the young woman. After the debacle with her marriage, she'd pushed away much of her maternal cravings because they hurt too much. And what she allowed herself to remember about that time in her life was minimal.

"When are you due?"

"Two weeks."

"So, the baby is just a little early," Ava began. "Let's think positive and focus on getting you to the hospital."

She heard a commotion and glanced up as two paramedics rushed in.

"Not going to make it," Rachel screamed. "He's coming."

"Stay strong," Ava encouraged, but who was she talking to—the baby, the mother, or herself?

The paramedics lowered the stretcher and helped the expectant mother onto it. But when they lifted it to rush out the door, Rachel wouldn't let go of Ava's hand.

"Come with me, please."

"But ..." Ava began, except one look into Rachel's big eyes, and the word no refused to come out. Instead, she looked to the paramedics for guidance. "Is it okay?"

"Sure, let's go."

As Ava followed the stretcher from the office, she ran into the person she assumed had been on the other end of the phone.

"You're going with her?" he asked, surprise evident on his face.

"I am," Ava retorted, hefting her carry-on bag a little higher on her shoulder. "Call Rachel's emergency contact and tell them what's happening."

He sputtered a few times, but Ava refused to back down and grudgingly he agreed.

"Thank you." She offered her saccharine sweet smile, meant to disarm even the biggest jerk. Then, once she was comfortable, he would follow her directive, she took off after the paramedics.

"Okay, Rachel," Ava said as soon as she'd caught up with the young woman. "He's going to call your family to meet us at the hospital."

Rachel's face contorted as another contraction hit.

"Breathe through the pain," the paramedic at the foot of the stretcher suggested.

Ava wanted to snap and ask him what in the hell he knew about breathing through the pain. Instead, she tried to guide Rachel's breathing. "Deep breath in," she encouraged. "Don't hold your breath, though. It makes it hurt more."

"Don't leave me." Rachel clutched Ava's hand.

"I'm here."

"Thanks," Rachel panted as another contraction hit.

Ava tried to stay close to her head and out of the paramedic's way. "I'll be here as long as you need me. Is the baby's father meeting us at the hospital?"

"No," Rachel murmured. "He wants nothing to do with his son. Besides, he joined the Army, and I don't ..."

"I'm sorry."

Words that sounded so trite even as they fell from her mouth.

"How about your mother, father?"

"My mom will come when she gets off work," Rachel explained.

The ambulance slid to a stop in front of the Emergency Department, and the slamming doors reminded Ava of when she'd been taken to the hospital. Alone and scared. Her father was away on business, and she didn't know where husband had been. She'd never asked him. But the sense of being alone had never been so great as when they'd rushed from one room to another.

The baby's heartbeat is erratic.

We need this baby born now!

When, hours later, after an emergency Cesarean section, they'd laid Emma in her arms, she'd felt an immediate connection.

Why hadn't she walked away from Peter? Why hadn't she told her father she didn't want to work eighty-hours a week?

Remember what you told Emma? You can't go backwards.

She knew that, and most days ... she listened.

The paramedics wheeled Rachel into the Emergency Department, and while they were checking on her, Ava stepped outside to call Emma.

"Hi Ava," Sadie, Emma's office manager, answered. "Emma's in surgery. Can I relay a message?"

"Everything okay?" Ava asked, thinking about the situation in Swan Harbor at the beginning of the year. "Not another..."

"No," Sadie assured her. "A dog ate a hard-plastic action figure, and Emma's working on removing it."

"That happen often?"

"You'd be surprised," Sadie said before disappearing to answer another phone call. Oh, hold on." Then she disappeared to answer another phone call. "Sorry about that. Anyway ....

"Listen, I won't keep you." Ava explained where she was and what happened. "Just let Emma know why I'm not on my way."

"Do you need a ride back to the airport?"

"No, I'll get a cab or an Uber."

"Okay. I'll let Emma know as soon as she gets out of surgery. Tell Rachel congratulations."

"Thanks, Sadie." Then she remembered she was supposed to meet Anita at the bonfire. "Will you do me a favor and let your mom know why I'm running late?"

"No problem."

Ava crammed the phone into her pocket and went searching for Rachel.

Maine Medical Center
October 31
6:00 p.m.

FINN STEPPED INTO THE LOBBY OF THE MAINE MEDICAL CENTER and glanced around to get his bearings. When Killian explained Ava's situation, he'd been only too happy to pick her up, but now that he was close, he had to wonder what she'd think. If he were to call her, would she look for another door out of the hospital hoping to avoid him?

He'd been given limited information. Her cell number, the name of the hospital, and 'Rachel' was having a baby. How was he supposed to find her with that?

Come on, mate. You've a knack for locating things.

The information desk, he decided, stepping around a woman with bright blue hair.

"Finley Reade."

Before he even gave her his attention, he knew the voice.

"Karen Adams." Finn turned his best smile in her direction. "You're quite far from The Lighthouse Inn, aren't you?"

"You know who I am?"

Finn's smile grew. "How can I forget the one responsible for giving me the room with the best view when I'm in Swan Harbor?"

She blushed. "I'm, uh, just doing my job."

"And you do it very well. What brings you this far from home?"

"I just found out I'm a grandma," she beamed.

Family Birthing Center. Could finding Ava really be that easy?

"Wow, congratulations! A lad or a lass?

"A boy." She ran her hand down her hair. "It's why I have a new color."

"That's quite the statement."

"You don't think it's too much, do you?" she asked worriedly.

"No, no." He directed her toward the gift shop. "Let's see what they have for the new mother and baby."

"Oh, you don't have to do that."

"Nonsense. It's my pleasure."

Finn picked out a bouquet of balloons and paid for it and the small blue bear Karen chose. Then he followed her through the line to get visitor's tags, thinking once they were on the right floor, he'd make his excuses and leave.

As they wound their way through the hospital, Finn asked questions meant to keep Karen talking. There was a part of him that felt a slight twinge of regret for using her to get what he needed. It still wasn't enough to force him to come clean.

"Let's see," she murmured. "It looks like this is her room."

Finn winked. "After you," he nodded, already making plans for his escape.

She pushed the door open. "Rachel, honey! Where's that baby?"

Rachel?

Finn stepped into the room behind Karen, already scanning for the woman who made regular appearances in his dreams. He found her sitting in a chair in a corner, holding the new baby. There was a look on her face that was a cross between joy, fatigue, and something he couldn't decipher.

"Hi mom," Rachel, the new mother, greeted Karen. "Come and meet—"

"—Ava King!" Karen squealed.

His eyes met Ava's briefly before hers bounced to Rachel and then Karen. "Would you like to meet Riley?"

"Can I?"

Karen waved in his direction and took the balloon bouquet from him.

"This is Finley Reade," she told her daughter. "Both he and Ava are frequent guests at The Lighthouse Inn."

Finn could see the questions on Rachel's face and jumped to answer them.

"I ran into your mother in the lobby." He sent her his most charming smile. "It was pure luck we were heading to the same place."

"Oh, that was nice." Rachel smiled. "Thank you for the balloons."

"My pleasure. And congratulations."

Karen sent him a measured look. "You never told me you were coming to Rachel's room."

"Didn't I?" Finn frowned. "Could have sworn I mentioned it."

"No, you didn't."

"I'm sorry about that." Finn stepped in to waylay any conversation tracks he didn't need. "I'm here on a rescue mission." His eyes sought Ava's again. "Killian told me where you were."

Ava raised a dark brow. "Killian sent you?"

Well, he'd volunteered as soon as he'd heard. But that was just a technicality.

"Said you still needed to go back to the airport for your luggage and rental car," he responded without really answering the question.

"Luggage!" Ava handed Riley to Karen.

Finn stepped close enough to peek at the babe. "He's beautiful, Rachel. I have two sons myself, and it seems like yesterday they were that size. Enjoy every minute, as they seem to fly by."

"Thank you, again." Rachel turned her attention to Ava.

While the two women were saying goodbye, he waved to Karen, who was cooing to the baby, and stepped into the hallway.

He didn't have to wait long before Ave came out to meet him. The look in her eyes was still there and, just as before, he couldn't decipher it.

"I'd appreciate a ride back to the airport," she retorted in a clipped voice.

Her tone surprised him, to where he snapped back, "By all means," before he could water it down. "Your carriage awaits."

She studied him through squinted eyes for a second before turning on her heels and heading toward the exit.

The entire way to his car, Finn asked himself what else he'd expected. He'd expected her to be annoyed he was there to pick her up, but a part of him had hoped he'd be wrong. That she'd smile and be happy to see him.

"Let me get that for you." He opened the passenger door and waited for her to slip inside.

She was quiet until they were pulling out of the hospital parking lot. "Did you know Rachel was Karen's daughter, or was that a lucky find?"

Finn winced. "What does it matter? Karen got to see her grandson. Rachel got a gift, and you're getting a ride."

"And what do you get, Finn?"

The words whispered over his skin, with goosebumps following in their wake. "I made Rachel smile, met her new son, and now have the pleasure of your company."

"And that's it?" Ava asked suspiciously.

She was looking for something specific, but he wasn't sure exactly what.

"At heart, I'm a simple man," he murmured. "There's nothing more important than family, a smile, kindness, and hope for tomorrow."

That she skipped a response to direct him toward the rental car counter.

"You can just drop me off. I'll be fine."

Finn looked at her as if she'd asked the impossible. "I'm not that big of a ponce. Once I know you have what you need, I'll leave."

"You expect me to believe that?" She blew out her breath. "Never mind. Just park."

"You're welcome," Finn tossed back as he pulled into short-term parking.

FOUR

Portland Airport
October 31
7:00 p.m.

As Ava walked next to Finn toward the airport, she kept hearing his response.

"At heart, I'm a simple man. There's nothing more important than family, a smile, kindness, and hope for tomorrow."

His answer was not unlike the same thoughts she'd had since January. But that didn't fit the man she knew him to be. When she'd decided to purchase an apartment in New York City, she'd done her homework. She knew how much he'd made last year. How much his home in Tarrytown and apartment in the City were worth. Where he shopped, and the specifics of his business. None of those fit the needs of a simple man.

Look in the mirror, Ava. Remember what Emma said to you when you visited her in February?

"We're both good at pretending. Aren't we?"

Maybe just as she brought out her corporate persona when she was unsure about something, he had one as well.

"You didn't tell me you were coming to Swan Harbor," she threw at him, hating the petulance in her voice.

Finn looked taken aback by her statement for just a second, and then his affability kicked in and he smiled. "You didn't ask."

No, she hadn't. Nor had she told him she was coming to Swan Harbor, so she couldn't accuse him of following her, unless ....

"Did you know I was going to be in Swan Harbor?"

He took her arm and pulled into an area away from the flow of traffic. "Are you asking if I followed you?"

"Did you?"

His jaw tightened, and he placed a hand on the wall next to her head, boxing her in. "While I will admit there is something between us, and I want nothing more than for you to give us ... no ... to give me, a chance. I'm not going to chase you like a little puppy begging for attention. So, no, I didn't follow you. Did you follow me?"

He was so close Ava was having a hard time keeping her thoughts organized. His cologne was heady, his lips were near, and she wanted ....

"Follow you?" Ava forced out. "You wish."

Finn took a step backwards. "You're right. I do."

Her heart stuttered because of the way he made her feel. It was the same, yet not the same as when she'd been young and foolish.

"Why?" she whispered. "Why are you going to Swan Harbor again so soon?"

"To spend time with Killian and Liam," he offered. "No ulterior motive."

Did she trust him?

While he'd put a little distance between them when he'd stepped back, he was still close enough to make her head swim. So, while she could say she trusted him with her person, she didn't trust him with her heart.

"Okay," she conceded. "I'm sorry I was so—"

"—Bratty. Snooty. Snotty," Finn offered.

"Bitchy," she corrected. "It's just ..."

His lips twitched. "It's just?"

"Never mind," she waved it off, tired of listening to herself. "I need to go check on my rental car."

"And your luggage?"

"My luggage ended up going to Portland, Oregon. I hope to get it tomorrow," Ava explained. "I'll need to stop and pick up something warmer for the bonfire, though."

"I could loan you a sweater."

There was something about the offer that was tempting. A man had never offered her his shirt. Which was saying something, especially since she'd been married for years.

Yours wasn't a real marriage. Isn't it about time you acknowledged that?

"If you had warmer pants and shoes." She waved at her slacks and heels. "I might take you up on that."

"Can't help you there, I'm afraid."

"I'll figure something out." She stepped to the car rental counter for her turn. "Ava King. I have a reservation."

The person took her driver's license and credit card, then clicked on the computer. But the more his fingers flew across the keys, the more nervous Ava grew. "Is there a problem?"

"It seems someone canceled your reservation, Ms. King," the man told her.

"Canceled?" Ava fought to keep her voice calm. "By whom?

He shrugged. "It doesn't say."

"Okay," she stretched out the two-syllables, and mentally regrouped. "Then just give me whatever you have."

"Well," he hummed, and she knew she wouldn't like what he had to say. "We have nothing right now. But we will have something for you tomorrow."

"Then I'll just check somewhere else."

"There aren't any available," he responded. "There was a convention, and their transportation fell through, so ..."

Finn gently touched her shoulder. "Ava love, I'll bring you back tomorrow."

"I hate—"

"I'm offering," he interrupted. "Besides, you have to come get your luggage, right?"

Their eyes met, and in them she saw nothing that said he was trying to trick her.

"You're sure?"

"Positive." He grinned. "Now hurry. I'm eager to get to the bonfire. I've never had a s'more."

"Me either," she whispered, trying not to stare at his mouth.

Finn's eyes dropped to her lips, and it took every ounce of Ava's strength to turn back and reserve a car for the next day. "You don't mind taking me to pick up a few things for tonight?"

"My pleasure."

"Okay." Her breathless response gave away what she was feeling, but for the next few hours, she was looking forward to her first bonfire.

And spending time with Finn ... she just wasn't ready to acknowledge that.

Swan Harbor Beach
October 31
7:00 p.m.

KILLIAN CARRIED THE ARMFUL OF LOGS ACROSS THE SAND AND dumped them near the circle where they were building the bonfire.

"Why is it you aren't helping cart the wood around?" he asked Liam, who was sitting nearby tuning his guitar.

Liam grinned. "Because they asked me to be the entertainment."

"Bullsh—"

"—hockey," Elsa laughingly substituted. "He volunteered to play with Tyler, Killian. Do you play too?"

"Haven't played in years," Killian admitted.

"It's just like riding a bike," Tyler added. "Do you have an instrument?"

"No."

"But I have one," Emma reminded him. "It was my father's. Plus, you sing in the shower."

He felt the tips of his ears turn red when Liam snickered. "Wanker."

"Tosser." Liam blew him a kiss.

"Knob head."

Rusty strolled up and dropped the wood he'd been carrying. "Quit being a lazy sod and get to work."

Killian wanted to stick his tongue out at his partner, but when Rusty's son came scampering up, he kept quiet. Besides, he'd volunteered to help with the bonfire ... even though he'd never actually built one.

'It couldn't be that hard', he thought as he cleared a circle and tossed logs into the center. After all, he'd built fires in fireplaces.

He'd just balled up several pieces of newspaper when he noticed how quiet it had gotten.

"What?" Killian glanced up to find Dylan and Gray staring at him as if he'd grown two heads.

"What is that?" Dylan pointed at the circle.

"A pile of wood?" Killian looked at the others for support.

"It's a pile of something alright," Dylan retorted. "That's not how to make a bonfire. Weren't you a Boy Scout?"

"Oh dear," Gray laughed. "You're in for it when Dylan pulls out the Boy Scout stories."

"You know I wasn't a bloody Boy Scout," Killian groused. "And what's wrong with my bonfire?"

"It has to breathe." Dylan rearranged the logs, then grabbed a handful of dried grass and some smaller pieces of wood. "You set the stage, and let it fly."

"Carry on then." Killian moved aside and dropped onto the blanket next to Emma. "He shouldn't have bloody asked me to help if he was going to redo it."

Emma kissed him. "You can build a fire for me any time you desire."

"Oh, I can?" He nibbled on her neck and felt her shiver slightly. "How am I doing?"

"How do you think?"

His blue eyes clashed with her green, and in them he saw promises that had him wishing the festivities were over.

"Later."

"And voilà." Dylan presented the fire. "See, earning that Eagle Scout came in handy."

"You earned that Eagle Scout by the skin of your teeth," Gray snickered. "Dylan had a hard time sticking with the oath."

It was as if a shadow crossed over Dylan's face. "You seem to have memory issues, Gray. From where I'm sitting, I believe that was you and James who had difficulty following the Scout's laws."

"True." Gray gave a long-suffering sigh. "James had a knack for leading me astray."

"That he did." Dylan brushed off his hands and stood back, admiring his work. "I even ended up finishing his project."

"Typical," laughed Gray, and then the conversation veered off in other directions.

Killian glanced at Liam, and the confusion in his brother's eyes had him leaning over to whisper, "James was Dylan's twin, and killed in the same accident as his parents."

"Ouch."

"Aye."

But with Dylan's wife pregnant with twin boys, they were planning on remembering James by naming one of the twins after him. *Life comes full circle'*, he couldn't help but think.

As the fire grew larger, so did the number of people surrounding it, sending Killian's awareness into overdrive.

Emma nudged his shoulder. "Stop that."

"Stop what?"

"Surveying the crowd like they're all suspects."

Killian leaned back on his hands, stretched his legs in front of him, and tried to appear relaxed. "Is that better?"

"What do you think?"

He responded with a grunt and went back to studying the cluster of people around the fire.

Sally and several others were setting up a folding table and spreading out crackers, chocolates, and marshmallows. Tyler and Liam were playing soft music, and even Dylan was laughing and having a good time.

But since everything with Santora had happened, Killian couldn't completely let down his guard.

Emma waved, and he immediately sought the group. "Who's that?"

She sent him a sideways look, as if she knew what he was doing. "The group on the right are people from Swan Harbor University. Linda, Sylvia, Phoebe, Harper, Beau, Aiden, and a couple I've not met."

"And the group on the left?"

"Students that help Maggie at her sanctuary."

Killian grunted again, but that tingling on the back of his neck was present. He casually scanned the perimeter around the circle he'd cleared. When his gaze reached the far side of the fire, the feeling grew stronger, but the shadows were too great.

"Doc, can you see who that is?" He nodded toward the shadow. Then it moved, and he realized it was Hayden, Jason, Jared, Peyton, Diane, and a few college aged kids he didn't know.

Emma sent him a disgruntled look, making him wonder if he was being paranoid. "Sorry, Doc."

"We're here, and safe," she reminded him. "Except Finn. Where is he?"

"I'm assuming he's with Ava."

"With my mother?" Emma's brows arched, and she pulled out her phone to send a quick text. "How did he end up with my mother?"

Killian shrugged. "When dad called, I mentioned what happened, and he volunteered to stop by the hospital."

"Well, they're on their way."

"Now, look who's worrying." He sent her a grin.

"It's just ..."

"I know, Doc."

Killian wrapped his arm around her and tugged her close. With her mother coming to town and her father reaching out after thirteen years, the unknown was making her nervous.

"It's going to be alright."

"Will it?"

He tilted up her chin and kissed her. "Aye, Doc. I promise."

Swan Harbor Beach
October 31
9:00 p.m.

Finn sent a sideways look at Ava as they walked down the beach toward the bonfire celebration. It felt as if they'd entered a truce since driving away from the airport. But he was hesitant to say much, worried it would topple the peace.

That's not you.

"You've never had a s'more?" he asked, more for something to say than because he didn't know the answer.

"No," she sighed. "Another one of those things my father didn't want me to do."

"Why?"

She didn't immediately respond, making him wonder if he'd stepped too close to her personal space. When she started talking, he found he not only had to listen to the words but to how she said them.

"My father took over King Industries right after he graduated from college. He was very rigid in his beliefs, and the expectations of what it took to be a King. Unlike his brother." She dimpled, and he was instantly charmed. "But that's a story for another time."

'Will there be other times?'

"My mother, Grace, was just eighteen and working in the offices of King when my father met her."

"So, it was an office romance?"

"Something like that," she chuckled. "They had a whirlwind courtship and a high society wedding."

"It's a lovely story so far."

Ava's lips twisted, and he thought she was going to say something else, but she surprised him and continued her story. "I gather my mother's pregnancy with me wasn't an easy one. Then, when I was eight months old, she ended up with pneumonia and even with the best medical care, there was nothing anyone could do. It left my father with an infant and a corporation to run."

"Did he hire help?"

"He did," Ava conceded. "But dad was a stubborn old fool and didn't trust anyone with my care. And as soon as I could entertain myself, he started taking me to the office."

"That's no place for a child."

Of course, his childhood wasn't much better.

"It wasn't awful." Her voice died, and it was almost as if she was trying to decide what she wanted him to hear. "As a teenager, I pushed my father to the brink a time or two," she continued. "And there were more times than I can count when I disagreed with his decision. As an adult looking back, he did the best he could do."

"Which we never understand until we're parents."

"And sometimes even then it takes a while," she added.

Ava smiled, and he had to fight not to take her into his arms. Her childhood had been almost the opposite of his and yet, something told him, they had more in common than they both knew.

Once again, he wished she would take a chance on him.

"Looks like a big crowd." She turned her attention to the bonfire, and the personal moment was lost.

"Just point me to the s'mores," Finn laughed.

Ava giggled. "Race you."

He watched her scamper off, only to get lost in the group crowded around the bonfire. It struck him that once again he'd seen another side of Ava King. That she'd changed was evident. But what had precipitated the changes? It was a question he was determined to answer during their time in Swan Harbor.

Finn found Liam and Killian standing away from the fire, both with their mouths full. "I was going to ask if you'd waited for me, but I see you didn't."

"Sorry, dad." Liam licked chocolate off his thumb. "I'm part of the entertainment, and we were on a break."

"Which is a worthy excuse. And you?" He waited expectantly for Killian to swallow.

"What can I say?" Killian popped the last bite in his mouth. "I didn't want to miss out."

"Then I'd better go get one of my own."

"Need some help?" Liam asked before he'd gone far.

"Think I can handle it," Finn assured them.

He was looking over the contents of the table when someone shoved a stick toward him. "Need this?"

Finn looked at the object in his hand. About three feet long, made of metal, one end two prongs and the other a plastic handle.

Based on the sticky mess on the prongs, what he used to melt his marshmallows.

Finn glanced at the end of the table nearest to where he was standing, but realized if he wanted some of his own, they were on the opposite end. He'd only gone a few feet when Ava stepped in front of him.

"Looking for these?" She gave him an impish grin and opened her hands to reveal four of the plump puffs of sugar.

"I might be. Are you looking for this," he wiggled his stick, "by any chance?"

"I might be." She tossed his words back at him. "Want to trade?"

He had to bite his tongue to hold in the suggestive comment that begged to fall free. "Alright. Would you like to roast them, or do you trust me?"

"It depends," she tilted her head teasingly, "how do you plan on cooking them?"

Finn looked around for answers, before finally admitting, "How the bloody hell do I know?"

Ava grinned and stuck the marshmallows, two on each prong, and took his hand, leading him toward the fire. "Now hold them in the flames," she instructed. "It won't take long."

He followed her directive, the heat from the flames pushing him back a half step. "I thought you said you haven't had one of these."

"I haven't," she told him, never taking her eyes from the fire. "YouTube."

"Cheater."

Her giggle was once again light and carefree, and he tucked the sound away to remember later.

"Pull it out!" She grabbed his hand and yanked the marshmallows away from the flames.

Again, he had to shove down the suggestive remark. "They're on bloody fire," he exclaimed, blowing on the flames.

"Perfect!" Ava blew across his hand, her hot breath mingling with his.

Finn's eyes met hers, and he had to fight the pull. "Crispy on the outside is perfect?"

"And gooey in the center," she quipped.

He didn't say anything but stood by and watched as she constructed their s'mores. "Aren't they beautiful?"

The fire brought a flush to her cheeks and caused her eyes to sparkle, and he had to agree. "Just beautiful."

She rolled her eyes and, handing him one of the concoctions, took a large bite of hers. Her moan of delight had his jeans tightening, and he had to look away and hand off the marshmallow roasting device to settle down.

"You'd better hurry and eat yours," she teased. "I might steal it."

"You wouldn't," he narrowed his eyes in challenge and took a bite.

"Don't tempt me."

Which was exactly what he wanted to do, he thought. But, just as when they were at the zoo, he found he enjoyed watching her. She dug into her s'more, and when the last bit disappeared behind her red lips, all that was left was a smudge of chocolate.

"You forgot something." He wiped his thumb across her lip as she'd wiped off his chili mess at Central Park and sucked it into his mouth.

"I was going to lick that off."

"You were too slow."

"Too slow?" she purred, but there was pure devil in her eyes. "Maybe for that bite. But ..." Before he could anticipate what she was going to do, she snatched his last piece and dropped it into her mouth.

"Now who's being unfair?" He took a step closer and invaded her space. "That was mine."

"What are you going to do about it?"

Finn's gaze pinged around them and, while no one was watching, he didn't think Ava was ready for what he had in mind.

"You know what I want to do," he whispered. "For now, though, I should cool off. Thank you for the s'more's lesson." As quickly as he could, he faded into the crowd, and found a grouping of boulders to hide behind for a brief respite.

Face it, mate. She's going to think you're a nutter for walking off like that.

He'd make it up to her, he decided. But the temptation had been too great.

The wind blew the cobwebs from his head, and he'd decided to return the way he'd come when he heard a shoe scrape on the rocks.

Had she followed him?

Finn positioned himself, and when the person stepped around the corner, he swung her into his arms and murmured, "You felt it too?" before swooping in for a kiss.

His lips had barely touched down when he realized it wasn't the mouth he wanted under his. He heard a gasp and lifted his head, meeting Ava's shocked eyes. Before he could say anything, she'd turned and run away.

FIVE

Lighthouse Inn
November 1
7:00 a.m.

AVA ROLLED OVER AND GLANCED AT THE CLOCK, KNOWING SHE wouldn't get any more sleep. Damn the man, she thought, for being so charming and then disappearing to make out with another woman.

Are you sure that's what was going on?

That's a stupid question, she tried to tell herself. A kiss is a kiss.

Are you sure about that?

It was just like all those times with Peter.

Is it really?

Why would you ask that?

Think about it.

Except she wasn't willing to delve too far into that relationship. She'd shoved the memories and the feelings so far down inside they didn't affect her any longer.

Dealing with them is one thing. Just don't lie to yourself.

With a huff, Ava tossed the blanket aside and slipped out of bed. It was obvious she wasn't getting anything done until her brain had made peace with the thoughts swarming around inside.

You could have talked to Finn.

When?

Well, duh. Where were you when he knocked on your door?

She'd been hiding in the shower, but that was beside the point.

Chicken.

Unfortunately, she agreed. She was willing to face a hostile room of stockholders, but the thought of dealing with feelings terrified her.

Without second guessing her decision, Ava pulled on her clothes from the previous night and stepped outside.

Since she would be in town longer than usual, she'd opted to stay in one of The Lighthouse Inn's cottages. The little house was perched on a slight incline from the main building, and looked out over the Atlantic Ocean. And, with large windows lining two sides, she had a beautiful view of the beach.

As she walked, her thoughts were a mash-up of the times she'd spent with Finn. The way he talked, the look in his eyes, and the way he made her feel. That was what scared her. Out of control, as if the only thing that mattered was being with him, kissing him, loving him.

But she'd felt the same things with Peter, and look ....

Stop! You were twenty-two when you fell for Peter. You're a fifty-year-old successful woman. Aren't you in control of your future?

Was she?

Ava moved farther away from the water and sank onto the hard sand. The longer she sat and listened to the rhythmic back and forth of the waves, the freer she felt. With her negative thoughts being pulled away, it left her with the optimism she'd chosen to focus on since January.

The barking of a black and white dog as he chased birds along the water's edge shattered the morning quiet.

"Good morning, Ava." The dog's owner, an older man she'd seen but never met, greeted her. "Are we disturbing you?"

Ava smiled. That he knew her name wasn't completely surprising. "You're fine."

He studied her for a second, and Ava had the strangest feeling he was trying to decide something. "May I?" He indicated a spot next to her.

"Sure," she told him. "You have me at a disadvantage, I'm afraid. I don't believe I heard your name."

"Folks call me Captain Jack." He grinned, and she instantly felt a connection. "It stuck after my years in the Navy."

"It's a pleasure to meet you, Captain Jack." Ava went back to watching the dog. "Who's your friend?"

"That's Bandit. He loves to run on the beach."

"He definitely looks like he's having fun," she murmured.

"What brings you down here this early?"

Ava glanced at him, a bit surprised by his directness. "Couldn't sleep, and thought perhaps a walk would clear my head."

"The ocean has a way of doing that." He hesitated before continuing, "I've done my share of staring at it through the years. Hoping it would take away the pain, calm my anxiousness, or give me peace."

"Did it always work?"

"It did," he inclined his head, "and it didn't."

She laughed. "I'm not sure how to respond to that."

"Isn't that how life is sometimes?" he went on. "You say one thing, but later wish you would have said something else? Or you see something and think it's one thing, but later you learn, it wasn't."

Ava arched a brow, thinking he was talking about something specific. "I get the feeling you're going somewhere with that statement," she pushed him in her own direct way.

He pulled out a pipe. "Do you mind?"

She shook her head, and after lighting it, puffed on it a few times. "During my San Diego assignment, I met Edythe, fell in love with her, and proposed. We had the biggest plans, but then ..."

His words faded and a sense of melancholy washed over Ava at the pain she could hear in his voice.

"What happened?"

"I saw her in a clench with another man and allowed my mouth to get away from me," he admitted.

Except it wasn't disgust she heard in the words, but sorrow.

"When I calmed down," he went on. "I learned it wasn't her hugging someone else, it was *him* hugging her. An earlier encounter with the fairer sex skewed how I viewed the situation."

The words swirled around in Ava's head, but she refused to allow them to settle. "Did you work things out?"

"That time. Communication is the key." Then he stood and whistled for Bandit. "Listen to your heart, Ava. It's trying to tell you something."

She started to ask how he could know that, but Captain Jack looked over her shoulder and nodded a greeting. "Good morning, Finn. I see you changed your mind about moving to Swan Harbor."

Ava's breath caught, and she slowly turned her head to meet Finn's dark eyes.

"Now, Captain Jack," Finn lightly admonished. "I'm not moving here, just spending time with my boys for the holidays."

"Good, good," Captain Jack murmured, almost to himself. "We need the hope." He turned his gaze back to Ava. "Thank you for the company this morning. Remember the key." Then, with a wink, he was gone.

She waited until the Captain and his dog had walked away before taking a deep breath and looking back at Finn. The way he was staring at her made her think he was waiting to see what she was going to do.

But as Captain Jack's words coalesced in her head, she had to wonder if there was some truth in them. Good communication skills were imperative in business, and had helped her develop her relationship with Emma. If she used them with Finn, what then?

"You're up early."

"I could say the same to you."

"Touché."

"Can I sit?"

Ava's heart raced and even though the cold was seeping around the edges of her warm clothes, her palms began to sweat. She opened her mouth to say something flip and instead, only one word fell from her lips, "Yes."

Finn sat on the cool sand and brushed his hands off on his jeans. "What did Captain Jack have to say? I always feel I'm being given a riddle when I talk to him."

"That sounds about right," she agreed. "He was telling me a story of a scene not appearing as it looked."

Finn ducked his head, his lips threatening to curve as he'd bet money Captain Jack had known exactly what he was saying. "Did you tell him?"

"No, but somehow I think he knew."

"Wouldn't surprise me," Finn responded quietly and then jumped in with what he'd tried to explain the night before. "What you saw wasn't exactly what it looked like."

"It wasn't?"

"No. I tried to explain last night."

"I wasn't ready to hear."

"Are you now?"

"Yes."

There was nervousness in her voice. But the only reason he could come up with for her to be nervous was if his explanation mattered. "You know what I wanted to do when you asked that question after stealing my s'more, right?"

"I, I think so."

Finn arched a brow. "Know this. I wanted to haul you into my arms and kiss you senseless."

A gentle blush crawled across her high cheekbones. "That's what I thought."

"I escaped behind those rocks to keep from embarrassing you," he admitted. "Bloody hell ... from embarrassing our kids. I was just getting ready to return when I heard someone coming."

"You thought it was me?"

"I thought it was you," he agreed. "I'd hoped you wanted that too. Bloody hell, I don't even know that woman."

"You don't?"

"No!" He shook his head. "Knew it wasn't you the minute my mouth met hers. Your lips are softer."

She smiled and something inside him relaxed, making it easier to breathe.

"I'm sorry."

Her apology surprised, but pleased him, as he hadn't expected it. "Why, Ava?"

She sighed, and it seemed as if an internal dialogue went on for several minutes before she replied, "What do you know about Emma's father?"

"His name is Peter Foster. He's coming to visit soon, and Emma is nervous. Why?"

"You haven't asked Killian for more than that?"

"I thought about it," Finn acknowledged. "Then I decided, one ... I wasn't comfortable sounding like a gossip and, two ... it was your story to tell. Why? Have you asked Emma about my marriage?"

The blush once again dotted her cheeks. "I'll admit," she replied primly. "I wanted to, but other than asking a question or two, I bit my tongue."

His heart flipped at the endearing look on her face, and he felt like a schoolboy instead of a man in his fifties. "Ask me, Ava. Whatever you want to know, I'll answer it."

Her lips twitched. "You really don't know the woman you were kissing?"

Finn chuckled, as that certainly wasn't the question he'd expected. "I really don't. Do you?"

"Her name is Heidi," Ava laughed. "She's friends with Becca."

"I'll apologize to Heidi the next time I see her," he muttered. "I normally don't kiss someone before introducing myself."

Ava rolled her eyes, making him relax even more. "Emma's father, Peter Foster, was an actor when I met him." She gave him a self-deprecating grin. "When I look back on that time, I'm embarrassed by my behavior. But let's say that I was young and naïve and imagined a happy ending with my Prince."

"He was the Gothel in your story," Finn murmured.

Her eyes twinkled. "How did you go from not knowing who Rapunzel was a few days ago to suddenly knowing the name of the villain?"

"Umm, well," he stuttered, trying to come up with what to say.

"Yes?"

"After I left you in your hotel the other night, I watched it."

"Really?"

"Is that so surprising?"

"More than you can imagine."

Ava glanced at him, and he had to fight not to get lost in her blue eyes. "I'm going to infer Peter did something when you were married that caused your reaction last night."

"That's right."

Her voice was so close he had to lean close to hear what she was saying.

"When my father found out I was pregnant," she revealed. "He was so angry, I was afraid he was going to have a heart attack. Instead of turning the anger toward me, though, he ruined Peter's career and blackmailed him into marrying me."

Finn winced, finding that wrong on so many counts. Somehow, he could understand the anger of the father and the embarrassment of the child.

"I gather Peter didn't take that too kindly."

"Hardly," Ava scoffed. "Took great delight in rubbing my face in the many women he had." She was quiet for several seconds before continuing, "I no longer believed he was part of my happy ending, but I'd never been so embarrassed and hurt in my life. Those weren't feelings I knew how to handle."

"Why didn't you tell your father you didn't want to be married?"

She looked at him as if he'd just suggested the impossible. "You'd have to know Leo King to understand," she explained. "I had Emma and became a damn good corporate CEO. And I try not to look back."

"But as my sons and I have learned," he noted. "Sometimes it's necessary to look back before we can move forward."

She shivered, and a quick glance at his watch told him they'd been sitting in the sand for a couple of hours. Finn pulled off his jacket and draped it over her shoulders. "Are you ready to start back?"

"Yes, thank you."

He stood and took her hand, pulling her up and into his arms. Ava's eyes flared, and he held his breath, waiting to see if she would back away.

The wind kicked up the ends of her dark hair. Her cheeks and the tip of her nose were red from the cold. And her eyes seemed an even brighter blue in the morning light.

Time stopped as they stood there, so close together he could feel the gentle puffs of air as she exhaled. He waited, wanting, hoping she would take the next step.

"Finn," she whispered, her breath blowing across his lips. "I ..."

His heart raced as he waited to see what she was going to say, worried the words would be ones he didn't want to hear. Worried his dream of being the one to rescue her from the tower were just fanciful thoughts that never stood a chance.

"I'm ..."

He bit off the need to rush her and worked to remain patient.

Her eyes dropped before once again locking with his, and he wanted nothing more than to hear ....

I want you.

I need you.

"I'M SCARED."

As soon as the words fell from her mouth, she wanted to call them back, but then she heard her inner voice cheering her on.

You go, girl! You're in charge of your own future.

What was Finn thinking? There were times he was hard to read, but then other times ....

He tightened his arms around her, pulling her closer to his warmth. "Tell me, love. What has you so afraid?"

"I'm afraid of the way I feel around you. I'm afraid of the way you make me feel. I'm afraid of taking a chance. I'm afraid of not taking a chance. I'm afraid of failing. I'm afraid of not trying. I'm afraid something will affect my relationship with Emma. I'm afraid she's not set a wedding date, because she doesn't want to end up like me."

The words spilled from Ava's mouth and once she started, it was like she couldn't find the off switch.

"I'm afraid of dying in the tower alone, because I'm too afraid to take a chance. I'm a mess."

Ava glanced up under her brows, expecting to see a horrified expression on Finn's face. What she saw couldn't have been farther from that. "What are you thinking?"

His expression was so sweet and sexy, her heart melted. And the huskiness in his voice had her tightening her hold on his waist, to keep from sinking back onto the sand.

"Last night, when you shared a little about your past, the thought that perhaps we have more in common than either of us realize crossed my mind."

"We do?"

"We do," he nodded. "I wasn't born with a silver spoon in my mouth. Nor was I brought up to run a large corporation."

"And you're not female," she teased.

He tugged her closer to his hard, male body. "No, I'm not."

"I'm glad."

"Me too, love." Finn licked his lips before continuing, and Ava's knees shook. "But to add to what I was saying, you are not alone with your fears."

His comment took her aback. "You're afraid?"

"Bloody hell, yes."

He kissed her on the tip of her nose, and for a split second, she forgot to breathe.

"I'm afraid something will happen to my relationship with Killian and Liam. I'm afraid I'll disappoint them. I'm afraid I'm always going to be alone." His voice dropped an octave, and he murmured, "And I'm afraid you won't allow me to be your Flynn Ryder."

Ava pushed the urge to scream down. "You want to be my Flynn Ryder?"

"I do." He dropped a quick kiss on her lips. "Will you trust me and give us a chance while we're in Swan Harbor? After all, remember what Captain Jack said."

Her lips curled up before she could stop them. "Captain Jack said a lot of things."

Finn turned them back toward the resort, but left his arm draped around her shoulders. Somehow, it didn't surprise her to see they walked in sync.

"Captain Jack told both of us to listen to our hearts. Does that sound familiar?"

"I'm sure there've been people I've worked with through the years who wondered if I had a heart."

"Really?" He dropped a kiss just below her left earlobe, sending a shiver rushing from the point of contact directly to her core. "You feel pretty warm to me."

Do not invite him back to your room.

Digging into her bucket of willpower, Ava pressed her cheek against his shoulder. "Thank you."

"For what?" He stopped in front of her cottage door.

Ava shrugged off his coat and held it for him to slide into while she organized her thoughts. "Thank you for listening. For not laughing at my fears. For reminding me, I'm not alone in feeling the way I do. And thank you for giving me hope."

"What else are you saying, Ava?"

What was she saying?

You're saying you want to take a chance!

I am?

Heck yes! Build the future you want!

"I'm saying," she took a deep breath and jumped, "have patience. But ..."

Finn tipped up her chin. "Let's keep whatever this is between us until we know what it is."

Her entire body sagged with relief that he wasn't willing to push the issue. "You don't mind?"

"Bloody hell, no," he quipped. "I shudder to think what Killian would say if something happened, and it affected his relationship with Emma."

"Exactly. We're just two friends whose children are getting married."

"Two friends, you say. Then, would it be okay if two friends stopped for breakfast on the way to Portland?"

Ava tilted her head and thought about what he'd asked. "I think that would be okay."

"An hour?"

"Yes, please."

He planted a firm, but hot kiss, on her lips that left them tingling long after she'd shut the door behind him.

SIX

Sally's Diner
November 1
11:00 a.m.

"Wʜᴀᴛ's ᴡʀᴏɴɢ?"

Emma glanced up as Elsa slid across the booth from her at Sally's, but her thoughts were sluggish.

"Did Peter show up early? Is Ava okay?"

The questions bounced around in her head until Emma forced herself to shove each into the proper place.

"Earth to Emma." Elsa snapped her fingers several times. "You're scaring me."

Emma frowned. "Sorry. I just saw something, and I'm trying to make sense of it. I mean, it was ..."

"You saw something? Okay," Elsa leaned forward and crossed her arms on the table. "Was it a person or a thing? Something good or bad?"

"It was my mom," Emma offered, "and Finn."

Elsa shrugged. "So. He's taking her to Portland to get her luggage and a rental car."

"True," Emma nodded, still trying to sort through what she'd seen.

"Were they in here?"

"They were leaving."

"And?"

"I had to run a few errands before meeting you, so I parked down the street. When I rounded the corner, Finn was opening the car door for my mom."

"And that's a problem?" asked Elsa. "Liam opens the door for me. Killian opens the door for you."

"It wasn't that he was opening the door," Emma tried to explain. "But how intimate it appeared. I felt like I was watching a ... well ... a moment."

"A moment?" Elsa frowned, and then as if she finally understood the comment, she grinned. "Oh, I get it now. You caught your mother and Finn in a clench."

"Not a clench." Emma searched for the right words, finally settling on, "It was a ... tender, moment. That's the only word I can think of that fits."

"Ahh," sighed Elsa. "That's uhh, actually kind of sweet."

"It was sweet," Emma agreed. "But it looked so natural. They've only seen each other, what, maybe three times."

"Was the moment one of those you'd expect from a couple who'd been together a while?"

"That's it," Emma nodded.

"Maybe it's because they're older," Elsa suggested. "Maybe those moments just come more naturally."

"Maybe."

"What did he do?"

"He brushed her hair off her face."

Elsa grinned. "You're freaked because he brushed her hair off her face? Boy, I'm glad you didn't see them at the bonfire."

Before she could respond, Hayden set their food on the table. "Let me know if you need anything else." Then he walked away.

"That was weird," Emma murmured.

"He's certainly distracted, isn't he?"

"Something seems to be going on with him," Emma agreed. "Maybe I'll have Killian talk to him. Now, tell me what I missed."

"You missed the sparks Ava and Finn were generating."

"You didn't tell me this."

"Sorry." Elsa grinned. "I discussed it with Liam. He said it explained several things he'd noticed lately."

"But this is my mother!"

"And Finley Reade is a good-looking man," Elsa pointed out. "Plus, he has his own money, so you don't have to worry about that."

"In February, she did say she wanted her own Flynn Ryder."

"Which is quite comical," Elsa laughed, "since Finn's birth name is Flynn."

"Wait, what?"

Elsa took a bite of the fry she was holding and chewed it slowly, her eyes twinkling the entire time.

"Just swallow it," Emma grumbled.

"Liam told me Finn changed his name after they moved to the States. Flynn became Finley, and he even changed the spelling of their last name. In England, it was spelled R E I D E."

"Why?" Emma muttered. "And why am I just now hearing this?"

"Something about Flynn sounding like a peasant. But," Elsa asked the question, Emma had feared. "Would it matter if there was something between them?"

How did it make her feel? Her mother was young and beautiful and deserved to be happy. And if the man who made her happy was Killian's father? Who was she to stand in the way?

"If there's something going on, why hasn't she said anything?"

"Come on, Emma," Elsa scoffed. "When you were working out how you felt about Killian, did you tell her?"

"Well, no. But I thought we were closer now."

"You are," Elsa replied calmly. "Think about it, though. I imagine the older you are, the more complex it is to date because you're carrying around more baggage."

"And dad was a pretty crappy husband," Emma acknowledged.

"As Claire was a wife."

"Add that to the fact I'm engaged to Finn's son."

"And you've not set a wedding date," Elsa added.

"Wait!" Emma held up a hand in protest. "You know that has nothing to do with Killian, and everything to do with my father."

"I know."

Elsa sat there for a second, and the look on her face reminded Emma of the many discussions they'd had over the years. The ones where her friend doled out words of wisdom that had her backing up and rethinking the situation.

"Think about it, Emma," Elsa laid out. "Ava is scared and may be attracted to Finn. But she's dealing with all the baggage left over from Peter. Plus, if whatever is going on with Finn doesn't work, and one or both get hurt—"

"She's afraid Killian and I might take sides."

"Exactly."

Elsa took another bite of her salad, and while she was chewing, Emma could see the wheels spinning in her head.

"Liam thinks we should give them a push," Elsa grinned. "My fiancé's quite the matchmaker."

"Liam?"

Elsa hummed. "He has a good track record, too. But you never answered my original question. Would it matter if there was something between them?"

"Caught that, did you?" Emma winced. "I want my mom to have with a man what I have with Killian. If that's with Finn, I'm okay with that."

"Are you sure?"

"Yes. But, if they got married, she would be my mother-in-law and my mother. And she would be Killian's mother-in-law and stepmother. That sounds like some soap opera storyline."

"Quit looking for problems before they arise," Elsa scolded. "However, isn't Ava's birthday soon?

"It's the 4th. I figured we'd go to Captain Jack's."

"Why not make it a family party?"

A sneaky smile crossed Emma's face. "Then watch to see what happens?"

"Yes."

"What if Killian has issues with this idea?"

"He doesn't." Elsa pushed aside her plate and reached for her notebook. "Killian walked up when Liam was talking about helping them out. If he did, wouldn't he have said something?"

"Maybe," Emma murmured. "Unless he wasn't paying attention to the conversation."

"No." Elsa sat there deep in thought for several seconds. "He agreed with Liam that he thought Finn was lonely."

"But it's a pretty big jump to go from Killian acknowledging Finn is lonely—"

"—To being okay with Ava and Finn dating," Elsa replied.

"Yes."

"What do you know about Claire Reade?"

Emma thought back to the conversations she'd had with Killian about his mother. "Not much. I know when she left, and his father turned to the bottle, it affected how he interacted with females. He became the *'let's see how many notches I can get on my bedpost'* guy."

"And Liam became everyone's friend," Elsa added.

"But they seemed to have all made peace, don't you think?"

"I agree that Liam and Killian have moved on," Elsa continued. "There are times, though, when I can tell Claire's words still linger in the back of Liam's mind."

"So, if Claire's words still cause the sons to question themselves," Emma murmured. "Then what about the father?"

"Yes," Elsa nodded. "He has to have his own baggage."

"Does my mom need someone like that, though?"

"I think at the very least they understand each other, and will take things slowly."

Emma had to admit there was merit in what Elsa was saying. That maybe Finn was just the type of man Ava needed.

"So, we're back to the family party, aren't we?"

Elsa arched a brow. "Ava's your mom. Think she'd like a party?"

"I think she'd enjoy spending time with family."

"Sounds like you have your answer."

Emma grinned. "If this blows up in our faces, I'm blaming Liam."

"I'll tell him you said that," laughed Elsa. "Now ..."

"Wedding talk?"

Lighthouse Inn
November 1
5:00 p.m.

AVA LINED UP HER THREE SUITCASES ON THE BED, FLIPPED THEM open and began unpacking. Shoes in the closet, sweaters on a shelf, lingerie in the drawers. She'd spent so much of her life living out of a suitcase, the doing and undoing had become an art form.

When she heard the door open, a little thrill ran up her spine and the thought, *'Let the fun begin'*, rolled through her mind.

"Ava," Finn's sexy voice made her name sound like a caress. "Where do you want these bags?"

"Just set them on the table." She quickly stacked the suitcases together and shoved them in the closet.

With her unpacking completed, Ava returned to the front room to find the bags of baby paraphernalia waiting for her. She'd just sorted through them when Finn returned.

"You realize we went a bit overboard, right?" He dumped the rest of the items on the table.

"You think?"

Finn picked up one package and peered inside. "Hmm, let's see. Here's a brown bear, a red bear, a dog, a ball, a clown, a—"

"Okay," Ava held up a little blue onesie, "but look at this. It even says, 'I'm cute,'"

"Just adorable," he muttered tongue-in-cheek.

She continued emptying and sorting the bags for several seconds before impishly sticking out her tongue.

"Watch it."

That connection between them sparked. She didn't push him, though. Since their earlier talk, she'd thought about her behavior when it came to men. It hadn't been hard to see she was in danger of making the same mistakes with Finn. If they had a chance of going anywhere, she needed to take a giant step backward.

Except, he'd say something unexpected, such as suggest they stop and check on Rachel and Riley, and her heart would race.

Or do something, such as stop at the toy store and buy everything a new mother could need.

Then, he'd proceed to dance around her, seducing her with little touches, heated looks, and sexy words.

"It was very sweet of you to do all this for someone you've only met once."

He grinned, but there was a hint of shyness behind it. Almost as if he needed someone to assure him what he'd done was worthwhile.

"It was fun." He held aloft an outfit that said New York Giants. "I got the feeling Rachel was just getting by, and now with a new baby ..."

"You picked up on that too, huh?"

"It's a good thing she's going to stay with Karen for a few weeks. Taking care of a newborn on your own isn't easy."

He'd pulled another surprise on her by telling her a little about his wife and how she'd behaved when the boys had been born. Which had been basically to leave the care of a newborn to Finn.

It reminded her of the first few months after she'd brought Emma home. She'd wanted no one helping her in the beginning. Then her father had hired Johanna, who had taken over the infant's care. He'd played it off as giving *'the new mother'* a break. But that had quickly morphed into encouraging she spend time in the office. Which, thinking back, had her realizing she'd never had complete autonomy from her father ... making her wonder ....

Finn took her hand and tugged her into the living room and onto the sofa. "Ava love, didn't you tell me you try not to look backward?"

"Yes."

"Isn't that what you were just doing?"

"How do you know that?"

"Please," he grinned. "You get this expression on your face, and I know you're wishing you could have done something different."

"But I can't ..."

"No, you can't," Finn agreed. "And even if you could, you wouldn't be the same person."

"I know." Ava took a deep breath and prepared to step into the health territory. But worried she would freak out Finn. "Did you ever wonder what happened to me after our encounter in January?"

He barked out a laugh as if her question surprised him. "Once or twice."

She wanted to say only once or twice, but instead tossed it out there, "I ..." Then her throat closed, and she couldn't force out the words.

"Ava," Finn kissed the back of her hand, waking her nerve endings and sending a zip of electricity straight to her heart. "Just spit it out. I'm listening."

"I had a stroke."

There, she'd spit it out.

"You?" His gaze touched her head, nose, mouth, and neck before sliding down to their entwined hands. "But I don't see ..."

And just like when she'd recited the story to Emma, Ava couldn't sit still and stood to wander around the room.

"I was very fortunate in many ways. My stroke was a small one, and I got to the hospital quick enough to get the medication. Otherwise." she shrugged, as if it were no big deal, but couldn't stop the shudder that went through her.

"But everything is alright now?"

"Yes."

"That's why you left King's, isn't it?"

"Yes. When you face your own mortality, it makes you take a long, hard look at your life."

"And now you have an opportunity to create the life you want." He sauntered across the room toward her. "Not the one your father wanted for you."

"I'm working on it."

"What is it you want, love?"

The husky tenor of his voice had her heart feeling as if it were rolling around in her chest. "To be happy."

He cupped her elbows and tugged her against him. "Tell me what makes you happy."

Ava stared into Finn's dark eyes, and the feeling of free-falling had her heart racing. "Hmm, at heart, I'm a simple girl. Family, kindness, a smile, and hope for tomorrow."

"Minx."

His eyes twinkled but something told her he was pleased she'd tossed his words back at him.

"What are your plans for later?"

Ava grinned and stepped from his arms to check the time. "I'm meeting with Anita, Becca, and Maggie at a bar called Swan's Spirits. And you?"

"Are you now? Isn't that a coincidence?" However, before he could finish what he was saying, his phone buzzed.

He glanced at the screen and frowned. "Excuse me."

When his dark eyes met hers, and a hard look passed over his face, Ava was left to wonder who was on the other end. And what had happened to the easy-going man who had been standing in front of her?

"I'm sorry." Finn slipped his phone back into his pocket, but there was a tenseness surrounding him that hadn't been there before. "It seems there's been a break-in at my home in Tarrytown. I need to drive back to New York."

Ava immediately felt the loss. "Did the police catch who it was?"

"No." He took her hand and walked toward the door. "I'll be back as soon as I can."

"Be careful."

"I will."

With little more than a buzz on her forehead, he left. She didn't want to worry, but considering everything that had happened recently, that was a tall order.

Veterinary Clinic
November 1
11:00 p.m.

KILLIAN CLIMBED THE STAIRS TO EMMA'S APARTMENT, REPLAYING the events of the evening in his head. It had been over fifteen years since his mother had walked away from her family and gone back to England. Her absence had affected each of the Reade males differently, and not in an altogether positive way. But each man had finally completed their own journey, and, after many years, they were in a good place.

It had been during Liam's quest they had learned of her death. Except, even with the knowledge of her passing, there was still a part of him that wondered if they could have done anything differently.

While there had been happy times when he'd been a child, as he'd gotten older, it had become more difficult to make Claire happy. Looking back, he realized his mother hadn't allowed herself to embrace the life she'd been offered. Instead, she'd constantly wanted ... more, bigger, richer.

His father had appeased her, but even when he'd made changes in his behavior, her good moods hadn't lasted long. Finn's responses to both of his sons had been the same.

"Claire and I weren't right, but she gave me you."

Why had his father stayed in a situation where he was obviously unhappy? Was it something having to do with Claire? Or was that pure Finn Reade?

Killian walked from the kitchen to the living room to find Emma on the sofa, surrounded by their cats, Millicent, Trudi, and Nina. "I told you not to wait up for me, Doc."

"I know." She studied him for several minutes before continuing. "How was it?"

"It was," he searched for the right word, finally settling on, "cathartic."

"But?"

"Open book?"

Emma nodded, but didn't say anything until he'd sat on the coffee table in front of her. "You still have questions, don't you?"

"Aye." He searched his thoughts but couldn't come up with how to explain what he was thinking in a clear, coherent manner. "It didn't help that my father wasn't there."

"He wasn't?"

"No." The memory of the call still bugged him. "Said he needed to go back to New York but would return in a day or so."

"He didn't tell you why?"

"No." Killian frowned. "Just said he'd call."

"That's good." She tapped the box in his arms and tilted her head with curiosity, "What's this?"

Killian grinned and turned it so she could read the words, '*Killian's Childhood*' written on the side. "Liam found it when he moved everything out of his apartment in New York. I'd forgotten I'd stored it there."

"Memories of your childhood?" Emma sat forward. "Aren't you going to open it?"

"I hadn't planned on it," he told her. "Probably a few rocks, shells, and pictures. Maybe a report card or two. Nothing important."

"Then I'll open it." Emma reached for it.

Killian swung it away from her. "If I share what's in my childhood box, what will I get?"

"What do you want?"

"Well," his gaze touched on her lips, before raising to meet her eyes, "a wedding date?"

"That's it?"

"Aye."

"Okay."

"Wait a minute." Killian squinted at her. "That was too easy."

"Too late." She leaned in and kissed him, taking the box from his arms. "You should have thought about it before tossing out the question."

"Humph."

Emma giggled and ripped into the box, her eyes growing wide as soon as she'd lifted the flap. "What do we have here?"

Killian's heart tripped, wondering if it was a good idea to let her look before he'd double checked there wasn't anything embarrassing inside.

"Maybe I should see what's in there first," he offered.

"Too late."

There was a rustle, as if she'd pushed aside some paper, and then she pulled out an old box.

What's this?"

"I'd forgotten I still had that."

Killian took the box almost reverently and flipped open the lid, revealing a Polaroid photo.

"Is that you?"

"Aye." He handed her the picture in question.

"You're what, seven or eight?"

"Eight, and Liam had just turned ten." Killian pointed to his brother. "We were on holiday at the beach. That was one of the good times we had as a family."

"Your father looks very different." She pinned him with her green gaze, and he found he needed to fight not to squirm. "Why didn't you tell me your dad changed his name after you moved?"

Killian shrugged. "No big deal, I guess."

"New country, new name?"

"Something like that."

There was a part of him that was glad she didn't ask any further questions but went digging some more. Seashells, rocks, sports trading cards, ticket stubs. Items he'd saved to commemorate a moment, and yet years later, looking at the junk, most of it meant nothing. It was just junk.

Emma dove back into the box, this time pulling out a smaller container. "Jewelry?" she asked, shaking it, and hearing the rattling inside.

"Aye," he grinned. "An old chain, my I.D bracelet, and several other pieces."

She took out the silver identification bracelet that had his name spelled out in block lettering. "Did you give this to your flavor of the week?"

"Now, Doc." Killian tilted her chin and kissed her. "You know the answer to that question. You're the only one I've ever gone steady with."

"I know." Emma smirked. "It's just nice to be reminded." She fastened the bracelet around her wrist and moved the chain around to uncover a ring. "This looks old."

Killian took it from the box and held it up to the light. It looked like an old class ring, silver yet tarnished with the head of a lion on it.

"It was my mom's," he told her. "She said it had been in her family for generations." He tossed it back in the box and took out a cross necklace.

"And that?"

"It was my dad's." Killian weighed the cross in his palm. "He gave it to me when I joined the police academy. Told me it would protect me, as it had him for years."

"How did it end up in the box?"

Killian thought back on the day he'd placed it inside. "I left it behind when I was assigned the Santora case."

"Nothing to identify you?"

"Nothing I didn't want stolen," he corrected. "I bought another one I wore, which Weaver used to identify 'Ian Jones'."

"Want me to take these to have them cleaned?"

"Maybe," he shrugged, putting them back where they'd been.

She peered inside the larger box again and looked up with twinkling eyes. "Look here," Emma pulled out a pile of photos, "your prom picture. Do you even remember her name?"

"Candy." He sent her a *'so there'* smile.

Emma rolled her eyes. "Somehow, I knew in your past there was a floozy named Candy."

"Hush. She was a nice girl."

"I'm sure she was." Emma flipped through the pictures. "You know what I notice?"

"How dashing I was as a young lad?"

"No." She giggled, "That you never had more than one picture taken with any girl."

He humphed again, wishing she'd toss the lot of them back in the box.

"Who's this?" Emma shoved a picture under his nose. "She looks quite a bit older than you."

Killian glanced at the photo and felt the tips of his ears heat. "She's a little older," he admitted. "But not much."

"And who is she?"

"Barbi."

Emma frowned. "Barbi … as in Liam's friend?"

"How the bloody hell do you know she's Liam's friend?"

She met his question with raised brows.

"Elsa?"

"Yeah."

"Just drop them back in the box, Doc."

"If I do, what do I get?"

Killian took the pictures and tossed them aside. "Whatever you want."

"Let's start with this." Emma tugged him down onto the sofa with her, and as her lips met his, he settled in to stay awhile.

SEVEN

Tarrytown, NY
November 2
6:00 a.m.

Finn sat in the early morning light, with the ever-present silver coin rolling along the back of his knuckles. His focus was on trying to determine how someone had entered his home. Especially since he had a top of the line security system he'd been told was impenetrable.

Getting soft, Mate?

Apparently, he was. The question was what he was going to do about it.

He'd arrived home too late the previous night to speak to the officers who'd been first on the scene. But they were due to arrive sometime after 8:00 a.m. Should he tell them about the note?

Notes, he amended, looking down at the newest.

Same white linen envelope. Same white linen paper with a single fold and his name on the outside. And inside, written in block letters,

IT DOESN'T BELONG TO YOU. ISN'T IT TIME TO RETURN IT?

Except telling them about the notes would lead to questions he wasn't willing to answer. Questions he'd not thought about in the twenty years he'd been in the states. Questions that led straight to Flynn Reide, whose tracks he'd worked to cover. Was the past he so wanted to forget coming back to haunt him, just when he was on the verge of having it all?

Again, what are you going to do about it?

Finn ran up the stairs to his guest room and opened the safe he'd told no one about. He took a deep breath and reached inside, pulling out a photo and three spiral bound notebooks. Something told him the answer he was searching for was between the pages of one of these books. The question was, which one?

He also found copies of old passports and the paperwork for their name change. And in the back corner, the delicate gold chain that had at one time held the cross he'd given Killian.

What would his sons say if they knew the original story behind the cross? Would they forgive him for his past transgressions?

What would Ava say? Would she care for the simple man beneath the thousand-dollar suits?

Questions he hadn't thought he'd need to contemplate on his drive from Swan Harbor. But with the possibility in front of him, there were answers to be found.

He returned everything but the notebooks to the safe and made his way to his study. His phone rang before he'd even sat down.

"Good morning, Ava love. You're up quite early."

"I could say the same for you," her voice husky from sleep came across the line. "I thought I might have to leave a message."

"No need. I haven't been to sleep yet."

"Why? Did something happen with the break-in?"

"Not really."

"But?" She pushed a little more. "Did they take anything?"

"Not that I can tell."

"But ...?"

When she hesitated, he imagined the wheels in her head were spinning, worrying him for some reason. "Did they leave anything behind?"

Her question threw him, but while he didn't want to lie to her, neither did he want to tell her the complete truth. "Why would you ask?"

"Well, it just makes sense," she continued in her direct manner. "If they didn't take something, then there had to be another reason, and the most obvious is to deliver a message."

"Unless it was just kids," he offered another option.

"Maybe. Did you speak to the police?"

"I'm waiting for them," he replied. "Then I'll head back to Swan Harbor."

"No! You can't!"

"No? But ..."

"I'm sorry," she cut him off. "That didn't come out right. You can't drive back without sleeping."

Finn let out the breath he'd been holding. "I've stayed up before, love. You've no need to worry."

She chuckled and even through the line, the sound sent goosebumps along his skin. "I'm sure you have, but you're not as young as you used to be."

"Is that your way of telling me I'm getting old?"

"No, no," she sputtered. "I just ..."

"I know," he assured her. "I'll be careful."

"You'd better. Let me know what you decide."

"I like you're worried about me." His voice grew huskier. "Means you might care."

"Maybe." She chuckled again. "I'll talk to you later. I'm going with Becca to Sally's kickboxing class this morning."

"Bye, love."

When he hung up, the sound of her laugh still reverberated in his ears. Her image still lingered in his mind. What was she doing to him?

You're not meant to be alone.

He'd said similar words to Liam when he'd been searching for answers. Had Claire's passing been the push he'd needed to move forward? Or was seeing his sons happy making him want that for himself? Or was it ...?

Ava.

There was just something about her.

But until he could follow his heart, he needed to find the answers to who could be ....

Finn opened the first book. Meticulous notes, observations, dates, diagrams, dating back to 1980. As he flipped through the pages, nothing stood up and shouted, *'I'm what you're looking for.'* He felt he was spinning his wheels, and once he'd reached 1983, he needed a break and dialed the office.

"I thought you were on vacation," Kim's cheerful voice greeted him. "But I'm not surprised to hear from you."

"Someone tripped the alarm on my house," he offered.

"Did they take anything?"

"Doesn't look like it." Then, because he wanted to move the subject off his home break-in, he asked about work.

"Nothing major, but Mrs. Connor would like to speak to you when you have time."

"I'll call her later. Are there any showings out my direction today? Maybe someone who could stop by the office and pick up my mail?"

"Let me check."

Finn could hear her clicking through the schedule for several minutes before she returned.

"Owen has a showing not far from you," she told him. "I'll call and see if he can stop by the office first."

"Thanks, Kim."

He'd just disconnected when the doorbell chimed. He shoved the notebooks and notes into his briefcase, then went to answer the door. "Good morning, Officers."

They introduced themselves as Officers Rhodes and Montgomery, and handed him a black-and-white photo. "Do you recognize him?"

Finn glanced at the picture and wanted to laugh. How was he *'supposed'* to recognize someone in a hooded coat, with only a quarter size piece of skin on the back of their hand visible?

"That was a joke, right?" Finn studied the officers. "Where did this picture come from?"

"Neighbors." Officer Rhodes waved toward the south of his home. "Were you able to ascertain if anything was taken? And how they were able to get around your system?"

"Nothing was taken," Finn began. "But, let me show you."

He led them upstairs to his bedroom and took them out onto the balcony. "The intruder climbed the trellis and jimmied the terrace door."

Flynn popped the lock on the patio door and quietly slipped inside.

"The bedroom was quickly searched, but not finding what he wanted, he went looking for my home office."

He didn't find the safe in the first room, and made his way toward the study.

"Once inside my office, he looked through my filing cabinet and my desk drawers, before locating the small safe."

The safe was an older model, hidden in a closet and bolted to the floor. With little room to manipulate, Flynn squatted in front of it and went to work on the combination. He got lucky on the second try, as the gentleman of the house had used the birthday of his daughter. When he opened the door, the brilliance of the silver coins sent his heart racing. "Come to papa." He reached for the tray they rested in.

"Did he get into the safe?" Officer Montgomery asked.

Finn shook his head. "No. He tried one combination, and it locked up. Then I'm assuming he heard sirens."

One by one, he moved the silver pieces of eight into his satchel. He'd just moved the last piece in the first row from its resting place when the phone rang.

They're not home, he reminded himself. But then he heard someone coming.

"Did he leave the same way he arrived?"

"No." Finn led them from his office into the front room and pointed to the doors leading to the terrace. "He left through those French doors."

"How do you know?" questioned Officer Rhodes.

Finn's eyes briefly touched the spot on the floor where he'd found the linen envelope.

As soon as she hung up, Flynn slipped from the room and back out onto the patio, knocking over a brick planter in his haste. His heart raced as he ran into the night, the silver weighing heavy in his pocket.

"They broke a vase right outside the door and knocked over a chair."

"We're going to check with your neighbors and find out if there's been any other break-ins," Officer Rhodes replied. "But since they took nothing ..."

He left that hanging, but Finn understood completely. As he walked them to the door, he knew they'd never find his intruder. The answer was between the pages of one of his books. Was he ready for a visit to the past?

Sally's Diner
November 2
11:00 a.m.

AVA MET HER FRIENDS IN FRONT OF SALLY'S AND FOLLOWED THEM inside the diner. She'd enjoyed the kickboxing class and was looking forward to a little female solidarity. That wasn't something she'd had much experience with in her lifetime. A friend in college, but then she'd graduated, chased after Peter, and ....

"It's crowded," she noted. "Are you sure this was a good idea?"

"We're fine," Becca assured her.

"Sally always has a table saved for us," Giennie added. "Here she comes."

"Right this way, ladies." Sally led them toward the back of the diner, where someone had shoved two tables together. "I'll be back with menus."

"Oh my gosh," Becca groaned, dropping onto a chair. "I'm not sure I'll be able to get out of bed tomorrow."

"I know I won't," Giennie grumbled. "It's a good thing I don't have any showings today."

"I don't know why you're complaining," Anita laughed. "That class was nothing."

Ava shook her head as the gentle grumblings went on around her. Each woman could express differing opinions without having to worry about the others.

"Mom."

"Emma." Ava smiled at her daughter. "I didn't see you when we arrived."

"We were over there." Emma waved toward a corner of the diner. "What have you been up to?"

"Sally kicked our asses," Anita offered.

"Kickboxing," Ava added. "It was fun."

"I tried to get Elsa to go—"

"Hey, stop that," Elsa laughed. Then she played the peacemaker and turned to Becca. "How's Gavin?"

"He's been very subdued," Becca explained. "I'm not sure if that's because of the injury, because his father left, or if there's more going on."

"What about Harrison?" Elsa turned to Giennie.

Ava saw Giennie exchange looks with Becca before she replied, "The same."

"Sounds like typical teen behavior," Maggie responded with a laugh.

"Could be," Elsa agreed. "But if there's anything I can do, let me know."

"Will do," Giennie assured her.

Becca agreed, and the conversation swirled around Ava for several minutes.

Enough so she finally learned the boys had found and experimented with dynamite a few months earlier. And Elsa, as their pediatrician, had been involved in their care.

"We'd better go," Emma nudged Elsa. "The clasp broke on my bracelet, and Elsa has a necklace that needs Al's magic."

"Have fun."

Ava had just tuned back into the conversation when Emma called out again.

"Mom, Finn went back to New York suddenly. Do you know why?"

"Me?" Ava practically squeaked, her blood freezing in her veins.

Does she know?

"Sure," Emma shrugged. "You're staying at the same hotel, and he was with you yesterday."

"Oh, yes," Ava forced herself to breathe again. "Right. Uh, something about a possible break in."

That sounded normal, right?

"Oh no," Emma frowned. "I wonder if he's called Killian."

"Wouldn't know," Ava answered and when Emma didn't follow up, let out the rest of the breath she'd been holding.

"Finley Reade," Anita sighed. "He is one fine looking man."

"Yes, he is," Becca agreed. "I bet he's like Dark Chocolate. One taste and you're addicted."

Ava had to fight to keep from agreeing with the analogy.

"And the way he fills out a pair of dress slacks," Anita pushed some more, causing Ava to fight not to fidget in her chair. "It makes my mouth water."

"Did you see him in his jeans the other night?" Giennie tossed out.

While they discussed how Finn's jeans had hugged his body in all the right places, Ava searched for a new topic.

"I heard he kissed Heidi," Becca added. "I'm not sure if I believe that or not. Could be just gossip."

Gossip, thought Ava. Perfect.

"So, ladies." Ava commanded their attention, as if she were conducting a business meeting. "Speaking of gossip. The diner is full."

And they were off, allowing Ava to relax.

Captain Jack was at one table, and after several whispered conversations, they learned he was interviewing a new employee, named Noah.

The owner of the local newspaper, Sydney, was at another table with a reporter, Quinn.

Their server, Hayden, wasn't his usual cheery self, but no one knew what was going on and quickly grabbed Sally.

"What's going on with your nephew?" Maggie frowned. "I've never seen him this disgruntled.

Sally looked over their heads, Ava assumed, waiting until he was out of earshot.

"Hayden is a gifted computer programmer, and wants to please the girls he dates. That's why they kicked him off his scholarship and he's living upstairs."

"And doing community service," Giennie added. "I saw him when I was at City Hall the other day."

"He is," Sally agreed. "Updating the computer systems for both the Swan Harbor Police and the Sheriff's department."

"I could have used him at the Sanctuary," Maggie replied, referring to the menagerie of animals in her care.

"Hayden and animals," Sally laughed. "I can't see that."

"Me either," Maggie agreed. "But I wanted to help."

"You have students helping you, don't you?" Ava asked, hoping her friend wasn't doing all the work alone.

"I do," Maggie's eyes twinkled. "But the more the merrier."

Everyone laughed and for a few minutes, Ava basked in the newness of the situation, and let down her guard.

"Ava." Sally gave her a smile that said, W*ouldn't you like to know what I know*? "I heard you and Finn have taken an interest in Karen Adamses' daughter, Rachel."

Ava glanced around the table at the five women and felt more pressure than she'd ever felt as head of King's.

"We did," she agreed, pulling her corporate persona out to help her get through the next few minutes. "I was there when Rachel went into labor. Did you know that poor girl doesn't have much?"

And just as she'd hoped, the women took the bait and were off.

Sheriff's Department

November 2
4:00 p.m.

KILLIAN FINISHED THE REPORT HE WAS WORKING ON FOR JUDGE Coleman and checked the time. Was it possible for him to leave a little earlier than normal? Rusty was out with Roland, Dylan was at an appointment with Molly, and he was done with his work. He sent his report to Amy's printer and grabbed his phone to send Emma a text.

Before he could send his message, it rang. "Hello."

"Killian, it's Hayden," the younger man replied. "Are you busy?"

"You're in luck," Killian told him. "I was getting ready to leave."

"Umm, do you have time to talk?" Hayden blurted. "I, I could use a little advice."

"Advice, you say," Killian hummed, "would this have anything to do with how mopey you've been lately?"

"You heard about that, huh?" Hayden grumbled. "Are there no secrets in Swan Harbor?"

Killian chuckled. "You should know better than that."

"I know," Hayden grunted. "It's just annoying when all your mistakes are out there for the whole town to talk about."

"I guess I can understand that."

"So, do you have time to talk?"

The slight pleading tone in Hayden's voice wasn't something he'd expected to hear. The younger man was a *what you see is what you get* type of person, but usually self-reliant.

"I can make the time," Killian assured him.

"Thanks." The tenseness in Hayden's voice relaxed a little. "I'll wait for you in the stairway at Sally's."

"Alright," Killian agreed. "I'll be there in a few minutes."

As he packed up his desk and signed the report before leaving the department, he couldn't help but wonder, what now?

When he stepped outside, he was greeted by the gentle rumble of Emma's precious Volkswagen, as she slid into a space across the street.

"Looking for me, Doc?" he called as soon as she'd opened the car door.

"Maybe." Emma smiled flirtatiously.

"Then what are you doing way over there?"

"No no no," she wagged her finger. "The question is, what are *you* doing way over there?"

Killian laughed and jogged across the street to tug her into his arms. "Is this better?"

"It's getting there," Emma offered her mouth.

He kissed her, meaning for it to be just a quick peck. But once his lips touched hers, he couldn't make himself let her go. She tasted like those chocolates she kept on her desk, and something that was uniquely Emma.

"Better?"

"Yeah," she replied breathlessly. "Much better."

"Glad you liked it."

"What's not to like?"

Killian nuzzled her temple and grinned down at her. "I was just going to text you to see if you were busy.

"I'm on my way to Swan Harbor University to see a couple of friends." Emma stepped out of his arms and continued, "Sylvia and Linda need me to help with a research project. We're going to tattoo *Sylvilagus floridanus*.

"Rabbits?" he quipped, showing off his knowledge of scientific names.

"Very good. But why aren't you in the office?"

"Hayden called," Killian explained, "and asked if I could talk."

"Good. The last two times I've seen him, he was grumpy."

"Maybe I'll find out why."

"Good luck." Emma nibbled on her lip for a bit before tossing out, "My mom was in Sally's too.

"Oh?"

He'd been meaning to talk to her about Liam's ideas, but ....

You were chicken.

"I asked her if she knew why your dad went back to New York."

"Because the alarm was tripped," Killian offered, having spoken to his father earlier.

"What did your dad say?"

"Not much," Killian admitted. "The conversation was a bit unsettling. I wasn't getting the whole truth."

"How do you know?"

Killian smirked, "I'm an investigator." Emma arched a brow, pushing him to add, "There was a hesitation in dad's voice. It's his tell, but I bet he doesn't even know he has one."

"I hope ..."

"Stop worrying, Doc. I'll get to the bottom of what's going on."

"Okay." Emma kissed him again and climbed into her car. "See you at home."

He waved her off, thinking home was another subject they needed to talk about. *'Soon'*, he promised himself.

With Emma's music ringing in his ears, Killian turned back toward Sally's, ready to see what Hayden needed.

When he rounded the corner of the diner, Hayden was pacing in front of the door, his hair going in multiple directions.

"Bloody hell," Killian mumbled, "what's going on with you?"

Hayden's eyes met his and in them, he could see a swirl of emotions. "I thought you weren't coming."

"Sorry." Killian's curiosity kicked up a notch when he got a closer look at the younger man. His eyes were bloodshot, and his clothing was a mess. "Emma stopped by for a few minutes."

"That's nice," Hayden muttered, but Killian could tell there was something weighing on him.

"I know you took Emma to Lover's Cove a few months ago," Hayden tossed out.

Lover's Cove was a grouping of boulders and a small cave with a legend behind it. The legend stated if a couple made love there, they'd be engaged before the end of the year.

"How did you know about that?" Killian asked without coming right out and answering the question.

Hayden rolled his eyes. "Please."

"Right." Killian nodded. "Swan Harbor's infamous gossip line."

"You know the legend about Lover's Cove, right?"

"Aye," Killian nodded his head slowly.

"I was surprised when you got engaged," Hayden's voice trailed off. "I mean ... why would you settle for one when you could have so many?"

A laugh escaped before Killian could catch it. "Why, indeed?"

The same question he'd asked himself when he was twenty and then again at thirty. But a yellow flash had captured his attention.

"I'm serious, Killian. What is it about Emma that had you …?"

Killian studied his young friend, and something told him the question had nothing to do with him and Emma. "This isn't about me, is it?"

Hayden swallowed hard as he suddenly found something on the ground to study.

"I'm the last person to judge, Hayden," Killian replied, wishing he'd had someone to talk to when he was twenty.

"Nothing to judge, yet," Hayden mumbled. "It's just some kids think the legend is so romantic, and they're pushing to go, and I—"

"—Don't want to push the legend?" Killian hesitated a beat. "Or is it you're not sure you're ready to take a girl there?"

When Hayden blew out a breath, Killian patted himself on the back for guessing correctly.

"Yeah. Peyton and I just started dating, and well …" He looked away. "Jared keeps telling me how stupid I'm being, but …"

"Tell Jared to stop being a dick," Killian snapped. "You'll know when it's the right person."

"Right." Hayden laughed, sounding more like his old self. "Besides, this is Swan Harbor, and I'm supposed to listen to my heart."

"You said it," Killian pointed out, and then added, "but it's true."

"You sound like my Aunt Sally," Hayden groaned.

"Or Captain Jack, or …"

Hayden pulled open the door. "Thanks, Killian. I'll talk to you later."

That wasn't so hard. Killian headed to his car, his father's problem once again on his mind.

EIGHT

Lighthouse Inn
November 3
2:00 p.m.

WHEN AVA GLANCED AT THE TIME AND ONLY FIVE MINUTES HAD passed since she'd last looked, she gave up trying to concentrate. She was nervous. There, she'd admitted it. Once she acknowledged it, though, the nerves didn't go away.

What she couldn't figure out was why she was nervous. It wasn't like she hadn't seen Finn before.

But this is the first time you've seen him since ….

Since she'd told him about her stroke.

How am I supposed to behave?

You do what comes naturally, but do not ….

Don't worry, she wanted to assure her inner voice. She'd made a list of do's and don'ts, and had no intention of trying to bypass any of them.

What do I say?

Really? After spending hours on the phone with him last night?

What if ….

Stop!

Another check of the time propelled her across the room and onto the balcony to stare out over the beach. The wind whipped her hair around and while the view mesmerized her, her nerves were still there ... waiting.

"Ava."

The sound of his voice grabbed her breath and before she could tell herself to be cool, she whipped around. "Finn!"

He was standing just outside the patio doors, and the word *Sexy* resounded inside her head.

Tight jeans, and a cream color sweater she couldn't wait to sink her fingers into. Wind-blown hair and eyes so dark she felt as if she were drowning.

"You're back," she forced out through a throat that wanted to close.

"I am."

"That's nice."

Come on! You're a King. Is that the best you can do?

Finn lifted a brow, as if he were thinking the same thing. "What are you waiting for?"

"I don't know what you mean."

"Don't you?" He took a couple of steps closer to where she was standing. "Think back, love. What did you promise me last night?"

She thought back on their conversation. There had been a lot of getting-to-know-you talk, but it was laced with innuendos. And those spoken with a sexy British accent had her heart racing and made her feel like a teenager experiencing the first blush of love.

Then, as they'd prepared to say goodbye ....

"I wish I was there."

"Why?" she whispered, not wanting to break the spell.

"Because," his voice grew huskier, "I really want to kiss you."

"Oh, you do, do you?"

He hummed. "I do. Would you let me?"

"What do you think?"

It was quiet for several seconds, and she could hear him breathing.

"Tell me," he commanded.

Ava wanted to tease him, but there was something in his voice that had her telling the truth. "Yes."

A single word, but the way he gasped told her more than if he'd given her words. "Save it for me?"

"My kiss?"

"Yes, love," he murmured. "I want it as soon as you see me."

"You do?"

"I need it. Promise me."

She tried to lighten the conversation. "If it means that much."

"You have no idea. Promise."

"I promise."

"Ava," Finn was prompting again when she came back to the present. "You promised."

"I did, didn't I?"

She took three steps, stopping just shy of touching him, and slid her hands up his chest to rest lightly on his shoulders.

"Welcome back to Swan Harbor, Finn," Ava whispered against his mouth. "Is this what you wanted?"

Their lips met and meshed, and Ava's thoughts scattered. *'Soft, yet firm'*, she couldn't help but think.

Finn groaned and crushed her against him, his mouth creating a swirl of emotion in the center of her chest.

Her arms slid around his neck as his mouth plundered, stealing her breath. He grabbed her rear, pulling her into the cradle of his thighs, and her softness rested against that hard wedge behind his jeans.

"Ah love. What you do to me." Finn whispered a kiss across her cheek and latched onto a sensitive spot just below her ear.

She understood that, as the way he was making her feel had her wanting to climb inside him. "Wait."

It took willpower she didn't know she had to step back and walk several steps away. Her lips tingled, and she could still taste him. Heck, she thought, she could still feel him.

Finn stepped behind her and wrapped his arms around her, dropping his chin on her shoulder. "Too fast?"

Ava tried to gather her thoughts, but knew she owed him an explanation. "I'm sorry—"

"Stop," he demanded. "There is nothing for you to be sorry about."

But with him wrapped around her, she couldn't think straight, and tugged him down onto a chair. "I know we've already …" she hesitated, unsure how to label their encounters.

"Made love," he whispered, his dark eyes digging into hers.

"Was it?" she whispered back. "Or was it just sex?"

"I told you before, it was more than sex, or it wouldn't scare you," he reminded her.

"So, you did." Ava licked her lips and prepared to enter the scary territory. "But if we're going to … secretly date," she settled on. "We can't end up doing any more of that."

"That?" Finn's lips twitched. "You mean make love?"

"Whatever you want to call it," she retorted primly. "None of that."

"Ever?"

Ava rolled her eyes. "Stop being cute. You know what I mean."

He grinned and leaned forward enough to give her a firm, but very thorough kiss. "How about that?"

"That … that." She licked her lips. "That is fine."

"And." He nuzzled her ear, and his lips grazed down the side of her neck. "How about that?"

Her stomach was swirling and somehow, she knew he could continue to find '*thats*' she'd definitely approve of.

"How about a walk?" Ava jumped up and headed inside to get her coat without waiting for an answer. "I think I could use some cold air."

FINN HAD TO CONSTANTLY FIGHT THE SMILE THAT WANTED TO break free as he walked next to Ava. Since deciding she could use some colder air, she'd not stopped talking, rattling on and on. Something he found completely charming.

"Did you find out more about the break-in?" She changed topics yet again.

"Caucasian," he offered. And neither had he discovered anything between the pages of his notebooks.

"That's it?"

"Yes. The security company came out yesterday and added some lights around my property."

"At least they didn't take anything."

Except, he couldn't help but think, his peace of mind.

"I noticed the table in the cottage was devoid of baby paraphernalia," he changed the subject to a more comfortable one.

She sent him a sideways look, as if she knew what he'd done. "I told the girls at Sally's yesterday Rachel had very little …"

"And that was it?"

"Oh yes," Ava laughed. "Before we'd left Sally's, they'd organized a list of what people had on hand, who to call, etc. Then yesterday evening, we took it over to Karen's and gave it to Rachel. I think she was overwhelmed."

"So, there are places in the world where people are genuinely nice."

"Small town charm."

"Is that what it's called?"

Ava shrugged. "It sounds good to me. Think you could live here full time?"

There were aspects of Swan Harbor that reminded him of living in Blyth England when the boys were young.

"Full time would be difficult, with my business in New York City," he opted for instead of directly answering her question.

"You don't think you want to work with Giennie?"

"Giennie is the town Realtor?"

"Yes," Ava laughed. "She keeps hinting she has several homes she'd *love* to show me."

Finn smiled, noticing how red the tip of her nose was becoming. "Are you cold?

"Maybe a little."

"Come here." He tucked her against his side, grinning when she crammed her hand into his back pocket. "I take it your hand is cold."

"I can't just put my hand on your tush?"

Her comment took him aback for a second. "Does that go both ways?"

She giggled and didn't answer his question. But as they continued walking, the idea of pressing her against one of the boulders in the distance grew more vivid. So much so, he began searching around for another innocuous topic.

"How are Liam and Elsa's wedding plans going?"

"Good," she smiled. "In fact …"

Finn lost track of what she was saying when he glanced down. The twinkle in her blue eyes, and the sight of her red lips kept distracting him.

"You're not listening to me again, are you?" She grinned, and when a dimple appeared in her cheek, he had the strangest desire to ....

"Come here."

Finn grabbed her hand, tugged her behind a large boulder and into his arms. His lips toyed with hers for several seconds, before she opened and allowed him inside.

The waves crashing close by ceased to matter. And the sound of the cars faded as their lips met and engaged in a conversation all their own.

His heart raced, his body tightened, and while there was a lone brain cell screaming this might be too much of '*that*,' he couldn't stop.

Someone moaned, and Finn glanced around, the mouth of a cave beckoning them. "What have we here?"

Ava hummed. "A cave?"

"Aren't you smart?" he teased, leading her inside. Before he could press her against the wall and pick up where he'd left off, a plaintive sound raised the hairs on the back of his neck.

"What's that?" Ava whispered.

"I don't know."

Finn took a step deeper into the cave and heard it again. A whimper, he thought. "It's an animal."

An animal that's hurt, his thoughts played out as he inched toward the sound.

"Do you have your phone?"

He mentally smacked his head for not thinking of that himself.

You were thinking with the wrong head ....

The flashlight from his phone was powerful enough for him to pinpoint the location of the sound. "Over there." Finn pointed to a pile of rocks and an old box. "Why don't you stay here?"

"For heaven's sake." Ava took off without him. "It's hurt and won't come after us. If it was planning to, it would have already happened."

He realized there was some truth in what she was saying and caught up with her just before she reached the rocks. "Be careful."

"Oh, Finn," Ava's voice broke. "It's a mother dog and puppies. We need to call Emma."

He handed her the phone and peered behind the rocks again. In the dim light, his eyes met those of the mother dog's and in them, he saw equal parts fear and relief. "It's going to be alright," he assured her softly.

"Yes, Sadie," Ava was saying. "In a cave close to The Lighthouse Inn."

"I don't know, Sadie," Ava continued. "Hold on."

"Was there a parking lot on the other side of the rocks?"

Finn shrugged, as he hadn't been thinking about anything but kissing Ava. "Let me check."

He jogged from the cave and climbed around the rocks until he could see the road. "Tell her yes," he called, retracing his steps.

"Okay, Sadie," Ava was saying when he returned to the cave. "Tell Emma to hurry. We'll be waiting."

His eyes met Ava's and without saying anything, he spread his arms, and she flew into them. "She's going to be alright," he tried to assure her.

"Will she?" Ava mumbled against his shoulder. "How did she even end up down here?"

"I don't know, love. But Emma's on her way, so I'm going to wait for her. Do you want to go with me?"

"No." She stepped from his arms, and he couldn't miss the tear tracks on her cheeks. "I don't want the mother thinking we're leaving her behind."

He'd guessed as much. "I won't be long."

She swiped a hand across her cheek. "Hurry back."

Finn kissed her lightly and left to wait for Emma. He hoped he was right, and the dog and her puppies were going to be fine because if not, then ....

AVA SANK ONTO A LARGE ROCK AND STUDIED THE MOTHER DOG. SHE knew nothing about breeds or what went into caring for puppies. But each time their eyes met, she sensed trust.

"Don't you worry," Ava assured the mother dog. "My daughter will know exactly what we need to do."

The dog whimpered a few times, but as much as she wanted to touch, she refrained. Then, for the next few minutes, talked nonsense, not thinking too hard about what was falling from her mouth.

It wasn't long until she heard the scrape of shoes on the rocks and went to help.

"Emma." Ava reached for Emma's backpack and led the way into the cave. "The mother and puppies are back here."

Emma gave her a half-smile and handed her a flashlight. "Here, mom, hold this for me."

Ava stepped to the side and aimed the light on the dog family, silently urging Emma to hurry.

For the next several minutes, the only sounds were of Emma as she gave directives. "The mom is a retriever mix," she murmured. "There's four puppies, but two of them, I ..."

When her voice trailed off, a little piece of Ava's heart broke, and she had to wonder how her daughter could do this day after day.

"The mom's hind leg looks infected." Emma continued with her examination.

"Is she going to be okay?"

"She's needs it thoroughly cleaned, but she should be fine." Then Emma pointed to the smaller crate, "Put these warmers in there for me. The puppies will go inside."

Ava moved the smaller cage and quickly added the warmers, holding the door for Emma to transfer the puppies."

"How old are they?"

"A few hours."

"Here, love." Finn took over holding the flashlight until all four puppies were inside.

Hurry, hurry, Ava chanted silently.

"Now, the mom."

Emma dug into her medical pack and took out a syringe and a bottle.

"It's just something for pain," she told them. "Once the dog is relaxed, we'll move her into the cage."

But it wasn't an easy process, taking all three of them to make the transfer. Then, once it was done, Ava's nerves were frayed.

"Okay, I'll help Finn grab the large cage." Emma zipped the backpack. "Can you get the rest?"

"I think so," Ava readjusted the cage so she could carry everything. "Let's go."

They made their way to the parking lot where Emma secured the cages in the back.

"I'm going with her," Ava told Finn.

"I thought you might."

"You don't mind?"

"No. I'll go get the car meet you at Emma's."

"You will?"

"Go." Finn held the door for her. "I'll be along in a bit."

Emma was talking to Sadie as they drove out of the parking area, and a little kernel of dread formed in Ava's stomach.

"Call Leroy for me, Sadie," Emma requested. "I'm going to need help in surgery. I should be there in fifteen."

"So, mom." Emma began after she'd hung up, and something inside Ava said, *'ah-oh.'* "It's quite fortunate you and *Finn* found the new family."

Did she just imagine the emphasis on his name?

"Isn't it though?"

You're a King. Don't let her see you sweat.

"You were just taking a walk," Emma continued, "and happened upon Lover's Cove?"

"Lover's Cove?" Ava repeated. "That's what those rocks are called?"

"It's what the whole cove is called," Emma explained. "It has quite the reputation."

Ava's heart raced. "Well, as you said, it's the mother's lucky day we found her. Do you think the puppies will survive?"

She held her breath, hoping Emma would move away from the *'why'* she'd been in the cave with Finn.

"I don't know," Emma sighed. "I hope so."

Leroy, a rather short, gruff man, helped Emma carry the large cage into the clinic. Ava followed with the smaller objects.

"Let me help." Sadie, Emma's leggy office manager, took the top object, leaving Ava to follow. "Emma said we need to warm the puppies."

"I can do that." Ava set the box and bag she'd been carrying on the floor and took off her coat. "What do we need to do?"

"Wait—" Sadie began before Emma raced into the room.

"Let me check them first."

Ava wanted to tell her no, don't open the cage, but before she could say anything, Emma picked it up and disappeared.

"She's taking them to a treatment room," Sadie answered the unspoken question.

"Oh."

While they waited for Emma to return, Ava had never felt so helpless in her life.

"Ava," Sadie sent her a sympathetic look, as if she knew exactly what was going through her mind. "I'll go check on Emma."

"Okay."

FINN FOUND HIS LADY IN EMMA'S OFFICE, STARING OFF INTO SPACE. "Ava?"

When she didn't respond after a few seconds, he dropped on one knee in front of her and took her hands between his. "What's happening?" he asked, when their eyes finally met.

She dropped her head and for a split second, he thought the worst.

"Leroy is getting the mom ready for surgery, through there," she indicated a door to their left. "And Emma's checking the puppies."

"Are they?"

"I don't know."

Her chin quivered and instead of pulling her into his lap like he wanted, he settled for an awkward hug.

Ava's hot breath blew across his neck and only the sound of someone approaching kept him from taking her mouth.

"Good news."

He and Ava jumped apart just as Emma entered the room carrying the cage with the puppies.

"Three of the puppies are healthy, but they need to be warmed. The fourth is dehydrated and needs an I.V."

"What can we do?"

"Sadie will set up the warmers and get some bottles. I'll be back."

"She didn't say anything," Ava whispered, as soon as Emma was gone.

"About what?"

Ava tilted her head as if to say, '*really*,' making him smile.

"You know very well what."

Finn grinned and leaned in, kissing her quickly. "Maybe we're making it a bigger deal than it is."

"None of that—"

"You said that '*that*' was alright," Finn interrupted.

Ava took a step closer and lowered her voice, "None of that '*that*' here."

"Spoilsport," Finn pouted. "You liked it when I ..."

"Here we go," Sadie came into the room causing him to swallow his words.

Ava sent him an impish smile, making him want to kiss her more. *It's going to be a long night'*, he thought, following the ladies across the room.

NINE

Lighthouse Inn
November 4
6:30 p.m.

FINN OPENED THE CLOSET AND REACHED FOR ONE OF HIS SUITS, BUT something had him bypassing it in favor of black tweed slacks and a black turtleneck. He slipped on his boots, then brushed back his hair and stared at the image in the mirror. And the anticipation he'd managed to keep tamped down all day sparked to life.

What was she doing to him?

Reminding you of what it feels like to fall in love.

There was some merit to that, he thought as he grabbed his coat and Ava's gifts.

Will she like it?

Relax! You're not a schoolboy!

Even with the pep talk, it took several deep breaths before he worked up the courage to knock on the door of her cottage.

"Finn! Come in."

Ava's breathless voice when she opened the door, sent his heart racing, and words lodged in his throat. "You look lovely," he forced out with a tongue that felt too big for his mouth.

"Thank you," she smiled, and the dimple in her left cheek popped. "And you look ..."

At her hesitation, a spurt of uncertainty roared through him. Should he have worn the suit? "Ava?"

"Good." She kissed him lightly. "Really good."

"That's all I get for looking *'really good'*?"

"For now. I'll get my coat."

It wasn't until she'd turned away, he realized he'd forgotten to give her the gifts he'd brought. "Hey." Finn waylaid her and settled her on the sofa. Then he held up the long-stem, red-tipped yellow rose.

Her eyes lit up, and he had to wonder if she understood the significance of the color.

"It's beautiful."

"And also, this." Finn handed her a small box.

"You bought me a present?"

She was saying something without saying the words, but he wasn't sure what it was.

"It's not much, but," he shoved it into her hand, "just open it."

Her gaze locked with his for a heartbeat, and then another, and then, as if there was a magnetic pull, their lips met. The kiss was different, in a sense that he didn't feel out of control. But there was an all-consuming rightness to it, as if he were where he was supposed to be at that point in time.

"Wow."

"Wow works."

Ava grinned and rubbed her thumb across his bottom lip. "It's not your color."

A corner of his mouth ticked up. "You're saying, I'd probably look better in a brighter red?"

"Probably so," she agreed. "Should I open it?"

He tipped his chin and waited for her to untie the bow and open the box.

"Oh, Finn." She lifted the charm bracelet and looked at him with glistening eyes. "It's beautiful."

"I didn't know—"

"It's perfect," she assured him. "I've always wanted one."

"Really?"

"Really. Put it on me."

Finn took the chain, fastened it around her arm, and placed a kiss on the inside of her wrist.

She studied the charms he'd added, a mother and child, a carousel, a carriage, a tower, and a puppy.

"It's us."

"I bought it before returning to Swan Harbor," he explained. "But I had to visit Joanne's Gems earlier today for the puppy."

"Thank you," she cupped his face, "it's perfect."

"You're most welcome," he murmured against her lips, not caring if her lipstick ended up on his face.

She tasted sweet, and he didn't need to think twice about what he wanted. His lips toyed with hers, and when she finally opened for him, he dove in. It was a hot, heady moment that could quickly spin out of control—and since they were due for dinner, he put some distance between them.

"That probably wasn't a good idea."

"Oh, I quite liked it." Ava stepped in front of him and swiped at his lips again. "But unless you want our kids knowing exactly what we've been doing, come with me."

Finn followed her into the bathroom and stood, watching her in the mirror while she wiped some cream over his mouth.

"There." She rubbed the cream off with a tissue. "The evidence is gone."

There was a part of him that wanted to say, '*Would it matter, if they knew?*' But while he thought his sons would be supportive of whatever happened, he understood Ava's concerns.

"I reserve the right to wear more of it later."

She tossed a grin over her shoulder on the way out of the room. "Maybe. We're running late."

"True." Finn waited while she put her rose in a vase of water, and held her coat for her to slip into. "We can't have the birthday girl being late."

"Exactly."

Ava was quiet, both on the way to the car and then on the drive to the restaurant. While he was content to hold her hand, he couldn't help but wonder about the night ahead. Was she nervous?

"Have you been to Captain Jack's?" he asked, when he drove into the marina where it was located.

"No." Ava leaned forward to get a better view of the seventeenth century Spanish galleon that housed the restaurant. "I wonder how Captain Jack ended up with a pirate ship."

"Who knows?" Finn pulled into a parking space. "I'm sure there's a story there."

"I'm sure there is," she agreed.

"Are you ready?" He squeezed her fingers in support.

Ava met his gaze and even in the dim light, he could see the twinkle in her eyes, which in a way surprised him. "It depends."

"On?"

"You." Her lips curved into a sexy smile.

"Moi?" Finn sent her a devilish grin, finally understanding where she was going.

She pointed her finger at him. "Stop that. No flirting."

He gave a long-suffering sigh and kissed her fingertips. "No flirting. Got it. Anything else?"

"None of that." She waved her loose hand in front of his mouth.

"No promises on that." He winked.

She made a face at him through the windshield, and as soon as he opened her door, he warned her, his voice low and dangerous, "You know you're playing with fire, don't you?"

"Maybe."

"Are you going to push my buttons all night?"

"Maybe."

"Minx."

Finn shut the door and had to fight not to grab her hand or place his arm around her as they walked.

"We're the last to arrive," she noted.

"And whose fault is that?"

She sent him a quick look, and he had to wonder what she would have said if they weren't close enough to be heard.

"We were wondering if you were coming," Liam quipped.

"Liam!" Elsa exclaimed.

"Sorry about that," Finn smiled. "As you get older, it takes longer to get dressed."

"Who are you calling old?" Ava exchanged looks with him.

"You look beautiful, Ava." Liam kissed her cheek. "Happy Birthday."

"Thank you, Liam."

But as birthday wishes were given to Ava by Elsa, Killian and Emma, Finn glanced up to catch Liam watching him. There was a glint in his son's eye that was only present if he were up to something. Dare he guess what that could be?

Captain Jack's Fine Dining
November 4
9:30 p.m.

AVA PUSHED BACK HER PLATE AND GAVE THE HAPPINESS BUBBLE inside permission to break free. Her birthday parties as the only child of Leo King had been ostentatious moments. Time for her father to show off his daughter. They hadn't involved the games and cake she'd desired.

She could remember celebrating with friends in college, but once those days were over, gone were the intimate get-togethers. Since then, she'd always been on the go and rarely acknowledged it was her birthday. But on the rare chance she allowed herself to hope, it was to be surrounded by family and friends.

And Emma, Killian, Finn, Liam, and Elsa were making her dreams come true.

"What do you need to be happy?" Finn had asked.

"At heart, I'm a simple girl, and all I need is family."

The night had flown by and, mostly, she'd relaxed and enjoyed herself. With their kids surrounding them, she'd struggled against Finn's pull. From gentle touches to lingering looks, she'd had to fight not to reach for him more times than she cared to count.

As the night wore on, he grew more difficult to resist. When he laughed, the sound would ripple across her skin. Or the heady scent of his cologne would make her dizzy. She reached a point where the fight to not give in became almost a physical ache.

"Are you ready, mom?"

Emma's question startled Ava, as she wasn't ready for the night to end.

"Sure, honey. This has been wonderful."

"Oh, it's not over, Ava," Killian explained.

"It's not?"

"No, mom." Emma smiled up at Killian, as he pulled back her chair. "There's dancing."

"And cake," Liam added.

"Dancing and cake?" Ava's gaze clashed with Finn's. "Did you know about this?"

"Maybe."

Her breath caught at his flirtatious comment and before she could stop, she poked him in the stomach. "Watch it."

Finn's eyes flared, and she could tell he was losing the fight with the sexy smile that wanted to break free. "Is that a threat?"

"No, a promise," she whispered, for his ears only.

"Ava," he growled.

There was a dark undercurrent that said more than words. His frustration at being close but not touching mimicked hers.

"I'm going to freshen up."

But as she pushed open the door to the lady's room, she glanced back to see Emma and Elsa following.

A brief moment of fear zipped through her. She knew it was irrational, but if Emma had issues with her and Finn being involved, it would be heart-wrenching. Because as much as she'd tried to keep her feelings for him in check, she was failing. Little by little, he was working his way into her heart.

Ava ducked into a stall and locked the door. The emotions inside continued to build. Especially when she watched how affectionate Emma and Killian, and Liam and Elsa were with each other. In a way, it made her jealous. The idea of her and Finn as a couple was getting too easy to see.

She took a deep breath and, for appearance's sake, flushed. She washed her hands, then mimicked Emma's stance in front of a mirror and reapplied her lipstick.

"So, mom," Emma began, and Ava fought to keep her neutral expression. "I like your bracelet. Was it a gift?"

"It was." Ava smiled, trying to remain nonchalant. "It reminded me of the one I gave you."

In May, she'd mysteriously received a package in the mail and inside had been a tarnished charm bracelet. There had also been a picture of her Grandmother Rose holding a two-year-old Ava and a note with her name on it.

Emma grinned, as if she knew exactly what Ava was doing.

"It is a little like mine," Emma agreed. "Did you ever find out who sent mine to you?"

Well, that was a bust, Ava thought, when the topic circled back. She'd given the bracelet to Emma the day before her engagement to Killian, and had ended up in Finn's bed again afterward. The fear and excitement of that encounter had her forgetting everything else.

"Not yet," she settled on. "I'm hoping to have more time to track that down while I'm here.

Emma nodded. "That would be nice."

"Did you get the clasp fixed on yours?"

"I left it at Joanne's."

Before she could come up with another topic, Elsa snapped shut her bag and pointed to the bracelet. "Can I see your charms?"

Ava wanted to say no, afraid there would be questions she couldn't answer. But unable to sidestep, she held up her arm.

While they looked at each charm, her stomach swirled with what ifs.

"Look, a puppy," laughed Elsa. "He must have been at Joanne's early this morning."

Ava bit her tongue to keep from asking why they assumed a '*he*' gave it to her.

"A tower?" frowned Emma.

"I like Rapunzel," Ava shrugged, as if it was no big deal.

"Very nice." Elsa grinned. "Finn has good taste."

And there it was again, Ava thought. The assumption it was from Finn.

But it is!

"Killian has good taste too," Emma glanced at the diamond on her hand. "He must have gotten it from his father."

"As does Liam." Elsa led the way from the lady's room. "Is Finn romantic like his sons?"

Ava had been in the middle of swallowing when the question rolled off Elsa's tongue. "Wh-Why would you ask me that?" She glanced up to see Finn heading her way.

But before anything else was said, he whisked her onto the dance floor.

"You looked like you needed rescuing."

"Do you know what you've done?"

He gave her a cheeky smile. "Saved you from answering questions?"

"Well that too," Ava conceded. "But you just gave them ..."

Then she got lost in his dark eyes, and her voice faded. Wasn't she where she'd been dreaming of all night?

"Would it be so bad if they knew?"

His husky baritone whispered against her temple, sending a shiver up her spine.

Would it?

WHILE HE WAS WAITING FOR HER ANSWER, FINN'S HEART RACED, and he had to hold his tongue to keep from pushing.

And then ... the most amazing thing happened. She wilted into his arms.

What was she doing to him?

"Thank you," he murmured against her temple. He swung her around the room in several intricate steps, mostly to show off.

Ava laughed, and the sound sent a zip of electricity straight through his body.

"Where did you learn to dance?"

"A lovely debutante or two in London shared their services," he offered slyly.

"I'm sure they did." She leaned back far enough he could see the twinkle in her eye. "They did a good job."

"I'm a quick study." He swung her around again.

Of course, she didn't have to know the real reason he'd been in some of those ballrooms.

"In fact, one time," he began.

But a tap on his shoulder had him looking back. "Yes?"

"Can I cut in?"

Finn wanted to tell the other man, bloody hell, no, but it wasn't the time to make a scene.

"Alright?" he whispered, hoping Ava would say no, thank you.

She squeezed his hand and stepped into the arms of the newcomer, and his heart twisted.

There was no way he could say more without looking like a twonk, he decided. But as he made his way to their table, he was glad the kids were still on the dance floor.

"Someone steal your woman?" Captain Jack quipped.

Finn gave the man a disgruntled look. "Stole my dance partner. Do you know that bloody bloke?"

"Aaron Fowler," Captain Jack responded, never taking his eyes off the couple. "He's the Chief of Police."

"He has bloody bad timing."

Captain Jack chuckled. "Isn't the first time. You need to decide if you're going to fight for her." Then he winked. "Now, I'm going to dance with your woman."

"Wait."

"I'll bring her back."

"But."

"Oh, look," Captain Jack nodded toward the server. "Peyton has the cake and champagne you ordered.

Finn settled back while a server placed the dessert in front of Ava. He wanted to sit and glare at the dance floor and instead forced his attention to the champagne.

"Where's mom?" Emma asked when she returned to the table.

"She's dancing with Fowler," Killian growled.

"Your tone says you have a problem with that," Finn noted.

Killian relaxed and rested his arm on the back of Emma's chair, all the time watching Fowler.

"There's just something about him." He shrugged. "Fowler's just a little too slick for my taste."

"Takes one to know one," snickered Liam.

"Wanker," Killian tossed back.

Finn exchanged looks with Emma and Elsa. "Some things never change."

"Were they always like this?" laughed Emma.

"Always." Finn smiled. "They were always trying to one-up each other."

"And I always won." Liam retorted.

Killian barked out a laugh. "In your dreams."

"Liam," Finn searched for a change of topic, "how's your new job?"

Liam laughed. "Trying to get us to make nice, dad?"

"Is it working?"

"Is what working?" Ava slid into her chair.

"Trying to make Killian and Liam behave," Finn groused. "Would you like champagne?"

Ava's blue eyes bore into his, making him feel he needed to spill all his secrets.

"Please."

Finn filled her glass and just as he set the bottle aside, the music transitioned into the birthday song.

"No!" Ava's eyes locked with his. "You didn't!"

"I didn't?"

As the music swirled around her, and the simple song was sung, Ava's response surprised him. He'd expected her to be used to the grand gestures and the attention. Instead, a blush covered her beautiful cheekbones, and her eyes sparkled with unshed tears.

He got lost in watching her, and when Peyton cut the pieces and Ava handed him one, and their hands touched, he forgot to breathe.

"Finn?" Ava murmured. "Cake?"

Her eyes widened, her nostrils flared, and her red lips beckoned. If he leaned in, just a little, he thought, he could taste.

Ava's brow arched, and her eyes almost dared him to follow through. But with the sense of being watched, he sent her a silent message *...later,* and took the plate.

While they were enjoying the dessert, he forced his attention to the table at large. He even participated in the conversation going on around him, but holding her and tasting her red lips were the only things on his mind.

"We're going to leave." Killian pulled out Emma's chair. "We have an early day tomorrow."

"Us too." Liam and Elsa followed suit.

Finn glanced at Ava. "Are you ready to leave?"

"Don't let us rush you." Emma hugged Ava goodbye. "I hope you had a good birthday, mom."

"It was the best. Thank you."

There was a huskiness to Ava's voice, telling him she was fighting some powerful emotions.

"Would you like one more dance before we leave?" he asked quietly when they were alone.

As soon as she nodded, he took her hand and led her to the dance floor. "Just so you know," he told her, "no one is cutting in this time."

Her chuckle was husky, but the way she tucked herself against his chest told him she was more than okay with his comment.

He held her as they moved to the music, and a multitude of thoughts flew through Finn's mind. But even though his mind and body knew what he wanted, he also realized she wasn't ready for most of them ... yet, anyway.

"Thank you for the birthday." Ava's hot breath blowing against the underside of his chin ratcheted up his need even more.

"You're very welcome."

She rubbed her cheek against his chest, and her fingers toyed with the hair at the nape of his neck. "Are you ready to go?" he asked, and even he could hear the tenseness in his voice.

Ava lifted her head and must have seen something in his expression, because she nodded and followed him from the restaurant.

The ride back to the Lighthouse Inn was quiet, the air around them thick with tension. Once they arrived, with every step closer to her cottage they drew, the anticipation inside rose.

Finn took her key and opened the cottage door. It would be so easy, he thought, to continue the celebration inside.

She looked up and in the dim light he could read the many expressions flying across her face. She wanted him, but that hint of fear was still there. Until it was only a memory, he would wait.

"Finn?"

"Happy Birthday, love." Finn crushed her against his chest. "Thank you for sharing your day with me."

"Oh, Finn." Ava's lips slid across his. "Thank you ... for everything."

She tugged him closer, offering her mouth, and he was helpless to resist. Their lips clung while their teeth and tongues clashed, fighting for the upper hand. Finn's body tightened, and the air swirled around them, until he could think of nothing but carrying her away.

He dropped his arms and stepped away. "I'm sorry." Then he tried to tease, needing to break some of the tension. "You said none of that *'that'*."

"That that was …"

Her words hung around them, but he agreed. It was impossible to describe how her kisses made him feel.

"Goodnight, love."

Because he couldn't resist, he kissed her once more. Then started back to his room. The walk served to cool his ardor, but once inside he was too keyed up to sleep. His mail from work had been delivered while he was gone. As he began to sort through it, the monotony of the task had him relaxing. Until a familiar sight sent a cold ball of fear through him.

He opened the white linen envelope and pulled out a single sheet of paper with two pictures printed on it.

"Bloody hell," he murmured.

One of them was a picture of him, holding a painting of the English countryside. One that had been stolen not once, but twice. The second time by Flynn Reide.

TEN

Randy's Arcade
November 7
7:30 p.m.

AVA SAT IN RANDY'S ARCADE, WITH ELSA'S MOTHER, PATTY, ON ONE side, and Sadie's mother, Anita, on the other. They'd gathered at Randy's for Elsa's bridal shower, and the more time she spent in the large building, the more she loved it. Which meant her father would have hated it.

"Imagine the germs, Ava," Leo King would try to reason. *"It's not a fitting place for a King."*

But there was something about the old, multiple-story home-turned-into-an entertainment-center that she loved.

The first floor had everything from pinball machines to the latest combat video games. A second floor housed multiple pool tables, and the top offered dining and dancing. And in the center of it all, a grand staircase led from one floor to another.

The longer she sat next to Patty, the more difficult she found keeping up the happy, everything's okay facade. When she'd offered to help Elsa plan her wedding, Emma had tried to warn her that Elsa's mother wasn't the same woman she'd been when they'd first met.

It had been over ten years since they'd arrived at Brown, first-time parents of freshman. Ava remembered Patty had a quick wit, sharp comments, and thoughtful suggestions. But that woman was gone, reminding her of her own good fortune regarding her health.

Alzheimer's Disease was slowly robbing Elsa of her mother. It was also taking from Patty the joy of watching her daughter prepare to marry the man she loved. The whole situation wasn't fair. But then again, life wasn't always fair.

"Look at that!" Patty exclaimed when Elsa pulled a gossamer nightgown out of a box. "You could read a book through that material."

Anita snickered and leaned over. "If she's wearing that, I certainly hope there's no reading going on."

Patty looked at Anita and for a second, Ava wasn't sure if she understood the joke, but then a twinkle appeared in her eye.

"Oh!" Patty chuckled loudly at Anita's comment.

Ava was taken aback for a second, as she never knew how Patty was going to behave. That she'd understood the comment enough to laugh was a good sign.

The feeling of being watched had her searching the room. Emma was staring, her brow raised in question.

It's nothing, Ava tried to convey with a subtle shake of her head, and went back to observing the women in the room.

Elsa had more friends attending her shower than Ava could ever remember having at one time. What did that say about her?

That the little girl in the tower analogy fits, in more ways than one, her inner voice uttered.

"Who's the woman with the strawberry blonde hair, next to Sadie?" she whispered.

"That's Jessie Prince Hunter," Anita began. "Her and Sadie have been friends since kindergarten."

"Related to the Sheriff?"

"His sister," Anita went on. "It was awful when their parents were killed. Jessie is married to Sadie's husband's brother."

"Okay." Ava's gaze traveled around the room, over Emma, her friend Molly, to an older blonde woman sitting next to Sally. "Who are the women over there?"

"Next to Sally?"

"Yes."

"The blonde is Mary Hunter. She's a psychiatrist at Swan Harbor General."

"And Sadie and Jessie's mother-in-law," Ava guessed, recognizing the last name.

"Right," Anita continued. "And the woman next to her is Rene Langley, the mayor."

"That's right," Ava remembered. "I met her briefly at Killian and Emma's engagement party, but she didn't stay long. Their little boy was sick."

"Roland," Anita grinned. "He has the cutest big brown eyes and dimples."

Just like Finn.

"And the younger women? Ava asked, trying to ignore her inner voice.

"There's Audrey, who is Elsa's nurse," Anita continued. "And Paula, who owns the pastry shop, and—"

"—Rachel," Ava said with a smile. "I'm glad she came."

"She was a year or two behind Sadie and Jessie, but I remember she had the voice of an angel."

"Really?" Ava studied the new mother sitting in the middle of the group. "She seems unsure of herself, to me. Did she want to be on stage?"

Anita frowned. "I don't think so. Teaching, maybe. But don't hold me to that."

"She fell in love," Ava sighed, "and the jerk left her pregnant."

"Sounds like Sadie's dad," Anita grumbled. "Men can be such jerks."

"Oh, not my Max," Patty gushed. "He was such a handsome man. And such a gentleman."

Patty had been so quiet, Ava had forgotten she was there, but she remembered Maxwell Winters very well.

"I concur, Patty," Ava agreed. "Your Max was a very handsome man."

But not as handsome as Finn.

Patty looked at her with confused eyes. "How is it you know my Max?"

Ava sighed, the sorrow weighing heavy on her heart. "I met him at the college one time."

"Okay," Patty nodded. "That makes sense. He was a fine professor."

She hadn't understood, Ava realized, but it had been suggested she not try to correct Patty's timeline.

"He was."

When Patty didn't continue the conversation, Ava sighed with relief. Trying to make sure she always said the right thing so as not to upset the other woman was exhausting.

While most of the younger girls played several bridal shower games, Ava had Patty help her pack the gifts into boxes.

"Now, how do you know the bride again?" Patty asked when the last gift had been packed away.

Oh, Patty.

"She's been my daughter's best friend for years," Ava explained, not for the first time.

"Right." A frown appeared between Patty's brows. "I wonder where her mother is. Mothers should really be involved in helping their daughters plan their wedding."

Oh, Patty.

Ava's heart hurt, and when Anita grabbed their hands and pushed them into empty chairs, she didn't fight too hard.

"What's this?" Ava looked around at the chairs set in a huge circle.

"A game," Anita smirked. "Just listen."

"This is just like musical chairs," Emma was telling everyone. "While the music is playing, keep the bouquet moving. When it stops, the one with the flowers takes their chair out of the circle."

The music started and every time the bouquet passed through her hands, Ava grew nervous.

Was it because of what the arrangement stood for?

Was it because she'd been brought up *King's must win*, and she didn't want to lose?

Or was it because she could imagine marrying again?

Marrying Finn.

The answer eluded her as the game continued, until it was down to her and Audrey, Elsa's nurse.

"Here we go." Emma started the music.

Back and forth they passed the bouquet, Ava's heart racing. A zillion thoughts flew through her head.

Should she let the younger woman win?

But then her inner competitive drive would kick in.

Back and forth, again and again, the music speeding up, sending Ava's heart skyrocketing. Something told her the music was coming to an end, and just after she'd given the bouquet away, there was silence.

"Congratulations." Audrey handed over the bouquet.

"Thank you." Ava's eyes met Finn's, as he and his sons had just arrived. But as he glided across the room, she forced herself to look away.

"Would you like to dance?"

His voice sent a thrill through her, and she wanted to turn his direction. And then, her imagination continued, she'd fall into his arms, and he'd kiss her like a man starving for her taste. Except, when she looked over her shoulder, it wasn't her, he was asking.

"Are you asking me?" Patty tittered.

Finn winked at Ava. "I am. Will you?"

Patty placed her hand in Finn's and followed him into the middle of the dancers, taking a little more of Ava's heart with him.

She was in so much trouble, she thought, watching him swing Patty around on the dance floor. Because the more she got to know him, the less she found she could compare him to Peter.

Listen to your heart, Captain Jack told her. It always knows.

Was the magic of Swan Harbor getting to her? Or was it Finn? Or was it love?

Can't it be all the above?

For some reason, that felt closer to the truth. Ava placed her prized bouquet with her bag, and grabbed the gifts for the attendees.

"Psst."

She glanced up, thinking she heard something, but when she didn't see anyone, continued her task.

"Psst."

This time, she localized the sound and found Finn hiding behind a pillar.

"Why are you hiding?"

"Come with me?"

She studied him for a minute. "Why?"

"You know why." He tapped his bottom lip.

A little thrill skittered through her body as she left her task and followed wherever he was leading.

⚘

Over Emma's head, Killian watched Ava disappear behind a pillar and sent a subtle nod to Liam.

"Killian," Emma nipped the skin just under his chin, "what's going on?"

"What are you talking about, Doc?" He feigned ignorance. "I just noticed Liam was dancing with Elsa's mother."

"He is?" Emma looked over her shoulder. "I thought Patty was dancing with Finn. Where did he go?"

Killian pretended to look for his father, but since he *literally* didn't know where he'd disappeared to, he wasn't really lying.

"Not sure. Men's room?" he offered just as the music ended.

"Okay," she shrugged. "I'll be back. I have maid of honor duties."

"Have fun."

As soon as she'd walked away, Killian caught Liam's eye and nodded toward where their father had disappeared.

"Where do you think they went?" asked Liam when he caught up.

Killian shrugged and led the way around the pillar. "Who knows, this place has more holes to hide in than Swiss Cheese."

Liam made a face. "That was bloody awful."

"You work with what you have," Killian quipped.

"Then you need more to work with," Liam retorted. "Do you see them?"

"No," Killian stepped fully around the wall, into a long narrow passageway, "and I've no idea where this goes."

"So, they could be anywhere?"

"Aye," Killian agreed. "But it was ingenious of you to cut in when he was dancing with Patty. How did you know he would head for Ava?"

Liam shrugged. "Intuition. Maybe I need to go into matchmaking full time."

"Right!" snorted Killian. "I'm sure that would go over with Elsa."

"She wouldn't care," Liam grumbled. "As long as I'm happy."

"Full time matchmaking won't pay the bills," Killian pointed out. "But it does give the Swan Harbor gossip line something to do."

The sound of a door opening had them ducking back around the wall.

"Is it them?" Liam whispered.

"Let me look."

Killian peered around the corner again, spotting Finn and Ava. "It's them."

"What are they doing?"

Once again, Killian looked around the wall. When he saw his father in a tight clench with Emma's mum, he began having second thoughts.

"Alright." He whipped back around, taking several steps away from the wall. "There are just some things a child shouldn't be privy to."

Liam grinned. "I want to look."

"Go right ahead." Killian moved out of the way. "But don't say I didn't warn you."

"How bad can it be?"

Killian counted to ten slowly, waiting for Liam to back away from his spying. "Well?" he snapped when he reached ten, and Liam still hadn't turned around.

"Our dad has some moves," Liam replied, holding his hand up. "High five, my plan was bloody brilliant."

"Alright." Killian grudgingly slapped his brother's hand. "It was bloody brilliant."

They hurried back toward the party, not wanting to be caught. "I just hope he doesn't hurt her. Emma would kill me."

"It could go the other way," Liam pointed out. "She could hurt him just as easily."

"Not bloody likely," Killian quipped. "He's our father, after all."

"True," Liam nodded. "And we do know our way around women."

"Other than Emma," Killian grimaced, "I'd rather forget those other encounters."

"That's probably a good idea," Liam muttered.

They stepped around the wall to find Emma and Elsa waiting for them. "There you two are."

"Doc!" Killian tugged her into his arms. "You shouldn't sneak up on a man like that."

"Where have you two been?" Elsa asked, pinning Liam with her blue-eyed gaze.

Liam grinned at his fiancée. "Just looking for the little boy's room."

"Don't be cheeky, Liam." Emma grumbled. "What did you do?"

"What makes you think I did something?" Liam held his hands up as if surrendering. "I am perfectly innocent."

"Since when?" Finn stepped around the corner with Ava close on his heels. "You've had that glint in your eyes lately."

Liam put his arm around Elsa's waist and pulled her close. "I'm happy and getting married. That would put a glint, as you call it, in anyone's eye."

Killian studied his father when he exchanged smiles with Ava. As was expected, the evidence of their tryst was written on Finn's face for everyone to see.

"Emma and I were just going to dance."

Killian rubbed his thumb along his bottom lip, trying subtly to send Liam a signal.

The glint in Liam's eyes grew brighter, telling Killian his message had been received.

"Elsa, love. Let's go dance," Liam added in a rush.

"But," Finn began, "we wanted ..."

"It's our song," Killian tossed over his shoulder, hurrying Emma into the crowd.

"Killian!" Emma sputtered. "What's going on?"

He glanced into her upturned face and, as always, felt the truth bubbling up. "I can't have any secrets?"

"You know the answer to that as well as I do."

"Aye, Doc. I do." He sighed and jumped in, "There's something going on between our parents."

"I know."

Killian tilted his head in thought. "So you've been keeping secrets too?"

Emma opened and closed her mouth several times. "But, but," she stuttered.

"See, Doc." Killian swung her across the floor before saying any more, "It's not so easy to talk about, is it?"

"What if?"

He kissed her, effectively shutting her up. Then the thought of what had sent him scurrying onto the dance floor bubbled up, and he couldn't stop the laughter.

Finn frowned. "They're definitely up to something. Did you see how fast they ran off?"

"Maybe they just wanted to dance." Ava shrugged. "Don't worry about it."

"But," he sputtered, turning away from the dancing and back toward her. "It was bloody odd."

Ava looked at him, and the smile on her face fell. "Oh no!" She grabbed his hand and tugged him back behind the pillar. "I told you *that* was a bad idea." The entire time she was lecturing, she was wiping her thumb across his lips.

"I'm wearing your lipstick?"

"Yes!" She continued to wipe. "There. It's not perfect, but better."

Finn grinned, thinking about all the times he'd caught his sons sneaking in from dates with lipstick smears. "Are you alright with this?"

Ava studied the floor for several minutes, and he'd have given anything to know what was going through her mind.

"I'm okay," she began, but there was a slight hesitation in her voice. "Just no more of *that*." Ava waved her hand in front of his mouth.

He couldn't help himself and grabbed her arm to kiss the inside of her wrist. "How about that?"

"Oh, you." The way she looked at him had her dimple popping, and his heart flipped several times. "Let's go give Elsa and Liam their gift."

They stepped back around the pillar, and when she tugged her hand free, he wanted to say something, but instead shelved it for later.

"Do you see them?"

"They're over there." Ava pointed to where a group of women had congregated. "My guess is saying goodbye to the guests."

"How did the shower go? Did you have a good time?"

She laughed. "It doesn't matter if the guests have fun. What matters is if the bride had a good time."

"And did she?"

"I think so, but ..."

He grabbed hold of her fingers without realizing what he was doing, only wanting to comfort her.

"But?"

"Patty."

That one word said it all, as the thought of the beautiful woman's decline was a punch in the gut. "Did she make a scene?"

"A scene? No." Ava squeezed his fingers and pulled her hand free. I'm not sure she ever really understood Elsa was her daughter. It just makes me sad."

"What can I do?"

Ava's gaze met his. "You're doing it."

"What am I doing?"

"Listening," she smiled. "And now, let's grab the kids."

"Lead the way."

They found Elsa giving instructions to Liam, Emma, and Killian regarding the wedding gifts.

"Can we grab you two for a minute?" Finn asked after Killian and Emma left with a stack of boxes. "We have something for you."

Liam set the bags he'd been holding back onto a table. "What is it?"

Finn slipped his hand into his jacket and pulled out an envelope he'd stuck in there earlier. "We hope you haven't booked a honeymoon yet."

"No," Liam opened the envelope, "with the move and all, we thought we'd wait."

"Now you don't have to wait," Finn told them, hoping they were okay with someone else doing the planning.

"This is for us?" Elsa glanced up, her eyes shining with unshed tears. "I don't know what to say."

"You say thank you," Ava suggested. "And take a lot of pictures."

The look Liam and Elsa exchanged had a lump forming in Finn's throat. His son's happiness had been a long time coming, and it was a joy to see.

"Thank you," Elsa whispered.

"What she said," Liam concurred. "Really, thank you."

"You're very welcome."

"Liam, quit being a lazy sod," Killian barked, returning from the trip to the car.

"Sorry about that," Finn began.

But Liam interrupted, "Quit being a knob head. We're on our way. Thanks again, Dad, Ava." He hugged them both.

Finn couldn't keep the smile off his face, as they helped organize the rest of the gifts. Every time his eyes met Ava's, he kept thinking of his statement to her.

"At heart, I'm a simple man. There's nothing more important than family ..."

Once Liam and Elsa, and Emma and Killian had driven off, the thought of returning to his hotel alone had Finn grabbing Ava's hand. "Come with me."

"Slow down," she laughed, following him to another floor. "Where are we going?"

He threw a grin at her, slowing his step slightly. "To play pinball."

"Pinball?"

"Yes!"

Finn led her into the room of old-fashioned pinball machines he'd discovered earlier. "Remember these?"

"Well," Ava looked around the room, "I remember them." She stretched out the word. "But I've never actually played them."

"You are in for a treat then. Wait here." He winked. "I'll get tokens."

While he waited for his tokens, he watched her move from machine to machine. And he couldn't help but think, it was as if she'd never been in an arcade before.

"Which one?"

Ava glanced around, her almost giddy smile threatening to break free. "That one." She pointed to a brightly colored machine in the corner.

He waved toward the machine. "Ladies first."

"I don't know ..."

"You've really never played?"

"No." Ava shook her head self-consciously. "A boy I liked in college played, but I just watched."

Finn's voice grew dangerous. "Well now, Ms. King. Let me show you."

He inserted the tokens into the machine, and as soon as the balls slid into play, he tugged her in front of him.

"Finn."

"Yes, love?"

Finn layered himself against her back, his hands covering hers, his head next to hers, and their cheeks pressed tightly together.

"Ready," he whispered against her temple.

"What do I do?" she asked, settling against him.

"You launch the ball." He showed her how to pull back on the lever. "When the ball bounces close to these," he covered her hands, showing her how to use the flippers, "you push them, keeping the balls in play."

"Sounds good." She bent forward slightly to get a better look at the ball bouncing around on the table.

But as the game wore on, Finn realized, it wasn't just the machine's balls that were in play, his were as well. For with every push of the flipper, her behind met his zipper placket to engage in more frottage than he'd experienced in quite some time.

"You're killing me here." He finally called uncle after almost an hour. "How does ice cream sound?"

"Ice cream?" Ava questioned. "But it's winter outside."

"So? It's never too cold for ice cream."

Ava stopped on the sidewalk and tugged on his hand. "Finn, did I do something wrong?"

"No, love." He pulled her into his arms and aligned their hips. "I just needed to cool off, unless ..."

Several expressions crossed her face before she leaned in and kissed him softly. "I get it now. I'm sorry."

"Don't be sorry, love." He kissed her back. "It's not that I don't enjoy it ..."

"But blue balls aren't your favorite."

He barked out a laugh. "No, they aren't. So is it ice cream or ..." Finn left it hanging, wishing she would choose the or ....

Ava sighed. "Ice cream ... for now."

Her kiss took the sting out of the sliver of disappointment her words had him feeling. However, it was progress.

ELEVEN

Veterinary Clinic
November 8
5:30 a.m.

"Doc."

"I'm right here." Emma replied as soon as Killian walked into the living area.

He studied her for several seconds and, just as always, she felt he was seeing inside her soul. "Are you alright?"

"I'm fine. Just couldn't sleep."

Killian climbed on the sofa behind her and tugged her into his arms. "You could have woken me."

"I know. But I just …"

"Have a lot on your mind."

"Yeah."

"What specifically?"

"Can't I just think and keep those thoughts to myself?"

"What was it you said to me when I asked about keeping secrets?"

"My thoughts aren't secrets though," Emma pointed out. "Just thoughts."

"But these thoughts are burdens, aren't they?" Killian continued working to ferret out what she was thinking.

"Maybe." Then she changed her mind, unsure about the word he'd used. "I'm not sure they're really burdens though."

"You're not worried about your mother and my father? Or about your father's visit?"

"Do you believe in destiny?"

"Like in things happening for a reason?"

"Yeah."

"If you would have asked me that question before everything that happened with Violet, I would have said no."

"And now?"

She felt Killian shrug before settling in with his answer, "I think we're in charge of our destiny, to a point." he went on. "But where did that question come from?"

Emma reached for her phone and pulled up the photos. "Do you remember the first picture of us I sent to you?"

"From the masked ball?"

"That's the one." She held up her phone, so they could both look at it. "What do you see?"

The picture had been taken by Elsa while they were dancing the previous New Year's Eve. They were dressed in evening wear, their faces and identities hidden by masks. Before that night, their conversations in Swan Harbor had been contentious, it was evident there was a connection between them.

"I take it you're looking for something other than how devilishly handsome I looked that evening?"

"Yes, Killian." Emma gave an exaggerated sigh. "If you were '*investigating*' what would you think?"

"That they were lovers," he immediately responded.

Instead of responding, Emma slid her thumb across the photo, and stopped at one of her mother and dad. "And this couple?"

In the picture of her parents, they were posing for the cameras, and Peter had his arm around Ava. But they weren't touching in any other manner. In fact, they were leaning away from each other. Plus, their smiles were forced.

"That they can barely tolerate each other."

"And this one?"

Emma flipped through her photos, finding one of Peter and his new wife. In it, they were posed just as he'd been standing with Ava. But with his arm around

Amber, their body language was almost the exact opposite. They were turned into each other, and her hand rested over his heart.

"That they were in love." Killian skimmed his palm along her arm. "Where are you going with this, Doc?"

"One more," she promised. "Look at this one."

Emma pulled up the picture she'd snapped of Ava and Finn dancing the night they'd gone to Captain Jack's.

"When did you take that?"

"Remember when I told you, I'd forgotten my wrap?"

He chuckled. "Had you really forgotten your wrap or were you spying?"

"Does it matter?"

"So, spying," he tsked.

"Wait a minute," she giggled. "What was it you and Liam were doing at Randy's again?"

"What?" he exclaimed. "Liam told you what we were doing. Just looking for the little boys' room."

"Uh huh, right." Emma held her phone back up. "What do you notice about this couple?"

"That they only have eyes for each other."

There was a tone in his voice that said he was getting to where she was going with her question. "You understand, don't you?"

Killian was quiet for so long Emma wasn't sure if he was going to respond.

"Aye." He took her phone and tossed it aside. "I asked my dad one time about him and my mother. He said, 'we weren't right, but she gave me you'."

"Just like my parents weren't right, but here I am."

"And through circumstances in both of our lives," he went on, and she knew he was thinking about Violet, "we met and fell in love."

"And because we met," Emma added, "our parents met."

"And have fallen for each other. Are you really alright with that, Doc?"

Emma turned in his arms, so she was facing him. "I'll admit, sometimes it feels weird to see."

"Like you're the parent watching your child come in from a date?" He used the exact analogy she was thinking.

"Yes!" Emma thought back to their night at Captain Jack's. "It's kind of cute to watch them."

Killian humphed. "You sound like Liam. He thinks dad has some moves."

"You don't agree?"

"Doc," Killian wrapped his hand around her long blonde hair, "there are some things I don't want our parents seeing. And some things I don't want to observe in them."

"Really?" Emma readjusted on his lap and slid her hand up his shoulder. "And what would that be?"

His eyes glittered in the low light. "I think it's best if I show you."

"By all means," she barely got out before his lips covered hers, and talking was shelved for a long while.

Lighthouse Inn
November 8
7:30 a.m.

Finn sat with his feet propped on the balcony railing and watched the waves. With a cup of coffee in one hand and his ever-present silver coin walking along the back of his knuckles, his mind was free to wander.

But instead of mentally sorting through what he'd found in his notebooks, he kept seeing Ava's face. And instead of trying to figure out who had been in his room, while he'd been at Randy's, he kept replaying moments they'd shared.

Her girlish giggle when they'd ridden the carousel. The sadness in her voice when she'd told him about missing out on moments of Emma's childhood. How she'd opened her heart and shared her fears. And the way her breath caught every time he leaned in for a kiss.

What was she doing to him?

She was stealing his concentration and taking over his mind. And no matter how often he tried to convince himself to slow down, his heart wasn't listening.

Told you she was reminding you what it was like to fall in love.

There was the breathlessness, the way his heart raced, and the feeling of anticipation that was never far away. But the cold showers, he thought with a self-deprecating twist of his lips, he could definitely do without.

Except, until he'd solved the mystery surrounding him, it didn't matter how much she meant to him. It didn't matter how successful he was. And it didn't matter how much he enjoyed spending time with his boys. Because, until he discovered who was sending the notes and why, the future of the family he'd been searching for his entire life was in jeopardy.

"Close your eyes really tight, Flynn," Winnie whispered in his ear, *"and make a wish."*

"But Winnie," five-year-old Flynn cried. *"I've tried every night since mum died, and it still hasn't come true."*

Winnie tilted her head as a resigned look crossed her face. "Doesn't matter, baby brother. You can't give up hoping tomorrow will be different. Remember, the future begins with hope."

"Do you still hope for your happy ending, like in those books you read?" he asked curiously.

"No, Flynn." Winnie showed him the newest romance she was reading. "These days, I've decided I don't want a happy ending but a happy beginning."

"Is that possible?"

"Anything is possible," she pulled the tattered blanket over his thin frame, "with hope."

"If you say so."

"Promise me, Flynn," Winnie pleaded with him. "Don't ever give up on hope."

For more than fifty years, he'd kept hoping he'd find the future he was meant to have. The 'happy beginning' she believed in. And yet ....

The reminder of his promise to his big sister propelled him back to his desk, and the notebooks he'd spent the better part of the night revisiting.

There had been three notes, with the first one left on his office desk.

Where is it? We know you have it.

The second had been dropped on the floor of his home.

It doesn't belong to you. Isn't it time to return it?

And after receiving those, he'd focused on the fears revolving around his sons.

"I'm afraid something will happen to my relationship with Killian and Liam. I'm afraid I'll disappoint them."

Then he'd received the third note, which effectively had his present and his hope for the future colliding with his past. As printed on the piece of paper had been the photo of him holding the stolen painting. And one of him and Ava sitting on a bench in Central Park. What he'd told Ava he'd been afraid of had never been truer.

"I'm afraid I'm always going to be alone," he'd admitted. *"And I'm afraid you won't allow me to be your Flynn Ryder."*

While the notes seemed to come through his office mail, that didn't explain his room being searched. Had the danger followed him to Swan Harbor? If so, should he go back to New York, alone?

Was he ready to leave Ava behind?

The chirp of an incoming text had him reaching for his phone.

> Ava: Good morning. Do you have plans for later this evening?

And after reading one short text, he had his answer. He was no more willing to walk away from Ava than he was from Killian and Liam.

> Finn: When should I be there?

> Ava: You aren't going to ask what I have in mind first?

> Finn: Does it involve spending time with you?

> Ava: Maybe.

> Finn: Just maybe? Well, if that's the case, maybe I have plans.

> Ava: Oh you! Yes, it involves spending time with me.

> Finn: Alone?

> Ava: Not really.

He reread the text, and while he couldn't figure out where she was going, he knew it didn't really matter.

Finn: What do you have in mind, love?

Ava: I'm going over to see Rachel later and offered to babysit. I was wondering if ….

Finn: You want me to help babysit.

Ava: I thought you might want to see Riley again.

Finn: While it will be nice to see Riley and Rachel again, they aren't the main attraction.

Ava: No?

Finn: Are you fishing, love?

Ava: If I were, would I catch something?

Finn: You already have. Shall I pick you up?

Ava: Meet me at Rachel's.

Finn: See you then.

He tossed his phone aside with a new determination burning in his gut. And after a quick glance at the photo of him with the painting, opened to the notes he'd written over twenty years ago.

The painting, Poppies and Peonies, is believed to be Monet's first work, painted in 1857 when he was just seventeen years old. It was commissioned as a gift for Queen Victoria in honor of the birth of her daughter, Princess Beatrice. Completed during the summer, the oil painting measures 21 cm x 41 cm.

Following her mother's passing, the painting was moved into the Princess' residence, remaining until its disappearance sometime during World War II. At the time, the painting was estimated to be worth £3 million pounds.

For the next few lines, Finn had to squint to read his notes, but he knew the dates traced the painting as it moved through the underground circles.

Poppies and Peonies was acquired by Roman Sutton for his much younger wife, Ella, for £15 million pounds in 1987. The painting is hung in the Sutton villa, located near the Charing Cross junction in Westminster, London.

Finder's fee for returning the painting, £2 million pounds.

The next few pages, he'd drawn diagrams of the villa, including all seven bedrooms, eight bathrooms, and the surroundings grounds. Then he'd filled several pages with the comings and goings of the staff, Roman, Ella and regular visitors.

Party to be held on New Year's Eve. Enter through the kitchen. Wear tux. Contact Remy.

He wanted to resist, but the pull was too great, sucking him into the memory.

New Year's Eve
London
21 years earlier

FLYNN STOOD IN THE SHADOWS OF THE TREES LINING THE DRIVE, waiting for the alarm on his watch to give him the go. At exactly 11:45 p.m., he walked into the Sutton kitchen and took the back staircase, undetected.

The painting was in Ella Sutton's office, and when he was halfway there, the sound of footsteps sent him running for cover.

"I'll be right back, Roman," a woman's voice called. "I just want to say goodnight to the baby."

With multiple doors offered, Flynn ducked into the nearest room, just barely hiding before a very pregnant woman passed by.

Bloody hell, he thought, the adrenaline coursing through his system.

Flynn counted the minutes in his head, finally allowing himself to breathe again when she returned the way she'd come. As soon as the hall was clear, he darted from his hiding place and rushed to her office.

The painting was hanging behind the desk, complete with a security device connected to the back of the frame. With little time to waste, Flynn bypassed the security, removed the real Poppies, replaced it with a copy, and returned it to the wall.

He rushed back down the hall and took the stairs two at a time. As he walked away from the villa with the Poppies in his arms, the clock struck midnight.

The next day, he'd handed the painting, worth over £27 million pounds, to his contact, Remy.

Which gave him a place to start, he decided, powering up his computer.

Camelot Arms Apartments
November 8
6:30 p.m.

Ava surreptitiously glanced at her watch, and the thought that Finn would arrive in a half-hour sent a thrill up her spine.

"Do you have any more questions?" she asked Rachel, tuning back into the task at hand.

Rachel frowned and spread the papers across the table. "Let me see if I have this right." She organized the forms. "I fill out these. Then if you like my plan, you give me money to start a music school?"

Ava grinned. "While it's not quite that simplistic, you have the right idea. I'll give you money, but it will be from investors who believe in you. You start your business, pay them back with low monthly payments, and eventually it's all yours."

"Wow!" Rachel exclaimed. "You're like a fairy godmother."

"As long as you don't see me as the evil queen," chuckled Ava. "I'm good with the godmother analogy.

"Never that," Rachel assured her. "You've been wonderful."

Ava blinked twice, and her eyes misted over. "I'm glad I can help. And." She glanced over at the baby who was sitting in a bouncy seat close by. "That I was there when Riley was born."

"Me too." Rachel gathered the papers and slipped them into a file. "I'll start on this tomorrow. It would be nice to stay in Swan Harbor."

"No rush," Ava assured the younger woman.

"Have to pay the bills." Rachel shrugged.

"For what it's worth," Ava reassured her. "I really do think your idea is a good one."

"Thanks."

"But now," Ava tapped her watch, "don't you need to get ready?"

A worried look crossed Rachel's face. "You're sure you don't mind staying with the baby?"

"I'm positive. Just show me where everything is, and don't worry. We'll have fun."

For the next few minutes, Rachel showed Ava where the diapers, wipes, and clothes were stored. Then she led the way to the kitchen. "He'll want to be fed at 7:00 p.m." She pointed to where the bottles were kept. "After he eats, he should sleep for a few hours."

"We'll be fine. Don't worry."

"Just call me if there's a problem."

"I will," Ava assured her again. "Now, go get dressed."

As soon as Rachel disappeared, the baby began fussing, and a sliver of fear settled in the pit of Ava's stomach. She could do this, couldn't she?

It's just like riding a bike.

Except she hadn't been allowed to ride a bike.

"You might hurt yourself, Ava." Leo King grumbled.

"But daddy!"

"I said no."

And she'd played the dutiful daughter. Just like she'd played the dutiful daughter when he'd hired Johanna to take care of Emma. She hadn't fought hard enough.

"Are you hungry?" she cooed, taking Riley out of his bouncy seat.

He stared at her with his big blue eyes while she took a bottle and warmed it.

"Okay, I'm ready." Rachel came into the kitchen. "I should be home before 10:00 p.m.

Ava tested the milk, tossed a cloth diaper over her shoulder, and followed Rachel back into the front room.

"You're fine. Who are you going with again?"

"Harper Taylor and Eden Fowler."

"Have fun."

Five minutes after Rachel was gone, there was a knock on the door.

Finn! Anticipation inside slithered out and zipped along her skin.

Be cool.

But as always, when she got her first look at him, a goofy smiled crossed her face. "Hi."

"Hi yourself."

Ava was content to stare, but Riley made his presence known. "Someone is hungry."

"Go ahead," Finn scooted her inside. "I'll watch."

Ava settled in one of the chairs and offered the bottle to the baby. "Here you go, little guy."

Riley latched onto the nipple as if he were starving.

"He's a good eater." Finn knelt next to where she was sitting. "Reminds me of my boys. They were always good eaters."

"Emma wasn't," Ava remembered. "She was finicky. But not this guy."

"Definitely not, Riley." Finn laughed at the way the baby was inhaling his meal.

A peacefulness surrounded them while she fed and burped Riley that Ava had never experienced with Peter. And, as seemed to happen every time they were together, she gave Finn another little piece of her heart.

"All done." Ava handed the empty bottle to Finn and put the baby up on her shoulder, patting his back gently.

It wasn't long before he let out a loud belch. And as soon as she lowered him to her lap, she noticed the look of fierce concentration on the baby's face.

"Ah oh," Ava murmured.

"What?" Finn asked, returning to the room. Then a look crossed his face, and she knew he'd gotten a whiff. "I'd forgotten about that," he laughed. "When something goes in—"

"—Something must come out," Ava groaned.

"Think you remember how to change a diaper?" Finn helped her collect the supplies.

"Sure," she told him, but inside her stomach swirled with uncertainty. Could she do it?

Finn laid a blanket on the floor and as Ava put the baby in the center, she kept going through the steps in her head.

"Here we go." Ava unsnapped the legs of the pajamas Riley was wearing.

She pulled open the tabs on the diaper, and the smell grew stronger.

"You might want to—" Finn began.

Except his warning came too late. As soon as she removed the diaper, Riley presented her with a surprise.

"Oh!" Her startled eyes met Finn's laughing ones.

"You've never changed a baby boy, have you?"

Ava felt her face heat. "No, but ..."

"Experienced it a time or two with Liam," Finn chuckled. "You learn never to leave them uncovered."

"Well, that makes sense."

"But we do grow out of it," Finn deadpanned.

"Uh good," Ava stammered, working to regain her equilibrium.

"Here." Finn took pity on her and efficiently put a clean diaper on the baby.

"You're good at that," she said in awe.

"Practice," he winked, re-snapping the baby's pajamas and handing him to her. Then cleaned up the dirty mess.

Too good to be true, floated through her head. *He's a natural.*

"Did you want more children?" she asked when he returned.

Finn's dark eyes met hers, and in them she saw regret and wishes. He swallowed, and she had to wonder what he was thinking.

"I would have loved another one or two," he admitted quietly. "But circumstances didn't allow it."

She gave him a melancholy smile. "I know what you mean. There were times I wished Emma hadn't been an only child."

"But we can't go back."

"No, we can't," she agreed, noticing Riley had gone to sleep. "Let me put him down."

"Take your time."

Ava placed the baby in the cradle someone had loaned Rachel and, leaving a small light on, went to find Finn.

He'd turned the television to one of the music stations and lowered the lights.

"Would I be wrong in thinking you have something in mind for us to do?"

"Well, that all depends." He smiled so his dimples peeked out. "On what you think I have in mind."

"Dancing?" she guessed, thinking there was nothing she wanted more than to be held in his arms.

"No." Finn stalked toward her, and the look on his face caused her heart to race. "Come here." He took her hand and tugged her down onto the sofa next to him. "Have you ever had your boyfriend over when you were babysitting?"

Boyfriend!

"I never babysat."

"Me either," he acknowledged. "But in the movies ..."

Ava slid her arms around his neck and held on as he laid her on the sofa and stretched out next to her.

"It goes like this."

His lips hovered over hers, and his dark eyes mesmerized. They told her things she'd never thought to hear.

"Kiss me." She cupped his face, tugged him close and, with his mouth on hers, let herself get lost in the moment.

TWELVE

Lighthouse Inn
November 9
7:30 a.m.

Finn had a carrier with coffees in one hand, a bag from Paula's Pastries hanging from the other, and under his arm, his briefcase. But standing outside Ava's cottage door, he realized he had no way of knocking.

"Bloody hell," he muttered, looking around for somewhere to set the carrier. Except without options, he used his knee to make a passable knocking sound.

He'd just about decided she'd gone to a morning exercise class when the door was yanked open, "Finn!" Ava exclaimed breathlessly.

She had on one of the hotel robes, her hair was wrapped in a towel, and something green was smeared on her face. But she'd never looked more beautiful.

"Did I forget something?" She tightened the belt around her slim waist.

"Breakfast?" He advanced on her in such away she was forced backwards.

"Finn!" she exclaimed. "I look—"

"Beautiful." He kissed her quiet.

"But ..."

Finn set the coffee carrier on the table, along with the pastry bag and his briefcase.

"Look at it like this." He took her shoulders and turned her toward the bathroom. "If I think you're beautiful with a green face, you have nothing to worry about."

Ava sent him a dirty look, and something had him swatting her on her delectable behind.

"Finn!" she squeaked, scurrying out of the room.

He chuckled, tempted to follow her.

Have patience.

Her words were the only thing that had him finding plates and laying out their impromptu breakfast.

He felt her return before she said anything, and indicated the cup he'd set on one side of the table. "I didn't know how you liked your coffee."

"It smells good," she murmured, coming the rest of the way into the room.

"Here, sit down."

Finn pulled out a chair, and as he pushed her forward, he couldn't resist nuzzling just behind her ear. "*You* smell good."

"Thank you."

Ava took the cup he handed her and sipped, her shining eyes never leaving his. "How did you know?"

"That you took hazelnut creamer?" He thought about holding out a while longer and making her work for it. But since she didn't appear willing to eat until he answered, he capitulated, "I asked."

"Who?" She squinted and watched him closely, as if she were trying to get the answer before he offered.

"It's no secret," Finn told her, "Paula."

Ava's mouth dropped open. "Oh."

"You think it's all over town?"

"I know it is."

He couldn't decide what to make of the look on her face, but didn't want her to worry. "We're staying at the same hotel. Friends buy friends breakfast."

She tore a piece off her cinnamon bun and nibbled it daintily. "Did she tell you what pastry I preferred too?"

Finn grinned, but didn't answer her until he swallowed. "Guilty. Would you rather I asked Emma?"

"No, no," she reiterated. "It's just ..."

"Scary," he supplied.

Ava's blue eyes met his. "Yes ... but also exciting."

Her whispered response sent his pulse racing. "Do you mean that?"

"Maybe." Ava's eyes twinkled. "Thank you for breakfast."

"You're welcome."

"Are you on your way out?" She nodded at his briefcase.

"No, I was hoping we could spend the day together."

"But I have—"

He jumped from his chair and knelt next to hers. "I thought maybe ... we'd work together. Am I being too presumptuous?"

She grinned. "That's a sweet idea."

"I'm a sweet guy."

"You are," Ava agreed. "Now finish your meal. It's almost time to work."

"Anyone tell you what a taskmaster you are?"

"Maybe." Then she grabbed his face and kissed him as if she'd been starving for his taste. "Work."

"Yes, ma'am." Finn kissed her hard and fast before jumping up to finish his pastry.

For the next couple of hours, they each set up their work areas and, besides soft music, it was quiet. To his right, there was the view of the beach and to his left, Ava. He could find no other word to describe it, but perfect.

"Stop staring." She periodically pointed her finger at him.

He tried, even succeeding for several minutes at a time, as he searched for Remy French. The man whose job it was to return the painting to Princess Beatrice's family. Then, a week after he'd taken it, the 'recovery' had appeared in small print in the London Times.

Poppies and Peonies, a painting thought to be Monet's first masterpiece, was returned to the royal family over the weekend. To whoever returned this gift, the Queen thanks you.

So why was he being sent notes regarding a painting he hadn't seen in over twenty years?

Talk to Killian.

Except he wasn't ready to see that disappointed look in his son's eyes. And since Killian was the law, it just made the situation stickier.

"I've been waiting fifteen minutes," he heard Ava snap. "When do you expect Mr. Morton to have time to take my call?"

She was annoyed, Finn thought, watching her pace while listening to the person on the other end of the phone.

"I told you," Ava continued in a clipped voice. "There was a bracelet mailed to my home in Boston in May. I'm following up on it."

A gift in May? That would have been right before their encounter.

"An hour?" Her eyes met his across the room. "I'll call back. Thank you."

"Problems?"

"Not really problems," she denied. "A mystery I'm trying to solve."

"Can I help?"

Ava's eyes never left his, as she set her phone on the table and glided toward him. He closed his computer and pushed it away in time for her to lower herself onto his lap.

"You're helping."

Finn frowned. "How am I helping, love? I don't even—"

Ava covered his mouth. "You listen."

She cupped his jaw and kissed him softly, hesitantly, as if she were feeling her way and didn't want it to be over too fast. Her lips trembled under his, and he fought the need to pick her up and lay her on the floor. But this was her show, and when her tongue probed the seam of his mouth, he opened and let her in.

"You listen," she repeated when she came up for air.

"No one else listened?"

"My employees listen," Ava confided. "But when we were married, Peter never listened, and my father ..."

"His way or the highway?" he quipped.

"Something like that."

"You're supposed to call back Mr. Morton in an hour?"

Ava hummed, trailing her index finger along his bottom lip. "And do you have something you need to do in the meantime?"

"Well." Her lips whispered along his cheekbone to drop a peck on the tip of his nose. "I can think of a few things." She placed a light kiss on his lips before bouncing from there to deposit one on an eyelid.

"Ava."

"Too much?"

He'd told himself he was going to follow her pace, but bloody hell, she was killing him. "Not nearly enough," he groaned, carrying her to the sofa and following her down.

Sally's Diner
November 9
12:30 p.m.

KILLIAN AND LIAM WALKED INTO SALLY'S, FINDING THE PLACE already buzzing with the usual lunch crowd.

"Hey, Killian ... Liam," Hayden greeted them before they'd gotten far. "Need a table, or are you picking up?"

"A table, please." Killian noticed the younger man seemed to be in a better mood since they'd had their talk.

"Okay. Hold on." He bounded across the diner with a little extra swagger in his step.

"He seems happy," Liam noted.

"Aye." Killian watched Hayden clean a table while sneaking peaks at one of the servers. "Appears someone new has caught his eye."

"I thought he was dating Peyton."

"Same here."

"Okay." Hayden waved them over. "Having your usual?"

"Let us look." Killian took the proffered menu and flipped it open. "I thought you and Peyton were ..."

"Well," Hayden shrugged, "I'm not sure what's going on."

"Could it be, she's noticed you've been making eyes at someone else?"

Hayden gazed over his shoulder and turned back with a grin. "Isn't she just ..."

Killian exchanged looks with Liam. "Do you miss those days?"

"You're the one who had a new girl every week, Killian," Liam laughed. "But do I miss not knowing how the girl I liked felt about me? No. I'm perfectly happy with what Elsa and I have."

"She's cute, Hayden," Killian quipped as soon as the younger man turned back to their table. "What's her name?"

"Katrina," Hayden sighed. "I have her in a class. Think I should ask her out?"

The old Killian Reade would have said *go for it* considering no one's feelings. But the man who loved Emma cautioned, "I would make sure everything is done with Peyton before you do."

"Really?" Hayden sent him a disgruntled look. "I guess."

"It's not a simple thing to do, Hayden," Liam empathized. "But it is the right thing to do."

"Okay," Hayden grumbled. "Are you ready to order?"

Killian shook his head. "Give us a few."

Once he was gone, Killian glanced at the menu and shoved it away. Who was he kidding? He always got the same thing.

"Not that it's not nice to meet for lunch," Killian began. "But what's going on? Everything okay with Elsa?"

"Things are wonderful with Elsa," Liam confirmed. "I just ..."

When he hesitated, Killian's gut churned with worry. After everything that had gone down with Santora, he'd thought ... " Just spit it out, Liam."

"Do you ever feel paranoid? As if—"

"—You're being watched?"

"Well, kind of." Liam brushed his hands through his hair. "I've said nothing to Elsa. I don't want to worry her. But ..."

Killian studied his brother for several seconds. "Emma thinks my concerns are leftover worry, and I'll admit ..."

"Hi Killian." Morgan waved as she passed their table, with Tia, Chloe, and Catherine not far behind.

"You'll admit?" Liam prompted.

"A few times, I've thought I was being watched, and it's..." He gestured towards the table where several of his ex-girlfriends sat.

"I could see how that would get old," Liam agreed.

"But you act like something concrete happened," Killian prodded. "What was it?"

"That's just it," Liam grumbled. "I'm not sure ..."

"What happened, Liam?"

"You know the book that was mom's?"

He was talking about a journal the private investigator had brought back from England.

"Aye."

Liam took a deep breath. "I was looking for it the other day and couldn't find it."

"And not being able to find something is new?" Killian scoffed. "Bloody hell, between your boxes and Elsa's, I'm not sure how you find anything in your home."

"There is that," Liam acknowledged. "But the book was different, because I had it when we went to Swan's Spirit's that night."

"And when you went home, you tossed it on an empty surface," Killian guessed.

"On the hall table," Liam admitted. "But when I went looking, it was gone."

"So," Killian shrugged. "Elsa moved it."

"She swears she didn't."

"Come on. Maybe she forgot. You know they do that ... move things, but deny it and blame you."

Liam laughed. "Glad it's not just me. But in this case, no, she didn't move it because it showed back up ..."

"Don't keep me in suspense," Killian retorted. "Where?"

"On my desk at work."

"So, you're telling me," Killian's brows went up in surprise, "the book disappeared from your house but reappeared on your desk at the station?"

"Yeah," Liam nodded. "See what I mean?"

"That's cocked up," Killian agreed. "But this is Swan Harbor. Maybe you left in at Swan's Spirit's that night and someone dropped it by the station."

"Maybe." Liam chewed on that possibility for a few seconds.

"Do you want me to ask Krystal, the owner, for you?"

"No," Liam shook his head, "I'll take care of it later."

"Alright."

"Are you ready to order?" Hayden stopped back by their table.

"The usual," Killian tossed out.

"Me too," Liam added.

Hayden rolled his eyes. "I could have told you that."

"Sorry," Killian offered. "But you know how it is."

"Right," Hayden grunted and walked away.

"No idea," Killian answered Liam's unspoken question regarding Hayden's mood. "Anything else going on?"

Liam grinned, and his eyes twinkled. "I heard dad bought pastry and coffee for him and Ava this morning."

"How do you know it was for Ava?" Killian asked. "If he bought two, it could have been ..."

"No," Liam interrupted. "It seems he didn't know how Ava took her coffee—"

"So he asked?" Killian guessed. "Swan Harbor's gossip line is on top of things."

"You think he spent the night?" Liam quipped.

Killian sent him a disgusted look. "I'd rather not go there."

"Think we should ask him about protection?"

"Bloody hell, Liam!"

Lighthouse Inn
November 9
3:30 p.m.

Ava had been staring at the numbers on the application for Becca's knick-knack shop for twenty minutes. But no matter how many times she started again, her focus sucked. She wanted to say it was because Mr. Morton, from the attorney's office, hadn't called her back. Or barring that, she could claim it had to do with the fact Peter was due to arrive shortly. Except, she knew those weren't really the cause. Finley Reade was directly to blame for her lack of concentration.

Since he'd arrived early with coffee, he'd been bombarding her senses. The smell of his spicy cologne had surrounded her. His husky voice, and the taste of his kiss. But combined with his gaze, his actions were enough to overwhelm anyone. Even the most jaded individual.

She kept thinking of the visit when she gave Emma the charm bracelet. That she had walked in on something between her daughter and Killian had been obvious.

Ava's eyes twinkled over the rim of her cup. "Looks like you took my advice about Killian."

"Your advice?"

"That if you have something good, you should hold on tightly," Ava reminded her. "Looks like you were holding on tightly."

"Mother!"

"Sorry," Ava chuckled. *"I feel like I missed out on those awkward moments when you were growing up."*

"So, you're making up for them now?"

And with Finn in the picture, their roles were reversed. It was the daughter who was involved in a relationship. Whereas the mother was feeling her way into one, much like a teen. Another one of those things she'd missed out on growing up.

It's Finn.

He'd taken her to the Central Park Zoo, and on a carousel. She'd worn his jacket, played pinball, and been taken for ice cream. There'd been babysitting, and kissing sessions on the sofa. The way he made her feel was ... unlike anything she could remember. Giddy one moment, breathless the next.

And happy, incredibly happy, she thought, glancing over her shoulder to find his dark eyes on her.

"You're supposed to be working," she teased.

"I could say the same for you."

Her response was cut off when her phone rang and, not recognizing the number, she grabbed it. "Hello, this is Ava King."

"Ava," a deep male voice practically purred. "This is Aaron Fowler. How are you?"

"I-I'm fine. And you?"

Ava glanced across the room to notice Finn had completely given up the pretense of working and was listening to her conversation.

"I hope you don't mind my calling," Aaron went on. "Killian gave me your number."

Ava's brows went up at the news. "Killian gave you my number?"

"He did."

It was silent on the other end of the line, and Ava chanced a look at Finn again. His eyes had gone hard, and he was clenching his jaw. He didn't resemble the carefree man she'd spent the day with.

"How long do you think you're going to be in Swan Harbor?"

"I'm planning on being here through the holidays, at least. Maybe longer. We'll see."

"Good." Aaron's voice grew huskier and there was something about it that left her uncomfortable. "I'd like you to go out with me."

She wanted to laugh and ask him who told him he was such a catch. But the other part of her worried he could make things difficult for Killian.

"You'd like me to go out with you?" Ava repeated. "Like on a date?"

Her phone pinged with an incoming text, but she ignored it.

"Yes, like on a date," Aaron asserted. "You're a gorgeous woman. I believe we could make beautiful music together."

"Thank you, Aaron."

Her phone pinged again, and curiosity had her looking at the message.

> Finn: Tell him no.

> Finn: Tell him you're involved with someone.

"What would be a good day for you?" Aaron barreled on.

Ava could feel Finn's dark eyes burrowing into her back, as she turned away from him to focus on the man on the phone.

"I appreciate you thinking of me Aaron," Ava began working to keep her voice even. "But I'm ... I'm seeing someone."

"Oh, you are." Aaron muttered, almost in disbelief. "I didn't know. Well, if anything changes."

"I'll be sure and let you know," Ava assured him, even though if things didn't work out with Finn, Aaron Fowler wouldn't be her first choice. His blond hair and blue eyes reminded her too much of Peter.

"Bye now."

Ava hung up, the realization she'd just had another one of those '*teen*' moments. Being asked out by one man while she was '*involved*' with another.

She powered down her computer and pushed her work stuff aside, mulling the 'how' Aaron had gotten her number. Had Killian given it to him because he didn't want her and Finn seeing each other? Or was there some other reason?

"What was that about?" Finn suddenly materialized at her side.

"What?"

He raised a brow as if to say, *You're going there?*, and she couldn't stop the giggle that had been threatening for a while. "Oh, you mean the phone call?"

"You know bloody well the phone call." Finn tugged her into his arms. "That Aaron was the one you danced with at Captain Jack's, I presume."

Ava slid her arms around Finn's neck. "You presume correctly."

"And?"

"You heard," Ava went on. "He asked me out. I told him I was involved. End of story. Except."

Finn side-eyed her. "Except?"

"The way he got my number."

A muscle in his jaw jumped, pushing her to soothe her thumb over it. "Killian?"

"Yes." Her troubled eyes met Finn's. "You don't think it was Killian's way of warning me away from you, do you?"

Her confused thoughts must have transferred themselves to Finn, as his expression morphed from jealousy to worry. "Or was it Killian's way of warning me to stay away from you?"

A sick feeling unfurled in her stomach. "What are we going to do?"

Their eyes clashed for several minutes and then in one fell swoop, he crushed her to his chest and covered her mouth.

That dizzying, flying feeling that always washed over her when she was in his arms didn't disappoint. The way he held her, kissed, touched, and treated her was what she'd been searching for her entire life.

"Hold on to me, love," Finn murmured. "I'm too old for games, and want you to know that slowly, but most assuredly, I am falling for you. I do not plan on letting you go."

Her heart jumped at his declaration. "Good. Because I feel the same."

"That's bloody good to hear." Finn kissed her lightly. "Now, I can't help but notice you packed up. Were you interested in some more ...?" He looked over at the sofa where they'd spent time earlier.

Ava glanced in the same direction. "I wish. But I told Emma I'd be by to check on the puppies."

"That sounds like a good idea. Should I go with you?"

"I'm sorry." She kissed him to take the sting out of her words. "I need to talk to her, and it would be better if ..."

"I wasn't there." He studied her for a second. "Is this about Peter?"

"How did you know?"

"Just a feeling."

While he hadn't asked any specific questions about what she was thinking, she knew he had them.

"I, I just want to make sure Emma's going to be alright."

"She will be," he told her. "After all, she's your daughter."

Tears immediately sprang to Ava's eyes. "That's the nicest thing anyone has ever said to me."

"I keep telling you," he grinned. "I'm—"

"—A nice guy."

"You said it." He winked. "Are you busy for dinner?"

"No, why?"

"I thought maybe I'd make you dinner at my place."

"But," Ava frowned. "Aren't you staying in a suite in the hotel? Last I heard, they didn't have kitchens."

"I moved into the cottage next door," he admitted. "So, will you ... come for dinner?"

"I'd like that. Should I bring anything?"

"Your appetite. 7:00 p.m.?"

"I'll be there."

He kissed her goodbye, and once again she couldn't stop the thought, he'd taken another little piece of her heart.

THIRTEEN

Lighthouse Inn
November 9
4:00 p.m.

Finn recreated the exact workspace he'd been using all day. The same type of desk, the same type of chair, and if he looked to the right, he could see the same beach. Except ....

"I'm afraid I'm always going to be alone."

He was alone. And he was lonely.

He tried to remind himself, if he didn't get to the bottom of the note mystery then there would be no future. And that frightened him more than anything.

It was that fear which propelled him to open his computer and once again locate the thread he'd been following. He found Remy French's fingerprints on many "recoveries" across England until 2012, after which the older man disappeared. It wasn't until he'd tried several unsuccessful paths through his usual channels, he'd given up and dove into the dark web. There, he finally found what had become of his old friend.

. . .

London Times

April 7, 2015

Remy French was found in the King's Cross Tube Station, shot six times. He was pronounced dead at the scene. Scotland Yard asks anyone with information to contact them. Investigation is ongoing.

Beyond the death notice, Finn couldn't find out more, including whether the police had caught a killer. On the one hand, that Remy had been murdered didn't completely surprise him. It did, however, leave him with a dull ache in the center of his chest. The older man had walked the line between right and wrong for as long as they'd known each other, but he'd played an undeniable role in Finn's life.

In fact, where would he have been if the grizzled older man hadn't warned him about ....

Don't go there, Mate.

But he needed to figure out his next step. He still had notes that came from someone, and with Remy dead, he wasn't sure where he should look.

Are you sure about that?

Yes! I can't risk my boys.

It's no longer just your boys.

He knew that, which made it more complex as the size of his family was expanding to include Emma and Elsa.

And Ava.

Each time they were together, she became a little more lodged in his heart. And, while the reasoning behind Killian giving Fowler her phone number was curious, he didn't think the reasons were nefarious. But even if they were, he'd meant what he said to her. He wasn't willing to give her up. She was coming for dinner, and what happened behind the doors of their cottage was between them ... and only them.

Thirty minutes later, he strolled through the A&P, and knew his every move was being monitored. It was a new and not altogether comfortable feeling, as he was used to the anonymity of living in a large city.

"How can I help you, Mr. Reade?" an older man behind the seafood counter asked.

"Half pound of shrimp, please," Finn said, not even bothering to ask how he'd known his name.

"Just half a pound?"

"That's right."

The man smirked, leaving Finn feeling he was missing something.

"Here you go. Anything else?"

"That's it for now, Abe," he read off the man's name tag. "Thank you."

"Enjoy yourself."

Finn nodded his thanks and picked up oil and spices before deciding on a pasta.

Should he go with ...?

"What are you making?" a woman to his right asked.

When there wasn't an immediate answer, Finn glanced sideways, into the smiling eyes of a woman who looked vaguely familiar.

"Krystal Salas," she introduced herself. "I own Swan's Spirits."

"That's right. Pleased to make your acquaintance." Finn offered her a perfunctory smile, and went back to studying the pasta.

"So," she hesitated a beat until he looked up, "what are you making?"

"What am I making?" Finn was trying to wrap his head around the idea a stranger wanted to know what he was going to cook.

"Shrimp Scampi," he finally answered.

She hummed for several minutes before tapping a box with one long red fingernail. "I'd go with the Penne. It's much neater."

"Ahh, thank you." Finn took the box she handed him and checked it off his list.

"You're very welcome," Krystal smiled. "Have fun."

Finn said goodbye and made his way to the produce section. He'd just picked up an all-inclusive bag for creating the perfect Caesar salad when an older woman snatched it from him.

"Bloody hell, what was that for?" was out of his mouth before he could call it back.

She laughed. "You sound just like your sons."

"You've got that wrong, Madame," he smiled. "It is they who sound like me."

"*Touché*," she quipped. "I'm Lois Duncan. Your son Liam saved my life a few months ago."

"At your anniversary party, right?" Finn remembered Liam telling him the story.

"That's right," she agreed. "Fifty years."

Finn winked. "He must have caught you when you were just a girl."

"Oh, you're full of blarney," Lois giggled. "Anyone ever told you that?"

Ava.

"A time or two," he acknowledged.

"Now," she exchanged his Caesar salad bag for one of mixed greens and a bottle of dressing, "these pair better with the Scampi."

"Thank you," he tossed them in his basket. "I just need wine."

"What about dessert?"

"I hadn't planned—"

"You need dessert." Lois took his hand, and Finn had no choice but to follow her back through the store. "Frozen berries aren't the best, but they'll do in a pinch." She tossed a bag in his basket and then pulled a can of spray whipped topping out of the refrigerator. "Put a few of those berries in a dish and a spray of this, and *Voilà.* Easy peasy dessert, and the cream can be used for other activities, if you know what I mean."

"I ..." Finn swallowed, and tried again, "I thank you."

"You're quite welcome. Have fun." With a wink, she disappeared.

Well, that went well, Finn thought, as he checked out. And while they exchanged coy looks and knowing winks, as if aware he was dining with someone, they didn't mention any names. Their secret was safe.

Veterinary Clinic

November 9

6:00 p.m.

Ava sat in front of the cage, housing the dogs she'd helped rescue and had to laugh at the puppies' antics. "I told you my daughter would make you feel better," she whispered when the mother dog's expressive eyes met hers.

The mother dog heaved a sigh and rolled a little farther over on her side, her brown eyes sending a look that said, "Children."

"They look like they're a handful alright," Ava laughed at the dog's expression. "But at least you're feeling better."

One puppy moved away from its siblings and rolled over the mother dog's paw. The mother nudged it several times, but when the puppy wouldn't move, Ava took pity on it. "There you go, little guy." She placed it between the others and, by the contented grunts, she assumed it found what it was looking for.

When the mother dog's eyes thanked her, Ava had to grin, "You're welcome."

She'd never spent much time around dogs, but after just a few minutes could completely understand the role they could play in easing loneliness.

"Is Paris keeping you company, Mom?" Emma rushed into the room in a rush and sank down onto the floor.

"Paris?" Ava glanced from Emma to the canine family. "The mother dog?"

"I thought I told you that was her name."

"Maybe that's what you were going to tell me, before Leroy ran in here the first ... or was it the second or third time?"

"Maybe." Emma leaned back with a sigh. "It feels good to sit down ... even if it is on a dirty floor."

"Are you always this busy?"

"No. Doctor Delaney, who owns Pets and Pals on the other side of town, asked if I could cover for him for a week."

"He's taking vacation in November?"

"In a way," Emma smiled. "He went to meet his new grandchild. I thought it was a good cause."

"Oh!" Ava blinked several times, suddenly overcome by emotion. "That's really very sweet of you."

Emma shrugged as if it were no big deal. "As Killian would say, 'it's the right thing to do'."

Ava took a deep breath and prepared to wade into that emotional territory she was just learning to traverse. "I'm really proud of the woman you've become."

"Mom, I—"

"Let me finish," Ava interrupted. "I know it wasn't easy for you to grow up surrounded by parents who barely tolerated each other. But even with a demanding grandfather, a mother who was always working, and a father who spent more nights flaunting his unhappiness than home, you've grown into a remarkable young woman. I'm really impressed. And so, so sorry."

"Mom, where's all this coming from?"

When Emma hesitated, as if she were trying to decide what she wanted to say, Ava added, "I've just been doing a lot of thinking about the past."

She didn't say it was because the past needed to be dealt with before she could move into the future. A future she was thinking about more every day.

"Does this have something to do with ..."

Ava's heart raced with fear Emma would ask her something about Finn she wasn't quite ready to answer.

"... with dad coming to Swan Harbor?" Emma finished, causing Ava to let go of the breath she'd been holding.

"I know Peter hurt you," Ava began, "many, many times when you were a child."

"It was no big deal," Emma responded flippantly.

A corner of Ava's mouth ticked up. "Never kid a kidder," she retorted, using the same rebuttal she'd heard Emma use. "I've been there."

At her quiet admission, Emma's head popped up from where she'd been watching the puppies. "Really?"

"Oh yes," Ava replied, her heart squeezing as the memories washed over her. "When I returned from Europe, after spending close to three months with the great Peter Foster, I had stars in my eyes. He was my prince, and was going to rescue me. But then I hadn't been home twenty-four hours when the first bruise was inflicted."

"What happened?"

The quiet question had something unfurling inside Ava's stomach. "A picture," she admitted with a crooked smile.

Emma winced. "Of dad?"

"Yes." Ava blew out a dry laugh. "Peter in the arms of his costar for the next movie. I felt like such a fool."

"Then why did you marry him?"

Ava sent Emma a smile meant to say, '*you know why.*'

"So," Emma rolled her eyes, "you were pregnant. People have babies without being married all the time."

"Not a King," Ava told her. "It would have tarnished the image Leo built around himself."

Emma's brows rose in surprise. "You had no choice?"

Had she?

Ava shrugged. "Looking back, I can say, sure there were choices."

"But grandfather Leo took over and convinced you otherwise, didn't he?"

"He did," Ava acknowledged. "I didn't feel as if I had any choice but to go along with what he wanted. If I had it to do again …"

"Mom," Emma sent her a pointed look, "wasn't it you who told me you were trying to move forward? Dad can only have power if you allow it."

"Is that something living in Swan Harbor taught you?" laughed Ava. "For some reason, it feels like it."

"Maybe?" Emma replied. "But in my case, it turned out to be true. You were right in saying dad hurt me when I was a kid. In fact, it was one reason I ran from Killian in the beginning."

Like mother, like daughter, Ava couldn't help but think. As she'd done the same things when she'd compared how Finn made her feel to how she'd felt with Peter.

"And while I'll admit, I'm nervous about seeing dad again, I believe he's changed." Emma grinned. "As have I."

"Are you telling me I don't need to worry about Peter hurting you?"

"No, you really don't," Emma confirmed. "We're different people now. I think it's time to let go of the past and move toward the future."

A giant weight lifted off Ava's shoulders. If she didn't have to worry about Peter hurting Emma, then maybe it was time to …

"Does that mean you're ready to set a wedding date?"

"You sound like Killian," chuckled Emma.

"Well?"

"I—"

"Emma," Sadie stuck her head around the door, "last appointment just arrived."

"Wait," Ava chided, "you can't leave me hanging."

Emma giggled. "Yes, I can. I've left Killian hanging for a while. I'll be back."

"Fine, be that way," Ava sputtered, pretending to be annoyed.

The sound of her daughter's laughter as she left to do a job she so obviously loved had her heart spilling over with happiness.

"Nothing like waiting until you're over fifty for your dreams to come true," she murmured, thinking things couldn't be more perfect with Emma.

But with the main reason for her trip to the clinic out of the way, she could turn her attention to the evening ahead. And to the fact she smelled like dog.

Which meant she needed to leave, she decided, patting Paris goodbye and dropping into Emma's desk chair to leave a note. But, unable to find a piece of paper on the messy desk, Ava pulled open the bottom drawer.

Oh my, she thought, her eyes growing wide at the contents inside. A quick peek assured her she was still alone as she reached in and took out the magazine.

Another first.

The model on the cover of the *Rebecca's Fantasy* catalog was wearing a barely there nightie, holding a bottle of oil in one hand and in the other a …. *Oh, wow! Will you look at that?*

Ava turned the first page, her nerves pinging all over the place.

Why are you nervous?

What if someone catches me?

But you're an adult.

The pep talk had her flipping another page, but before she got far, the sound of footsteps sent her heart racing faster. She crammed the catalog back in the drawer and scrambled for a piece of paper just as Killian ambled around the corner.

"Ava?" Killian frowned, "Everything alright?"

"Uhh, yes, fine. Why do you ask?"

Killian arched a brow, "You're just a little—"

"I'm fine." Ava stood and grabbed her bag. "I was just going to leave Emma a note but since you're here, you can tell her I had to go."

"I hope it wasn't something I said," Killian began.

"No, no," Ava searched for an excuse, "I just have some things to do."

"Why don't you stay for dinner?" Killian invited. "You shouldn't have to spend so much time alone."

"No, no. I'm fine." Ava breathed a sigh of relief when Killian stepped aside and she could pass. "Tell Emma I'll talk to her tomorrow. Bye now."

KILLIAN COULDN'T STOP HIS CHUCKLE WHEN SHE SCURRIED DOWN the hall. But curiosity as to what could have caused the guilty look on her face had him searching through Emma's desk drawers. He finally located the culprit in the bottom one and pulled out a rumpled copy of the *Rebecca's Fantasy* catalog.

"Killian?"

"Doc," He dropped the catalog and sat on her desk, tugging her between his legs,. "Are you done?"

"Yes, but." She looked around him. "What are you doing with that catalog?"

"Shopping?"

She side-eyed him. "Right."

He picked up the magazine and tossed it back in the drawer. "When I walked in, your mom was looking mighty guilty, and I wanted to know why."

"My mom was looking through my lingerie catalog?" An expression much like she'd sucked on a lemon crossed her face, and she dropped into a chair. "I didn't need to know that."

"Told you, there are some things children don't need to know about their parents. But then ... other things ..."

"What have you done?"

"I had lunch with Liam." While he didn't plan on telling her about the book that mysteriously moved from Liam's place to his office, he'd share his gossip.

"I'm guessing by the twinkle in your eye, you didn't just talk about the wedding."

"Not once."

"So," she huffed. "Are you going to make me work for it?"

Killian grinned. "Oh, this news I might share for free, but the rest of it ..."

One of Emma's blonde brows popped up. "What do you want?"

He reached back into the drawer and grabbed the catalog. "I'm sure I can find a thing or two in here we both might enjoy."

"Okay."

Killian flipped through several pages. "These look interesting."

She took the catalog and studied the page for a few seconds. "Strawberry or Pineapple?"

His first thought was he should have asked for more, but smirked. "Yes, please."

Emma rolled her eyes and tossed the catalog back on the desk. "Now, what happened?"

"Did your mom tell you she had breakfast with my dad?"

"No," Emma frowned. "And I gave her plenty of opportunities. In fact, I was going to ask her to stay for dinner."

"She has plans," Killian shared, a part of him shocked he was in the middle of the Swan Harbor gossip chain.

"With your dad?" Emma guessed.

"Aye. Dad went to A&P and—"

"It was all over town before he checked out."

"Aye."

"What's he making?"

"Does it matter?"

"No." A contemplative look flitted across Emma's face. "I bet she's never had a man cook for her."

"My dad's a good cook." Killian tugged Emma a little closer. "Are you ready to go up? I thought I'd make omelets, and then I want to show you something."

Emma frowned. "Is everything okay?"

"It's fine, Doc. I've been wanting to talk to you for a few weeks and—"

"You're just now bringing it up?"

"We'll talk about it after we eat."

"Okay. I'll be up in a minute."

"Alright," he laughed. "And I can tell you about giving your mother's cell number to Fowler."

"You did what?"

He kissed her cheek and left her standing in the center of her office, knowing her curiosity would push her to hurry.

But as he gathered the ingredients to make dinner, Killian pushed the gossip thoughts aside and brought out the housing issues. Would she be upset, or would she understand?

Why are you making this such a big deal?

He'd asked himself that several times, and every time the only answer he'd come up with was this was her home. Was she ready to give it up?

Guess you're about ready to find out, his inner voice whispered.

Then Emma rushed through the door, and Killian took one look at her face and knew their talk would have to wait. "What happened, Doc?"

"Oh, Killian. I'm sorry, but Rene called and thinks Ruari has colic."

"And I take it that's not a good thing?"

"No." She hesitated for several seconds, before stepping closer to wrap her arms around his waist. "I'm sorry."

Killian tightened his hold. "Don't worry about it, Doc. There will be other times to talk."

"Do you want to go with me?"

"No." He kissed her on the head and stepped back. "I'll stay here with the girls."

"Are you sure?"

"I'm sure. Can you eat before you leave?"

"Keep it warm for me?"

"Hurry back."

Once she was gone, Killian took out the plans he'd picked up on his way home and spread them on the table. "Alright girls," he shared with Millicent, Nina, and Trudi when they jumped up to see what he'd unfurled. "I need a little help here."

FOURTEEN

Lighthouse Inn
November 10
10:00 a.m.

Ava had been trying to work for several hours but, just as if he'd been sitting across the room from her, Finn was ruining her concentration. She'd read a line from a proposal and something he'd said would flit through her mind. Once that happened, she'd get lost in the memory.

When she knocked on the door of Finn's cottage, Ava noticed her palms were sweating. What was wrong with her?

"Good evening, love," Finn greeted her when he pulled open the door. "You're right on time."

"I'm a King," she dimpled, "being on time has been instilled in me from birth."

"From birth, you say?"

Finn's lips toyed with hers, and the way he made her feel had what she was going to say fly away. "It's not as important as this." She offered him her lips.

"Good." He took her up on the offer, giving her an open mouth kiss she was sure had left scorch marks.

Ava blew out a breath and tried reading out loud, thinking maybe it would help her focus. "In order to maximize the number of people I can serve, I'd like to offer a menu ..."

"Are you sure I can't help with anything?" Ava asked when Finn had seated her and returned to the kitchen.

"You're helping." He handed her a glass of white wine.

Ava side-eyed him. "How am I helping?"

"You've improved my view." He winked. "And besides, it's all done. I hope you like shrimp scampi."

"It smells delicious."

"Thank you." Finn set a plate in front of her and dropped a light kiss on the top of her head.

Cherished, she thought. *He makes me feel cherished.*

But when her thoughts once again floated away, she pushed the proposal aside and pulled out another.

"Sassy Smoothies," she read the name of the business the person wanted to open.

Catchy, she decided, reading on.

"Berries are loaded with antioxidants and have been known to help with lowering blood sugar, lowering cholesterol and ..."

"I hope you saved room for dessert." Finn took her hand and led her to a blanket in front of the fireplace.

"Are we having s'mores again?"

Finn sent her a look of confusion. "No, why?"

She waved at the flames. "I just thought ..."

"Oh!" He leaned forward and nibbled on her neck, sending shivers throughout. "I just wanted to do this."

Ava tilted her head, giving him better access. "I do like how you think." She carded her fingers through his silky dark hair and guided his lips to hers. Kissing him was becoming addictive. "I could get used to this."

The light of the fire caused Finn's dark eyes to glitter. "That's my hope."

He kissed her again, and while a part of her was ready for him to carry her away, the other, more rational part reminded her to slow down.

"I should get dessert," he murmured.

That he seemed to read her mind was something exciting and scary, too. No man had ever paid that much attention to Ava, the woman.

"Berries?"

"And," he showed her the can of whipped topping and shook it, "tell me when to stop."

He sprayed the cream on the berries, and Ava got lost in watching him instead of paying attention to what he was doing. "Stop," she giggled, when she looked down and realized the cream had completely covered the berries and was in danger of spilling over the top of the bowl.

"You weren't paying attention," he scolded playfully. "That could have been a big mess."

"I was too watching." Ava swiped her finger through the cream and licked it off. When his eyes flared, something had her gathering more, but this time, sliding the cream over his lips. "Well, look at that."

His tongue peeked out to lick off the confection, but Ava dropped her finger on his lips. "No, let me."

She sipped, licked, and nibbled her way around his mouth until both were panting. "There."

Finn's eyes were closed, and the way the flames flickered, casting his features in and out of shadows had her breath catching. "Where have you been all my life?" she murmured, not realizing she'd said it out loud until he opened his eyes.

"Waiting for you to find me."

His whispered response brought tears to her eyes. "Isn't that my line? After all, I'm the one who grew up in the tower."

He took her hand, kissing her fingertips, and then laid it on his cheek so she was cupping his jaw. "I think we've been waiting for each other."

"I like that."

She could tell he wanted to kiss her again, but he surprised her with only a tempered peck, then handed her a spoon and her dessert. "Your cream is melting."

Ava widened her eyes. "We couldn't have that, now could we?"

"Definitely not." He picked up his own dessert and settled back against the hearth. "Tell me about your visit with Emma. Are you still worried?"

He'd listened as she talked about her time with Emma. Had he always been perfect?

She glanced at the clock and while she had time before she was to meet with Becca to look at several spaces along the pier, she gave up trying to make sense of any new proposals.

Instead, she turned her attention to the mystery surrounding the charm bracelet, and trying to get in touch with Mr. Morton, the owner of the law practice.

"Morton, Timmons, and Jade," chirped the always happy receptionist who answered the phones. "How can I help you?"

Ava sighed and prepared to launch into the same speech she'd given the other fifty times she'd called, "This is Ava King. I'm calling—"

"Oh, Ms. King," the woman interrupted, "I was just getting ready to give you a call."

"You were?" Ava retorted skeptically. "Did you find the answers I'm searching for?"

"Well ..."

Here it goes, thought Ava, *the blow-off.*

"I'm not sure if he found all the answers or not," the woman went on, "but Mr. Morton instructed me to call you. Let me connect you."

Her comment surprised Ava to the point she almost forgot those manners she'd had instilled in her since birth. "Uh, thank you," she tossed out at the last minute.

The brief wait surprised her again.

"Ms. King," a deep voice boomed across the line, "this is Will Morton. I'm sorry you've had a difficult time getting through. Stephanie said you were calling about a bracelet?"

Ava wanted to say something about good customer service begins with following up in a quicker manner, but bit her tongue. "Yes, Mr. Morton. In May, someone sent me an old charm bracelet and a picture. I'm trying to track down where it came from."

"There wasn't a note inside?" he asked, and while she might have been imagining it, she thought she detected a touch of curiosity in his voice.

"Not really," she hedged. "Just a piece of paper that said, 'For Ava.'"

"And you need to know what, exactly?"

"Mr. Morton, the picture is of my grandmother and me, when I was around two years old. I'm trying to figure out where the bracelet came from."

"It sounds like your grandmother left it for you."

His offered response had Ava rolling her eyes and thinking, *Gee, I could have come up with that answer.*

"My grandmother passed before I was three. I just turned fifty-one," Ava retorted. "So, if she didn't send it from the great beyond, where has it been for the last forty-eight years?"

He chuckled, and for some reason the sound set her teeth on edge. "That is a mystery."

"I could have told you that."

"I'm sorry." His voice lowered and grew more somber. "This practice was my dad's home away from home for almost sixty years, and since his passing, I've been trying to make sense out of some of his notes. I bet your bracelet was one of those situations. Hold on and let me check something."

He was gone before she could say any more, but the possibility she was finally going to get some answers had her grabbing a piece of paper to make notes.

"Okay," he came back on the line, "you said your name was Ava King, right?"

"Yes."

"And your grandmother was Rose Dawson?"

"Yes," Ava stretched out the single syllable word.

She could hear the rustle of pages for several seconds before he returned.

"There are two notes in my father's handwriting from 1970, and one of them says, "Mail the contents of my safe deposit box to Ava King on her fiftieth birthday. Then there's a date and an address."

"But it arrived months after my birthday," Ava pointed out.

"That's my fault," Will explained. "That was around the time my father got ill, and then it took a few months before—"

"I'm sorry for your father's passing," Ava interrupted him. "It just seemed odd when the bracelet appeared seemingly out of nowhere."

"I can understand that," he acknowledged. "But maybe the letter will explain everything."

"The letter?"

"Forgive me," he said again. "I should have mentioned this at the beginning. I told you there were two notes in your grandmother's file. One to send the contents of the box and the other ..."

"Yes," Ava pushed, wishing he would just spit it out.

"There's a letter, and attached to it is another note. It says, 'If Ava contacts you after she's received the bracelet, mail her this letter. If she doesn't, send it to her heir.'"

"My heir?" Ava asked, confused by the wording. "But how were you supposed to locate my heir?"

"The firm has always had an investigator," he told her. "I'm sure your grandmother knew that."

"Okay," Ava backed away from questions about the origins and focused on the note. "Can you send me the letter?"

"Where should I send it?"

She rattled off the address of the hotel, and wrote a note to alert them at the front desk. "Thank you for your help, Mr. Morton."

"It's my pleasure, Ms. King. I hope the letter brings you the closure you're looking for. Have a good day."

Ava had barely disconnected when there was a knock on the door.

Finn, she thought, answering it.

"I stayed away as long ..." Then he must have seen something in her expression. "Hey, what happened?"

She tugged him inside, slammed the door and fell into his arms.

FINN TIGHTENED HIS HOLD ON HER, AND FOR THE FIRST TIME realized just how delicate she felt in his arms. He'd not experienced this Ava. One who was weeping uncontrollably, but who had willingly turned to him for comfort. And he was at a loss as to what to say ... or do.

He found his hands unerringly soothing up and down her back, while he whispered nonsense words. Her fingernails dug into his skin, and her silky hair tickled his face, but he had no intention of pushing her away.

The wind whipping around the cottage, the distant sound of the waves, and the soft snuffle as she worked to get herself under control surrounded them.

"I'm sorry." Ava stepped away from him and reached for a tissue to blow her nose. "I rarely do that."

Finn studied her carefully for several seconds. "What? Throw yourself in the arms of handsome men, or cry?"

"Both."

Ava sniffed and blew her nose again, and even with her face blotchy and her eyes red-rimmed, she was beautiful.

"Do you want to talk about it? I'm a little early before we have to leave."

"You still want to go with me to look at real estate for Becca's business?"

"I want to be with you," he offered her the truth. "Should I apologize?"

Her face lit up at his confession. "Not at all. I just didn't know if you had something to do."

The thought of what he'd been working on in his cottage floated through his head. "Nothing is more important than this." He took her hand and pressed it against his chest.

She lifted a black brow. "You really are full of blarney, aren't you?"

"And you love it," was out of his mouth before he weighed the words.

She gasped and their eyes locked, but when she didn't bolt, he took it as a positive sign. "Talk to me."

"I finally spoke to the attorney's office that mailed my grandmother's bracelet." Then, as if she couldn't stand still, she wandered into the living area, and settled onto the sofa before continuing, "My grandmother Rose left it in a safe deposit box, to be sent to me on my fiftieth birthday. Why wouldn't she just give it to my father for me?"

"How old were you when she died?" He joined her on the sofa.

"Almost three." Ava reached for her phone case and pulled out a picture. "This photo came with the bracelet."

Finn took one look at the picture and whistled. "Emma looks like her."

"She does." Ava studied the picture again. "Except she has Peter's coloring. Mr. Morton said there was another note that if I contacted them, to send me a letter. But why?"

"Maybe she was an eccentric old woman," he tossed out. "Do you know anything about her?"

Ava shook her head. "Nothing. My father refused to talk about my mother or her family. His excuse was it was too painful for me, but I think it was too painful for him."

"Do you have anything of your mother's?"

"I have a scrapbook she started for me when she was pregnant." Ava smiled at the memory. "And her wedding pictures. But there are people in the pictures I don't know. Were they family or friends?" She shrugged. "No clue."

Finn tugged her into the bend of his arm and heaved a sigh of relief when she settled against his shoulder. "Everything you've told me is a step closer to solving the mystery of the bracelet. Except that doesn't explain the tears."

"No." The tenor of her voice changed. "I don't know where those came from. Maybe it was just the knowledge of all the loss my family has suffered. My mother was in her early twenties, and my grandmother was in her mid-forties. Emma is older than my mother was when she died, and I've lived longer than any female on my mother's side in generations. And I—"

"—Had your own health scare," he finished what she was thinking.

"Yes."

"But you're alive, and thriving," he reminded her. "Remember, no looking back."

"I'm trying not to," she murmured against his shoulder.

"Is the letter being sent here or to Boston?"

"Here. Maybe it will fill in the holes." She sat up and brushed her hair off her face. "But enough of my pity party for now. We need to go. I'd better fix my make-up."

Finn squeezed her hand and ran his finger over the red marks on her neck. "While you're in there, you might want to put on a sweater with a higher collar."

Ava covered his hand with hers. "Why?"

"Let me show you."

He winked and promptly latched onto the side of her neck he'd discovered the night before. Her moan and the way she tilted her head, offering him easy access went straight to his gonads, and if he had his way they'd be staying inside.

"Did you give me a hickey?" she exclaimed, but there was a little giggle in her voice.

Finn laughed. "Wait. Are you exasperated or exhilarated by the prospect?"

An impish grin crossed her face, and her eyes sparkled. "A little of both. I've never had a hickey."

"Never?"

"No." She giggled, "But I'd better cover it, or the gossip line in Swan Harbor will have a field day."

"That they will." He stood and pulled her to her feet. "Next time, I'll be sure and leave my mark where no one can see it."

She dimpled, and he thought she was going to say more. Instead, she tossed a smile over her shoulder and sashayed into the bedroom.

His heart flipped several times and as soon as she was out of sight, he opened the patio doors to cool off. The closer they got, the more he had to fight to have patience. Following her into the bedroom was tempting.

Instead, while he was waiting, he reminded himself of several unsettling events he'd added to the growing pile.

The feeling of being watched when he'd walked Ava back to her cottage the night before.

Sounds, as if someone was trying to get into his cottage early in the morning.

Footprints outside the window closest to the cottage door.

And the new note,

GETTING THE PICTURE YET?

Same linen paper and envelope, but this one apparently hand delivered.

"Bloody hell," he murmured, more frustrated than he'd been in he couldn't remember how long.

"Finn."

He schooled his features and turned to face Ava. "Ready?"

"In a minute." She glanced down and when he followed her gaze, realized he'd pulled the silver coin from his pocket. "How do you do that?"

"Walk it across my fingers?"

"Yes."

"Practice." He shrugged. "I've done it so long I no longer pay attention."

"Can I?"

Finn took her hand and showed her how to move the coin from finger to finger and then stepped away. She managed to get it up on her index finger, but every time she tried to move it, the coin fell.

"Here." Finn placed it on her thumb and patiently touched each finger she was to move. "It just takes practice."

Ava laughed. "I'll never be as good as you."

"Probably not," he chuckled at her outrage.

She took the coin and laid it flat in her palm and studied it for several seconds. "It looks old."

"It is."

"Where did it come from?"

Finn's heart raced, and he fought to maintain a neutral expression. "I picked it up in Edinburgh," he murmured. "It reminds me of how far I've come."

When she smiled and handed it back to him, he let go of the breath he'd been holding.

"I get that." She dimpled and crossed the room to dig into a large bag he'd seen her with. "I carry this around to remind myself of how far I've come."

Ava tossed the coin, and when he caught it and laid it in his hand, he noted it was old and corroded, and had an almost greenish cast to it. "An old penny?"

"Yes," scoffed Ava. "Peter found it on a road in Austria, just before he asked me if I wanted to go to France with him. I thought it was so romantic. Looking back, though, I realize a penny was about all my feelings were worth to him. I keep it to remind myself I'm not that naive girl any longer."

Ironic they both carried coins to remind them of how far they'd come.

Finn trailed his finger down Ava's soft cheek. "You're stronger than you think you are."

She gave him a crooked smile. "I told you some people wonder if I have a heart. I've been called a bitch and a ball-buster more times than you can imagine."

"I'm not talking about that kind of strength, Ava." Finn cupped her face and gently kissed her, first on each eyelid, then on her lips. "You've had to be a strong, forceful female to keep King Industries on top. But I'm talking about what's inside of here."

He touched her chest, just over her heart, and the way it was racing mimicked his own. "You care, and even though you've had some knocks in your life, you've picked yourself up and reinvented Ava King."

"You keep saying the nicest things."

"Just speaking the truth. Now, come here. While we're in public, I won't be able to do this." Finn caught her mouth with his and feasted on her lips like a starving man searching for his last meal.

FIFTEEN

Sheriff's Department
November 10
12:00 p.m.

KILLIAN STROLLED INTO THE SHERIFF'S DEPARTMENT AND TOSSED
the book he'd just read to Molly's first grade class on Dylan's desk. "Bloody hell,
"he grumbled. "I don't know how your wife does it."

Dylan glanced up from his computer screen. "What did she do now? Last I
heard, you enjoyed reading to her students."

"I'm not complaining about reading to them," Killian tried to explain. "It's
your wife's uncanny ability to choose books that tap into whatever's going on in
my life."

"Wait a second," Dylan laughed. "Are you saying the books Molly chooses
for her first graders *speak* to you?"

Killian sent his boss a disgruntled look before admitting, "Some of them ...
yes."

Dylan picked up the book and read, "*Wemberly Worried*. Does this mean
you didn't talk to Emma last night?"

"No, I didn't get to. She had an emergency."

"What was it this time?" Dylan wanted to know. "Kittens, puppies, or ...?"

"Ruari was sick."

"You're telling me you didn't talk to Emma because Rusty's horse was sick?"

"It was late when she returned and—"

"*Bwack Bwack Bwack*," Dylan imitated a chicken. "What are you afraid of?"

The atypical response had Killian studying his boss carefully. Dylan enjoyed being a sounding board and always offered words of wisdom, whether they were wanted or not.

"What's going on, Dylan?" He watched closely for a sign he was on the right track.

"What?" Dylan frowned. Then immediately started moving things around on his desk, as if he were looking for something.

Killian tapped into his experience questioning perps and waited, somehow knowing his friend would cave.

Dylan huffed and tossed his pen on his desk. "You're getting quite good at ferreting out 'burdens,' aren't you?"

"I have my moments," Killian agreed, thinking it was still easier to listen than to share.

"You know Molly is having twins, right?"

"Aye," Killian smirked. "It's been a regular topic of conversation for several months. Is everything alright?"

"Yes," Dylan hurried to assure him. "Molly and the babies are fine. It's just …"

"It's just," Killian prodded, thinking it took just as much work to get his boss to talk as Emma.

"Molly wants to name one of the boys James."

"After your brother," Killian knew. "Is that a problem?"

"No," Dylan shook his head. "It's the other baby's name I'm struggling with."

Killian frowned. "Well, unless she plans on naming the baby after her ex-boyfriend, I don't see the issue."

"She wants to name the other baby after me," Dylan mumbled.

"I'm sorry, Mate," Killian shrugged. "I still don't see the problem. If I have a son someday, I'm sure he'd feel honored to be named after his father."

"Are you sure about that?"

Killian rolled his eyes. "Aye, I'm sure. But this isn't about my son, it's about yours."

"When you're a twin," Dylan began, "it's difficult to be your 'own' person. Growing up we were always, 'the twins', 'the boys', or 'Dylan and James.'"

"And based on a few stories I've heard from Gray about your youth, I'm guessing you were the 'responsible' twin."

"I was the oldest," Dylan sighed. "It was my job to be responsible."

He sounded just like Liam, but Killian didn't think that was what he wanted to hear. "You worry if your son is named after you, he'll feel pressured to behave a certain way."

"I guess," Dylan huffed. "It's hard to explain, but there's already been one set of Prince twins named Dylan and James. I want the boys to be able to find their own identity."

"Tell Molly. She'll understand."

"Sometimes it's easier said than done."

Killian nodded in agreement. "I understand. But maybe you think it will be a big deal, and it will turn out like the camel who took a walk."

"You're talking about another children's book, aren't you?"

"Aye," Killian quipped. "If you're going to be a father, you need to bone up on your children's books."

"Thanks for the advice."

"Don't be cheeky, Dylan."

Dylan laughed. "Now back to your problem. Why haven't you talked to Emma?"

"She has a lot on her mind," Killian used the excuse he'd been falling back on for weeks. "I know she's worried about our parents—"

"I heard your dad made dinner for Ava last night," Dylan grinned. "How did it go?"

"Why are you asking me?"

"Are you okay with it?"

Killian sighed. "I want my dad to be happy. If Ava makes him happy then, I'm alright with it. But, bloody hell, it's an odd experience."

"I can imagine," Dylan conceded. "Is that your only excuse?"

"Emma's father's coming to Swan Harbor soon."

"Peter Foster is coming to Swan Harbor?" Amy handed Dylan a message. "My mom will flip."

Killian winced. "I hadn't even thought about Peter having groupies."

"How long will he be in town?" asked Dylan.

"No idea." Killian made a face. "I'll watch him."

"Good idea," Dylan agreed. "So, Emma's worried about her parents. Which, okay ... is a lot. But what's the real reason you don't want to talk to her?"

"It's her home," Killian admitted softly. "And I know how much she loves her home."

Dylan studied him for several seconds. "Have you considered the possibility that it's not her apartment, that's her home? That perhaps her home is Swan Harbor ... or you?"

"So, what you're saying is I should be more like Wemberly and just talk to Emma."

"You said it, I didn't," Dylan pointed out. "I would have said, 'quit being an idiot and talk to Emma.'"

"Yeah, yeah," Killian groused. "I get the message."

"Good. And now," Dylan held up the note Amy had dropped on his desk, "grab Rusty and follow up on this. Captain Jack thinks there have been intruders on his ship."

"What the bloody hell were they looking for? Their next meal?"

"No idea."

He grabbed the note and was halfway out the door when Dylan called him back, "Don't forget this," he held up the book *Wemberly Worried*, "you might need some pointers."

Killian thought about tossing out a succinct response but at the last minute, grabbed the book and winked, "Thanks, Mate. I just might."

Swan Harbor Pier
November 10
1:00 p.m.

FINN HAD BEEN FOLLOWING AVA AND BECCA IN AND OUT OF SPACES along the pier for two hours. In that time, he'd lost count of how often he'd wanted to take her hand, brush her hair off her face, or slip his arm around her. And every time he'd stopped himself and refocused on the business at hand, he'd learned something.

Ava was a sharp businesswoman, with an uncanny ability to ask the right questions, and getting to the heart of the matter quickly. And, while the business was going to be Becca's, Ava had boosted her confidence. If he hadn't already been half in love with her, just watching her in action would have pushed him over the edge.

The outing had also opened his eyes to new possibilities. With the Swan Harbor pier anchored on one end by the pirate ship and on the other by a music club, there were still empty spaces to be filled. While he could easily see Becca's shop taking one of those, there were others that begged for just the right business. A bicycle shop, a boutique, a candy store, even another ice cream place.

Giennie, Ava's friend, led them into another building closer to Captain Jack's restaurant, redirecting his attention. While he listened to her explain the benefits of the space, Finn realized what had been missing from their tour. She couldn't paint the picture of what a thriving, energetic pier looked like. What he could do ….

Wait! Where did that come from?

"What do you think of this space?" Ava asked when Becca and Giennie had walked away.

"Location wise it's perfect," he offered, in what he hoped was a voice that said he was paying attention.

"But?"

Her blue eyes locked with his, and the sparkle in them said she was on to him.

"With empty spaces on both sides, I'd worry." Finn shrugged, his thoughts traveling back to what he would do if the space were his.

"Are you okay?"

No, he wanted to say. I just had an epiphany that plays into my hope for the future. Instead, he smiled and took her hand. "I'm fine, love. If it's okay, I'm going to take a walk while you finish."

"Okay."

Her eyes dropped to his mouth before bouncing back up, pushing him to prompt, "I know."

"You know what?"

He sent her a lazy smile, dragging out his response, "What you want."

"Oh, you do?" One black brow rose in question. "How can you know?"

Finn's smile grew larger. "Because I want it too." He peered around her to make sure the other women weren't paying attention and blew her a kiss. "That will have to do for now."

"Oh you," she shook her head, "you're awfully sure of yourself, aren't you?"

"About some things," he agreed. Then the search for answers he'd been working on crossed his mind, sobering him. "But not others. I'm going to take that walk. Alright?"

"Okay."

Before he could say any more, Becca asked for Ava's opinion, and he stepped outside. The day was cold and with the pier empty, he wondered at the viability of businesses through the winter months. Could they make enough to survive, or was there a way to bring visitors to Swan Harbor year-round?

What are you doing?

He was thinking long-term, planning with his heart and not with his head. Which was how he was fairly sure he'd gotten into the situation he was in regarding the notes.

A dog chasing a bird interrupted Finn's internal thoughts, and something had him finding a bench to watch their antics.

The sign of freedom and lack of cares, he couldn't help but think.

"Finn," Captain Jack waved, "I hope Bandit didn't disturb you too much."

"No. He's fine. I was just thinking how he appears to have not a care in the world."

Captain Jack watched his dog for several minutes before turning back. Finn could feel the older man's scrutiny and worked to keep his neutral mask in place.

"You're at loose ends," the other man stated.

Finn relaxed, thinking that seemed to be a fairly safe topic. "I'm not used to sitting around so much."

The older man inclined his head toward the bench. "Mind if I sit?"

"Please."

"What is it you do again?"

"Real estate," Finn offered. "Manhattan and the surrounding area."

"Different way of life," Captain Jack noted. "It took me a while to adjust to life after the Navy. What do you think of small-town life?"

A corner of Finn's mouth curved up. "Is that your way of asking if I'm going to stick around?"

The older man chuckled. "Well, are you?"

"I don't know," was out of Finn's mouth before he could call it back.

"You've piqued my curiosity."

Here goes nothing, Finn thought, trying to formulate what he wanted to say. "Your pier looks pretty new. Is it?"

"A couple of years," Captain Jack frowned. "The property belonged to a fellow who didn't treat his misses as well as he should have."

"Divorce settlement?"

"Death," Captain Jack corrected. "Contested will, probate. Finally, the Hunters could purchase the land and build what you see."

"I wondered," Finn murmured.

Captain Jack gave him a sly look, as if he knew exactly what Finn was trying to find out. "What would you do with it?"

"I don't deal in commercial real estate," Finn began. "But maybe a bike shop, a candy store or two, pizza, ice cream. I'd use the boardwalk in Atlantic City as my model."

"It would change the look of the place," Captain Jack muttered.

"Is that not a good thing?" Finn asked, thinking of his thoughts regarding winter activities.

Captain Jack shrugged. "Change is inevitable. But with the influx of more people, I think we'd need to find the key first."

The key?

"Communication?" Finn repeated what Captain Jack had told Ava was the key.

"Oh, that's one key," the older man agreed. "I'm just not sure it's *the* key."

"I see," Finn replied, even though he didn't know where the conversation had gone.

"In fact." Captain Jack snapped his fingers. "I should have thought of that when Rusty and Killian stopped by."

"Rusty and Killian stopped by?"

"Someone was in my office," huffed the Captain.

"Did they take anything?"

"No," Captain Jack's voice grew soft, as if he were mentally looking around his office. "Books rearranged, files put back in a different order, my computer moved."

His description of his office reminded Finn of how someone had moved his objects. "Pictures out of order, pencil and pen cup moved?"

"That's it," Captain Jack confirmed. "But if they were looking for the key, they came up empty. Been looking for that since I was a boy."

"Maybe it doesn't want to be found."

"You couldn't have said it better." This is Swan Harbor, where things happen when they're meant to happen."

"Destiny?"

"That's right," Captain Jack nodded. "In fact, I heard you were shopping yesterday."

Finn barked out a laugh at the segue. "A man's got to eat."

"How was your shrimp scampi?" Captain Jack turned his twinkling brown eyes Finn's direction.

"My shrimp scampi?" Finn repeated, trying to figure out how much the older man knew.

"Did your lady friend enjoy it?"

"My lady friend?" Finn echoed, beginning to feel like a rat trapped in a maze.

Captain Jack turned away from the dog's antics, his dark eyes making Finn feel as if he were reading his thoughts. "I told you the other night you have to decide if you're going to fight for her."

"You did," Finn acknowledged. "But it's complicated."

"Love is complicated."

"But does it have to be?"

"Do you appreciate things that come easily?"

"I want to say yes, but," Finn shrugged, "who knows."

"What makes it complex with the lovely Ms. King?"

"Family."

"They don't approve?"

"Ava doesn't," he started to say, but then realized he'd admitted too much.

"She's worried your relationship could affect Emma and Killian's?"

"Something like that," Finn conceded.

"Is there more?" the older man prodded.

"Let's just say," Finn hesitated, unsure how much to offer, "Sometimes sins from the past get in the way of moving forward."

"Do you want to end up alone?"

His blunt question took Finn aback for a minute. But since the older man never wasted an opportunity to make a point. "Is that a rhetorical question?"

Captain Jack laughed. "Perhaps. But do you?"

"Bloody hell, no," Finn retorted.

"Good, because it's lonely."

There's a story there, Finn realized. "What happened?"

"Edythe was told something about my family she wasn't ready to hear. That if she married me, it would be the biggest mistake of her life."

"And she listened?"

"Yes." Captain Jack stared out at sea, and Finn had to wonder at what his lady had been told. "She didn't have enough hope."

"The future begins with a little hope," Finn repeated the statement Winnie had instilled in him.

"It does." Captain Jack shrugged. "It's why it's so important to find the key."

"Do you know what happened to Edythe?" Finn brought the conversation back to the woman Captain Jack had loved.

"No. And not a day goes by I don't wish I would have fought for her and ..."

Finn had gone back to watching the dog chasing the birds, but when the older man's voice broke, he looked toward him. The emotion on his face was evident.

Captain Jack sniffed and pulled from his pocket a silky handkerchief and loudly blew his nose. "I'm sorry," he apologized. "I usually try not to look back, but this year, I've spent more time realizing what I missed."

"I had moments like that, after my wife left and returned to England," Finn admitted. "Then one day, I stopped caring."

"Easier said than done," the Captain noted. "Especially since ..."

"Something reminded you of what you missed, didn't it?"

"You could say that." Captain Jack wiped his nose again and stuffed his handkerchief back into his pocket. "We were to be married in November," he finally offered. "It would have been fifty-one years this month."

"I still don't understand why you never went after her," Finn pressed. "If you loved her, then why didn't you fight for her?"

"Stubbornness, pride, sorrow, and so many other emotions I've never acknowledged. When she left, she took my heart and for years, I waited for her to walk back into my life and tell me she was sorry."

"Did you really expect that to happen?"

"No." Captain Jack's voice faded, and Finn had to lean closer to hear the whispered words. "But losing Edythe wasn't the worst thing that's happened in my life."

"What could be worse than losing the woman you loved?"

"Losing your child," the older man whispered. "When she walked out of my life, she was pregnant."

It took Finn a second to process the other man's last words. "Wait a minute. You're telling me that somewhere out there you have a son or daughter you've never met?"

Captain Jack cleared his throat and stood. "That's what I'm saying. But Finn, I didn't tell you, so you'd feel sorry for me. I told you, hoping it would propel you to decide what's important to you. If that's family and love, then do whatever you need to do to fight for your future. You've got the hope ..."

Finn watched him walk back toward the restaurant, the words resonating in his mind. Wasn't that what he was doing by searching for the answers on his own? Protecting his family and fighting at the same time?

SIXTEEN

Swan Harbor Pier
November 10
2:00 p.m.

AS SOON AS GIENNIE AND BECCA DROVE OFF, AVA LOOKED DOWN AT the business card in her hand. Was she *really* considering this?

You're happy here.

She was! In fact, she wasn't sure if she'd ever been happier. Even when she was twenty-two and flew across the ocean searching for Peter, she'd still held a part of herself back. But it hadn't stopped her from going after what she'd wanted. That had been Peter, and she'd chased him with a single-minded mentality only someone who always got what she wanted understood.

When she examined her feelings she could admit, deep inside, she'd expected her father to burst her happiness bubble. She was a *King*, and had been groomed to take over the family business.

Except, those were his dreams and not hers and, as always, Leo King won. It had been a battle of wills until she'd just ... given up.

And now?

I'm building the life I ... Ava Rose King ... want.

It's about time.

She found Finn sitting on a bench close to Captain Jack's restaurant, staring out at the gray sea. He appeared deep in thought, and she had to wonder what was going on inside his head. Was he thinking about business? Or was he thinking about her?

"A kiss for your thoughts," she teased when she was close enough, and he still hadn't noticed her.

Their eyes met, and the heat in his stole her breath. "Are you sure that's a safe offer out here in plain view of anyone?"

"I didn't say when I'd pay, now did I?"

Finn tilted his head in acknowledgment. "*Touché*. Becca and Giennie leave?"

That he didn't tell her what he was thinking didn't escape her notice. "They did."

"Are you ready to go back?"

Ava glanced at the card in her hand again and took a chance. "Not quite."

Finn pushed up from the bench and sauntered in her direction. And the look on his face touched something so deep inside, she had to turn away.

"You feel it too, don't you?" he murmured.

"The tightening of a cord pulling us together?"

"Yes."

Goosebumps worked their way up her spine, but she knew it had nothing to do with the cold and everything to do with him. "Why do you think I looked away? I thought—"

"—You could break the connection."

"Yes."

"Did it work?"

Ava chanced another look at him. "No. But I'm an adult."

He took her elbow, and turned them in the direction of the car. "If you're not ready to go back, where to?"

"I can't believe I'm even considering this, but," she blew out a breath, "would you look at a house with me?"

Finn frowned. "A house?"

"Giennie happened to mention a cottage she thought I might like, and ... well ..."

"Ava, love," he opened the car door, but took her hand to keep her from slipping inside, "why the hesitation? If you want to look, let's look."

He's right, she thought. *If it's what I want, then ....*

"Good." She smiled, allowing the bubble of excitement to grow. "Let's go."

"Tell me about the cottage," he requested as soon as he'd climbed into the car.

She waited until they'd left the marina parking lot and pulled up Giennie's link. "It's a four-bedroom cottage on a cliff not far from the Inn."

"Does someone live in it now?"

"No. It's been a summer rental for years, but the owners are tired of taking care of multiple homes."

"Would you stay here full time?" he surprised her by asking.

"I don't know," she admitted. "My home base can be anywhere, but if I want to be hands on, I'd have to travel."

He turned onto a side street that wound around homes and large pine trees lining the road. The closer they got, the more excited she felt, and once he pulled into the driveway, she was out of the car before it had even stopped.

"Oh, Finn, look!" Ava stopped to take in the view.

The ocean spread out in one direction, and while the sky was gray and the water dark, she could picture it on a summer day. A blue sky reaching for the blue of the ocean, so clear it would take her breath.

"Did Giennie give you the combination to the lock-box?" he asked when he caught up with her.

Ava handed him the card, and by the time she tore herself away from the view, he had the door open and was waiting for her. One look and she knew the cottage was meant to be hers. Windows lined the back wall, and as she wandered from room to room, she pictured meals, fires in the stone fireplace, and evenings on the covered porch.

Finn wrapped his arms around her waist and propped his chin on her shoulder. "It's you."

"It is, isn't it?" She laid her hands on top of his and pressed her cheek against his head. It was peaceful and felt right. But she had to bite her tongue to keep from asking, '*but is it you?*' Because if whatever between them continued to grow ....

He said he was too old to play games. Ask.

"What's going through your mind?"

"How do you know I'm not just enjoying the view?"

"You're tense."

"How do you know that's not because I'm trying not to throw myself at you?"

Finn nipped her earlobe, sending a current zipping along her skin. "I just know."

"You're stronger than you think you are."

His words had her pulling up her big girl panties and jumping, "When you said you were falling for me, did you mean it?"

"Bloody hell, yes."

THEN HE TOOK A BREATH AND TEMPERED HIS RESPONSE. "I ALSO meant it when I said I wasn't willing to let you go."

He'd told her his plan was to spend the holidays with the boys, but had there been a part of him that knew how being in the small town would affect him? Had he hoped it would affect her the same way?

"I think I know where your thoughts are going."

"You do?"

Finn took her hand, led to a chair, and sat on the ottoman in front of her. "You're wondering if I could see myself here too, aren't you?"

Ava had been staring at their clasped hands, but as soon as his question was out, she lifted her head. "Maybe ..."

He gave her a look as if to say, *'really?'* "No games," fell from his mouth because somehow, he realized this was one of the most important conversations they'd ever have.

"Yes," she murmured. "You said it was me, and I immediately wondered—"

"—If it was me too?"

"Yes."

There was so much he wanted to say to her, to promise her. But until he'd discovered the reason for the notes, he couldn't give her the future he thought they both wanted.

No, but you can give her hope.

"Do you know what I was thinking while Giennie was showing us the spaces?"

"How you wished you were anywhere else?"

"No." He squeezed her hands but couldn't sit still and stood to move around the room. "How I could bring the pier alive if I were showing it."

"You don't sell commercial real estate," she pointed out.

Finn shrugged. "I might not have to. There are other ways I could be involved. As an investor, as a mentor ..."

"Like I am?"

"I don't know exactly," he admitted. "Right now, it's just a thought bouncing around in my head. But while I realized I could work *and* live in Swan Harbor; the full picture hasn't formed yet."

She cupped his jaw and kissed him slowly. When she stepped back, her smile took his breath. "I like how you think."

"Good." Finn kissed her again.

"But I'm not going to tell Giennie you think you could do a better job selling the pier."

"Probably wouldn't be a good idea," chuckled Finn. "And now ..."

Ava grinned, as if she knew what he was thinking. However, before he could settle in for another kiss, something pulled her attention away, and she jumped up. "How handy are you around the house?"

He glanced around at the paneling covering the walls, and the old carpet on the floors. "It depends, love. What are you thinking?"

For the next hour, Finn followed her around the cottage and took notes while she rambled, "I can do some of these," he told her, looking at the list. "But it would take forever."

Ava snatched the piece of paper out of his hand and a pucker developed between her brows. "You have very neat handwriting ... for a man."

Finn didn't want to tell her it had come in handy when he'd needed to take meticulous notes for a job, instead offered, "Many hours practicing my penmanship when I was a lad."

"You never talk about your childhood." Ava cocked her head and pinned her blue-eyed gaze on him.

"What do you want to know?" he asked softly, even though a part of him hoping she wouldn't pursue the topic.

"You once said you weren't born with a silver spoon in your mouth ..."

"Hardly," he offered. "My mum was the housekeeper for a family like yours."

"And your father?"

"Never knew him," Finn admitted. "Mum said he was a rail worker, there one day, gone the next."

"I'm sorry."

"You can't miss what you never had."

"Liar." She slipped her arms around his neck and pressed her body against his. "I never knew my mom, and I missed her every day."

Finn hugged her and got lost in the feel of having her in his arms. It would be so easy, he thought, to distract her. *Patience!* He leaned back enough so their eyes met, then kissed her softly, and stepped away from temptation.

"My mum died when I was five, but I had an older sister, Winifred, Winnie, who essentially was my mother. She loved to read, and dreamed of her prince coming along and rescuing her."

"Just like me," Ava murmured. "Was she looking for her happily ever after?"

"No," Finn smiled, remembering one of their last conversations. "Winnie was looking for a happy beginning. She made me promise I wouldn't stop searching for my happy beginning."

"The first day to the rest of your life."

"Emma said the same thing when I mentioned it to her."

"I don't remember what we were talking about," Ava confessed. "But Emma told me you had suggested a happy beginning. I like that idea."

"As do I." Finn tugged her back into his arms. "And you make me quite happy."

"I know exactly how you feel."

He kissed her, and while he'd kissed women before, there was something different about kissing Ava. She fit in his arms, as if designed just for him, and when their lips met, the rightness never ceased to surprise him. While a part of him felt as if he'd been kissing her forever, the other part grew as giddy as a boy falling for his first crush.

"Now," he stepped away from her again, promising himself no more distractions, "is there anything else we need to do here?"

Ava glanced around and shook her head. "Not now. I'll tell Giennie to get the paperwork started. Maybe I can be in here by Christmas."

"With all the work you want done," he barked out a laugh. "I think that's ambitious."

"Really?" Ava pouted. "Oh, well. Maybe next year."

Could he give her the changes she wanted by the new year? he couldn't help but wonder.

You need to solve the mystery.

I'm working on it, he wanted to snap.

"Are you hungry?" Ava asked when he climbed into the car next to her.

"Do you want to stop for something?"

"No," she leaned on the console just enough so when he turned his head, her hot breath blew across his lips, "let's stop at the store and cook."

Finn's lips kicked up. "You know, if people see us shopping together there will be talk, don't you?"

"So," her eyes glittered in the dim light inside the car, "let's live dangerously."

Finn tugged her forward for a hard kiss. "You're on."

She leaned back, fanning herself. "Be still my heart."

"You haven't seen anything yet."

"Promises, promises."

Hold on, he wanted to tell her, it might get rocky.

Giennie's Gym
November 10
8:00 p.m.

"Jab, jab, jab, cross, knee, kick," Sally yelled in time with the music.

Emma followed the instructions, but her thoughts were pinging all over the place.

"And here's the finale," Sally called when the music transitioned. "High, low, high, low ..."

Punches, twists, turns, pushing her muscles to the point of exhaustion and then ... the cool down and the feeling of euphoria as her endorphins kicked in. Emma loved that high, and with her busy schedule hated she hadn't been able to experience it more often. But as she stretched, allowing her heart rate to lower, she realized she needed to try to make more time for herself.

Sadie sent her a toothy grin as soon as Sally dismissed them. "See, aren't you glad you came?"

"Yes," Emma blew out a breath, "I needed a good sweat."

"You needed to blow out all that negative energy," Sadie grumbled. "You've been awfully grouchy lately."

"Ah oh." Elsa followed them across the room to where they'd left their water bottles. "What's going on, Em? Is it Peter, your mother, or your mother and Finn?"

"Does it have to be any of those?" Emma retorted.

"No." Elsa pushed through the door to the exercise room, and when Emma walked past, whispered, "What's really going on?"

She searched for a word and finally decided on. "I'm unsettled."

"But it's not about Ava and Finn?" Elsa prodded.

"No," Emma assured her. "While it's a little weird, I'm really okay with it."

"Good," Sadie giggled. "Because I saw them at the A&P earlier and oh my goodness, they are just so dang cute."

Emma pulled her jacket from her locker and tugged it over her head before asking, "They were shopping together?"

Sadie nodded. "I rounded a corner and saw your mother looking at the cheeses and had taken a step toward her when she giggled.

"My mother giggled?"

"She did," Sadie confirmed. "And do you know why?"

Emma exchanged looks with Elsa. "Do I want to know why?"

"Well, if she doesn't, I do," Elsa announced.

"Now don't hold me to this." Sadie lowered her voice when several other women entered the locker room. "But there's a good possibility Finn was nuzzling her ear."

"That's so," Emma winced, "cute ... and really, really freaky at the same time."

"Why is it freaky?"

"My dad left when I was fifteen," Emma explained. "I've never seen my mom 'date'."

Sadie's brows rose. "Never?"

"Never. And my parents' marriage wasn't really a marriage so ..."

"I think it's romantic." A goofy smile crossed Sadies's face. "I've seen my mom go in and out of relationship after relationship and yet, I don't even think she knows what she wants."

"Does anyone until it hits them over the head?" laughed Elsa.

"Some of us do," Sadie quipped. "Later girls."

"Do you find it weird the whole town knows what's going on with my mom's relationship?"

Elsa raised a brow. "You're asking *me*? Remember the gossip line texts before Liam and I figured out our relationship?

Emma giggled, some of her unsettled feelings dissipating. "True. And when I'd say something to Killian, he'd roll his eyes. Yet now, he's right in the middle of it."

"Killian?" Elsa slipped her bag over her shoulder, as they left the locker room. "I thought it was just Liam. What did Killian do?"

"He gave Fowler my mom's cell number," laughed Emma. "Seems Fowler used it and asked my mom out."

"Oh, no," Elsa cried. "Poor Finn."

"Oh, don't go poor Finn," chuckled Emma. "My mom blew Fowler off, and last night Finn cooked for mom, so ..."

"Ahh, that's so romantic. It's a good thing Liam made sure they'd have to spend time together."

Emma frowned. "What did Liam do?"

Elsa put her finger over her lips. "Shh, don't tell Liam I told you, but. ..."

"But?"

"It was Liam who canceled your mom's rental car."

"That was *Liam*?" Emma shook her head at the Reade boys' antics to push their father and her mother together.

"It was Liam," Elsa confirmed. "I wonder what's next?"

"I just hope it doesn't backfire."

"Me too," Elsa winced. "See you tomorrow."

"11:00 a.m., right?" Emma asked, thinking she'd need to move a few things around to make time for the dress fitting.

"That's right. See you then."

Emma crawled into her car for the drive home. While talking to her friend had her feeling better, there was still an unsettled feeling inside. It distracted her just enough so when she pulled into her drive, she narrowly missed an exiting car.

A part of her thought there was something she should have done, and the other part just wanted to get inside. But when she found Killian's messenger bag propped against the door, her nerves settled as she assumed they'd just delivered it.

"Killian," she called, as she climbed the steps to their apartment. "Why was your—?"

"Doc," Killian stepped into the doorway, "why do you have my bag? I've been looking all over for it."

Emma handed it to him. "I assumed the person driving the car I passed left it."

"What did you say?"

Emma had taken a few steps away, but Killian's usual gentle tone had gone sharp, causing her uneasy feeling to return full force.

"When I drove through the gate," she explained, "a car was leaving."

"Who was it?"

"I don't know." Emma studied him for several seconds. "What's going on?"

He set his bag on the table and when he looked at her, she could tell he was fighting some inner battle. "I don't know, but ..."

"But?"

"Liam lost mum's journal, and it appeared somewhere else. And—"

"—You lost your messenger bag, and it appeared on our porch."

"Aye."

"Anything taken from your bag?"

"Nothing in it to take." He took out a tube she recognized, but wasn't sure where she'd seen them, and passed it back and forth between his hands.

"Is that what you've been trying to talk to me about?"

"Aye."

"Killian, what's going on?"

He took her hand to lead her into the living room. When she couldn't quite read his expression, something told her he was worried, but she had no clue why. Was it the whole wedding date thing?

"Doc," he took her hands between his, "remember when you stopped by my apartment and I was packing?"

"And were grouchy?"

"Aye."

"And you told me it had to do with Santora," she reminded him.

"That was only half the reason."

"Oh?"

"I was thinking about having to move in here."

Emma's heart sped up. "You didn't want to move in with me?"

"I'm sorry, Doc." He kissed her hands, "I'm making a mess of this. I want to live with you, but not here. I want to live with you here." He handed her the tube.

She frowned, but instead of saying anything, opened the tube and took out a rolled-up piece of paper. *Blueprints* floated through her mind as she unrolled it.

On the paper there was the depiction of a home, similar in structure to how her clinic was built.

"It's the same style as this place."

"Aye." Killian took a breath and somehow, she knew he was weighing his words, "Cameron said it would complement the other structures on the property, but I don't want to presume ..."

"Presume what?" Emma set the drawing aside and scooted forward on the chair, taking his hands again. "I feel like I jumped from B to F without knowing what was between."

"My fault." Killian made a face. "I've been hesitant to say anything because this is your home."

Then it was a light went off inside her head, and she wanted to kick herself for being so selfish. "Are you saying you're worried I don't want to leave this *apartment*?"

"Aye. I know how much you love it here," he explained. "And you even waited until you had a home before adopting Millicent."

Emma kissed him softly. "Killian, *you* are my home. Yes, I love my clinic and Swan Harbor, but wherever you are, that's my home."

"Really?" His eyes lit up. "You're really alright with us building a new home on the other side of your property?"

"Yes." She grinned at the boyish excitement on his face. "I'm really okay with it. Besides," she looked around at the boxes stacked in the corners, "we could use more storage."

"Among other things," he agreed.

"Think we can put in one of those oversize tubs with the massaging jets?"

"You want massaging jets, Doc?" Killian kissed her and tugged her up. "I'll see what I can do. In the meantime, how about one of the good old-fashioned kind?"

Emma grinned. "I need to shower ..."

"I can help with that." Killian chuckled, taking off for the bathroom before she'd even completed her sentence.

SEVENTEEN

Lighthouse Inn
November 11
10:30 a.m.

Ava studied her image in the mirror, and the memory of the day she'd suffered her stroke washed over her. She should have listened to her body and gone to the doctor's office. But she hadn't. There had been an international teleconference she'd needed to be a part of, and it had been during that everything had fallen apart.

Her head had hurt, she'd been dizzy, and her thoughts had circled around in her mind. She'd thought it was a simple headache, and had excused herself to go to the ladies' room. Except, when she'd looked in the mirror, she hadn't recognized the person staring back at her.

"Who are you?" she'd whispered, just before everything went black.

Hours later, she'd woken in the hospital and been told she'd suffered a stroke. They'd also told her she'd been given a shot of the drug meant to reverse any effects.

"Why didn't I know the person in the mirror?" she asked the doctor, even though she was terrified of what he was going to say.

"Prosopagnosia," he explained. "It's the inability to recognize your own face."

"Is it permanent?"

"Your staff called 911 quickly, and you were given the medication well within the window. I'm hopeful. But your blood pressure was high. You need to take better care of your body."

"Okay."

He handed her a mirror, and as she lifted it, the sick feeling inside grew. Then, when she recognized her own face, she relaxed.

"It's me."

"That's good to know." He smiled. "You should rest now."

Once she was alone, Ava lifted the mirror and while it was her, the woman in the mirror was alone.

"And look at you now." Ava brushed her hair back, thinking it seemed to shine more than usual. "You've got the relationship with Emma you've always wanted. You're buying your first home, and you're crazy about a man." There was a bruise on her neck, accompanied by other marks she assumed were whisker burns that showed how close they'd grown. Except she had no regrets.

"I just need to hide them." She pulled a bright red cable-knit sweater over her head and adjusted the high neck.

Satisfied she'd covered the signs of her make-out session, Ava grabbed her bag and keys and locked up. As she passed the cottage Finn was staying in, her feet slowed, but she knew if she stopped to say hello, she'd be late.

She entered the lobby through the side door of the Lighthouse Inn and walked down the short hall. Her intension was to stop at the desk and ask about her letter. But as she rounded the corner, the person Karen was checking in had her taking several steps backward and peering around the wall.

It was him. The sick feeling in the pit of her stomach swirled. It had been thirteen years since she'd seen him, and he looked the same. Thick blond hair, tall, well-dressed ....

"Who are you spying on this time?" Finn whispered in her ear.

"Shoosh! She hooked her hand in his jacket and pulled him through a door which happened to be a storage room.

"Ava, love ..." He wrapped his arms around her waist, and tugged her close. "If you wanted to be alone, you just had to knock."

"You saw that, did you?"

"That you walked right by? Yes," he pouted. "Now give me a proper good morning kiss."

Ava kissed him but fought allowing it to suck her into the abyss as it usually did. "I need to go." she murmured against his lips.

"You didn't appear to be in a big hurry just now," Finn pointed out. "Who were you spying on?"

"Peter was checking in," she admitted. "I didn't want him to see me."

"Why?" His dark eyes studied her, making her feel like she was under a microscope. "Do you still have feelings for him?"

"No!" Ava sagged against him and kissed him to back up her words. "I know it's irrational, but I'm not sure what to say to him. So, until I figure that out, it's easier to hide."

"Alright," he replied hesitantly. "Where is it you're off to again?"

"Elsa's wedding dress fitting," she reminded him. "What are you doing while I'm gone?"

"Missing you." Finn dropped a kiss on her lips. "And since you're a King, who's never late, you'd better go."

Ava kissed him again. "I know. Now, let me leave first, and you wait a few minutes before you follow."

"Yes, ma'am," he dimpled.

"Oh, you." She kissed him again. "You're too charming."

Before he could say more, Ava stepped into the hallway, just as Karen rounded the corner.

"Ava!" Karen gave her a confused look. "What, what are you doing in the storage closet?"

"I, I," Ava searched for a good excuse, and held up her bag, "I was looking for something and thought that was the ladies' room."

Karen pointed to the sign on the door. "But it says storage closet right there."

"Silly me," Ava shook her head. "I wasn't paying attention. But listen, I needed to ask you something, anyway."

"Sure," Karen murmured. "What is it?"

"I'm expecting an important letter from an attorney's office. Can you check to see if it's here yet?"

"Sure, let me get—"

"Actually." Ava directed Karen away from the closet and crossed her fingers Peter was already on his way to his room. "I'm running late for Elsa's wedding dress fitting. Can you look, please?"

When Karen nodded and took off toward the check-in counter, Ava let out the breath she was holding.

You need to keep your hands off him.

Except it was hard, because being with him felt so right.

Then tell your family.

There was a large part of her that wanted nothing more than to shout their relationship from the rooftops. The other part, though, liked the thrill of dating secretly. It was as if they were in their own bubble, and with no one else knowing about them ... they were free to shut out the world.

"No," Karen brought Ava back to the task at hand, "I don't see a letter. Maybe it will come in tomorrow."

"Okay, thanks for looking."

Ava chanced a peek back toward the hallway. Finn was leaning against the wall with his arms crossed over his chest. The heat in his eyes grabbed her heart, and it was only her sheer stubbornness that carried her out to her car and not across the lobby into his arms.

Lighthouse Inn
November 11
1:30 p.m.

GETTING THE PICTURE, YET?

FINN TOSSED THE NOTE ON HIS DESK IN DISGUST. "No, BLOODY hell, I'm not getting the picture."

Except, what was he missing?

He took Poppies and gave it to Remy.

Remy returned it to its rightful owners. He knew, because of the 'thank you' from the Queen.

Then he'd left England and Flynn Reide behind.

But before that ....

Remy had warned him ....

"Listen, mate," Remy's voice came over the line. "I need to tell you something."

"Bloody hell," Flynn snapped. "I told you I was done. I'm out of that business for good."

"I know," Remy's voice softened. "It's not a job I'm calling about. It's to give ye a warning."

Flynn scoffed. He knew what he was doing, and while his most recent jobs were the first in years, he hadn't lost his step. "What's the warning?"

"The man who owned Poppies, Roman Sutton, you know what he does?"

"Banking," Flynn retorted.

"International Banking, to be precise," Remy corrected. "Word has it he's involved in laundering large sums for several big names out there."

"So," Flynn scoffed. "What does that have to do with me?"

"Deep pockets," Remy told him. "There's also talk he's being investigated."

"I still don't see how this affects me."

Remy sighed. "I'm trying to keep my promise to your mum and keep you safe. Take your family and get out of sight for a while. I'll do what I can on this end."

"Do you really believe I need to leave?"

"I wouldn't have called if I didn't," Remy told him solemnly. "Godspeed, Flynn. Take your family and grab that happy beginning one more time."

"Alright, Remy. Be well, my friend."

He'd packed up his family, and they'd left England behind. And until Liam had asked him to locate Claire, his life as Flynn Reide had stayed in the past.

The notes pointed to Poppies, which pointed to Remy. But with that being a dead end, Finn sat down to dig into Roman Sutton.

When he'd researched the other man while preparing for the job, he'd only paid attention to the basics. This time, he decided, he needed to be more thorough.

Before he'd gotten far, there was a knock on the door, and his heart kicked up its speed. He shoved his files into his briefcase, shut his computer and ran to answer it.

"Did you mi–" he began, before realizing it wasn't Ava. "Killian … and Liam too. What brings you by in the middle of the day?"

"We need to talk, Dad," Killian told him. "Can we come in?"

A cold kernel of dread formed inside Finn, worried that they were coming to warn him away from Ava. Especially since it had been Killian who'd given Fowler her cell number.

"What's this about?"

Killian exchanged looks with Liam and Finn thought, here goes. "Dad, has anything odd been going on?"

"Odd going on?" Finn's blood froze for a completely different reason. "Like what?"

"Things moved," Liam offered, "or disappearing and reappearing."

Finn's thoughts went back to his office. "Do they leave anything behind," *like letters,* "or just move things?"

"Leave something behind?" Killian arched a brow. "Besides what they've taken, you mean? No. Mum's book disappeared from Liam's home and ended up at his office. My messenger bag disappeared from my car and ended up on my front porch."

"Someone took Claire's book?" Finn frowned at Liam. "I didn't know you'd kept that."

Liam shrugged. "I almost didn't, but Elsa tossed it in the box and told me to show it to Killian."

"But other than a name here and there." Killian took up the story. "I saw nothing of value in it."

Which, Finn thought, had been his conclusion.

"Captain Jack said someone had been in his office, moving things around," Finn tossed out.

"You saw him?" Killian leaned back and rested one foot on the other knee, his action deceptively calm.

"At the pier, just after you left," Finn offered, not explaining why he'd been there. "Said he should have mentioned the person was looking for the key."

"The key?" Killian barked. "To what? His house, his office?"

"Hope," Liam murmured.

"Hope?" Killian repeated. "What the bloody hell are you talking about?"

"Didn't Emma tell you about her conversation with Captain Jack about Jonesy and hope?"

Killian shrugged. "She told me he visits the swan daily and fills her in on Jonesy's behavior. But hope?"

"I only remember this because one time Jonesy ..." Then, as if he'd changed his mind, Liam hesitated a second. "Captain Jack believes Jonesy holds the key to Swan Harbor's hope." That he's given all his 'hope' to the town's lost hearts."

Finn laughed. "Which explains why he told me it's a good thing I've been staying in Swan Harbor. That the town could use some of my hope."

"When Rusty and I stopped by the restaurant," Killian added. "We weren't sure we believed him."

"You think he was making it up?" Finn shot back, not realizing how defensive he sounded.

"We just weren't sure he hadn't forgotten a few things," Killian explained.

Finn's mind swirled with how to explain his obsessiveness with knowing exactly where everything was located. That in his past life, it had been necessary for his safety.

"Captain Jack was a captain in the Navy for many years." Finn took the easiest explanation route. "I would think that required him to be very precise with knowing the placement of his belongings."

"Alright," Killian acknowledged that Captain Jack could have had an intruder. "So back to my original question, Dad. Have you noticed anything out of place?"

Talk to them!

"I'm not telling you my story, so you'll feel sorry for me," Captain Jack told him. "I'm telling you so if you decide family and love are the most important things, you will fight."

"I wasn't sure," Finn sighed, "which was why I didn't say anything. Then, after talking to Jack and hearing your stories ..." He picked up his phone and forwarded a couple of photos to his sons' phones.

Killian opened the text. "This is a hotel room."

"Yes, in the main building," Finn acknowledged.

"It's your closet, bathroom counter, and desk," Killian named each picture. "I fail to see what you're trying to show me."

Finn's eyes met Liam's, when he'd glanced up from his phone screen. "You see it, don't you?"

"Follow me, Killian." Liam led the way toward the bedroom.

Finn sat back and crossed one leg over the other, hoping to appear much more relaxed than he was feeling inside.

"Your shirts and slacks had been switched, your cologne bottles reversed, and your hairbrush is on the other side of them," Killian rattled off when they came out of the bedroom. "It could have been the housekeeper, though. Right?"

"The cologne and brush, yes," Finn agreed. "But not the items in my closet. Which is why I'm out here. Housekeeping comes when I request it and they're the only ones allowed inside."

"Alright," Killian's jaw tightened with annoyance, "we have someone who is moving objects around, possibly looking for the 'key,' to save the town's hope. Bloody hell, what's next for this town? Losing its heart?"

Finn laughed. "At least you can't say you're bored."

"We'll get out of your way." Killian and Liam moved toward the door. "Do you want to have dinner with us tonight? We thought we'd go for Italian."

Will Ava be there? Finn wanted to ask. "Text me the details," he said instead. "I have some paperwork I want to get through, so maybe."

He waved them off and leaned against the door, his mind going in a million different directions. Had he brought his problems to Swan Harbor, or …?

"He's hiding something," Killian began before they'd gotten far.

"Bugger that, Killian," Liam retorted. "We know that. The fact he has the hots for the lovely Ms. King."

Killian winced. "Must you talk about my future mother-in-law like that?"

"Speaking of," Liam grabbed his arm and pulled him behind a large pine tree.

"Li–"

"Shh" Liam hissed. "It's Ava."

Killian almost stepped onto the path to say hello, but then something had him remaining hidden.

"Come on." Liam took off back toward the cottages, staying off the path behind trees.

"Bloody hell," Killian murmured. "What have I gotten myself into?"

"Look." Liam pointed to where Ava was going. "Someone isn't going home."

"They're adults," Killian reminded his brother.

A woman's laughter carried across the wind, and when Liam peered around, Killian followed suit.

Finn had his arms around Ava, his face was buried in her neck, and she was laughing.

Bloody hell, what am I doing? Killian thought, preparing to step back.

Then Finn lifted his head and laid a kiss on Ava that had Killian feeling heat climb up his face.

"Told you dad had some moves," Liam whispered. "Look."

Against his better judgment, Killian peered back around the tree to see Finn walking Ava backward into his cottage, and then the door slammed.

"Told you we should have checked for protection when we were in the bathroom," Liam murmured.

"Liam!" Killian shook his head, trying to remove the image of his father and Emma's mom in a clench. "Let's go."

"Spoilsport," Liam grumbled.

"Now, back to why we came in the first place," Killian reminded Liam when they were in the car. "Our moving objects. Which I guess includes Captain Jack now."

"And dad said someone moved things around in his hotel room," Liam replied.

"There was something in dad's voice." Killian thought back on the way his dad had spoken. "He asked *if* they left anything behind. Why would he ask that?"

"You think he was telling us someone left something behind when they searched his room?"

"Maybe," Killian nodded. "I also noticed he'd crammed a folder in his briefcase, and it was half sticking out."

"So?" Liam shrugged. "He's working on some real estate deal. In fact, guess where dad and Ava were yesterday afternoon?"

"How the bloody hell do I know?" Killian groused.

"They were looking at a house," Liam nodded. "Together. Here in Swan Harbor."

"Who told you that?"

Liam pulled out his phone. "Camille, you know, the owner of the French place on the pier, sent a text at 2:30 that they had driven out of the marine parking lot."

Killian sent his brother a disgruntled look. "So."

"Dorothy, she lives on the corner of Pine Ave and Sea Line Drive, exchanged texts with Paula that they had turned onto her road. They were up there a couple of hours before someone saw them at the A&P."

"Bloody hell," Killian sighed. "I wonder if this was going on when Emma and I were getting together."

"Most likely," Liam smirked. "I keep thinking of your comment about the Swan Harbor's spy line, giving the word informant a whole new meaning. When you're in the matchmaking business, it's important to be in the know."

"Is Elsa aware of this obsession of yours?"

"She loves me," Liam retorted. "Nosiness and all."

"Just remember," Killian reminded Liam as he pulled up in front of the fire station, "there are some things I don't want to know."

Liam opened his door and got out. "But it's so much fun to rile you. See you later, Little Brother." He winked and slammed the door.

"Bloody hell," Killian shook his head, wondering what was next.

EIGHTEEN

Lighthouse Inn
November 11
5:30 p.m.

Finn sat in Ava's living room, his feet propped on an ottoman, and his laptop opened in front of him. But for the past half-hour, he hadn't learned anything new. He'd been too busy staring at the view.

Ava's blue eyes met his. "Thirty more minutes."

"What?" Finn held his hands up in surrender. "I'm just sitting here and minding my own business."

She sent him a look that said, *You know exactly what you're doing.* "You're watching me."

"And that's not a good thing?"

"Not when I need to concentrate."

"Alright," he sighed forlornly, "I'll behave."

"Just thirty more minutes," she promised. "Then we can misbehave together."

"I'll hold you to that."

"I'm sure you will."

Finn tore his gaze away and refocused on the notes he'd made about Roman Sutton.

Roman had been born in 1940 to a British father and a Polish mother. He'd been twice divorced before meeting and marrying Ella Owens in 1987. There had been two children from his first marriage and four from his third.

He started working for the Association of Foreign Banks when he was twenty-two and became president at forty.

In 2007, Roman was being investigated for fraud but was cleared of charges. In 2010, he 'retired.'

In 2013, wife number 3, Ella, divorced Roman and disappeared. No mention of the children.

After that, Finn found the information was spotty until he jumped into the dark web. There he'd found Sutton's obsession with the man who'd taken Poppies never quite disappeared.

In 2012, Sutton had put out feelers looking for information on the Shadow Angel. He'd offered one million pounds if the information led to the 'Angel's' identity.

Then Remy had gone underground in 2012. Had there been a connection?

Each year, they raised the reward for information on the Shadow Angel. In 2015, it was worth five million pounds.

And then ....

In 2016, hidden on a back page of an obscure newspaper, Finn found a small entry that sent the fear inside to another level.

Dear Shadow Angel, It's just a matter of time until we meet. You took from me. Just wait to see what I'll take from you.

Finn's gut clenched, and when his phone buzzed, he was happy to shut down his computer.

> Killian: We're meeting at La Luna on the pier at 7:00 p.m. Let me know what you decide.

"From Killian?" Ava asked when he looked up to find her staring at him.

"Do you want to go eat with the kids?"

"As opposed to?"

Finn tried to shove aside his feelings of impending doom and focus on the here and now. "What would you like to eat?"

She grinned. "I'm not sure. A sexy man cooked for me the last two nights."

"Want him to cook again?"

Ava's eyes met his, and there was a different look in them than he'd seen lately. "If he does, what will it cost me?"

Finn fought to keep his thoughts from traveling into that *Don't go there space*, and without taking his eyes off her, packed his computer away. "I think." He sauntered toward her and tugged her up and into his arms. "I'll leave that up to you."

"Really?" She arched a black brow, and her eyes dropped to his mouth before lifting back up. "You'll allow me to decide what it's worth?"

"Yes, love." He whispered a kiss across her mouth. "I want it all, but the pace is up to you."

Her breath hitched. "I don't ..."

Finn kissed her, taking the words from her mouth and just like every time she was in his arms, his heart raced, and his body tightened. "No rush," he assured her. "I'm an adult."

"Yes, you are." Ava placed barely-there kisses wherever she could reach.

"You're killing me." Finn finally held her still long enough to capture her lips. Her unique flavor drew him, ratcheting his need to the next level, and if they didn't stop, he was fairly sure all thought of food would disappear.

He'd taken a step back, intending to lower them to the sofa when her phone buzzed.

Ava chuckled, "Think it's Emma asking about dinner?

"Good guess."

"What should I tell her?"

"Tell her you're tired and staying in."

"And what are you going to tell Killian?"

"That I'm tired and staying in," he winked, letting her go.

"Are we living dangerously?"

The information he'd uncovered briefly flitted through his mind, but he shoved it aside and smiled. "I prefer to think of it as going after what we want.

And Ava," he cupped her jaw and kissed her, fighting to keep it brief. "I want you."

Ava's eyes drifted open, and the gentle puff of her breath blew across his mouth, sent little shivers racing throughout.

He wasn't sure how long they stood there, but just as he was leaning in for another kiss, her phone buzzed again. "Saved by the text."

"Who says I want to be saved?"

Finn groaned, but stepped away and handed her the phone. "Here."

She took it, but there was a sexy blush dotting her cheekbones, and her pulse was fluttering, giving him hope they were on the same page.

"I'll look in the ..." He waved toward the kitchen.

The promises he saw in her eyes had him stepping away to send Killian a text.

> Finn: I'm going to stay in tonight. There are a few things I need to take care of.

When he didn't feel guilty for wanting to spend the evening alone with Ava, he knew he'd made the right decision. Except that didn't take care of dinner.

"What do you have in your kitchen?" He went to search her refrigerator.

"I have very little."

"You're right." He took out a carton of cream, some spinach and a pepper. "If we combine these with eggs and cheese, we can make a frittata."

"You can make a frittata?"

"Bloody hell, yes. The best frittata you'll ever taste," he promised.

"A little food, a little romance, and—"

"—Me." Finn kissed her.

"Perfect."

"Are you done with what you were working on?"

"Almost," Ava's eyes sparkled, "I'm submitting my offer for the cottage. Giennie thinks they'll accept."

"Then we have something to celebrate."

Her smile started slowly, almost as if she couldn't quite believe what she was going to say, "We do, don't we?"

That something different in her eyes was back, he noted, getting lost in them. "I'll just go ..."

He grabbed a paper bag from the A&P and shoved the ingredients into it. "I'll go start dinner."

"I won't be long."

"See that you aren't." Finn dropped a kiss on her nose. Then he reached for his briefcase and stepped outside.

The cold air cooled his libido, but the buzz left behind by whatever had been surrounding them in her cottage remained, simmering just under the surface.

"You're an adult," he murmured. "Not some hormonal teen." Except his body wasn't listening, because it ached and there was only one way to soothe it ... her.

❧

When the door shut behind Finn, Ava let out the breath she was holding. What was wrong with her? There was a new heightened awareness every time she was in his company. But when had it started?

Was it when he'd cooked dinner for her? Or did it have something to do with the feelings that had taken over her when she'd been in the cottage? How right it felt when Finn said she fit. Nothing had ever felt more right ... besides a certain someone's kisses.

Stop that! Get control!

But even after she submitted her forms, something new bubbled inside. And as she brushed her hair, and touched up her make-up, it sparked, threatening to erupt. Somehow, she knew, whatever '*it*' was, it wouldn't take much to sweep her away completely, taking over her very thoughts and feelings.

Ava used the walk to his cottage to have a talk with herself. Since she'd given them a chance, she'd thought she could control the feelings he ignited, but ....

"You can do this," she scolded as she knocked. "Don't throw yourself at him."

"Ava." His breathless voice, and the grin on his face when he pulled open the door, tossed her good intentions out the window.

"I did it!" She threw her arms around his neck.

"You submitted your offer?"

"Yes. You know this is the first house I've purchased?"

"Really?"

Finn tugged her inside and took her coat. Then, just as he had the first night he cooked, he seated her and did all the work.

"Yes, really." Ava smiled. "In Boston, I still live in the house I grew up in. And we know what happened to the apartment in New York."

"Was that when you were sick?"

She nodded. "Yes. Looking back, I think my reaction to you terrified me to where I refused to stop and acknowledge it."

Finn lifted a brow. "Are you saying before that moment you hadn't jumped a man you'd just met?"

Ava sucked in her breath, remembering the hot, visceral need to have him when she'd met him in January. "I'd never ..."

"Hey," he dropped the spatula and pulled her into his arms, "I was teasing you."

"So, you aren't asking for an apology?"

"Bloody hell, no!" he shot back so quickly, something inside relaxed. "It was the same for me. I think I was a little in lust with you just by hearing your voice."

"You were?"

"Most definitely. Ready to eat?"

Ava could have gotten lost in his dark eyes, but forced herself to look away, settling on the table. "Those are new." She noted the vase of roses.

"I made a quick trip to the small market inside the Inn," he told her. "Bought some flowers for my lady."

"Oh, you did?" Ava giggled at his choice of words.

"I did. Come sit."

She let him lead her to the table, and while they ate listened to him regal her with stories of when Liam and Killian were boys. And with every story, he took more and more of her heart.

Good things come to those who wait, she couldn't help but think.

His dark eyes shown with happiness, and his smile turned her inside out.

"You're not listening to me, are you?" he teased.

"I'm listening."

"Then what was I talking about?"

"You were talking about getting stung by a jellyfish." Ava giggled at the surprised look on his face. "When you run a company as large as King's, you learn to multitask. I became very adept at listening and daydreaming at the same time."

Finn laughed. "A good skill to have. Are you ready for dessert?"

"Dessert?" Her eyes lit up. "Frozen berries and cream?"

"No."

"No?" Ava glanced around to see if she could get a hint. "S'mores?" she squealed, spotting the ingredients beside the fireplace.

"You game?"

"For chocolate and marshmallow? Lead on. But shouldn't we clean the kitchen?"

"Later." Finn scooted her into the living room. "They didn't have those fancy roasting forks in the market, so ..."

"You cut sticks off a tree?"

He shrugged, and his face turned red. "I hope it works."

"It will work," she assured him, even though she didn't know if it would or not.

Finn held out a stick with marshmallows on the end. "Would you like to do the honor?"

But he licked his full bottom lip, and the way it glistened had something inside blooming. "Actually," Ava took the stick and laid it on the hearth, "I think I want something else now."

A light she hadn't seen lately glowed in his eyes. "And what do you want, Ava, love? If it's in my power, it's yours."

"Really?"

"What do you want?"

Her eyes watered at the emotions climbing inside and, in that moment, she handed him her heart. "You, Finn. I just want you."

He was quiet for so long she almost turned and ran and then ... the sexiest smile he'd ever given her graced his face. "I'm all yours."

Ava hesitated a heartbeat, and then another. Then, the invisible cord between them tightened, pulling her toward him.

"I've got you," he whispered when she crawled onto his lap.

"Is this okay?"

Finn cupped her hips, and settled her closer to the hard wedge behind his zipper. "If it was any better, I'd die." He pushed her collar away and latched onto that sensitive spot on her neck.

Every touch of his lips sent a spark of heat straight to her core. She groaned and scooted closer to his hardness. The movement of his hips set her on fire and as the heat climbed inside, she lost track of what burned the brightest.

Was it the line of fire his lips created skimming her neck? Or the way his fingers stoked the flames, as they whispered along her skin? He touched, and her body felt alive.

His hands slid up her back and swept her sweater up and over her head.

"You're beautiful." Finn almost reverently cupped her breasts.

"I'm—"

Whatever she was going to say was lost when he took one taut peak between his lips. "Beautiful."

Ava's breath stuttered in her throat, the feelings he was creating leaving her at a loss. She needed more, pushing his head away long enough to unfasten her bra and toss it aside.

"Lovely." He cupped her breasts, his lips traveling from one side to the other. Everywhere his gaze landed, heat sparked to life.

It feels too good. She pushed her hips against his hardness, and every thrust sent her a little closer to the top.

The feelings inside grew, and there was a part of her that kept thinking she should stop. Thinking they should move. Except, she couldn't make herself listen.

"Finn," she whispered, grinding against his erection.

"I'm here, love."

He licked her nipple and sucked it into his hot heat, and her hips moved of their own volition.

Her hands carded through his silky hair, holding him still while his lips toyed and sucked. The pleasure they were generating shot straight to that place between her legs that couldn't get close enough.

"I want ..."

"More." Finn released her long enough to swing her off his lap, and lay her flat. "Is this alright or ..."

Ava met his dark gaze as he hovered over her, and the intensity was almost too much. "Come here." She pulled his lips to hers.

With his talented mouth, he sipped, stroked, and sucked, pulling feelings from her she'd never thought possible. Fire, heat, the thought that everything inside was going to bubble over with the next stroke, the next kiss.

But he kept playing her as if her body were a well-tuned piano, and he was the maestro.

He pulled his sweater over his head, and when their bare torsos touched, every nerve ending sizzled.

Ava reached for the button on his slacks, but his swift intake of air had her eyes flying open to see the strain on his face. "Are you ...?"

"I'm fine." He backed away just long enough to remove his slacks. "Someone's overdressed," he smirked, barely giving her time to catch her breath before he stripped her leggings off.

But instead of lowering next to her, Finn hovered above her and everywhere his gaze touched, igniting a spark.

The words in her heart threatened to fly free, but what if ....

"I'm too old for games."

"I," her eyes locked with his, "love—"

"—Love."

"You," they sighed simultaneously.

Then his lips were on hers and all she could do was feel. A touch here. A caress there. His lips trailed a line of kisses down her stomach and her heart soared.

The storm inside raged and with every stroke, it pulled her higher.

"I can't ...."

"Don't," he murmured. The feelings were so consuming, she felt as if he were pulling her very soul from her body.

"I'm with you." Finn tugged her leg up over his hip.

"Oh!"

"Perfect," he purred.

Ava tightened her leg around his flank, forcing him into the position she wanted.

"Bossy, aren't you?" Finn chuckled, showing her exactly who was in charge.

"And you're risking insubordination," she told him, tightening her internal muscles.

"Oh, bloody hell, Ava," Finn cried, losing control and seating himself completely.

She looped her other leg over his. "That's better, but ..."

Finn bracketed her head with his hands, his face directly above hers, and the flames casting shadows over them. "I really love you," he murmured huskily. "No matter what happens, don't forget that."

There was a part of her that wanted to question what he meant, but then his lips touched hers, and he started moving, and all that mattered was what was happening in this moment in time.

While this wasn't the first time she'd given him her body, it felt brand new. Each time he moved, the feelings pulled from inside were more intense and with every stroke the storm raged.

Her senses heightened until everything around them disappeared, and he was all that mattered. The way he was holding her face, as if he never wanted to let her go, had her heart racing. And the way he was kissing her had her holding onto him for fear of being left behind.

A gentle thrust, a twist, and before she could catch her breath, the storm rushed over her, sucking her under. Ava tightened her hold on Finn's shoulder and just when she felt she was surfacing, his body shuddered and sucked her back under once again.

She wasn't sure how long she lay there, fighting the tears threatening until finally he rolled onto his side and pulled her close.

"Hey," he leaned back, tilting her chin up, "did I do something wrong?"

She couldn't get the words out and buried her face against his bare chest, letting the tears fall. He whispered words of love, and his hands soothed up and down her back until finally the tears faded, and she was able to get herself under control. How was she to explain to him what was going through her mind?

"I'm sorry," she sniffed, hoping she didn't sound like an idiot. "You did nothing wrong."

"Then why the tears?"

"I've just never felt so," she gave him a watery smile, "loved."

Finn brushed back her hair and placed a gentle kiss on one eyelid. Then the other before settling a tender kiss on her lips. "You are, you know? But if you need me to show you again, I'd be happy to."

Happiness bubbled up inside. "So soon?"

"Are you questioning my prowess?"

"Well, you are older and ..."

"I'll show you old." He nipped her earlobe. "Just give me a minute."

Ava brushed her thumb across his bottom lip. Her breath caught when he sucked it into his hot mouth. "Is that a real minute or a minute as in we can make and eat a s'mores minute?"

He chuckled, and the sound zipped straight to her heart. "Does it matter?"

She pushed him over onto his back and climbed on top to straddle his stomach. "No. But while we're waiting ..."

NINETEEN

Veterinary Clinic
November 12
8:30 a.m.

When Emma woke up, she knew the day was going to be different. Her father was in town, and after months of back-and-forth emails, he was coming to her clinic. And instead of facing him head on, as she probably should have, she'd scheduled an early morning patient.

But halfway through cleaning the canine's teeth, she'd finally admitted Killian had been right. While she believed it was important to face the past before you can move forward, it didn't make it any less scary. Except starting her day doing something she could do with her eyes closed, allowed her to stay in control ... for a little longer anyway.

"I can finish this, Doc," Leroy repeated, not for the first time.

While there was a part of her that wanted to stay and take over, she forced herself to step away from the table. "Okay. Let me know if you need me."

He gave her a look that said, '*I can do this*,' and went back to tending to the dog lying on the table.

Just go.

She tugged off her gloves, and her pulse spiked. It was then she realized she'd probably made a mistake. That meeting Peter as he walked into her place of business, would have given her more confidence. Just as it had when her mother had shown up unannounced all those months ago.

Too late now.

Like a coward, she'd left Killian to greet her father instead of listening to her own words. When she read his text, she decided she owed him something special, because as he had so many times, he'd read her mind and alleviated her fears.

> Killian: Peter arrived on time. I covered and told him you had an emergency. He's been introduced to Paris and her brood. I'll expect payment later. I love you.

Emma took a deep breath and opened the door, just enough to hear her father speaking to someone.

Was it Sadie?

"I arrived an hour ago," Peter was saying in a tender voice. "You're up awfully early."

He was quiet for several minutes before replying, "No, I haven't seen her yet. I met her Fiancé."

"Probably," he chuckled, and Emma had to wonder what he'd been asked.

"I'll let you know," he promised in response to some question. "I love you."

The small snippet of the conversation had Emma wondering why his wife, Amber, hadn't flown East with him. Had that been her idea, or had she not been invited?

When it was quiet for several seconds, Emma wiped her sweaty palms on her scrubs and stepped completely into her office.

Peter was sitting on the floor scratching Millicent's back and watching Paris nurse her puppies. His eyes met hers and in them, she saw the same fears she had.

What do I say?

Will she give me a chance?

Thank you for inviting me.

With the realization she wasn't alone, some of her fear disappeared. "I see you met Millicent." Emma laughed at the disgruntled look on the cat's face when Peter stood. "She thinks she runs the place."

"I get that," he acknowledged. "We have several who behave the same way."

"Really?" The comment reiterated just how little she knew about her dad and his new life, and had her making a mental note to change that.

"Amber collects strays," he admitted absently, making Emma think he was referring to more than just the four-legged kind.

"Maybe next time you come East, she could come with you." It was an idea she hadn't completely thought through, but once it was out there, she realized it was true.

Peter's smile grew, and he seemed to relax his posture slightly. "She'd really like to meet you too."

Their eyes locked, both understanding the step they'd taken with the admission. Emma wasn't sure how long they stood there before Peter cleared his throat. "Killian," his brow arched, "showed me what to do."

"Oh?" Emma glanced around the room, where besides the mother dog and her litter, there was only Boomer. A very pampered pug who was in a corner cage giving her a pitiful look.

"Yes." A pleased expression crossed his face. "I cleaned out the cages, fed your borders, and walked the new mom. That pug wouldn't let me near the cage."

Emma rolled her eyes. "He's pouting because he had to stay an extra night."

"Nothing serious, I hope."

"A reaction to a new food left him dehydrated," she explained. "He's fine, but I should take him out."

"Do you mind if I go with you?"

"It's cold."

"I think I can handle it."

There was something in his smile, she thought. Almost as if he were worried she wouldn't meet him halfway.

"I'd like that."

"Good."

Emma clipped a leash onto Boomer's collar, and they left the building. It was quiet at the outset of their walk, both trying to feel their way. But slowly, her father asked a question, and another one. About her business, her friends, Swan Harbor, each question digging a little more into her life, as if he were really interested in the person she'd become.

They hadn't gone far before Boomer decided he'd walked enough and sat, refusing to budge. Emma shook her head at the dog's expectant look. "Someone thinks he makes the rules."

Peter laughed and squatted to scratch the dog's ears. "I can see that."

It was quiet again, but not the uncomfortable silence she'd been worried about. She asked him questions about his life in Washington, and there were several times talking to him felt surreal. Her entire life, she'd imagined having a 'normal' conversation with the great Peter Foster. Now that she was, she kept thinking she should feel envious ... or like she'd missed out on something.

Peter Foster was her father, but at one time, he'd been an up-and-coming actor starring in box office romcom hits. That is, until he'd met her mother and because of her grandfather Leo, his career crashed, and he'd ended up married.

He'd been a father who wasn't present in his daughter's life until her grandfather died. Then Peter had taken part from the fringes. Pictures kept in albums, transferred to a blog sent to her the previous January. Since then, fear and stubbornness had stood between them.

"Do you ever wish you could have a do over?" she asked him quietly. "Have a chance to change things in your life?"

Peter said nothing for several seconds, but when he turned his blue eyes in her direction, she knew he was speaking from a place of conviction. "Emma," he sighed, "I would assume everyone who reaches their forties or fifties wishes they could go back and undo a stupid move or two. But ... you change one thing ..."

"And you change the person you are," she answered quietly. The same thing she'd discussed with Elsa, Killian, and her mother.

"Yes." He sent her a lopsided grin. "I'm in a really good place and from what I can see, you are too."

Emma's eyes misted over, and she had to blink several times to clear her vision. "You're right," she brushed off her jeans. "I am."

"I thought so." His smile turned devilish. "On the way back, you can tell me about Killian."

"Dad," she huffed, realizing her exasperation was partly pretense. "You sound exactly like mom."

"Does your mother like Killian?"

"She does." Emma hesitated a few steps and then tossed out. "Mom's in Swan Harbor, did you know that?"

"Your mother is here ... in town?"

"Staying at the Lighthouse Inn."

"Isn't that interesting?"

Her next patient was waiting for her when they returned to the clinic, so she didn't get to ask what he'd meant.

Should she warn her mother? Peter had hurt Ava more than once. Had she put that part of her life behind her in order to move forward? Or was she still holding on to the resentment and anger?

Lighthouse Inn
November 12
10:00 a.m.

Finn stretched, and the aches in his back reminded him he wasn't as young as he used to be. But when he opened one eye to see Ava staring back at him, he realized the pain was worth it. Especially if the outcome was to end up in bed with the woman he loved.

"Good morning." He tugged her against his chest.

The way she curled against him had his heart racing. "You know what this means, right?"

He kissed the top of her head. "That's a loaded question. I think it means we need to talk to our kids."

She sighed. "Okay, that too. But let's wait until Peter leaves. I don't want ..."

He wasn't sure how he felt about her fear of coming face to face with her ex-husband. But he understood her concerns regarding her daughter's feelings. "What did Emma say about Peter? Is she worried?"

Ava chuckled. "She told me he could only hurt her if she let him. That she's moved on and believes they've both changed."

"You sound skeptical."

"Stupid, huh?"

"Understandable."

"Really?"

Finn searched around for how to tell her about his marriage without bringing too much of his baggage into the bed with them. "I understand how it feels when the person you love throws your feelings back into your face."

"Like you don't matter."

"That sums it up. And just like Claire and I weren't right, neither were you and Peter."

"But she gave you Liam and Killian, and Peter gave me Emma."

"There is nowhere else I'd rather be, Ava."

"Me either."

He kissed her, and a part of him worried about morning breath. Except she was soft and warm, and he didn't want to stop.

"I love you," she murmured. "But I'm still going to have to do the walk of shame."

"The walk of shame?"

"Yes." She sat up, and the sheet fell around her, exposing her breasts for his perusal. "Walking back to my place in yesterday's clothing."

Finn had a hard time formulating his thoughts. Especially with Ava sitting next to him with her upper half bare. "Did anyone see you?"

"When?"

"In the clothes you had on yesterday?"

"Emma, Elsa, and Patty"

"And they aren't here, now are they?" Her smooth back drew his attention, and he couldn't keep from trailing his finger up and down her spine.

Ava shivered and goosebumps broke out on her skin. "N-N-No," she stuttered. "But I ..."

Suddenly, she tossed the sheets aside and jumped up.

"Honey, wait." Finn threw the sheet off and scurried after her.

She had her bra halfway on, and when she looked up at him, there was something in her eyes, he couldn't read.

"Regrets?" He held his breath until she answered.

"No!" Her eyes flared. "I just thought I'd—"

"—Leave before I asked you to?"

"Something like that."

"If I had my way, we'd stay locked away all day."

"That's not very practical, is it?"

"No." Then something had him knocking her hand out of the way and refastening her bra. "There. Now you know I don't want just one thing."

Ava slipped her red sweater over her head, its length hitting the top of her thighs.

"Sexy," he whistled.

"Oh, you."

Instead of stepping into his arms as he'd hoped, she picked up her leggings and slipped them on. "Do you have plans for today?"

"A few phone calls," he shrugged as if it were no big deal, "do you have something in mind?"

"How about I clean up and then grab Paula's for us?"

A corner of Finn's mouth curved. "You look fine to me."

Ava wrinkled her nose. "I'm pretty sure if I went to Paula's like this, the entire town would know where I spent the night."

He tugged her into his arms and nuzzled her ear. "How would they know that?"

"Because," she kissed him, "I smell like sex."

"I didn't notice."

"Maybe it's because you smell like it, too. Go shower." She popped him on his bare arse, and the temptation to toss her over his shoulder was strong. Before he could pick her up, though, she slipped on her coat. "I'll be back."

"Hurry. I'll miss you."

Ava blew him a kiss and was gone before he was ready for her to leave. He convinced himself that nothing could touch them as long as they remained in their little cocoon. But as he gathered his clothing and showered, he knew he was just fooling himself.

"I'm not telling you my story, so you'll feel sorry for me," Captain Jack told him. "I'm telling you, so if you decide family and love are the most important things, you will fight."

If he were going to fight was never the question, because he'd always fought. But the question was quickly becoming how long he was going to fight alone.

He'd just washed the last dish when there was a knock at the door, and while he wished it were Ava, he knew it hadn't been long enough.

"Karen," he greeted her, and when her eyes were stuck staring at the center of his chest, he pulled his robe closed. "You'll have to forgive me. I got a bit of a late start today."

"Finn," she gave him a coy smile and held out a large envelope, "your mail arrived from your office. I thought you might want it right away."

A sick feeling of dread formed in the pit of his stomach. Just why, he didn't know.

"You're too kind." He took the package and weighed it in his hands, hoping there were no surprises inside.

"It wasn't a problem. Have a good day."

After she left, it took several seconds before he worked up the courage to dump the contents on the table. Then another few before he was strong enough to sort through the real estate flyers. He'd almost relaxed when a white linen envelope stopped him cold.

Carefully, Finn removed the letter and read,

Wouldn't Scotland Yard be interested in knowing what happened to Flynn Reide, or should I call you the Shadow Angel?

"Bloody hell," he murmured. The time had come to stop running.

THERE WAS A PART OF AVA THAT WANTED TO JUST SIT AND RELIVE the past fifteen hours, but the other part was pushing her to hurry. Because the faster she moved, the faster she could return and relive the time with Finn ... in his arms.

She grabbed her coat and pulled open the door, just as Karen lifted her hand to knock.

"Ava, I'm glad I caught you."

"Karen, how are you? Do you want to come in?"

"No," Karen shook her head, "you look like you're on your way out. I just wanted to give you this."

She handed Ava a 5" x 8" envelope that she knew inside was a letter from her Grandmother Rose which had been waiting for her for forty-eight years. "Thank you, Karen. This means a lot to me."

"No problem, Ava. Have a good day."

The memory of how emotional she'd felt after hearing about the letter had her locking the door and taking it with her. Just before she turned on the path toward Finn's cabin, he turned in the opposite direction, apparently so lost in thought he didn't see her.

"Finn!"

When he ignored her and continued walking, a cold feeling formed in the pit of her stomach.

"Finn," she called again.

This time when he stopped, the cold feeling warmed, and she thought maybe ....

Slowly, he turned around. One look at his face and the kernel grew, expanding outward.

"I thought we were going to have coffee."

"Something came up," he replied, but while the words were coming out of Finley Reade's mouth, they didn't sound like him. Heavier accent, clipped, gruffer, a man she didn't know.

"Oh." The cold climbed, piercing her heart, taking all the heat, and squeezing. "Finn, I love you."

He stopped and turned back toward her, and the anguished look on his face had her wanting to run to him. "Talk to me."

Several expressions crossed his face, then with a subtle nod, he walked back toward his cottage and beckoned her inside.

Ava tightened her hands into fists and stepped across the threshold, then dropped the letter on the table.

"I don't know what to say."

"Bull," she snapped. "You are never at a loss for words. Tell me what happened."

A corner of his mouth kicked up before settling into a straight line. "This doesn't involve you." Again, he tried to push her away.

She wanted to argue with him but instead tossed out, "Do you love me?"

Finn was holding onto his briefcase handle so tightly, his hands had to be hurting. When he opened his mouth, she expected to hear she'd dreamed the whole thing. Instead, he whispered, "Of course, I love you."

"Then it damn well affects me."

Finn set his briefcase on the table and unbuttoned his coat. "It's just ..."

Ava stepped into him and hooked her hands in his lapels. "It's just what?"

"You asked about my childhood," he began in a voice so soft, she had to lean in to hear him. "I was born on the east side of London, the bastard son of a woman who worked for a rich family. My mum idolized the 'idea' of that family. Mother, father, three children, a dog, and a cat. Everyone on their best behavior."

"I sense a but coming ..."

"Oh, not yet," he denied. "My mum told me that someday I could have a family just like that. If I was good enough. If I worked hard. That someday there was a family meant for me. That would be my happy-ever-after."

"What happened to your mother?"

"She died when I was five," he whispered. "My sixteen-year-old sister, Winnie, took over our mother's job and raised me."

"Of the happy beginning."

He nodded and a faraway look crossed his face. "Winnie told me I had to search for the life I wanted. That once I found it to hold on tight. It would be the first day of my new beginning."

"What happened to Winnie?"

"The perfect family wasn't so perfect," Finn snapped. "The father drank, knocked the wife around, and if he couldn't find her, he went after his kids. But one boy was my age and hiding with Winnie and I, in our rooms."

Ava gasped, somehow knowing what was coming.

"He stormed into my room and had a belt. 'Let's see how many lashes you can handle, laddie,' he yelled, standing in the doorway. Winnie stepped in front of me and pushed the man, and he stumbled backward. 'Run boys, run!' my big sister cried. I took Miles's hand, and we ran. That was the last time I saw my sister."

His voice trailed off and Ava wanted to take him in her arms, but then he stepped back, putting more distance between them. "She died protecting me, and at six-years-old, I had to create another new beginning. Bloody hell, Ava, I'm tired of something or someone always coming between me and the life I want."

"What do you want?"

"A family, Ava. *My* family." He picked up his briefcase and took the steps to reach the door. "I'm fighting for *my* family." Then he was gone.

Ava's thoughts pinged all over the place, unsure what to do. "But he said he loved me," she murmured. "Doesn't that make me family too? Even if we're only connected through Emma and Killian."

She wasn't sure when she decided, but her keys were in her hand, and she was running toward her car.

"Hold on to me, love. I'm too old for games and want you to know that slowly, but most assuredly, I am falling for you. I do not plan on letting you go."

And just earlier when she'd asked, "Do you love me?"

"Of course, I love you."

His car was gone by the time she backed out of the parking space. Except, even in the small town, she had no idea where to look for him. She just knew she needed to get away and turned in the opposite direction of the Inn.

"Listen to your heart, Ava," Captain Jack told her. *"It always knows."*

"Well, Jack," she murmured. "My heart says to go home, and I'm going to listen.

TWENTY

Liam and Elsa's Cottage
November 12
12:00 p.m.

Finn was sitting at Elsa's kitchen table with a cup of coffee in front of him when Liam and Killian arrived.

"Help yourself, dad," Liam retorted. "Did we leave the door unlocked?"

"No," Finn's reply was succinct, but he wasn't in the mood for social niceties.

"We're here," Killian snapped. "What's so bloody important?"

"Have a seat." Finn reached for his notebooks and took a deep breath. When he started talking, rather than starting at the beginning, he started at the end. "I'm getting threatening notes." He tossed them on the table in the order they'd been received.

Killian raised a brow. "This is why you asked if anything had been left behind?"

"Yes."

"Killian's the investigator here." Liam flipped the letter with the picture of him holding the painting around. "But I'm assuming this is what you took?"

Finn tipped his chin in acknowledgment.

"You're the Shadow Angel?" Killian asked quietly. But something in his manner told Finn his son knew more about the Shadow Angel than he was letting on.

"I was the Shadow Angel," Finn admitted. "These might fill in some holes, and the sticky note is where the Poppies story begins."

Killian and Liam studied him for several heartbeats before each grabbed a notebook and began flipping through the pages. While they were digging into his past, Finn couldn't sit still, and wandered into the living room to stare out the window. The view of the town in the distance reminded him of Ava, and the view from her cottage. Would she forgive him? Did he even deserve her forgiveness?

The gentle rumble of voices from the other room had him wishing he'd stayed in there to hear what they were saying.

"Dad." When Finn turned around, Killian was leaning against the kitchen door frame. "You need to give us more information. Especially if you expect us to help you."

Finn's dark eyes clashed with his son's blue ones, but in them, he didn't see the judgment he'd expected. "You don't have—"

"Just stop," Killian snapped. "We're family."

Finn swallowed hard and followed his son into the kitchen. "What do you want to know?"

"Have at it, Killian," Liam replied.

Killian tapped the letter with the picture of the Poppies painting and flipped around the notebook with the information. "This was where you disappeared to before we moved, wasn't it?"

"Yes."

"Did you reach out to your handler," Killian wanted to know, "or did he reach out to you?"

"Does it matter?" Finn asked, wondering where the question had come from.

"To the case? No," Killian shrugged. "Humor me."

"I reached out to him," Finn conceded. "Before that time, I'd been out of the business a long time."

"You did it for mum, didn't you?" Liam had guessed the reason he'd jumped back into Shadow Angel's shoes without having to be told.

"Why would you think that?" Finn asked instead of answering, still used to shielding his sons from their mother's behavior and expectations.

"Come on, Dad," Liam scoffed. "I was old enough to know mum wanted more than you could give her on your pay from working in the shipyard."

"Alright, yes. I did it for your mum," Finn admitted quietly. "I just wanted to make her happy."

"How did she know?" Killian asked softly.

He hadn't wanted to get into this part, but since it didn't appear he had a choice, Finn pulled out his silver coin. "She saw this."

Killian flipped the coin around and studied it for several seconds. "It's a silver coin. You need to elaborate."

Finn took the coin again and habit had him sending it rolling across his knuckles. But telling his sons the story of how the coin had come to be in his possession was harder than he'd thought. "It was 1983, and I learned about a shipment of silver coins, pieces of eight, that were stolen in 1715. And part of that collection still resided with a family. My plan was to return it to the Spanish government, for a finder's fee."

"Did you tell mum the story?"

"No." Finn shook his head and jumped into where he never hoped he'd have to go. "It was your mother's family who had the collection."

Liam barked out a laugh. "You're telling us, you stole from Grandfather Jones?"

"Not quite," Finn denied.

"What are you saying exactly?" Killian prodded.

"I *planned* to steal from your mother's family," Finn conceded. "But in doing my homework, I missed one very important detail."

"Spit it out, Dad," Killian grunted.

"I knew the family went to dinner every Friday," Finn shared. "Except the last Friday night of every month, everyone went except your mother. Then, when I was in the middle of appropriating those coins, the phone rang."

"And mum saw you," Liam guessed.

"No," Finn denied. "It was I who saw your mother."

"I met Claire when I was 21 and she was just 17. With her long black hair and big blue eyes, I thought she was the most beautiful girl in the world. It wasn't long before we were inseparable."

Killian threw the words he'd used the previous January back at him. "What did you do?"

"I put all the silver back into the case, except for one, and snuck out as quickly as possible." Finn explained with a smile. "Then I got a job in the shipyard and put myself in your mother's path."

Liam chuckled and looked at Killian. "Told you he had some moves."

Killian gave him a disgruntled look, and Finn had to wonder about the missing pieces of that conversation. "So forward wind to years later, and …"

"Your mother wanted more and threw out a comment about my earning a finder's fee for returning items."

"And you contacted your handler," Killian added.

"Yes, Remy French," Finn offered.

Killian touched the notes. "Do you think he's the one sending these?"

"Remy died in 2015," Finn explained. "Six shots, found in a tube station in London."

"Did they catch who did it?" Killian asked, in full investigator mode.

"Not that I could discover," Finn admitted. "I was hoping …"

Killian ran his hand through his hair. "Dad, you once said we all need help now and then. That's what families do. They help each other."

"I agree, but—"

"No arguments," Killian interrupted. "And while I didn't know specifics, I overheard a fight between you and Uncle Alistair."

Finn glanced at Killian. "When?"

Killian shrugged. "I'm not sure. He tossed out a comment about sticky fingers. And you told him if he didn't keep it under his hat, you'd break his."

Finn winced. "Not one of my finer conversations with your uncle. But why didn't you ask me?"

"Then I'd have to arrest you," Killian quipped.

Finn studied his son, and the sick feeling in his stomach returned full force. "Do what you have to do."

"Dad," Killian laughed. "I was joking. From what I know of the Shadow Angel, he took objects from individuals who'd happened upon them in a nefarious manner. You just returned them to their owners."

It wasn't always that way. "Thank you, son."

"Have you told Ava?"

Finn glanced from Killian to Liam and back. "Ava?"

"Come on, Dad," Liam laughed. "We know you have the hots for her."

"Bloody hell, Liam!" Killian exclaimed. "I told you—"

"At least I didn't ask about protection," Liam snickered.

"Bloody hell, Liam!" Finn stared at his oldest. "Where did that come from?"

Liam smirked. "I'm practicing for when Elsa and I have a family."

Finn felt the heat climb up his face, but wasn't sure if he should admit anything about his relationship with Ava. Especially after ....

"We know you've been seeing her." Killian pointed to the picture taken at Central Park.

"She doesn't know what's going on," Finn admitted. "I was hoping I could solve this on my own and protect all of you. But when she finds out about my past, how can she look beyond the person Flynn Reide was? She deserves—"

"—A man who loves her and tells her what's going on in his life," Liam told him quietly. "Don't you think you owe her the chance to decide?"

"With this hanging over our head, though," Finn pointed out disgustedly. "How can I promise her anything?"

"You give her hope," Liam stated.

"After all, you are hope," Killian repeated Captain Jack's comment. "What the bloody hell does that mean, anyway?"

"No idea," Finn sighed. "So, tell me how to fight this, Killian."

"Tell me what you've found out," Killian suggested. "And we'll go from there."

While Finn couldn't say he was 100% relieved he'd shared his burdens with his sons, he could admit, the load had lightened.

"Here's what I've found out so far." He pushed his notes across the table. "Now what?"

Veterinary Clinic
November 12
4:00 p.m.

HER DAY WITH HER FATHER SHADOWING HER EVERY MOVE HAD gone better than she'd expected. He knew how to take direction, when to ask questions, and when to be quiet. Plus, he was a good listener, which probably helped since he was a high school drama teacher. But as the day wore on, she'd noticed he'd been careful to stay hidden. Which wasn't a behavior she'd expected, since the man she remembered adored attention.

Since their walk, though, Boomer had decided Peter was his newest friend and refused to leave her father's side.

"Are you sure you want to do this? I can just as easily bring his owner back here."

"No, I'll be fine," Peter assured her. "I just didn't want you to feel uncomfortable."

"Me?" Emma frowned, "Why? Because someone might recognize you?"

He switched his weight from one leg to the other, appearing ill at ease with the topic. "It's been a long time, and," he grimaced, "this *is* your place of business."

"We'll be fine." She waved away his concern. "If you're sure, you can grab his highness, and I'll get his medication."

Peter gave her a look that said, *I hope you know what you're doing*, and picked up Boomer. "I'm ready."

"I'm sure it will be fine," she repeated, leading the way to the front.

Once they stepped through the door, Emma realized she should have talked to Sadie. Because her waiting room held not just Boomer's owner, Alisa, but two of her friends, Heidi and Sadie's mother, Anita. Peter's reaction was interesting because, as she watched, he became the man she remembered from her youth. He stood a little taller, his stride became a little looser, and his smile seemed less sincere. "Hello, I'm P ..."

"Dax Blue," Alisa and Heidi screamed at the same time.

"We couldn't believe it when Anita called," Heidi began.

"And told us you were here," Alisa added.

"Sadie," Emma hissed, "you didn't."

"Sorry," Sadie whispered back. "I never expected ..."

"Alisa." Emma waded into the group. "I need to give you instructions." She held up Boomer's medication, hoping the dog's well-being would take precedence.

"Oh," Alisa waved, "just write it down. You know my memory."

Peter's eyes met hers over the top of the women's heads. '*See. I tried to warn you*,' they seemed to say.

"I'm sorry, Emma," Sadie pouted. "If you only knew how many times my mother has seen the original Dax Blue movie. I wanted her to meet her idol."

"It's okay," Emma sighed. "He seems to have it under control."

She jotted instructions for Boomer's care and then leaned back to observe. The man who was standing in her waiting room was the same man she saw when she was paraded around as a child. He was charming, charismatic, engaging, having developed a way to make everyone feel special. But after spending just a few hours with him, she realized he was wearing a mask.

"Hot, Hunky, Gorgeous," Sadie murmured.

"Eww," Emma mumbled. "That's my father, and I certainly don't want my father and Killian described the same way."

"Sexy?" quipped Sadie.

Emma grimaced, but then tried to look at him objectively. Thick, still-blond hair, bright blue eyes, and a chiseled chin complete with a dimple. She'd give Sadie handsome. Beyond that ... she wasn't willing to consider.

Several minutes later, he waved goodbye to his fans and sagged against the counter. "I'm sorry about that, honey," he confided. "Sometimes these things still happen."

"Thank you for being nice to my mother, Peter," Sadie smiled. "If I would have known it was going to be all three ..."

"No worries," he winked. "Maybe a head's up next time."

Sadie's mouth dropped open under Peter's intense gaze.

Emma laughed, not used to seeing her office manager at a loss for words. "Will wonders never cease. I believe you've rendered Sadie speechless."

"Oh, poo," Sadie huffed. "I'm just ..."

Peter exchanged a conspiratorial grin with Emma, causing her breath to lodge, but it wasn't because of his sex-appeal. It was the knowledge that reading each other's minds was something that occurred within families. She ... they had come far.

Ava's Cottage
November 12
6:00 p.m.

Ava sat on a lounge chair in the cottage and watched the sky grow darker. She knew she'd been hiding out for hours. But since she had nothing scheduled, and Peter was with Emma, she didn't worry.

And Finn.

There was a part of her that believed he wasn't meant to be hers. Experience had shown her the only man who had loved her enough to fight for her was her father. But his love had been suffocating, not only for her, but for others who might have wanted to love her. She'd tried with Finn … and failed.

Then why are you still hiding?

Except she didn't feel as if she were hiding. She'd done as Captain Jack had suggested … she'd gone home. At least to the place that would become her home as soon as she'd signed the paperwork. And while no one, except Giennie, knew where she was, Swan Harbor was a small town. If someone cared to find her, they could.

A soft knock caused her heart to race with the hope maybe Finn had come looking for her. But then she realized if he believed she was a part of his family, he would have told her what was going on. That he would have fought for *them*.

With that realization, she almost didn't answer it, preferring not to talk to anyone just yet. But the second, more forceful knock pulled her from the chair and across the floor to open the door.

"Killian," she exclaimed. "Is everything okay with Emma?"

"Emma's fine," Killian replied. "Can we talk?"

Ava studied him closely, and while he appeared a little somber, there was nothing in his expression to tell her why he'd stopped by. "Come in." She left the door for him to close and went back to the lounge she'd been sitting on all day.

He didn't say anything, but she tracked him across the room by sounds. The closing of the door, the clicking on of a lamp, and the scrape of a chair when he flipped it around and set it close to her.

"How did you find me?" she asked, more for curiosity than for something to say.

"It's Swan Harbor," he reminded her. "Even if you don't want to be, you can be found."

"I see." Ava chanced a glance at him, and his steady gaze was too intense, too caring. Tears simmered just beneath the surface and clogged her throat. "Why are you here?"

"My dad loves you."

Ava fought to keep her mouth closed, and one tear bubbled up, spilling over. "Oh, he does?" she retorted in her best corporate voice. "Did he tell you this?"

"Aye."

Her blue eyes met his and one brow popped up. "He did, huh? I see."

Killian's mouth curved into a mocking grin. "Now I know where Emma's 'tough lass' behavior came from."

She felt her lips twitch, but refused to set the smile free. "That doesn't answer my question. Why are you here?"

"Has my dad told you anything about my mother?"

"That they weren't right," Ava offered.

"But she gave him Liam and me," Killian smirked. "His pat answer, I'm afraid."

"I'm sure he didn't want to badmouth her in front of you and Liam."

"Maybe," Killian acknowledged. "My mother was a difficult woman."

Ava fought the need to ask questions, wishing it was Finn who was sharing this information. But the desire to know proved too strong. "How so?"

"Her family had money, but not quite on the same level as the Kings," he was quick to clarify. "In England, my father worked in the shipping yards, and mum was never happy. She wasn't kind."

"I'm sorry," Ava murmured. "He loved her, and she had two healthy sons. Why was she unhappy?"

"We never really understood why," Killian explained. "But my father stayed with her for his family. That was the most important thing to him."

"I get that," Ava huffed. "He told me he's fighting for his family. Fine. I'm certainly not stopping him."

"Except he's not only fighting for Liam and me," Killian's voice grew huskier, "he's fighting for you too."

"How can you say that?" Ava frowned. "I gave him the opportunity to let me in and you know what he did?"

"He walked out."

"Yes."

"I know little about my father's childhood," Killian admitted. "But I don't think anyone has ever loved my father enough to fight for him before."

Except his sister, she thought. *And look what happened to her.*

"Dad didn't want to tell us what was going on." Killian went on, "But he finally realized he needed my help to solve the problem. His not telling doesn't mean he doesn't love you. He's trying to protect you."

"You say that, as if you've been in his shoes."

"More than once," Killian scoffed. "And while it's not always the easiest thing to do, sharing with Emma brings us closer."

The fact the man sitting next to her was not only going to bat for his father but also loved her daughter reiterated her thoughts about him. "Thank you for stopping by, Killian. I'll think about what you've said."

He nodded once and, after returning the chair he'd moved, followed her to the door. "Will you be alright?"

"I'm fine."

As he backed out of the drive for the return trip to town, she couldn't make herself leave the safety of the cottage. Except, where did that leave her and Finn? If neither were willing to fight for the love between them, they were at an impasse. Was that the only thing left after such a promising beginning?

TWENTY-ONE

Ava's Cottage
November 12
7:00 p.m.

FINN PULLED INTO THE DRIVE OF THE COTTAGE, EXPECTING TO SEE Ava's car parked in front of the garage. When it wasn't where he'd thought, his heart flipped, and the acid in his stomach churned. He shouldn't have waited, he thought disgustedly.

Except, what if ....

Stop! What is it you want?

Ava.

And?

My family.

And?

A happy beginning.

Remember, Flynn. With hope, anything is possible.

But will Ava understand?

She loves you.

And he loved her, except how did he explain his thought processes?

Talk to her. Tell her everything.

First, he had to find her, and when she wasn't at the Inn, Emma's, the gym, or Sally's, he took a chance and tried the cottage. But where was she?

Text her.

What if she doesn't want to talk to me?

You're too old for games out his phone.

"Bloody hell." He pulled out his phone

Finn: I'm a cockwomble, love. Where are you?

She didn't respond right away and with every minute that passed, the sick feeling in his stomach grew.

Then his phone buzzed, and when he saw the picture she'd sent, his stomach settled, and his hope was given free rein. She was at the Inn, looking for him.

Ava: Where are you?

Finn: Waiting for you.

He sent a picture of the cottage, hoping she would understand what he was trying to tell her.

Ava: I'm on my way.

Finn: I can come to you.

Ava: Stay there!

His lips curved at her last text, as he could hear her saying those words as clear as if she were sitting next to him.

Ava: Start a fire.

Finn: Bossy.

Ava: Just wait. I'm driving now.

He didn't want to distract her and slipped his phone into his pocket. Then went to follow her orders.

Since he remembered the code on the lockbox, getting into the house was the simple part. But starting a fire proved a little more difficult. Instead of greeting her with a glass of wine and a cozy fire, when she walked into the house, the room was smokey and he was covered in soot.

"Finn!" Ava sent him a '*what the heck look*.' "What happened?"

"Don't ask."

"What happened?"

He looked down at his sweater with its streaks of black. "What does it look like? You wanted a fire, and well ..."

"Are you okay?"

"No, I'm bloody not okay," he snapped. "The house is filled with smoke, my favorite sweater is ruined, and I burned my finger."

"But you built me a fire," she murmured, taking the necessary steps to reach him.

Finn studied her up close and, while he couldn't read her thoughts, there was something about the way she was looking at him that twisted his heart. It was in her eyes. "I'm sorry."

A corner of her mouth kicked up. "And what are you sorry for?" she retorted. "Would that be walking out and leaving me standing in the cottage? Or would it be taking me to bed? Or—"

"No," he tried to interject, but she barreled right past him.

"Was it for pursuing whatever this is?" She waved her hand back and forth between them. "Or was it telling me you loved me?"

When her voice broke on that last question, he tugged her into his arms and murmured, "No, never that," over and over.

She held herself stiffly against him, and a little piece of his heart shattered. His biggest fears crawled around inside that she wouldn't listen. That it wouldn't matter what he said. That he'd failed with her, just like he'd failed with Claire.

Then, just as he expected her to step away from him, she sniffed, and wilted against his chest.

"I'm sorry," he repeated. "I don't deserve—"

"Stop it!" She stepped out of his arms and glared up at him. "Don't give me that '*You don't deserve*' crap. Not only are you belittling my feelings, as if I don't have enough sense to know what I want, but you're also selling yourself short."

That she was beautiful rushed through him. With her eyes flashing blue fire, and her face glowing from anger, he lost track of what she was saying. But it wasn't the words that resonated inside his head. It was the fact that someone he loved was willing to go toe to toe with him and fight.

"What gives you the right to turn those sexy dimples my way, say sweet things to me in that smooth as butter voice and," she snapped, "then walk away, leaving me to figure out what the hell happened?"

"I'm sor—" he tried to apologize. But she cut off his words with just a look, and Finn finally gave up and leaned back against the counter.

She jabbed her finger in his direction. "I'm fifty-one-years-old and can make my own decisions."

"I never said you couldn't."

"Didn't you?"

"Bloody hell, no!"

Ava scoffed. "Excuse me. Wasn't it you who stated you were '*fighting for my family*' and walked out?"

"Yes, but ..."

"So, you say the words '*I love you*' to just anyone?"

"Bloody hell," Finn cried. "You know that's not true."

He wanted to take her in his arms and beg his forgiveness. If he did, though, would she believe him or think he was just giving her the words she wanted to hear?

"Then why, Finn?"

Her question threw him, because she'd asked it in such a different manner than her previous words. It sounded ... defeated.

"Never doubt that I love you," he began, holding the counter to keep from reaching for her. "But something from my past has resurfaced and ..."

"You're trying to protect me."

"Bloody hell, yes."

"Yes, well, Killian said the same thing, and that's just stupid."

Finn's thoughts spun for several seconds, trying to decide which direction to go first. "Wait. You've talked to Killian?"

"Yes."

She hung her coat over a chair. Then, a crack in the fear he felt inside appeared, allowing the hope to seep up, covering a little of the darkness.

"He came by earlier," she went on. "Told me to fight for you."

Finn laughed.

"You think that's funny?"

"I'm sorry." He shook his head, "I'm not laughing at you. It's my sons. After I told them what was going on, they turned into busybodies and wanted to know what my intentions were."

Ava opened and closed her mouth a few times. "Was that when you told them you loved me?"

"Yes," he admitted softly, letting go of the counter to take a few steps toward her. "It was also when I told them what my intentions were, but I didn't think it was fair to offer you something that wasn't mine to give."

"What are you talking about?"

"The future." Finn forced the bile rising inside back down and took a few more steps. "I don't know what the future holds. How can I ask you—?"

Ava rolled her eyes. "Do I look stupid?"

"Bloody hell, no." Finn frowned. "Where did that question come from?"

She waved her hand in his direction. "Because there you go again. How can I ask … blah, blah, blah. I'm going to ask a question and, depending on your answer, I can tell you what the immediate future holds."

She'd pulled out her corporate persona and was setting a scene, but exactly where she was leading him, he wasn't sure.

"Alright, love," he complied. "What's your question?"

"Do you trust me?"

That wasn't the question he'd expected, but he didn't have to think about it. "Yes."

"Then trust me to decide what *my* future holds," Ava told him softly. "Trust me to know that if you weren't worthy of my trust and," she took several steps closer, "my love, I wouldn't be here. You said we were too old to play games."

"We are."

"Then stop playing games with my feelings."

"I'm not."

"Aren't you?" she pushed again before he could say more. "You claim to love me, yet you're '*protecting*' me."

"But …"

"I know you lost your mother at a young age, and your sister a short time later. I'm not sure what happened after that, but I'm not sixteen. Trusting me with the truth is the only way we can fight for what we both want. A happy beginning for all of us."

His emotions bubbled up, and he had to blink rapidly to push them back down. She was everything he'd ever wanted and more.

"It's not pretty."

"Let me decide."

"Alright."

He reached for her, intending to take her in his arms. "Don't!" She stepped back quickly.

"What?"

"You're covered in soot," Ava pointed out. "Go shower."

Finn glanced at his hands, to see the remnants of his fight with the fireplace remained. "Here?"

"Yes." She pushed him toward the stairs. "Then we'll talk."

He could argue, but while he understood telling her would be harder than telling his sons, it was the only option. Letting her go was not something he was willing to do. "Alright."

⁂

As soon as he'd disappeared up the stairs, Ava wilted. It had only been his words, *'You're stronger than you think,'* combined with Jack's comment about listening to her heart that had given her the strength to confront him. Even though she didn't know what he was keeping from her, it didn't matter. He was no longer that man.

But just saying that didn't mean she wasn't a little freaked out about what he was going to say. Nor did it mean she wasn't a little concerned that Killian and Liam knew about her and Finn. She'd wanted to be the one to talk to Emma, but now ....

"Ava?"

His soft voice sent a chill up her spine, and she stilled herself to be cool as she slowly turned toward him. Just looking at him took her breath at just how sexy he was.

"I didn't want to put my soot covered sweater back on," he explained the reason he was bare-chested.

"And you think I mind?"

Finn shrugged and stepped farther into the room. "Are you sure you want to hear what I have to say?"

The thought, *He doesn't think he's worthy,* crawled through her head, telling her she needed to break through whatever was holding him back.

"I was born on the east side of London, the bastard son of a woman who worked for a rich family. My mum idolized the 'idea' of that family. Mother, father, three children, a dog, and a cat. Everyone on their best behavior."

"Winnie made me promise that every time things got bad, I wouldn't stop searching for my happy beginning."

"If your sister were alive today, what do you think she would say?"

He looked taken aback by her question for a split second.

"She'd kick my arse and tell me to fight for the family I want."

"Then what's holding you back?"

"It's hard to put into words," he began.

"You asked me why I didn't want to see Peter. Do you remember?"

"Yes."

"And in all my," she made quotation marks with her fingers, "alone time today, I thought about that question. Do you know what I realized?"

"What, love?"

"That Emma was right. A person or a person's words can only hurt *if* you let them. But I realized something else too."

"What was that?"

"That you have to care to be hurt."

"Agree."

"When you talked to Killian and Liam today, were they mad? Were they hurt you hadn't told them before?"

"They," he hesitated, searching for the right words, "were alright."

"But that wasn't the reaction you'd expected?"

"No." Finn blew out a breath. "I don't know what I expected."

"Don't you? Have you shared your past with others?"

"Once," he admitted. "And it was used to push me to do something I didn't really want to do."

"Then why did you do it?"

"To make them happy."

He's talking about his ex, she realized.

"Were you really worried your sons would do the same?"

"Yes. No. I don't know," he grumbled, moving to stare out into the darkness. "I didn't want to disappoint them."

"Weren't you the one who told me without Claire and Peter we wouldn't be where we are?"

"Yes."

His response was so quiet, if she hadn't been watching his reflection in the glass, she wouldn't have heard him. Her hesitation in jumping into a relationship with him with both feet stemmed from what had gone on with Peter. Which reiterated her thought Claire had his past to hurt him. But how could she show him she wouldn't do that?

Ava was across the room, sliding her hands up his bare back before she'd even realized what she was going to do. He inhaled quickly, and when he didn't step away, she pressed her cheek against his smooth skin and placed a tender kiss on his spine.

"I'm here," she promised him.

"But for how long?"

She reversed her position, moving in front of him and laid her cheek on his chest. "As long as you want me."

Slowly, his arms closed around her, holding her so tightly she couldn't get a full breath. But when his body shook with emotion, she knew there was no way she was going anywhere, unless he pushed her away. They could have been standing there for a minute or ten before he loosened his hold.

"I love you, Ava," he murmured. "I'm not sure what I did to deserve your love, but somewhere along the way, I must have done something right."

She looked up and their eyes met. "Don't you think I feel the same way?"

His mouth hovered above hers, not touching, but with their breath mingling, it sent her heart racing. Before the thought *kiss me* had fully formed, his lips covered hers. The kiss was so desperate, her knees grew weak, and if he hadn't been holding her, she would have fallen.

He groaned and tightened his fingers on her back, tugging her against his firm chest. Their tongues dueled, and his lips crushed hers. Ava had no choice but to hold on and let him carry her along.

I'm here. I'll always be here.

When Finn lifted his mouth, Ava had to drag her eyes open. The way he was staring at her and holding her as if she were his lifeline had her brushing her fingers softly across his cheek.

He dropped his forehead against hers and even though she was tempted to push, somehow, she waited, hoping he would meet her halfway.

"Are you—?"

Ava placed her finger over his lips. "Stop." Then she led him to the blanket in front of the fireplace.

Finn glanced around and, just as she was going to ask what he was looking for, he grabbed a few pillows off the sofa. "The floor's hard," he explained.

"Are you sure it's not just that you're old?"

He pulled her into his lap so quickly she knocked them both over and sprawled across his chest.

"Are you okay?"

"I'm fine, and as much as I would like to see where this position can take us," he sighed and rolled her next to him, "it's not the best one for a talk."

Ava settled on his shoulder and waited. The proverbial ball was in his court.

Finn tightened his hold on Ava and kissed her fingers before settling their clasped hands on his stomach. With her in his arms, the sick feeling in his gut had lessened. But the memory of his past being used to hurt him in his first marriage had him wary.

She loves you. Trust her.

"After Winnie's death, I lived by the seat of my pants for what could have been weeks but felt like months," he began his tale. "There was a church that fed the homeless, and I snuck in the lines, pretending I belonged, and helped myself. Then one day, men from Scotland Yard came around asking questions, and I knew they were looking for me. I hid in a small storage room in the church for several days and tried to figure out what to do."

"Why didn't you go to the police?" Ava asked softly. "You were just a little boy."

Finn shrugged. "Fear is a powerful emotion. The family we'd lived with had money, and I was afraid they would somehow blame me for everything."

"Did you ever find out the complete story?"

"Years later," he told her. "I looked it up in the papers. There was a fight and both my sister and the man died that night."

"I'm sorry."

He kissed the top of her head. "Me too. But I survived."

"How? You were what? Six or seven?"

"I turned seven living in that storage closet." Finn smiled at the memory. "During the day, there were other homeless kids I talked to. They showed me how to blend in and out of groups, and how to steal when I was hungry."

"Was that often?"

"More often than not," he admitted. "Then one boy, Kenny, showed me how to steal things you could sell for money or food."

"That doesn't sound very safe."

"It's not," he conceded. "But looking back, it led to a situation that probably saved my life."

"How so?"

The more of his story that came out and the more Ava asked questions, the more Finn relaxed. Her voice wasn't judgmental, but curious.

"Every day, I woke up and thought '*today is going to be the day I find my family. Today will be the day I find my happy beginning*'," he went on. "But as the days passed, with each one the same as the day before, I began to lose hope it would ever happen. And then I spotted Joan."

"Joan?"

Finn chuckled. "Joan was one of the women who cleaned the church where I was hiding. I stayed out of sight when she was around, and thought she didn't know about me."

"She tricked you?"

"Yes, she did." And even years later, he could still hear the affection in his voice for the older woman.

"What did she do?"

"Set me up."

"Oh, no!"

"No, love." Finn squeezed her fingers, loving she cared about that homeless boy. "It was smart."

"What did she do?"

"At first, it was little things. A sandwich, a piece of fruit," he shared. "But then she took off the gold cross necklace I'd been eyeing."

"You were going to steal her necklace and sell it?"

"Bloody hell, yes," he exclaimed. "Winter was coming, and I needed a new coat."

"Oh, well, priorities," she mumbled.

"I hid and watched as she cleaned that night," he went on. "And when she finished, there was her gold cross necklace hanging from the hand of the blessed mother."

"A statue?

"Yes." He nodded, picturing the inside of the building. "A cherub statue of the blessed mother stood on one side of the door to the sanctuary. The holy water on the other."

"And she left the necklace hanging on the statue?" Ava questioned. "You didn't think that was weird?"

"I was seven, love," Finn replied. "What did I know?"

"Point," she acknowledged. "Did you take it?"

"Not immediately. I waited until the lights were out and then slowly, I approached the door where the statue was located. But as I stared at the cross, lights from outside hit the window just right, and it seemed to glow. Curiosity, more than the desire to steal, had me reaching out and taking it off the hand."

"Joan came up behind you, didn't she?" Ava guessed.

"She did," Finn chuckled. "But she didn't yell at me, didn't accuse me of stealing it."

"Did she want it back?"

"Joan was soft-spoken," Finn remembered, not answering the question directly. "And when she sang, she had the voice of an angel."

"You loved her."

"I did," he admitted. "When she saw me holding her necklace, she said, 'You have a choice, laddie. You can sell that cross for a few shillings, or you can come home with me. I think perhaps you were sent here to save me'."

"What did she mean?"

"Joan's only child and husband had been killed in an accident in which she'd walked away," he answered quietly. "I don't think she would have harmed herself, but I don't know."

"You saved her," she whispered, her voice thick with emotion, "and she saved you."

"That she did," he agreed. "And for ten years, she pushed me in school, insisted I drop the cockney accent, and taught me how to survive in the upper class of London."

"Hence the debutantes in London society who taught you to dance."

"Remembered that, did you? But yes. Joan was my family ... and then she got sick."

"Oh, Finn, no."

"She wouldn't go to the doctor," he sighed. "Said she knew the problem. Breast cancer. Told me her mother had it, and she'd known it was only a matter of time. When we couldn't afford food—"

"—You stole it."

"I did. And she would say, 'Laddie, the good book says you shouldn't steal'."

"But you didn't care."

"I cared about her," he tried to explain. "I told her the good book also says to honor your father and mother, and I was doing the best I could. But it wasn't enough."

"She died?"

"Yes." The sorrow he felt at her passing was just as fresh as if it had happened yesterday, instead of almost forty years previous. "And her friend, Remy French, told me Joan made him promise to make sure I was okay."

"I'm glad she didn't leave you alone," Ava murmured. "Did Remy keep his promise?"

Finn rolled over onto his side and looked into Ava's eyes. "I'm not sure what I expected you to say when you learned about my past. But the way you're acting isn't it."

"Our pasts mold us into the people we become," she began. "The man in my arms is a man who is kind, caring, smart, successful, loves his family, and," her voice dropped, "who loves me and makes me feel cherished. Plus, you are who you are *because* of everything you went through. How can I hold any of that against you?"

"I don't deserve you," he whispered against her lips. "But bloody hell, I'm not letting you go."

"Good."

His lips covered hers, and he wanted to sink in and stay awhile, but as much as he hated the thought, he had to tell her about Remy and Sutton.

When he lifted his head, she nipped his chin. "There's more to the story, isn't there?"

"How did you guess?"

"Because nothing you've said so far would lead you to think you didn't have a future." Ava pushed him back over and propped her head on his shoulder. "I have a question though."

"What is it, love?"

"The cross necklace," Ava circled back, "What happened to it?"

"The night she saved me," he told her, "she fastened it around my neck and told me it would always keep me safe."

"But you don't wear it."

"I gave it to Killian when he joined the police force," Finn explained. "The chain is in my safe."

"You saved it," Ava murmured. "That's so sweet."

"Let me tell you the rest of the story and see if you still think it's sweet." He took a deep breath and jumped in. "Remy turned me into the Shadow Angel."

"The Shadow Angel?" Ava pushed up, her eyes meeting his. "Who's that?"

"A thief who takes what's been stolen and returns it, for a nice finder's fee."

"I'm listening."

Here goes, he thought, "One day ..."

TWENTY-TWO

Veterinary Clinic
November 13
3:00 a.m.

KILLIAN TRUDGED UP THE STAIRS, HIS MIND AWHIRL WITH everything he'd learned in the past twenty-four hours. And everything he still didn't know. But as he tossed his shirt in the corner, left his jeans hanging over a chair and crawled into bed next to Emma, he vowed to put them aside for a few hours.

He bunched up his pillow, and his body had just relaxed when the mattress shifted and Emma rolled over. "Killian, is that you?"

"No. It's the Shadow Angel."

"What?"

"Of course, it's Killian, Doc. Go to sleep."

"Okay."

Except there was something in her tone that reminded him of how she'd spent her day. "I'm sorry, Doc. How was your time with Peter? He seemed a decent sort to me."

She giggled. "I'm glad you think my dad is a decent sort, Killian. My day was ..."

"Good?"

"It was good." She rolled over to face him. "But you know what?"

"No what?"

"I didn't take my own advice, and that annoys me."

"I'm sure it does, but what advice?"

"I told my mom she didn't need to worry about my meeting with dad," Emma sighed. "But I still worried."

"Gee, I wonder who told you that," he muttered tongue-in-cheek.

"Be nice." She playfully pushed him. "I feel annoyed at myself."

"Stop being annoyed." He kissed her. "Is he coming back to the clinic today?"

"I think so." She scooted closer to his chest and draped her arm over his waist. "I probably need to reach out to my mother today, and talk to her about dad."

Killian hadn't wanted to get into his father's situation, but with the opportunity to spread out before him, he decided he might as well. "Speaking of your mother ..."

"What?" He could feel her trying to read his expression, but knew it was too dark for her to see clearly.

"I don't know what to tell you first," he admitted.

Emma scrambled from his arms and flipped on the beside lamp.

"Bloody hell, Doc." He covered his eyes and waited for them to adjust. "Next time warn a man, will you?"

"Sorry," she retorted. "But you can't just say something like that and expect me to remain calm. What's going on?"

Killian scooted up in the bed. "My dad is in love with her."

Her mouth dropped open and then she closed it, and her lips gradually curved up. "Do you think she loves him too?"

Killian thought about the sadness he'd noted on Ava's face when they'd talked. "I would assume that's why she was angry and hiding out in some house up on the cliff."

"What?" She frowned. "A house on a cliff? And what did your dad do?"

"That's a loaded question," he murmured. Then, in as succinct a way as possible, he explained his father's past as the Shadow Angel, and how his past was impeding his future.

Emma said nothing for several minutes, and then she grinned. "What is with you Reade boys and your pasts getting in the way of the future?"

"Well," Killian pointed out, "even though part of my past involved Santora, the emotional hang-ups all stemmed from my mother."

"I'm sorry."

"Me too." He hesitated for several seconds, his mind filtering through memories and things his father had said. "Apparently, my father gave up his wayward ways for my mum, but she then pushed him back into the business."

"Why?"

"Money."

"But if he didn't want to go back to that way of life," she asked. "Why didn't he tell her no?"

Killian barked out a laugh. "*No one* told Claire Reade no. If you did, she would continue to badger and say really nasty things. I was too young to understand when we lived in England. And too self-absorbed to pay attention as a teen. Looking back, though, she was guilty of verbal abuse. How my father stayed with her, I'll never know."

"What does he say?"

"He says he did it for his family."

"Was he worried your mother would take you and Liam and disappear?"

He hadn't thought of that, because Claire never seemed to enjoy being a mother.

"Maybe," Killian finally conceded. "When Liam told me it was dad who'd told her to leave if she didn't like Liam's decision regarding college, it surprised me. Seems he'd reached his fill of her abuse."

"There are a lot of similarities between our parents and what they want, Killian."

"I know, Doc."

"Why did you go see my mom?" she asked. "And how did you find her?"

Killian sent her a grin. "Swan Harbor gossip chain."

"True," Emma agreed.

"I went to see her," he went on, "to tell her to fight for my dad."

"Do you think she listened?"

He chuckled. "According to Liam, it was almost as sweet as Della and Jim in *The Gift of the Magi.*"

"They went looking for each other?"

"Aye." Killian shook his head. "Last I heard, they were at the house. I'm not sure if they stayed the night or not."

"I didn't even know my mom was looking at a house in Swan Harbor." She frowned. "I feel out of the loop."

"You've been fretting about Peter."

"I know." Emma flipped the light off and pulled him down with her. "Now that I can stop fretting about that, I need to get caught up with the gossip chain."

"I'm sure Liam can fill you in."

"What has Liam done now?"

"He can be overzealous with sharing."

"And because he knows it bothers you ..."

"Aye," Killian agreed and added, "He shares more."

"I can see that."

"Now," he murmured against her lips. "Anything else, or can I kiss you?"

"Kiss away."

Killian dropped a kiss on her lips, and was getting ready to deepen it, when she pushed against his chest. "Bloody hell, what now?"

"Captain Jack's message suddenly makes sense," Emma told him, the skepticism still there every time she spoke of the eccentric older man. "He said having our parents here had given a major boost to the town's hope. But we still need to find the key. I bet he knows about their relationship."

"Bloody hell, Emma," Killian muttered. "The entire town knows about their relationship."

"Okay. Now kiss me."

"What if I don't want to—"

Her lips took the words right out of his mouth, and Killian had to admit there were definite advantages to sharing.

Lighthouse Inn
November 13
8:00 a.m.

Ava wrinkled her nose, hoping to push off whatever was tickling her face, and buried her head more in the pillow. But then the feeling persisted, and it was joined by the knowledge she was being watched. Slowly, she opened her eyes to find Finn staring, his expression somber.

"Good morning, Sleepyhead." He dropped a kiss on the tip of her nose. "Why did you leave my bed?"

It took a second for the morning fog to clear, but then she realized he was asking why she'd moved onto the sofa. "A few hours ago." She pushed up to a sitting position. "I woke up and couldn't go back to sleep, and didn't want to wake you."

"I wouldn't have minded." His eyes twinkled, and then it was as if a shutter came down over them. "Why couldn't you sleep?"

She grimaced. "I don't know. Just sometimes, I wake up, and it's an hour or more before I can go back to sleep."

He studied her, and she knew he was trying to decide if he believed her or not. "I promise. It has nothing to do with finding out you were this mysterious thief who somehow developed a romantic air."

Finn frowned. "A romantic air? Believe me, love. There was nothing romantic about all the research those missions required. And keep in mind, I started before technology was what it is."

"Oh, I know." She grinned. "But attending a masked ball, dancing with the hostess and then sneaking out to take paintings, jewelry, and silver coins ... you had some moves."

He dropped his head, and she could see the red tint covering his cheekbones. "Finn, look at me." Ava tilted his chin up, forcing him to meet her eyes. "You can sneak into my bedroom and use those moves any time you want."

"I'll show you my moves." Finn pulled her onto his lap and stole her thoughts with his kisses. "Are you sure you're alright with everything?"

"Am I alright with the fact some idiot is leaving you notes, threatening you and trying to interrupt what we're trying to build? No!" Ava smiled and placed a kiss on the corner of his mouth. "But am I okay with where you came from? I think I answered that last night. My question is, what now?"

Finn adjusted her on his lap, and Ava had to wonder if it was more to gather his thoughts than because she needed adjusting.

"Killian is following up some trails that were dead ends for me," he explained. "I'm hoping he has answers soon because ..."

He glanced around the room and suddenly his face hardened, reverting into the man who'd been on his way to talk to Killian and Liam the day before.

"What is it?"

"Someone was in here yesterday." He moved her back onto the sofa and stood up.

"When?" She looked around, but didn't know what he was seeing.

"After I came back from meeting with the boys." He pointed at his briefcase. "That's on the wrong side of the desk. Plus, someone rearranged the mail from my office.

"Mail?" His comment reminded Ava of what she'd dropped on the table. "Where's my letter?"

"On the kitchen counter," he told her, not even phased by her topic jump. "Did Karen bring it to you when she brought me my mail?"

"Yes." Her thoughts went back to his comment. "How in the heck did you know someone rearranged your mail?"

He shrugged. "Habit. For years, I had to make sure I left things exactly as I found them, and so—"

"—You always put things in the same place." He nodded, and she made a face. "I'm going to drive you crazy, then."

His brows rose. "More than you already do?"

"Yes." She went to look for her letter. "I might be organized in that I write everything I need to do. But—"

"—You squeeze the toothpaste from the middle, throw the dishes in the dishwasher haphazardly, never leave your shoes in the same place, and your clothes are all mixed."

"Well," she huffed. "How did you know?"

"Told you," he tugged her against his warm chest, "habit. But I can live with those things. Your side of the closet will just be a mess, and mine will be neat."

Ava's breath hitched, and she couldn't help but think that for a man who couldn't promise her a future yesterday, he was sure making some grand statements.

"Too soon?"

"You." Her heart raced, and she almost ran from the question, but, *'no games.'* "You want to live together?"

He tugged her hips into the cradle of his and dropped a kiss on her lips. "Ava, love, I want it all. But until this is over ..."

"—No promises."

"Let's hope for the best and prepare for everything else."

"I can do that." She threw her arms around his neck and rested against him, hoping with everything inside the future would give her a happy beginning with Finn.

"Do you want to open the letter now?"

Ava stepped out of his arms and looked down at the envelope. "I think so."

"Do you want me to stay?"

"Please."

"Whenever you're ready."

She nodded, and on trembling legs, made her way back to the sofa. "I don't know why I'm so scared."

"It's like you're receiving a letter from the beyond." Finn shrugged. "And since you never knew your grandmother ..."

Her hands were shaking so much, it took her several tries to get the outside envelope open. When she reached inside and pulled out the letter, the scent of flowers filled the air. "Can you smell that?"

Finn's gaze met hers. "Flowers?"

"Yes." She nodded, the smell triggering a memory, but she had no idea where it came from. "It's familiar."

"Our senses pick up things even when we don't realize it's happening. If it's important, the memory will return."

Something had her leaning over and kissing him.

"Not that I mind, but what was that for?"

"Just because."

"My pleasure." He chuckled, and the sound went straight to her heart. "Feel free to kiss me *'just because'* any time."

She grinned and turned back to the letter. On the outside, her grandmother had written, *For Ava* in her dainty handwriting, and the date of her fiftieth birthday.

"Here goes." She unfolded the paper and read.

Happy Birthday, my darling Ava.

Before I get into my reasons for writing this letter, I want to take a moment to tell you how excited I was when your mother told me she was pregnant. As a child, Grace spent hours alone, mothering her dolls (and the stray dogs or cats she'd drag home) and wanted a houseful of children. She loved you, and the day you were born was the happiest day of her life. It even surpassed the day she married Leo, and she loved him with her whole heart.

But then she became ill, and was taken from us way too young, and your father changed. I worry my time on this earth will be cut short, and I won't be there to protect you and teach you about Grace, our family, and where we come from. I've always been one to write my thoughts and have journaled for years. Someday, those will help you understand your heritage.

My family heralds from a small town in southern Maine, called Swan Harbor. I knew everyone's business, and they knew mine, and the town had a way about it. Granny's had the best milkshakes, and we'd go see the newest picture shows on Friday nights. But every time someone was born, or someone died, there was a sense of urgency. Was the town going to survive, or were we destined to disappear like so many other small towns had done throughout the years? I'd decided as soon as I finished with high school, I'd move to the big city.

Then, the summer before I graduated, your grandfather Dawson's family vacationed in Swan Harbor. And we fell in love. Ray was a kind man, and no one was more surprised than I, when he insisted we settle in my hometown. He told me the town needed our hope to help it survive. I thought he was crazy, but loved him and, since it meant being close to my best friend Terri, (who was busy planning her wedding to Dean Patterson), I was happy.

As time went on, there were whispers something hanging over the town. Some called it a curse, others said it was just bad luck, and with a lot of digging (and sneezing) through the library archives, we learned the story of your ancestor, Hope. She'd fallen in love with a man, but before they could grab their happily-ever-after, she fell ill and perished, leaving behind her infant son.

Through generation after generation, the women never survived to see their forty-fifth birthday. The key, they say, is to reunite Hope with her lover. But at this point in time, we haven't found the key, and its whereabout remain unknown.

After you were born, something different happened. The next summer, a swan appeared. He is pure white and beautiful, and swims in our harbor with his head held high. The 'something' that had always hung in the air seemed to disappear. The town began to thrive, the people began to communicate, the air seemed cleaner and the water bluer. He became our sign that Swan Harbor would survive forever. That swan brought us hope.

Except swans don't live forever, and the key needs to be found. Supposedly, the answer lies within the charms of this bracelet, as it's been in our family for years. But now, it's up to you and yours, my precious granddaughter, to reunite Hope with her lover. Until then, Swan Harbor is living on borrowed hope. Trust Jack. He knows.

All my love,

Your Grandmother Rose

WHEN AVA FINISHED READING THE LETTER, SHE THOUGHT BACK ON some conversations with her father. "Why didn't I know my mother was from Swan Harbor?"

"You said your father didn't like to talk about your mother," Finn reminded her. "Plus, your grandmother said he changed. Maybe he heard about the Swan Harbor 'curse' and blamed her family."

Ava slanted him a side-eyed glance, but something about his comment made sense. "No wonder Emma felt like it was home from the beginning."

"And you, love?" Finn tossed the question she'd been pondering for a while.

"Do you think anyone who knew my grandmother is still alive?"

"She gave you a few names to start," he pointed out. "Dean and Terri Patterson, and Jack."

"You don't think ..." Ava looked at the letter and then back at Finn, "Could that be Captain Jack?"

Finn shrugged. "Stranger things have happened. And," he added, almost as if he'd just thought of it, "Captain Jack did mention someone must be looking for the key."

Ava's heart expanded. "I need to go see Captain Jack."

"I would say so," he pulled her up, "how about a shower, I buy you breakfast at Sally's, and then we'll go talk to Jack."

"I like that idea." She busied herself folding the blanket she'd used and tossed it on the sofa. "An hour?"

He grabbed her hand and tugged her into his arms. "I could grab a clean set of clothes and we could shower together—"

"Stop." She giggled, and it felt like her heart flipped several times. "We'd never get dressed."

"If you say so." He helped her with her coat and opened the door. "I'll walk you back."

Ava planted a hand in the middle of his chest. "I can find my way. Go get ready."

She kissed him goodbye and practically skipped back to her cottage. Her family was from Swan Harbor. This was *her* town. Now, she had two important things to talk over with Emma, she thought, on her way to shower.

TWENTY-THREE

Captain Jack's Fine Dining
November 13
10:30 a.m.

Finn pulled into the marina parking lot and shut off the car. "Are you sure you don't want to wait for me?"

Ava squeezed his fingers, but never looked away from the huge ship where Captain Jack's restaurant was located. "I would love for you to be with me, but you need to take care of your mystery. And not hold my hand."

"But I like holding your hand." He kissed her fingers, sending little tingles up her arm.

"Another teen moment," Ava murmured with a laugh.

"Teen moment?" Finn frowned. "Is that a good or a bad thing?"

"Oh, it's definitely a good thing," she assured him. "Sitting in a car holding hands with my boyfriend is another new experience for me."

His eyes twinkled in the morning light. "Ever necked with your boyfriend in a parked car?"

"No," she exclaimed, but what felt suspiciously like anticipation sprung to life. "And I'm not going to start now. This town doesn't need more to gossip about."

"Who was it that said, 'let's live dangerously?'" Finn hooked a hand in the top of her coat and tugged her forward. He placed kissed, one that was so hot, it surprised her the windows hadn't fogged.

"Wow."

"You're welcome."

It took her several seconds to reorganize her thoughts and focus on the task at hand. "That's Captain Jack's car, right?" She indicated an older model Cadillac.

"I think so," Finn acknowledged. "I'm surprised he comes in this early, though."

"I think he's lonely." Ava thought back on the conversation she'd had with Jack regarding Edythe, the woman he'd loved. "It's sad he never married."

Finn sent her a look, and she had to wonder at what was going on in his head. "What?"

"Did you know Captain Jack had a child out there he's never seen?" Finn asked her softly. "He doesn't even know if it's a male or a female."

Ava's mouth dropped open, and her eyes immediately filled with tears. "Oh, Finn. That breaks my heart. Why?"

"He told me Edythe learned something about his family and took off." A distressed looked crossed his face. "That was the threat Claire held over my head. For years, I worried if I'd come home and she'd be gone and—"

"—You'd once again lose your family."

The look in his dark eyes melted any reserves she'd been holding onto, and that thread between them tugged her across the console. The kiss wasn't the hottest, nor was it really even an open mouth kiss, but when their lips met, it was like a current zipped from his mouth to her heart.

"Talk about wow," he murmured.

"I agree." She glanced back out the window, and the ship casting shadows on the dock reminded her of where she was. "You'll come here as soon as you see what Killian has to say, right?"

"With bells on." He kissed her again.

"No more of that." She pointed her finger at him. "When you kiss me, my thoughts get all muddled."

"I kind of like that," chuckled Finn, reaching for her again.

"No, no, no." Ava hopped out and blew him a kiss. "I'll see you in a few."

"Good luck, love," Finn winked. "I'll miss you."

Ava could feel Finn's eyes following her as she walked across the parking lot. Even though she wanted to relive moments spent in his company, she relied upon her corporate discipline and switched her thought processes. Her grandmother had written words over fifty years ago that, on one hand, seemed eccentric, but when combined with other things that had happened, gave her pause.

Just before she opened the restaurant door, Ava's discipline wobbled, and she glanced over her shoulder. Finn blew her a kiss, and her heart fluttered. Once again, she fought the giddy smile that was never far when she was in his company.

I'm here to see Jack, she reminded herself, allowing the door to close behind her. Except, instead of bright lights and music as had greeted her the night she'd come for her birthday, it was dark ... eerie ... silent.

Goosebumps slithered up Ava's spine, and she hesitated, wondering if she should have waited for Finn.

"Hello," she called, her voice echoing in the empty room.

She thought she heard running footsteps, then nothing but silence.

The urge to leave and return later was strong. With her grandmother's words ringing in her head, she went looking for Jack's office.

By the time she found it, Ava's heart rate was racing, and her palms were sweating. The creaking of the ship was making her anxious. And she kept hearing what sounded like breathing and the scurrying of feet.

"Hello," she called again when she turned into the last hallway.

Her shoes echoed and as she neared the office, the shadows were darker, pressing close to her.

"Captain Jack, it's Ava King," she tried again. "Do you have a minute?"

When she reached his office, and he still hadn't said anything, she hesitantly pushed on the door and peered inside. Jack wasn't sitting at his desk, but the sight of legs sprawled on the floor had her breath catching in her throat.

"Jack!" Ava pushed the door wider.

"Watch out!" someone yelled.

Ava heard a whistle close to her right ear and turned to see something swinging her direction, and then everything went black.

Sheriff's Department
November 13
10:45 a.m.

FINN STROLLED INTO THE SHERIFF'S DEPARTMENT TO FIND KILLIAN leaning back in his chair, his feet propped on his desk and a donut in his hand. "Isn't it a little late for breakfast?"

"Who said this is breakfast?" Killian licked his thumb. "Besides, I got a late start today."

"Everything alright?" Finn pulled a chair close to Killian's desk.

"Aye," Killian assured him. He wiped off his hands and dropped his feet onto the floor, before picking up a folder. "I was up late working on this."

"I'm sorry, son," Finn sighed. "I hate—"

"Stop it, Dad," Killian interrupted him. "I would help you no matter what, but this time it's not just for you. It's for all of us."

Finn studied the floor for several seconds. Multiple thoughts raced through his head, so many, he wasn't sure which to focus on. "I appreciate it, and I know Ava does too."

"Speaking of," Killian leaned on the desk and lowered his voice, "did you work things out with Ava?"

"We're getting there," Finn conceded, unwilling to go much farther until he knew Ava was alright with them being 'outed.'

"That's good to hear." Killian grinned. "If you need advice, just let me know."

"Thank you, Killian," Finn laughed. "I'll remember that."

Killian stared at him for so long, Finn caught himself looking down at his clothing. "Did I spill something on my sweater?"

"No." A thoughtful frown appeared between Killian's brows. "I was just thinking you look different."

"Different, how?"

Killian tilted his head, and Finn fought to sit still. He could feel the heat climbing up his face, and he cleared his throat several times. "Bloody hell, Killian," he snapped. "Quit staring."

"Sorry," Killian smirked. "I was just thinking of all those times I came home from dates, and you looked at me so carefully, it made me uncomfortable.

"You probably had something to be guilty of." Finn quipped. "I, on the other hand, ..."

"Right," Killian muttered tongue-in-cheek. "You didn't think you could tell us about you and Ava?"

"I ..." There were many things he could have said about his relationship with Ava, but he didn't wish to do anything that might make her uncomfortable. "My intentions are nothing but honorable, son. I just don't want to put Ava in a situation ..."

"She's not ready to be put into," Killian supplied.

"Right."

"Fair enough," Killian conceded. "But I've noticed something different about you since you've been in Swan Harbor."

"Oh?" The thoughts he'd had regarding the pier were still there, waiting for him to give them permission to grow. "How so?"

"You're ..." Killian shrugged, as if the perfect word still eluded him, but then offered, "more relaxed. And even with everything going on, that's saying something. You look happy."

Finn smiled, but fought to keep it tempered. "I am. And it's nice to be around you, Liam, and your fiancées."

"And Ava?" Killian grinned.

And Ava," Finn confirmed, thinking most definitely her.

"I'm happy for you, Dad." Killian returned to the task at hand. "Now, here's what I've been doing."

"Did you find out who shot Remy?"

"Not yet." Killian spread out several pieces of paper across his desk. "You tracked Remy's fingerprints to several discoveries until 2012, and then learned he was killed in 2015, right?"

"That's right." Finn scooted his chair closer to the desk and pointed to the notes he'd written. "Sutton started looking for information on the Shadow Angel in 2012 and seemingly stopped in 2015. That doesn't feel like a coincidence."

"To me either," Killian agreed. "Which is why I'm trying to find a connection to Remy and Sutton."

"Any luck?"

Killian handed him a piece of paper. "These six people can be connected to Remy at various times between 2012 and 2015. All of them are in the 'locating' business in some way." He pointed to three of the names. "Do you recognize any of those?"

"Ruben, Fraser, and Coby are familiar," Finn admitted. "They were in the same type of situation as I. Only took what had been stolen and returned the item to the original owners."

"And these other names?"

"I knew of Damian and Theo," Finn acknowledged. "But not Hudson."

"And were they also in the 'finders' business?" Killian wanted to know.

Finn had to dig into his memories of what he'd heard Remy say about Damian and Theo. "After I met your mother and walked away from the business, Remy expanded his contact base. Those were two of his newest acquisitions."

"From your tone, I gather that wasn't a good thing."

"You could say that again." Finn blew out a breath and sorted through his thoughts. "While I took from people, as did Ruben, Fraser, and Coby, we had a Code. Our targets were items stolen previously, unlike Damian and Theo, who only worked for the highest bidder. They took to take and sold for the money. I tried to tell Remy that, but he was stubborn."

"And his stubbornness could have been what got him killed."

"Could it be he refused to give up my name?" Finn tossed out an idea he couldn't stop thinking about. "And that's why they shot him?"

"Aye," Killian agreed. "I'm sorry, dad, but that's a possibility."

"Bloody hell," Finn spit out.

"Agree." Killian made a few notes next to the names and indicated the last one. "You didn't know Hudson?"

"No. Did you find out anything about him?"

"He's younger than the others," Killian explained. "And I can't find anything about him much before 2010."

"Could Hudson be an alias?"

"That's my guess," Killian noted. "Which makes me wonder why."

"You don't think ..." Finn began, while several thoughts in his head tried to connect.

"What?"

Finn dug around until he uncovered his notes on Sutton. "Could there be a connection between Hudson and Sutton?"

Killian stared at him and Finn assumed his son was probably thinking he was nutter, but then his lips curved up, his smile almost sly.

"That's the connection I was trying to make at 2:30 a.m." Killian shook his head in annoyance. "But it's a possibility. Sutton retired in 2010, and Hudson appeared. It gives me a place to start."

"I'll work on that today."

"Alright,"

"Anything else?" Finn asked, eager to get back to Ava and see what she'd found out.

"You have a hot date," Killian smirked.

"I—"

Then his and Killian's phones chirped simultaneously.

"Liam?" Finn pulled out his phone.

Liam: Fire at Captain Jack's!

"Bloody hell." Finn's eyes met Killian's, and his feet were already moving. "Ava's at Captain Jack's!" he threw over his shoulder on his way out.

"Dad wait!" Killian called.

Except Finn didn't stop to see what his son was going to do. All he cared about was the woman he loved was in danger, and she needed him.

***

Captain Jack's Fine Dining
November 13
12:30 p.m.

Ava held the oxygen mask over her nose and mouth and waited while Liam applied a bandage to her head.

"You won't need stitches," he told her, "but you might want to have a plastic surgeon check it out."

"It's at my hairline." Ava held the mask away temporarily. "I think I'll be fine." But when talking brought forth a coughing spell, she put the mask back before he even had to ask."

"Besides the cut," he questioned. "How's your head?"

"You know about the marching band, right?" she mumbled.

Liam grinned. "Seeing spots, nausea?"

"Only pounding," she admitted. "What about those other two people? And Captain Jack?"

Liam glanced over his shoulder where his partners were working on the two men who were found with her in Captain Jack's office.

"Concussions, I think," Liam replied. "Do you know who they are?"

"I've seen them around town." She shrugged, not remembering where or when though. "And Captain Jack?"

"I don't know," he began, before he was interrupted by the squeal of tires.

Ava glanced up to see Finn crossing the parking lot as if the hounds of hell were on his heels.

"How is she?" he fired the question at Liam and then immediately asked her, "Are you alright?

"She's fine, Dad," Liam told him calmly. "But she has a headache, so if I leave you alone with her, you have to be nice."

"Bloody hell, Liam," Finn retorted. "I know how to treat a woman."

"I'm sure you do," Liam smirked.

Ava ducked her head when he turned his twinkling blue eyes on her, but ignored him and focused on Finn. "It's a good thing my head's hard."

"Oh, love." Finn brushed gentle fingers on her head, close to the bandage, and tears sprung to her eyes. "I'm so sorry."

She thought she heard Liam murmur, "I'll leave you two alone," but her attention was solely on the man whose dark eyes mesmerized her.

"What happened?" He settled down on the curb.

The rattle of a stretcher as it was rolled out of the restaurant sidetracked her. "I'll tell you in a minute. Will you please go check on Jack?"

"But Ava ..."

"Please," she implored him to understand. "I didn't get to talk to him."

"Ava." Killian approached them before either could respond. "How are you?

"Headache. How's Jack?"

"I'm not sure." Killian glanced toward where Liam was talking to the older man. "What happened?"

Before she answered, Ava turned back to Finn. "Go check on Jack. Please."

"Alright." Finn squeezed her hand. "I'll be right back."

Killian pulled out a small notebook. "What happened?"

Ava removed the oxygen mask. "I stopped by to see Jack, and when I pushed open his office door, someone hit me on the head."

"You didn't see who it was?"

"No." Ava touched the bandage on her forehead. "I noticed Jack wasn't at his desk, saw someone was lying on the ground and then, lights out."

"Was Jack expecting you?"

"No, I ..." Then she second guessed how much to say to him because he was her daughter's fiancée. Finally, she opted for a partial truth. "I received the letter that should have accompanied the bracelet I gave Emma, and thought maybe he knew my grandmother."

Killian's blue eyes bore into hers, and she could tell he knew she was holding back.

"Do you know those other men who were with you?"

"Liam asked the same thing," she told him. "But while I've seen them around town, I don't know who they are."

"Alright." He looked up as Finn returned. "Do you need to go to the hospital?"

"Yes ..." Finn began.

But Ava drowned him out, "No. I just want to go back to the hotel and get out of these smoke covered clothes."

"Alright. I'm going to check on Jack, and see if I can find out about the other men." Killian nodded goodbye. "I'm assuming you're taking her home."

"Bloody hell, yes," Finn retorted.

"Alright then." Killian turned his attention back to Ava. "Do me a favor and give Emma a call, will you?"

"I will," she promised. "I don't want her mad at both of us."

Killian nodded once and walked away, leaving her alone with Finn. "How's Jack?"

Finn studied her for several minutes before squatting next to her. "He's fine. They're taking him to the hospital because of his age, just as a precaution, but let's get you home now. I'll tell you more later."

She wanted to argue, but then Liam came back, and she was more than happy to hand over the oxygen mask. "Are you sure you don't want to go to the hospital, just to be on the safe side?"

"No. I'll go home and rest."

"I'll see that she does." Finn slipped his arm around her, plastering her to his side, and she had to fight not to lean on him completely.

"Let me know if there are any problems," Liam told them. "Feel better, Ava."

She smiled, and leaned on Finn as he directed them to where he'd haphazardly left his car. "It's a good thing you didn't get a ticket."

Finn helped Ava inside. "Even if I had, it would have been worth it."

Her heart melted at the look in his eyes and she realized how he'd been holding himself in check while they were in public.

"Home?" he asked as soon as he was inside.

"I wish," she sighed. "But for now, the Inn will do."

For a second, she thought he was going to say more. Then he pulled away from the curb and turned toward the hotel. "I'm going to call Emma."

"Good idea."

"Mom!" Emma exclaimed as soon as she answered. "What happened? Are you okay? Do you need me to come there?"

The rapid questions didn't help Ava's headache, but she took a breath and jumped into the story. "I'm fine, Emma. Just a little knock on my head. And no need to come over. I'm going to shower and take something for my headache. I'll call you later."

"Are you sure?" Emma repeated, and there was something in her voice Ava couldn't decipher.

"Positive."

"Well, okay," Emma sighed, "I'll talk to you later."

"Bye, Honey." Ava let the phone fall, leaned her head back and closed her eyes.

"You didn't tell Emma why you were on your way to see Jack," Finn noted. "Why?"

She glanced sideways at him, as he pulled into the Inn's parking lot and tried to make sense out of why she's been so quiet. "I guess I don't want to say anything until I have something concrete to tell her."

"I can understand that." Finn unfastened his seatbelt, then leaned across the console and clicked hers open. "My heart stopped when Liam's text arrived."

Ava moved her head just enough to lean against his. "I'm sorry I scared you."

"Will you let me come inside and take care of you?" His hot breath blew against her temple.

"I hoped that's what you would say."

"Good." He kissed her cheek and jumped from the car."

When he opened the door and Ava swung her legs out, Finn took her hand and, as if it were perfectly natural, pulled her into his arms. "Hold on to me, love."

He was warm and safe. But there was still a part of her that refused to rely on him completely.

"I'm okay," she tried to assure him again.

"Stubborn," she thought she heard, when he shut the door and directed them toward her cottage.

"Very," Ava admitted with a laugh. "Is that going to be a problem?"

"Won't be for me," he chuckled. "If it's not for you."

She chose to ignore his comment and instead asked, "Tell me what Captain Jack said. And is he really okay?"

Finn opened her cottage door before answering, "Jack probably has a concussion and a few burns from where he tried to put out the fire."

"Do they know how the fire started?"

"Someone set it," Finn admitted. "And Jack was murmuring it was because they were looking for the key."

"The key to reunite Hope with her lover?" Ava questioned.

"Maybe." Finn tugged her into his arms and methodically began unbuttoning her coat. "Let's get you out of these clothes and into the shower."

"There's nothing wrong with my hands," she reminded him. "I can take off my clothes."

Finn hung her coat and turned her toward the bathroom. "I'm aware of that." He buzzed her cheek. "But I'm not ready to stop touching you."

Ava stopped and in a single move, wrapped her arms around him, and pressed her body as close as possible.

He lost his mom, his sister, and Joan. Was he afraid of losing me too?

Finn cupped her cheek and brushed his thumb over her bottom lip. "Don't scare me like that again." Then his lips covered hers and, as always happened, her thoughts grew muddled, and all she could do was feel.

TWENTY-FOUR

Lighthouse Inn
November 14
8:30 a.m.

Finn had his laptop open, and for the past two hours had been scrolling through information, looking for a connection between Sutton and Hudson. However, after hours of searching—and with too many links to keep track of—he'd found very little.

Hudson connected with Remy in 2011 in London, 6 months before Remy disappeared.

He was involved in the recovery of a necklace stolen from The House of Saud. But rather than returning it to the original owners, sold it for 10 million pounds to the Jaxson Harvey family.

Hudson stole a painting in 2014 from the Francis family and sold it to the Carters.

In 2015 there was spotty mention of him connecting with a woman named Matilda Newman.

And while it wasn't a lot of information, there were two names, requiring further investigating.

Jaxson Harvey had been a patron of the Association for Foreign Banks from 2000 through 2007. At which time Roman Sutton was the President.

Matilda Newman, old money, lived in Cornwall. The Shadow Angel had taken a statue from her home and returned it to the Vatican in 1982.

"You returned a statue to the Vatican?" Ava asked, having come silently into the room and was leaning over his shoulder.

"Don't you know it's rude to read other people's notes?" Finn turned enough in his chair to pull her down onto his lap.

Ava curled her arm around his neck and sent him a mischievous smile. "But then how do I learn all the juicy details about the Shadow Angel?"

"You ask, love." He kissed her softly. "Whatever you want to know."

She hummed. "So was Matilda Newman one of those debutantes?"

"Let me show you, Matilda." He opened a new browser and typed her name into a search engine. "There."

"She was born in 1921," Ava read. "A little old for you?"

"Just a little," he agreed. "How are you feeling?"

"Better," she assured him. "I want to call about Jack and go see him."

"I think that's a good ..."

His phone buzzed before he'd finished his sentence and, with a frown, he hit accept. "Killian, is everything alright?"

"Dad." The tenor of Killian's voice had Finn's muscles tightening, and his pulse picking up speed. "I need you to get down to the office as soon as you can."

"Killian," Finn tried again. "What's going on?"

"A few pieces of the puzzle have clicked into place," Killian offered cryptically.

"Regarding Sutton?"

"Maybe," Killian replied. "Just get down here. We could use your help. I'll see you when you get here."

"We?" Finn began, but Killian had already hung up.

"What was that? Did something happen?"

"Apparently so," he frowned. "Will you be alright?"

She laughed. "Although I love you want to take care of me. I'm perfectly capable. I told you. I'm going to pick up Jack and take him home. After that, I'm going to ask him about Rose."

"Alright, love." Finn shut down his computer and kissed Ava goodbye.

Except, as he drove away from the Inn, Killian's words kept floating around in his head. What had he meant by the cryptic response, '*a few pieces have clicked into place*'? And who the bloody hell was the 'we,' in his statement? Was it Liam?

Finn opened the door to the Sheriff's department to find Killian waiting for him.

"Dad, thanks for getting here so quickly."

"You made it sound like it was important," Finn replied. "And I have to say you have me a little curious ... and a little nervous."

Killian nodded his head in acknowledgment. "No reason to be nervous, but I get your curiosity. Whenever a case starts to come together, I feel like I'm on a roller coaster, searching for the rest of the answers."

"What's going on, Killian?"

"Do you know who Ian Jones was?" Killian tossed out, and his expression had Finn paying close attention.

"Of course I do, Killian," Finn replied. "I'm not daft. Ian Jones was your undercover persona. A womanizer and a two-bit thief."

"That's one Ian Jones." Killian led him down the hall. "But not *the* Ian Jones."

"*The* Ian Jones?" Finn and stepped into the conference room. "Bloody hell."

"Dad," Killian went on, "meet Quinn ..." he pointed to a dark-headed man, dressed all in black, his sardonic smirk firmly in place, "and—"

"Alistair," Finn murmured, staring at what could have been a carbon copy of Claire's brother, thirty years previous.

"Aiden Jones." The man he'd been staring at stepped forward, his hand outstretched.

His demeanor differed from Alistair's, Finn noted, shaking the man's hand. But in looks, he was the image of his father. Black, slightly wavy hair, blue eyes that held an intelligent but shy expression, and an average build. But unlike his father's tailored suits, the son had on a tweed jacket that was a few years old, over a faded sweater.

"But you are Alistair's boys?" Finn worked to get on the same page as the rest in the room.

"Yes sir," Aiden replied, his accent that of the Queen's English.

"Killian?" Finn sent his son a confused look. "You said you'd connected some of the loose pieces."

"Trust me, Dad." Killian pointed to a chair. "Have a seat, and we'll tell you what we've figured out."

Finn glanced around the room once more before finally pulling out a chair and dropping into it.

"Aiden and Quinn were the other two people in the restaurant yesterday," Killian began.

"You were?" Finn looked from one to the other. "Why?"

"We had an appointment with Captain Jack," Aiden explained. "But someone jumped us and …"

"So, there were two uninvited guests on the ship?" Finn looked to Killian for confirmation.

"More than likely," Killian agreed.

"But how did you end up in Swan Harbor?" Finn asked the room, not caring if it was Aiden or Quinn who answered. "And where's your mother, sister, and father?"

Aiden exchanged looks with his brother and began their story, "About the time you and your family moved to the States, my mother took Quinn, Sarah, and I, and moved to London."

"Miriam left your father?" Finn exclaimed, surprised Alistair would have allowed such a thing to happen.

"Yes," Aiden winced. "There was a huge fight, and while I don't know what happened, I believe she was holding something over my dad's head."

"We could only see my father when he visited us in London," Quinn added. "Aiden and I believe she was afraid he'd try to take us from her."

"Fast forward to this past spring," Aiden went on. "I have a Doctorate in English, and found a visiting position listed in a professional journal. That position was at Swan Harbor University. It turned out I'd met someone from the town when I was in graduate school."

"Who?"

"Cameron Hunter."

Finn was familiar with the name, but rather than digging more into the acquaintance just nodded. "I'm with you so far."

"I'm a freelance journalist," Quinn took over, "and was doing a piece on stolen objects and the black market. One lead led to another, and I ended up following a path from Roman Sutton to … our father."

"Alistair?" Finn's brows went up with surprise.

"Yes," Quinn nodded. "Turns out I wasn't the only one, as the Serious Fraud Office (SFO) was in the middle of their own investigation."

Somehow that didn't shock Finn, and he sat back, allowing Quinn to go on with what he was saying.

"When they took dad into custody," Quinn continued. "Our sister moved into his house—"

"—And uncovered what brought us here." Aiden laid several pieces of paper on the table. "We found out dad and Roman Sutton were looking for the rest of the silver coins which were part of the collection grandfather Jones had."

"There were more?" Finn asked, surprised he'd never heard that before.

"Our father believed so," Quinn nodded.

Killian slid another piece of paper across the table. "The pieces of eight came from a ship sailing to Spain from Cuba, in 1715, by a pirate whose name was," he hesitated a beat and his eyes met Finn's, "Ian Jones."

"Ian Jones was a pirate?" laughed Finn, fighting the desire to pull his silver coin out to check the date.

"Aye." Killian's eyes twinkled, as if he knew what Finn was thinking.

"What you're telling me," Finn tried to sort out what he'd learned, "is the Jones family had a pirate who stole silver in 1715. Some of it stayed with the family, and Alistair and Sutton were looking for the rest? But how did that lead to Swan Harbor, and Jack?"

Aiden laid a plastic bag with a smaller piece of paper inside on the table. The page was old, yellowed, and looked ripped from a journal. "Because we have reason to believe Captain Jack's restaurant was Ian Jones' ship at one time."

Finn frowned, thinking that was a tremendous leap. "What makes you think that?"

Quinn shrugged. "Sarah has made it her mission to find out everything possible about this pirate. Somehow, she discovered people had seen him in the waters nearby.

"In the 1700s," scoffed Finn," there were plenty of pirates in these waters."

"Look at the picture." Aiden pointed at the bag. "We think the page was from Ian's journal."

Finn studied the men carefully, and their steady gaze convinced him to pick up the bag holding the page. There was a crude drawing at the top that could easily be Jack's ship. The name of the ship, "Hope's Haven," was painted on the hull for all to see. Just reading the name sent a chill up his spine.

"We assume that was the name of Ian's ship," Aiden explained.

The key, they say, is to reunite Hope with her lover.

Words from Ava's letter rushed through Finn's mind, but that was her story.

"Jack's ship has no name," Finn pointed out.

"We know," Aiden agreed. "But look at the drawing again."

Finn went back to studying the picture, and while the ink was old and faded, he could tell the ship was docked. But it was the image drawn on the pier that convinced him the men were on to something. "It's a swan."

"Aye," Killian's eyes met his. "Was my ancestor led to Swan Harbor long before me?"

Killian's words caused a chill to work its way up Finn's spine, and spread to his fingertips. Similar to words he'd thought after speaking to Elsa and Emma at Liam's engagement party rose inside.

Was there something to Emma and Elsa's thoughts about Swan Harbor? Was he being guided by a force more powerful than him?

"But," Finn frowned, "if you believed I could help, why the cryptic notes? Why didn't you just ask?"

"Notes?" Aiden repeated. "What bloody notes?"

Finn sent Killian a look before turning back to Aiden and Quinn. "You haven't been leaving me notes?"

"No!" Quinn exclaimed. "Until we started talking to Killian, we didn't even know who he was."

Finn knew Claire and Alistair hadn't been close, and after they'd gotten married, things hadn't changed.

"I'm sure whatever your father had to say about me wasn't pleasant," Finn retorted.

"You were always *'that bastard,'* who stole Claire away from the family," Aiden offered, unsurprising words. "And your sons were *'the bastard's boys.'*"

"So, if you weren't the ones searching the ship." Finn's frightened eyes went to Killian. "Someone else set the fire."

"Which means someone out there is still looking for this *'key'.*"

"Bloody hell," Finn mumbled, his thoughts going to Ava, and what she'd planned for the day.

Killian pointed to some lines written beneath the picture. "Could the answer to the riddle tell us where to find the key?"

Maybe, Finn thought. Then a conversation with Captain Jack could tell them if his and Ava's families' mysteries were converging. Could tell him if they were being directed by a force larger than them all.

***

Captain Jack's Cottage
November 14
11:00 a.m.

AVA HAD ONLY BEEN WITH CAPTAIN JACK FOR AN HOUR, AND HE was exhausting her. She understand he was angry about what had happened to his ship, but the doctor had given her instructions to take him straight home. He'd complained, pitting his stubbornness against hers, until finally, he'd capitulated and gave her his address.

It surprised her to learn his cottage was just down the street from the one she was buying, and had hoped being home would improve his attitude. Except once they were inside, neither the view of the sea nor the rambunctious greeting from his dog had quieted him. He didn't calm down until he was assured his ship was intact. But now that he wasn't full of bluster, dare she bring up the letter?

"You've been tiptoeing around me since you picked me up at the hospital," he retorted in his direct manner that never failed to surprise her. "Just spit it out."

"It can wait," she began.

Before he cut her off, "Is 'it' what you wanted to talk about yesterday when you stopped by the ship? I'm sorry about that." He waved his hand toward her head, where the cut was still visible.

Ava absently brushed her hand across the bandage on her forehead. "Are you sure you're feeling alright?"

"Bah," Captain Jack snapped. "I'm grouchy because someone dared to mess with my ship. They hit me over the head. And then I had to spend the night in that blasted hospital. How the hell do they expect you to rest when they're waking you every few hours? I told you, I'm fine."

"I was wondering, if you know." Ava tugged the letter from her pocket and held it out for him to see.

The color leeched from his face, and she wanted to kick herself for listening to him. "Where did you get that?"

Ava glanced at the letter, her grandmother's handwriting the only thing that could distinguish her envelope from another. "Someone sent it to me."

"When?"

Briefly, she told him about her call with Will Morton from the attorney's office. "I got the bracelet in May, but just received the letter yesterday. Did you know my—?"

"Rose," he sniffed, and she could swear there was a catch in his voice.

"Yes," Ava nodded, her heart racing. "She died when I was young, and my father refused to talk about my mother or her family."

"Of course, he did," he murmured, so softly she wasn't sure she'd heard him correctly.

"You knew my father?"

Captain Jack blew out his breath and pushed up from his chair to storm across the room.

"Yes, I knew your father," he replied, his voice cracking.

Ava studied Jack's posture. He was holding himself ramrod straight, his hands clenched into fists, as if he were fighting not to hit something. But she wasn't sure what to make of his behavior.

She knew her father had enemies. While he'd been controlling, and there'd been times she'd tried to get away from him, she'd known he'd loved her. But most of Leo's enemies had been because he'd bested them in business. Jack had been in the Navy, and his hate seemed personal.

"What did my father do to you?"

"Besides destroy my life?" Jack retorted. "Isn't that enough?"

Like he'd done to Peter, floated through her mind.

Ava slowly approached and touched Jack's arm. "I'm sorry. My father could be difficult. But he's been gone a lot of years."

"How long?"

"Thirteen."

"Good riddance."

She gasped and stepped back as if she'd slapped her. "Jack, again I'm sorry.

But the letter mentioned a Jack in this letter, and I'd hoped you might have known my grandmother."

"I knew your grandmother," he acknowledged quietly. "Can I see the letter?"

Ava handed it to him, and when he took it, his hand was shaking and the sadness on his face had tears filling her eyes.

He ran one finger over the words printed on the front, and a single tear rolled down his cheek and Ava couldn't help but think he'd loved Rose. But while she wasn't sure exactly how old he was, she knew he was significantly younger than her grandmother would have been.

Jack sat, and when he brought the letter to his nose and inhaled deeply, the tears she'd been holding spilled. "You smell it too, don't you?" she asked. "What is that scent?"

"Lavender."

Where had she smelled it before? The scent was familiar, but she knew there was no way her father would have allowed it in their home. He'd told her he was allergic, never allowing flowers or perfume inside their house of any kind.

Somehow, though, she knew the smell was a part of her past. That it had surrounded her at one time. Finn's words gave her hope.

Our senses pick up things even when we don't realize it's happening. If it's important, the memory will return.

Jack's eyes met hers across the room as he folded the letter and returned it to the envelope.

"It's obvious you loved my grandmother, Jack," Ava pushed him for answers. "What was she to you?"

He didn't answer but laid the letter on the table. Then he collected a folder and a picture frame from a desk across the room.

"It's time you learned the truth." Jack handed her the items he'd gotten off his desk.

Ava glanced down, and the image was like a punch to the gut and her knees almost gave out. "That's you ..."

"Yes."

"And my grandmother."

"Yes."

"And *me.*" Ava looked away from the picture that showed her in Jack's arms while he stared down at her, wearing a huge smile. Looking over his shoulder was her grandmother, her smile so big it was as if she'd just won the lottery.

"When was this taken?"

His expression had the tears returning to her eyes, and she wasn't sure she was ready to hear his answer.

"In Boston," he told her quietly. "It was your first Christmas."

And the only Christmas she'd had with her mother. "Who are you?"

"My name is Jack Swan," he whispered.

TWENTY-FIVE

"Jack Swan?" Ava repeated. "You're grandmother's—"

"—Brother," he replied.

"You were my mom's uncle?"

"Yes." Jack lowered into a chair, his ever-present companion, Bandit, sitting faithfully at his side.

Ava tilted her head and studied him, trying to decide what was suddenly so different about him. Did he look older? Or younger? Relieved the secret was out? Or terrified?

How did she feel? *Besides pissed?* she thought, tuning back into what he was saying.

"Rosie was born less than a year after my mother and father were married," he explained. "I was born not long after my mother's fortieth birthday. Then ..."

"She died when you were young, didn't she?" But Ava knew the answer, even before he responded. Her grandmother's haunting words about the women never surviving beyond their fortieth-fifth birthday echoed in her head.

"I was four," Jack told her. "Your mother was just a few months old, but with no hesitation, Rosie took me in. She raised me as if I were her son and not her brother. Grace was like a sister."

"But why?" Ava cried. "Why am I only now learning about you ... and Swan Harbor?"

Jack toyed with the folder in his hands for several minutes before bringing it to her. "I was hoping ..."

"What? That I wouldn't find out?" Ava threw at him, her stomach churning, and the bile climbing into the back of her throat. "Were you angry when Emma moved here? I bet the first time you met her, it freaked you out, didn't it?"

He looked at her with eyes that begged her to understand, and a corner of his mouth kicked up. "I had no idea who she was when I took Bandit to see the new vet. Then I looked into her green eyes, and she looked so much like Rose, I very nearly wept. But she had no idea who I was ... and I tried to tell myself that was how it was meant to be. Then ..."

"You saw me."

"Yes." His smile was melancholy, and while she was still so angry, something inside of her twisted. "You look just like I imagine Grace would have looked had she lived."

Ava squinted, her thoughts trying to connect several things flying around in her head. "Do I really? Look like my mom, that is?"

Jack's eyes met hers, "Yes. Surely you noticed that growing up when you'd look at her pictures."

She set the folder aside and wandered to the window, noting his view was angled more toward the lighthouse than her new home's. "My father hid all the pictures of my mother, except a few taken just before she died. It wasn't until after he was gone, I found them. And by then—"

"—You had no idea who the people were."

"None," Ava agreed. "Maybe mom had planned to write who were in the pictures someday, but ..."

"That day never came."

"No."

"I'm sorry."

"What are you sorry for, Jack?"

She turned the stare she'd always used when she'd needed something in the business world on him. But the good Captain didn't behave as she'd expected. Instead of jumping to do her bidding, he smiled, even though it was obvious he was fighting his emotions.

"I fail to see why you find this situation funny."

"I'm sorry, Dear," he apologized. "The expression on your face reminded me of the look your mother used to give me when she wanted me to do something."

Ava sniffed, refusing to melt into a puddle of emotions like she wanted ... at least until she was alone. "Tell me about the lavender."

"That's not the question I expected."

"Humor me."

"Rosie loved the smell," he told her, and goosebumps broke out on Ava's arms. "She planted it all along the back patio, and had pots of it all over the house."

"Did my mom like it?"

"Very much so," he admitted. "It was the first thing I smelled when I stepped into your house in Boston. She said it was calming."

"But my dad never allowed flowers inside," Ava began.

"Your dad wasn't always a mean son of a ... gun," he opted for. "In fact, he had a wicked sense of humor, was whip smart, and worshiped the ground your mother walked on."

Ava wasn't sure she could remember her father ever laughing, much less telling a joke. He'd been austere, rarely cracking a smile. "Grandmother said he changed."

"He did."

"Tell me what happened," she insisted, even though there was a part of her that knew what he was going to say.

"I was stationed in San Diego," he began, his voice thick with emotion. "Edythe and I had flown to Swan Harbor in April and announced our engagement. We were in the middle of planning our November wedding, when I got word Grace had died. As you can imagine, my world fell apart. We flew back to Boston for the service and, your father was disengaged. He barely made it through without falling apart."

"My father?" Ava frowned, as the man Jack was describing didn't sound like Leo King.

"Your father," Jack confirmed. "In fact, he sent you home with Rose."

He was quiet for several seconds, and the expressions that crossed his face had Ava's stomach knotting. Somehow, she knew she wasn't going to like what he had to say.

"My mother died in the summer, right?"

"Yes, July." Then he continued, and little pieces of her heart broke with each word he uttered. "Edythe and I had decided to have a small wedding here in Swan Harbor. She told me the town needed hope that life went on, because there was still a pall in the air over Grace's death."

"Had my father taken me back to Boston?"

"No," Jack shook his head. "You were still staying with Rose and Ray, and the very apple of their eyes. They were spoiling you rotten."

"Are there pictures?" Then she remembered her grandmother's line in her letter. "And journals?"

"There's an entire trunk-full, upstairs." He swallowed hard and continued, "When you're ready, we'll get Finn and the boys to move it. It was your grandmother's hope chest."

"I'm buying the house at the top of the hill," she told him, something she hadn't even told Emma. "I know exactly where to put it."

"The house at the top of the hill?"

"Yes," she frowned. "Why? Do you know it?"

"That was the house Ray built for Rose, not long before you were born." His smile said the memories were good ones. "It's fitting the hope chest will be returning to the place it rested for so long."

There were a million questions she wanted to ask about her mother and grandmother, but forced herself to wait. "Finish the story, Jack."

"Edythe and I returned to Swan Harbor in November, and were making last-minute preparations for our wedding. A few nights before the ceremony, Leo arrived. He seemed to be back to his old self, unless you looked closely, and then you could see it in his eyes."

"What?"

"Nothing," Jack told her, sending a chill up her spine. "The boys took me out for my '*bachelor party*,' and Leo drank more than I'd ever seen him. I don't know whom he spoke to, but someone told him he shouldn't have married a '*Swan woman*'. That they were one of Swan Harbor's cursed families."

"Oh no," Ava murmured, and she knew where the story was going. "What did my father do?"

Jack sent her a look that said, '*I really wish I didn't have to tell you this*'. "He told Edythe if she married me, it would be like signing her own death warrant. That if she valued her life and that of any children she planned to have, she'd run and not look back."

"And because she was pregnant, she did," Ava guessed, thinking it would be the only reason Edythe hadn't stayed and fought.

"Yes," Jack nodded. "Then he took you, said some vile things to Rose and Ray. Told them he'd see to it they had nothing to do with you, and if they tried, he'd ruin them. And make sure Swan Harbor became nothing but a ghost town."

"But in the picture that came with the bracelet," Ava murmured. "I was bigger, closer to two."

"Rose let your father go." He sighed and wandered back to stare out at the window. "She thought once he was back in Boston, he'd calm down."

"Right," Ava scoffed. "That just gave him more time to plot."

"For an entire year, she went without seeing you, her heart breaking every day. On the morning of your second birthday, she woke up Ray and told him they were going to Boston."

"My dad let her in?"

"No. Leo wasn't home." He was silent, and she had to wonder where he'd gone. But then finally he continued, "Rosie showed up with an armful of gifts and told the sitter she was expected. She and Ray spent the rest of the day with you ... and then your father returned home."

Ava's stomach clenched, and the sour taste in her stomach grew stronger.

"As you can imagine," Jack sighed. "It wasn't pretty. They returned home and within a few months, Ray's business dried up, and he died. Rose followed a few months later. Afterward, Swan Harbor seemed swayed back and forth, as if undecided about leaving or staying. I went back to San Diego and, until I retired, only returned to Swan Harbor to keep an eye on the tourist boats and the Spanish galleon."

She wanted to ask him about that, but she was still trying to wrap her head around the fact he'd just remained silent. Her thoughts were pinging all over the place, and while she wanted to run, Ava picked up the folder he'd handed her earlier. "I still don't understand, Jack. Why didn't you fight?"

He looked at her with watery, resigned eyes. "You have to understand, Ava. In the beginning, I had no way of knowing who Emma was. Her last name is Foster."

"Okay, I'll give you that," she conceded. "But then you saw me."

"A part of me wanted to grab onto you with both hands, but I had no way of knowing if you were like your father. Then I got to know you, and I didn't know what to do. On the one hand, there was the possibility of a family again …"

"But on the other hand?"

His voice dropped, and she realized he was more affected than he wanted to admit. "I had Swan Harbor to think about. Especially when Jonesy started showing signs of losing hope. And someone started searching for the key. I had to protect both, and the ship. Because while I only knew a part of its history, I was the last living Swan."

The only thing that kept floating around in her head was that once again, her father had taken from her, and she hadn't been important enough to fight for.

"I need to go." Ava snatched up the folder and practically ran out the door, tears already flooding her eyes.

"Ava, stop!" Jack cried. "I was wrong!"

Except, she wasn't in a place to forgive him yet, and hit the gas, causing the car to fishtail up the street.

Captain Jack's Cottage
November 14
1:00 p.m.

Finn drove into Jack's drive, a little surprised Ava wasn't still there. But since he had a few questions for the older man, decided he'd call her once he had some answers.

After he rang the bell and the door didn't open immediately, he wondered if they'd gone somewhere. He knocked again and had just turned away when the door suddenly swung open.

"Oh, it's you," Captain Jack mumbled and, leaving the door open for Finn, disappeared down a side hallway.

"Bloody hell." Finn pulled the door shut behind him and went in search of Jack. He found him sitting in a chair, staring out the window, the pier and ship visible in the distance.

"Was Ava here?"

"Yes.

Finn frowned, not used to one-word answers from the older man. "And did you talk?"

"Yes," Jack muttered. "She needs you."

Finn's breath caught. "What did you say?"

"She needs you."

"And I need her," Finn offered. "But something tells me there's more to the story."

"You could say that," Jack acknowledged. "She found out I was her grandmother's brother."

"*What*?" Finn snapped. "And why the bloody hell is she just now finding this out?"

"Because of her father," Jack replied, his answer not the one he'd expected.

"What's the bastard done now?"

"It's what he did almost fifty years ago," Jack told him. "But it's more imperative than ever the key is found."

Finn wanted to ask more questions about Leo King, but he could get those answers from Ava. Now he needed to find out about the ship.

"Jack," Finn pulled a chair closer to where the older man was sitting. "Where did your ship come from?"

"The restaurant?" Jack frowned. "It's been in the Swan family for generations. Why?"

"You don't know who left it to the Swan family?"

"I would assume it was a gift for Hope's son—"

"Did you say Hope?" Finn interrupted.

"Yes," Jack confirmed. "We assume it was a gift for her infant son from his father."

The key is to reunite Hope with her lover.

"Bloody hell," Finn murmured. "This Hope had an infant son? But she died. The son didn't go with the father?"

Jack looked at him as if he thought he were daft, but thankfully added pieces to the story, "Hope and the father weren't married. When she died, and no one came forward to claim the babe, he was raised by one of his uncles."

"Why didn't Hope's parents raise the infant?"

Jack shrugged. "I'm not sure what happened, but Christine, Hope's mother, had died, leaving behind a grieving husband. After Hope's death, the baby was given the last name Swan, after her mother."

"What was the baby's first name, Jack?" While he waited for the answer, Finn's heart raced, because he knew what it was without being told.

"Ian," Jack murmured. "Ian Swan. But he didn't live beyond his fifteenth birthday."

"But," Finn hesitated, trying to fit everything together.

"Oh, he never married," Jack clarified. "Christine had a brother, and as I'm the only Swan left, it's my job to protect the ship."

"What if I told you I think I know who Ian's father was, and might know how we find the key?"

Jack scoffed. "Come now, son. I've looked my entire life for that key. How can you come into town and know more than I do in such a short time?"

A corner of Finn's mouth curled. "I listened to my heart."

And something beyond my control is in charge.

Captain Jack stared at him, making Finn feel like he was reading his mind. "Who's the father?"

"Ian Jones," Finn replied quietly. "We think the ship was called Hope's Haven."

"Why do you think this?"

Finn shook his head, still wigged out by the turn of events. "Because the men you were meeting with yesterday are my nephews. Their father is Killian and Liam's uncle."

Jack went back to staring out at the ship for several heartbeats, and then it was as if a light went off, and he broke into a smile. "That's it," he suddenly exclaimed. "I need to see Jonesy, and you need to go find Ava."

Before Finn could say anything else, Jack yelled, "lock up behind you," and then the door slammed.

"Bloody hell," Finn murmured, as he locked the door and left Killian a voicemail. "What did I say?"

Instead of immediately following Jack's command to find Ava, Finn called Sally's and ordered food. On the way to town, he stopped a few times, and then drove to the cottage where he assumed his lady had run. But after he'd parked and knocked, he couldn't help but wonder which Ava he would encounter.

When she opened the door and smiled at him, he studied her carefully. Although her eyes were red, she appeared composed, as if she had already decided what to say about the information. As *if* she'd made peace with everything she'd learned.

"It's been hours since I saw you." He tugged her toward him with his empty hand. "Don't I deserve a better greeting?"

"That depends on if you brought me something to eat. I'm starving."

"And if I did?"

Her eyes lit up. "You brought me food?"

"I'm still waiting to see what my prize is."

"What do you want?"

Finn wanted to tell her he wanted everything, but settled for kissing her and then handing her the Sally's bag.

Ava held up the bag. I get this for only a quick kiss?"

"That's right, and this is free."

She took the red rose he'd picked up from the florist and side-eyed him. "I sense a but coming ..."

Finn chuckled and held up the last thing he'd brought. "What are these worth to you?"

Ava glanced at the folder and launched herself into his arms. "Already?!" she exclaimed when she saw the logo for Giennie's real estate business.

"I thought you would need some cheering up." Finn tossed the folder on the table and focused on Ava. "But it looks like you're handling the news better than I expected."

She stepped away. However, instead of immediately responding to his comment, began setting their lunch on the table. Finn followed suit, but it wasn't until they'd sat, and she'd taken a few bites, she said anything, "Jack's my great-uncle."

"I know."

"Do you also know my father destroyed my grandfather's business, blamed my grandparents and Swan Harbor for my mother's death, and wouldn't let them see me?"

"I didn't know all of that." Finn enclosed her smaller hand between his and kissed her fingers. "I'm sorry, love, for what your father took from you. But the question is, what are you going to do now?"

Her gaze met his and in them, he saw peace and curiosity. "What are you thinking?"

"Emma has always said there's something about this town, and now we know why. It's *ours.* For fifty years, my father tried to keep it from me, but no longer."

He grinned, his heart suddenly lighter than it had been for days. "That's my girl."

"Am I?" She laughed, the sound almost carefree. "Your girl?"

"Bloody hell, yes!" he confirmed, thinking he wished she were more than just his girl.

Ava dimpled. "Another teen moment. I've never gone steady either."

"I'm happy to give you so many firsts," he winked. "But what are you going to do with the knowledge you learned today?"

She took another bite of her sandwich, her eyes never leaving his face. I'm finally going to do what my father denied me as a child.

"And that is?"

"Did you know my grandfather Ray built this house?" she tossed a new question at him instead of answering his.

"No. But maybe that explains why it fits you so well."

"Maybe so." Ava pushed her plate aside and picked up the folder he'd brought with him. "I'm going to sign the papers making this house mine, and read my grandmother's journals. And help my uncle find this key, whatever it is. I feel like I've just started my life—"

"Your happy beginning," he murmured.

"Yes."

Her eyes met his and the way they sparkled had him taking her hand, and tugging her up and into his lap. "I love you."

"I love you, too."

Finn gently rubbed his thumb under her eye. "You've been crying, love. Don't bury those feelings. Talk to me."

He wasn't sure she was going to listen until she framed his face with her hands and placed a tender kiss on his mouth.

"You're right. When I left Jack's house, I was so ... hurt, I cried. But then, I read everything my father had done and realized I can't go back and change the past. Am I angry? Yes! And if my father were alive, I'm not sure what I would say." She paused, her face a canvas of fleeting emotions as she continued, "However, it all relates to my health scare and the choice I made. I have the power now. I can create the future I want."

"And what do you want?"

"I want a home, not just a house. A home filled with love, family, hope, and—"

"—Kisses," he interrupted, kissing her soundly.

"Definitely," she giggled. "Lots and lots of kisses."

He could help with that, he decided, settling in to show her. Then he'd fill her in on what he'd learned today, and together, they'd look for the key.

TWENTY-SIX

Swan Harbor Zoo
November 14
4:00 p.m.

Emma pulled into a parking space at the zoo, her mind spinning with everything she'd just learned from her mother. On one hand, she had a hard time wrapping her head around the information. However, on the other, it helped several things click into place. Swan Harbor wasn't just *a* town she'd happened upon when looking for a business to buy. It was *the* town waiting for her family to find again. Which explained why she'd felt an instant connection.

While gaining the knowledge about the town was one thing, it was the other piece of information giving her pause. The concept of family had been a difficult thing to understand growing up. Hers had been dysfunctional and distant. Since living in Swan Harbor, though, her ideas had changed and grown. Little by little, she understood families came in all sizes and shapes and sometimes they took work. She'd made peace with her mother ... with her father, and now she had an uncle.

Except, Jack wasn't just some arbitrary person she knew nothing about. He was trying to drag her into his beliefs about the town's hope being tied to a swan. And to convince her a 'key' needed to be found for the hope to survive. While she found him charming, he was also eccentric and confusing. Besides, how did one reconcile believing fanciful thoughts with their scientific minds?

You can't measure love, and you believe that.

Although not guaranteed of a happy ending, you're willing to take a chance.

She understood she'd changed, and change was good. However, the old Emma peeked out periodically, especially when changes were coming one after another. Lately, though, her need to control the pace was taking a stronger stance.

Between her mother, her mother and Finn, her father, and Jack, the changes were coming at such a fast pace it made her feel like ....

How?

Like she was a snowball on its way down a mountain. That with every roll, someone new would jump on, her circle growing larger with each passing day.

And would that be so awful?

She didn't think so, but if the changes happened one at a time, they'd be easier to handle.

Would they really? Or is that just an excuse?

Maybe a little of both, she decided, as she pushed open the door to the aviary.

As she'd expected, Emma found Jack sitting on a bench with Jonesy floating nearby. But when her eyes met the older man's across the room, the unexpected occurred. Something inside blossomed, because he was no longer just an older man who loved a swan. He was *her* older man. And that made a difference.

"Why didn't you say anything?" she asked him, after she'd sat and he'd remained silent.

"About the fact I'm your uncle?"

"That would have been a good place to start."

"When I brought Bandit to you in February, I didn't know."

"That's what mom said." Emma blew out a breath. "It's just so ..."

"Amazing?" He sent her a crooked, albeit hesitant, grin. "Mind-boggling, awful ..."

"I was going to say confusing," Emma offered, "and overwhelming."

"Now you know how I've felt for years. Swan Harbor and Jonesy have depended on me, and I've floundered."

But his feelings were about the town ... and a swan, and not about family. There was a difference. Wasn't there?

The town seems to be prosperous. "How is that floundering? How is that overwhelming?"

"Jonesy." He pulled the answers back to the swan. "I can just tell he's waiting for something, because his hope is waning."

Emma wanted to tell him he wasn't giving her answers she could understand. That it wasn't just him floundering, but her as well. "Tell me about Hope," she opted for, thinking a different direction might make more sense.

"I'll tell you what I know." He moved around on the bench, and she couldn't help but notice he was pale, with several bruises dotting his face.

"I'm listening." As he talked, Emma tried to keep an open mind.

"A handful of families founded Swan Harbor in the early 1700s," he began. "Prince Geoffrey, or Geoffrey Prince, as he became known—"

"Dylan's family?"

"Yes," he nodded, his voice growing softer. "They too are affected by the same pall that's hung over the Swan family for years."

"That the women don't live beyond forty-five?"

"Yes. Your mother has outlived the females in both families."

"She almost didn't," Emma murmured.

Jack looked at her, the shock on his face telling her he hadn't known. "She appears to be in good health."

"Mom's fine now," Emma assured him, happy when his expression relaxed. "I promise. Anyway, Geoffrey ..."

"Fell in love and married Christine Swan," he continued. "We know little about their marriage, but it was a happy one. Then, when his wife died, Geoffrey fell apart and Hope ran a little wild. No one knew she was seeing the pirate—"

"Ian Jones," Emma supplied, still completely weirded out by the recent development.

"Hope gave birth to the babe, Ian, in the fall, but then died weeks later."

"And no one knew why she was alone?" Emma questioned. "Or why Ian didn't take his child?"

"No one knows. But," Captain Jack added. "Sometime later, they docked the ship, and left a large amount of silver with a note for the Swan family."

"Wasn't there a way of tracking him?"

Captain Jack shrugged. "Who knows if they even wanted to look? The important thing was Christine's brother, Philip, cared for and raised the son."

"Mom said Ian died when he was young."

"He did." Jack slanted a look in her direction, his color changing as he grew more animated. "The destinies of the Swan and Jones's families were decided long ago."

Emma laughed. "Right. You're trying to tell me Killian and I were *destined*, to meet?"

"You don't think so?"

"When your heart speaks, it's best to listen," Molly had said.

"This is Swan Harbor, Emma," Sadie told her. "Things happen when they're meant to happen."

"Hope and Ian never had their happy ending," she replied, not answering his question.

"Which is where you and Killian come in," Jack replied, his voice growing excited.

"Okay." Emma stretched out the two syllables, wondering where Jack was leading her, and if she really wanted to follow. "Well, we are engaged so ..."

"It's a start," Jack assured her. "But I'm not sure it's enough. You need to have a baby."

A bark of laughter escaped before she could hold it back, as somehow she'd known that was where he was heading. "That's a nice thought. But it's not in the cards for a while, anyway."

"I was afraid you were going to say that," Jack sighed. "Maybe since Hope and Ian could never marry, that would give the town a boost of hope. When are you getting married?"

Emma grinned, thinking about the visit she'd taken with Elsa to the small church in the middle of town and how she'd actually chosen a date. But she hadn't told Killian. Should she tell Jack?

"What about mom and Finn?" She moved the talk away from herself. "Jonesy is doing better."

While Emma, the veterinarian, had no explanation for why, there was no denying the swan appeared healthier.

"True." Jack nodded, and Emma let out the breath she'd been holding. "But while their union has given the town a boost of hope, it won't last forever. We still need to find the key."

"Killian believes solving the riddle will reveal the key."

Captain Jack stared off, lost in thought. "Perhaps. It just feels as if Swan Harbor is on a precipice, waiting for something ..."

That uneasy feeling Emma had fought for weeks settled back over her shoulders. Why, she wasn't sure.

Sally's Diner
November 14
7:00 p.m.

Finn opened Ava's door and held her hand as she stepped from the car. "Are you ready for this?"

"What?" She dimpled, and he had to fight not to pull her into his arms for a kiss. "To be stared at by our children?"

"For starters," he acknowledged. "I'm sure by now it's all over town that you and Emma are Jack's family."

"I'm sure it is," Ava agreed. "But I'm still the same person I was before I found out."

He studied her carefully and seeing no sign she was holding anything back, shut the door but kept a possessive hand on her as they went inside.

"People are staring," she murmured when the diner door shut behind them.

"They're admiring your beauty," he grinned.

"There's that Blarney-stone talk again."

"No, love," Finn whispered for her ears only. "I only speak the truth."

Her eyes locked with his, and it was only when someone cleared their throat, he was able to tear his gaze away. "I'll hang our coats in the back."

"Okay, thanks." Ava slid into an empty chair.

But as he hung their coats and returned to the group, he had to wonder why he hadn't asked her if she'd told Emma about them. If she had, it would make it easier to get through the next few hours.

"Killian," he asked, deciding he wanted to toss the attention elsewhere. "Did you learn anything new from Aiden and Quinn?"

"Speaking of Aiden and Quinn," Liam interrupted before Killian could answer. "Why did I not know they existed? And do you really believe it's just coincidence they showed up in Swan Harbor now?"

"I wondered the same things," Killian added. "But I can't find any holes in their story."

"None?" Liam pushed, surprising Finn, as he was usually the most accepting of the two.

"I've met Aiden a few times," Emma offered. "He's been at the University since August. Seems to get on well with the staff, but he's quiet."

"Much like his mother," Finn murmured.

"It's your turn, Dad," Killian handed the conversation back. "Why didn't we know we had cousins?"

Since before his meeting with the Jones' boys the day before, Finn hadn't thought about Alistair in years. "By the time Claire and I were an item, her brother had married and moved his family to Cornwall. There had been a disagreement between him and his father. After our marriage, I know your mother talked to her brother a few times, but they didn't agree on much."

"What about the conversation I overheard?" Killian asked, reminding Finn of the 'sticky fingers' comment.

"Alistair came to Blyth asking to borrow money," Finn shared. "You walked into the room at the end of that conversation. It wasn't long after that Remy suggested we leave the country. Which I gather was when Miriam took Aiden, Quinn, and Sarah, and moved to London."

"What about grandfather's money?" Liam wanted to know—something Finn had asked himself. "If Alistair didn't have it, and mom didn't. Where did it go?"

Finn shrugged. "I'm not sure. Poor investments, maybe. But if I had to guess, I would say Alistair gambled away any money he made."

"Anyone hungry?" Hayden arrived, holding a tray of food aloft and temporarily halting the conversation.

"It's about bloody time," Killian grumbled, but the twinkle in his eye belied he was really angry. "We're starving."

Hayden set a couple of plates down and, with a little wave, walked away.

"What the bloody hell?" Killian exclaimed.

"Looks like your talk didn't solve the boy's woes," Liam quipped. "Perhaps I need to have a go."

"Sorry about that." Sally looked off across the room toward where Hayden had disappeared. "He's been moody lately. A big project in one of his classes. And something's going on between him and Peyton."

"Katrina," Killian offered. "That's what's going on between them."

Sally sighed. "If that's the case, having Peyton working here again doesn't help. I'll have a talk with him. Let me know if you need anything else."

Finn thought about saying something about young love. But since everyone was eating, took a bite of shrimp, just as Ava laid her hand on his thigh. Her touch was so ... surprising, his food caught in his throat, and he almost forgot to breathe.

His body tightened, his muscles jumped, and he could have sworn the thread connecting him to Ava had wrapped around them both. But when he glanced her direction, she was calmly eating her soup. Did she not feel it? Was he the only one?

"Huh-Huh-How," Finn cleared his throat and tried again. "How are the wedding plans coming?" He looked up into Liam's twinkling eyes and could feel the heat climbing.

"They're good, Dad." Liam's smile grew. "Anything new ... with ... you?"

Ava's finger hit a particularly sensitive spot on Finn's thigh, and it took every ounce of his willpower to respond in a neutral voice. "No, nothing new with me." He picked up his napkin with his left hand and stopped a wandering one with his right. "But Killian, you never said what you learned from Ian Jones' journal page."

Liam's eyes briefly met his, and Finn arched a brow, daring his son to say something. When he went back to eating, Finn trapped Ava's wandering hand and placed it back in her lap. She snickered, and a thousand thoughts flew through his head, none of which would be appropriate in the middle of Sally's. Except, the longer he sat next to her, the need to touch her grew stronger.

"We think answering the riddle may lead to 'the key,'" Killian was saying. "But we're no closer than we were when you left."

"What riddle?" Ava asked, reminding him he hadn't told her everything. He'd thought about it ... before they'd gotten side-tracked.

"Dad didn't tell you?" Killian's blue-eyed gaze said, '*I bet I can guess why.*'

"No."

Finn's eyes met Ava's and in them, he saw understanding—and that she was fighting the same needs as he.

"On the journal page," Finn explained. "Besides the drawing of the ship, there were several passages, and another drawing."

"And," Killian repeated. "Someone suggested the riddle's answer would lead us to the key."

"Makes as much sense as anything else," Liam grunted. "This town seems to drop pieces of information on its own timetable."

"Sadie says the same thing," Emma murmured. "That things happen in Swan Harbor when they're supposed to happen."

"Bloody hell," Killian mumbled. "Why did I move to Swan Harbor again?"

"It's your destiny," Emma quipped. "At least that's what Jack thinks."

Ava's quick intake of air had Finn glancing in her direction, but she was watching Emma. It made him think she'd heard something he hadn't.

"Read the riddle, Killian," Finn prodded.

Killian glanced at the two women, but the look on his face said he too was in the dark.

Finn gave a subtle shrug, just as confused by the situation as his son. When he leaned back, almost before he'd completely thought it through, he draped his arm along the back of Ava's chair.

"As dad said, under the first picture it says, '*When reunited with my Hope, my heart will soar. And I will be alone no more.*'"

"Oh, that's so sad," cried Elsa. "He never knew his son and lived the rest of his life alone."

"I agree." Finn's eyes met Ava's. "We're not meant to be alone."

She smiled and, as if it were the most natural thing in the world, leaned into him. Finn's heart raced, and he couldn't help but think, '*small steps*', as Killian continued, "The riddle goes like this ..."

My bounty can be found.
In a place that's safe and sound.
It is close, within your reach.
But, the security you must breach.
Find the one to set it free.
Only they will have the key.
Hurry, the hope is fading inside my heart.
It's up to you to know where to start.

"What the bloody hell does that mean?" Liam grumbled.

"We don't know." Killian hesitated a few seconds and slid his phone back into his pocket before continuing. "I sent it to Jack to see if he had any idea. The consensus is this '*bounty*' is on the ship."

"But Jack's been searching for it since he was a kid," Emma pointed out. "Don't you think he would have found it by now if it were on the ship?"

"The ship has a lot of ... space." Ava shuddered, and when their eyes met, Finn couldn't stop his head from dropping against hers. He could have lost her.

I'm okay, her eyes said, but it didn't stop him from inhaling deeply. Her perfume washed over him, settling him, making him feel everything was going to be alright in the world.

"What about the fires, Liam? Did the investigator find out anything?"

"There was only minor damage to the ship," Liam reported. "The fires were small, almost as if they were meant to create more smoke than damage."

"Trying to cover up something?" Killian tossed out.

"Maybe" Liam conceded. "And ..."

But as he continued to explain the discoveries about the fire, Ava found her mind wandering. She'd become used to touching and being touched by Finn, and suddenly having to watch that had thrown her. So much so, she'd unconsciously leaned into him several times. And yet ... it was as if no one noticed. Was she worrying about something she shouldn't? At least, as far as the man beside her was concerned.

Her daughter, on the other hand ....

"How was your meeting with Jack?" she asked Emma quietly, while the men continued talking.

Emma wrinkled her nose and sighed. "It was okay. But I just have—"

"—A hard time with the whole concept of a key saving hope," Ava nodded in understanding.

"Yes." Emma blew out a breath. "I'm a scientist, and the idea that this '*hope key*' is going to save the women in our family is just ..."

"Ridiculous?" Ava supplied.

"Maybe." Emma hesitated, apparently working her way somewhere. "But really, the whole *It's your destiny* talk freaked me out more than the key talk."

"You don't like the idea Killian is your destiny?"

"Yes. No. Ugh," Emma groaned. "I want to think Killian and I were in charge of our destinies. That we chose to fall for each other. It just feels like added pressure."

Ava frowned, unsure where Emma's thoughts were going. "How so?"

Emma rolled her eyes and whispered, "Captain Jack told me Killian and I needed to have a child to save the town."

"Oh!" Ava chuckled. "I can see how that would definitely add pressure. Did you tell him you'd get right on it?"

"No. I told him that wasn't in the cards yet."

"Good for you," Ava grinned. "See, that's how to be in charge of your destiny."

"How do you think Jack feels about finding us?"

Emma's question surprised Ava, but she threw out the only word she'd been able to come up with, "Scared."

"Scared?"

"Yes." Ava hadn't expected needing to clarify her thoughts, and paused briefly before responding. "For almost fifty years, family hasn't been something he thought was possible. Then suddenly, he's presented with us, and the possibility of finding this 'key' at the same time. I think in his head they're tied together."

"That if he finds the key, the family will stay?"

"Something like that." Ava shrugged, because she wasn't even sure where her thoughts stemmed from. "It just feels like he's scared, we'll hurt him like my father did."

"Does it feel surreal?" Emma glanced around the table. "All the changes?"

"Surreal?" Ava smiled, and the heat of Finn's hand against her shoulder felt so natural she fought not to lay hers on his thigh, "Maybe sometimes. But I feel as if I've finally found the life I was meant to have."

"I'm glad, mom. And," Emma's eyes skimmed over her to land on Finn before popping back, "I think it's wonderful you're buying a place in Swan Harbor."

"Really?" Ava asked, holding her breath, she'd heard Emma correctly.

"Yes! Tell me about the house."

Ava's whole being relaxed and, with Finn's thumb running rhythmically back and forth along her shoulder, she shared.

TWENTY-SEVEN

Terri Patterson's Home
November 15
1:30 p.m.

SHE'D HAD NO DIFFICULTY LOCATING TERRI PATTERSON, HER grandmother's best friend. But the next day when she knocked on her door, Ava found her palms were sweating. Then the door opened and instead of a woman, she was staring at Captain Jack.

"Terri's expecting you," he explained quietly. "But you have to wait until she's finished watching her soap opera."

"You're serious?" Ava gave a half-laugh.

"Damn straight."

Jack held the door and as soon as she stepped inside, a sense of familiarity overwhelmed Ava. It wasn't just the smell of lavender, but the design of the house, and the paneling on the walls. Exactly like the ones in her cottage.

The largest television Ava could ever remember seeing in a person's home overshadowed the room. "Wow!"

"It's a doozy, isn't it?" Terri glanced toward the door when her program switched to a commercial. "It was my birthday present."

"Impressive," Ava agreed.

"You look just like Grace." Terri pointed to the sofa. "Have a seat. I'll be with you in a minute." Then her show returned, and her gaze once again went to the large screen.

Ava gradually made her way around the room, taking the time to look at the pictures adorning every surface. She recognized Sally, Hayden, and a younger version of Rachel with a group of girls. And in the center of a credenza was a picture of Terri at her 90th birthday party, surrounded by her family.

"How does she keep them straight?" she murmured.

"She doesn't." A woman about Emma's age giggled. "You're Ava King, aren't you?"

"I am." Ava smiled at the younger woman. "But you have me at a disadvantage."

"Sorry." The young woman gave a self-deprecating smile. "I'm Harper—"

"—Rachel's friend," Ava remembered.

"Yes. Rachel calls you her fairy godmother."

"I was in the right place at the right time," Ava replied, but the happiness bubble inside grew, threatening to burst.

"You're being modest." Harper grinned. "It was really nice, and I'm excited Rachel is staying in Swan Harbor."

"Her idea for music classes is a good one," Ava replied. "What do you do?"

"I'm a professor at Swan Harbor University," Harper answered. "I teach in the Education department. Since I'm newly back in town, Grandma Terri offered me a room."

"And she's been a pleasure to have around." Terri clicked off the television.

"Thanks, Grandma." Harper buzzed the older woman's cheek. "I'll see you later."

"Bye, Dear." Terri waved the younger woman off. "Drive safely."

Harper rolled her eyes and called, "It was nice to meet you," before leaving through a back door.

"She's a sweet girl," Terri whispered to Ava as if she were telling a secret. "Had her heart broken a while ago."

"Haven't we all?" Ava commiserated.

"Harper seems happier these days though," Terri went on. "Maybe she's met someone."

"Swan Harbor is full of nice people," Ava offered.

Terri sent her a sly grin. "I hear you have a nice young man these days. And he's a looker, too."

Ava swallowed hard, pulling out her corporate persona for the first time in days. "Where did you hear that?"

"It's like that, is it?" Terri giggled, almost girlishly.

Her face heated, but Ava was determined to play dumb until she'd spoken to Emma. "That's a beautiful quilt," she settled on, after searching for a change of topics.

"You sound just like Rosie." Terri gave her an indulgent smile.

"I do?" Her planned questions for the older woman were suddenly mixed up in her head, causing her to ask a general question. "Tell me something about my grandmother."

"Rosie was feisty," Terri's eyes took on a far-away look, "and the best friend a girl could have. As you can imagine, when Ray decided they were going to live in Swan Harbor, I was ecstatic. Selfish maybe, but at the time I couldn't picture life without her. And now, I've lived more of my life without than with her, and yet I still miss her. In fact, look what I found." Terri unfolded the material she'd been holding and spread it across her lap.

Ava ran her hand over it and instantly felt a connection. "It's a quilt, right?"

"It is." Terri pointed to the interlocking circles that decorated the blanket. "This is a double wedding ring pattern, and your grandmother started it for you when Grace told her she was expecting. "Rosie or Grace cut the fabric for each of these blocks," she said, pointing to the squares connected to form the rings.

"Really?"

"Oh yes," Terri laughed. "This pink material was from a dress she bought for Ray's thirtieth birthday. They went to Portland to a fancy restaurant, and it ended up with grease on the skirt ..."

"And she didn't just throw it out?"

"Oh, no," Terri exclaimed. "It was gorgeous material, and your grandma was a terrific seamstress. She loved designing clothing, and then trying to make them. Definitely ahead of her time."

"I can't even sew a straight line," Ava grimaced. But growing up, her father had bought her the finest clothes available. He'd considered homemade things beneath a King. "How did you end up with grandmother's quilt?"

"Rosie and I had a deal," Terri shared. "She'd sew all the squares together with her magic machine, and I'd do the hand quilting. I got half-way through and then ..."

"Grandmother died."

"Yes. Then every time I tried to work on it, my heart broke," Terri admitted. "And now ..." She held up her hand, her fingers bent and arthritic.

Ava's heart bled at the news of the loss. But then Terri grabbed her hand. "Would you like to finish it?"

"Me?" Ava fought to keep her mouth from falling open. "I'd love to, but I don't know ..."

"Oh, it's easy," Terri assured her. "Here."

Before she could make any more excuses, Terri had dumped the quilt into Ava's arms and disappeared down the hall.

Ava heard her ask a question, and Captain Jack appeared. "Any word from the boys?" he asked, since the Reade and Jones' men were searching the ship.

"Nothing new," Ava admitted. "It surprised me when you answered the door. I assumed you would have wanted to keep an eye on your ship."

"I'd promised to install a couple of shelves for her." He winked. "Besides, I've searched the ship for years, and something tells me I'll be there when the key is found."

"I'm sure you will." Terri patted Jack on the cheek when she returned. "How are those shelves coming?"

"Almost done," he told her, and Ava had to duck her head to hide her smile.

"I swear," Terri shook her head. "He talks about the ship as if it were alive."

"Talks about Swan Harbor that way too," Ava added.

"True," Terri agreed. "But there's some truth in that. Now ..."

For the next hour, Ava gripped the needle as Terri painstakingly showed her what to do. She stuck her finger more times than she could count, and her stitches were not nearly as precise as the ones the older woman had done years before. But she'd done it, and the feeling inside was one she was hard-pressed to label.

"Any word from the boys?" Captain Jack asked again, on his way through the room.

Ava exchanged indulgent looks with Terri. "Same answer as last time, Jack."

"Damn," he muttered, disappearing again.

"What's happening on his ship?" Terri asked. "Are they cleaning up from the fire?"

"I think some of that is going on," Ava confirmed. "But the boys, as Jack called them, are searching for the key. It seems the ship belonged to the pirate Ian Jones."

"It's kind of romantic, isn't it?"

"A love story that ended tragically," Ava sighed. "Maybe if we find the key, Ian and Hope can rest in peace."

Jack stuck his head around the corner. "Ava, how did that riddle go again?"

She handed the needle to Terri and pulled her phone out of her bag,

"My bounty can be found,
In a place, that's safe and sound.
It's close, within your reach,
But the security you must breach.
Find the one to set it free,
Only they will have the key.
Hurry, the hope is fading inside my heart,
It's up to you to know where to start."

"What the hell does that mean?" he grumbled.

"I think I know," Terri's eyes twinkled. "Ian was a pirate, right?"

"Yes!" Jack came farther into the room. "How can you know the answer that quickly?"

Terri shrugged. "I read those historical romance novels. Anyway, the answer is in the first four lines."

"My bounty can be found,
In a place, that's safe and sound.
It's close, within your reach ..."

"But the security you must breach," Jack muttered.

"Yes," Terri confirmed. "Where's the most secure place on a pirate ship?"

"The captain's quarters?" Jack guessed.

"No," Terri scoffed. "The brig. If someone is bad enough to get thrown in the brig, they aren't getting out."

Jack's eyes met Ava's, and in his there was a light that hadn't been there in ... ever.

"Let's go."

Ava looked down at what she was doing. "But ..."

"Go on, now." Terri shooed them off. "But come back and tell me about it."

"We will." Ava grinned and spontaneously kissed the older woman on the cheek. "Thank you for the lesson."

"My pleasure, dear. Bring your young man with you next time."

Ava waved goodbye and followed Jack's car as he wove through town and pulled into the marina parking lot.

"Why is it we didn't call and tell them where to search?" she asked Jack on the way inside.

He looked at her as if she had three heads. "And let them have all the fun? You've got to be nuts."

"Oh, well." Ava laughed, thinking he seemed to have extra pep in his step suddenly. "Carry on."

"I intend to." He grinned. "Come on, boys. Let me show you where the answer to this riddle lays."

Ava took a few steps to follow, and then, Finn hauled her around a corner and into his arms.

"Where are you off to?" he muttered, just before kissing her thoroughly.

Ava grinned up at Finn. "I was going to find the key. It's in the brig."

"The brig?" Finn shook his head, as if he weren't sure he'd heard her correctly. "How do you know that?"

"I don't know for sure," Ava explained. "But that's what Terri thinks so ..."

"Here you are."

"Yes."

"How was your visit?"

Another little thrill ran through her when she thought about her time with Terri. "Wonderful."

"I'm glad." Finn kissed her again. "I want to hear all about it."

"Definitely." Ava wiped her lipstick off his mouth. "Any more leads on Remy and Sutton?"

"Killian is expecting a call from Scotland Yard any time," he told her. "I'm ready for this to be over so we can—"

"Hurry you two." Jack stuck his head around a corner. "We need help."

What had he been going to say? Ava wondered, as they ran to see what was happening.

Captain Jack's Fine Dining

November 15

4:30 p.m.

KILLIAN TOOK THE BOX OF CANNED GOODS FROM AIDEN AND carried them to the island in the center of the kitchen, then set it next to the other items. There was a part of him that thought what they were doing was as ridiculous as he knew Emma believed it to be. The other part, though, needed it to be true. Needed to think finding a 'key' would not only reunite Ian with his Hope, but save Emma. He couldn't think about the possibility of losing her before they'd had fifty or more years together. That happy beginning his father always talked about.

"Okay." Captain Jack began as soon as they reached the pantry. Which, at one time, had been the brig, but was now empty. "Are we ready?" He flipped on the light, picked up a flashlight, and stepped inside. "Since a key is mentioned, I'm assuming we're searching for a keyhole."

Killian exchanged looks with Liam and made a subtle nod toward where his father and Ava were huddled.

"What do you think, Dad?" Liam questioned, causing the pair to jump apart. "Any suggestions for finding a secret … keyhole?"

Finn cleared his throat and stepped closer to the pantry. "Any built-in areas?" he tossed out, as if he'd been paying close attention.

"Nothing," Jack grumbled. "And the walls are smooth and even."

"How about the floor?" Quinn offered. "Could there be a moving plank?"

Killian leaned back against the island and watched his newly found cousin step into the pantry. Minutes later, Quinn exited, wearing a disgruntled look.

"There's no bloody keyhole in there," Quinn griped. "Who told you it would be in the brig?"

"A ninety-year-old who reads historical romances," Ava pointed out. "Do you have a better idea?"

"She's got you there," Aiden murmured.

While they were arguing, Killian kept thinking about how a brig might have compared to a jail cell. "Jack, is that the original door?" His thought stemming from the only place in a cell where one might find a keyhole.

Jack poked his head out of the small, box-shaped room. "Yes. Why?"

Killian sauntered closer and grabbed hold of the door, thinking it was probably 8" thick. "Was this always here?" He indicated a window that was about 12" long and 8" wide, stretching mid-way on the door, between five and six feet.

Jack frowned. "No. There were rusty iron bars. I was just happy we could keep the door." He knocked to show how sturdy it was.

Killian's gaze jumped from Jack to meet the eyes of the others in the room. "You heard it too, didn't you?"

"Knock again," Finn instructed.

Jack knocked again, but this time, the slight echo Killian thought he'd heard earlier was missing.

"Show me where you knocked." Killian pushed open the door, so he could see.

"Here." Jack knocked, just under the window.

"And the first time?"

"Closer to the doorknob." Jack knocked again, and just like the first time, there was the slight echo.

"Bloody hell." Killian adjusted the door and focused on the edge just above the lock. "Look."

On the edge of the door, a couple of inches above the latch, there was a set of grooves. And on either side, thin lines could be traced up about 8" before joining in the middle.

"It's a secret compartment," Jack chortled. "How did I miss that?"

"But how is it opened?" Liam asked what they were all wondering. "That isn't a normal keyhole."

"It looks like a bloody lion," Killian muttered.

"What did you say?" Aiden asked, coming closer.

"A lion." Killian pointed to what he was talking about.

Aiden took Jack's flashlight and shone it on the wood. "Could it be ...?" Then he handed the light back and took out his phone.

"What are you searching for, Aiden?" Quinn peered over his brother's shoulder.

"The family crest," Aiden slid his thumb across his phone screen.

"The family crest?" Killian echoed.

Aiden showed Killian his phone. "My father has a huge picture of the family crest in his great room. Could that be what it is?"

Killian looked back and forth between the picture and the door, excitement growing inside despite his need to stay calm. "It could be. So, the key isn't a traditional one. Do you have anything with the crest on it?"

Quinn frowned. "Like what? I'm not in the habit of carrying the family crest around."

"I don't bloody know," Killian grumbled. Except there was something swirling in his head. Like a piece of a puzzle searching for its mate.

Ava looked closer. "It's small. Jack was anything left in the Captain's desk?"

"Like what?"

"I don't know," she shrugged. "Maybe one of those stamps used to seal letters with wax."

"Or a ring?" Killian met Ava's questioning glance. "Like a signet ring?"

"Maybe," she nodded. "Especially if it has a raised area."

"I have it." His eyes met his father's, and his heart raced with the realization. "Mom gave it to me. I found it a few weeks ago."

"Well, what are you waiting for," Jack shooed him along. "Go get it."

As he ran to do Jack's bidding, he could hear the other reciting, "Find the one to set it free. Only they will have the key."

Killian tossed his light on his car and took off toward home, glad the roads weren't icy. By the time he'd pulled into the driveway, his heart was racing and Emma's *Rhopalocera* were swarming in his gut.

"Killian," Emma met him at the door, "you found the key, didn't you?"

"*I* have the key, Doc." He took the stairs two at a time to their apartment.

"Wait, what?" Emma followed him into their bedroom. "How do you have the key?"

He brought the box of his things out of the closet and hurriedly sorted through, finding the smaller container. "There's a secret compartment in a door on the ship. We think this ring," he pulled it out and slipped it on his index finger, "will release whatever's inside."

"And save hope?" she murmured.

And save you, he wanted to say. "Aye, Doc. Can you come with me?"

"Try to keep me away." Emma exchanged her scrubs for a sweater, jeans, and boots. "I'm ready."

Her face was glowing, and while he knew he needed to hurry, he couldn't keep from pulling her forward for a hard, and way-too-short kiss. "Let's go."

Captain Jack's Fine Dining
November 15
6:00 p.m.

Finn leaned back in the chair, his arm resting on Ava's, watching Liam, Aiden, and Quinn get acquainted.

"What are you thinking?" Ava's quiet voice broke through his concentration.

He slanted a half grin in her direction. "I'm just enjoying life."

Her eyes met his, before going across the room and back. "Me too. I just wish ..."

"I know, love." Finn took her hand, unconsciously kissing her fingers. "With a little luck, we'll have a few answers and put everything behind us and move forward."

"Wait a minute." She poked his leg playfully. "In one breath, you told me you were enjoying life, and in the next are ready to move forward. So, which is it?"

Finn slowly turned his head in her direction and had to clamp hold of her shoulder to stay in his own space. "I think you know what I mean."

She blushed and dropped her eyes. "Finn, I—"

But she was interrupted when Killian and Emma rushed into the room and he cried, "I've got it."

"It's about time," Liam groused.

"Wanker," Killian shot back.

"Where's Elsa?" asked Emma. "I thought she'd be here."

"Patty fell," Liam explained. "Elsa met Lilly at the Emergency Department. I've been waiting for this tosser—"

"Boys," Finn brought them back to the task at hand, "can we get on with this?"

"Bloody hell, yes." Killian pulled off the ring and held it out for Jack. "I believe you need to do the honors, since you've been searching for years."

"I have," Jack acknowledged. "But you have the key, Killian. You're the one who's meant to set it free."

Killian grabbed Emma's hand with his left, and holding the ring in his right, fit it snugly into the notches carved in the door. "Are we ready?"

"Just turn the bloody thing," Liam groused.

Slowly, Killian turned, forcing the design in the door to follow. By the time it had moved a quarter turn, and nothing had happened, Finn began holding his breath. At halfway around and still nothing, he grabbed Ava's hand.

"Oh, look," she whispered.

Finn watched as Killian guided a slim drawer from the center of the door.

"That's not the silver my dad thought was hidden," Quinn retorted.

"No." Killian removed a book and held it out for everyone to see. "I think it's a journal."

"Ian's?" asked Jack, almost reverently.

Killian laid the book on the counter next to to Jack. "You should check."

Jack's hands were shaking as he opened the top cover and leaned close to read the words written inside.

"*Property of Captain Ian Jones,*" he read, his voice thick with emotion. "And then it says,

> *Close your eyes, heart of mine,*
> *And feel my arms, one last time.*
> *Wait for me, I'll soon be near.*
> *Wait for me until I'm here.*
> *I promise you Hope, I'll find the key,*
> *And on that day, we'll both be free.*

"It's dated *18 December 1718.*" Jack finished quietly.

Finn heard Ava sniff and pulled her against his chest.

"Hope died in his arms," Ava murmured. "He's asking her to wait for him. Why?"

"Because he didn't want to go on without her," Finn whispered.

Ava lifted her head, and when his eyes met hers, all he wanted to do was kiss her. But since they weren't alone, settled for pressing her tighter against his chest.

"Is it missing a page?" Killian indicated the journal page that had led them to the door. "Could that be the key? Reuniting the book and the page with the ship named Hope's Haven?"

Jack shrugged, and his anxious eyes met Finn's before touching on Ava and then Emma. "I hope you are right, son."

He opened the book and as he flipped through looking for a missing page, Finn's thoughts were traveling along the same ones as Killian's. While it made very little sense, what else could it be? Hope wasn't something that a 'key could control.' It was a feeling inside that motivated and pushed people. A feeling that was strong in some and weak in others. A feeling that gave you strength to fight.

"Does it match?" He stepped closer to the book and watch Jack slide the page back into place.

"It matches," Jack told them in a voice that was soft and tremulous. "And you asked if this was all. Look."

On the left side of the page, there was a picture of the ship, its name missing. It was docked, and there was a drawing of the same swan. But it wasn't alone. Instead, a chest was close by, its top open to show it was empty. The date at the bottom of the page was *18 December 1718*.

The page Aiden and Quinn had brought fit on the opposite side. But the name of the ship adorned the hull, and the chest lay below the words, this time its top closed. The date at the bottom of that page was *14, February 1720*.

"Is that the last entry, Jack?" Ava asked, her fingers digging into Finn's arm, as she waited for the page to be turned.

"There are more drawings." Jack pointed to the book. "A chest similar to the one drawn before a heart with a lighthouse and ..." The color drained from his face as he turned toward Emma.

"What is it, Jack?"

"Jonesy."

"What about Jonesy?"

"Jonesy has to be set free."

TWENTY-EIGHT

Lighthouse Inn
November 16
9:00 a.m.

Finn tugged his black sweater over his head and strolled from the bedroom to find Ava staring out the window. He wrapped his arms around her from behind and propped his chin on her shoulder. "What are you thinking?"

"That it looks like snow." She closed her hands over his arms and pressed her head against his temple. "And about Emma and Jack."

"That's what I thought." He hesitated a beat, the memory of the argument between Emma and Jack still fresh in his mind. "They'll work it out."

"Will they?" She turned around and looped her arms around his neck. "It really surprised me."

"How so?"

"Emma has been," she grimaced, "tolerant of Jack's eccentric behavior regarding Jonesy."

"Haven't we all?" When her eyes met his, he wondered if he'd disappointed her with his admission.

"I know it's far-fetched to believe hope can be given or taken from a town, but ..."

"Your emotions are all mixed up in the possibility," he offered. "Intellectually you realize it makes no sense, but emotionally–"

"I can't stand the thought of losing Emma."

"Ahh, so the real reason comes out." Finn sat and pulled her onto his lap. "I know Killian feels the same way. And I don't want to lose any of you. But maybe this is a good thing."

"A good thing?" she exclaimed. "How can you say that?"

"Think about it, love. Emma and Jack are family now, and they need to work that out. Families disagree, but they talk and move forward ... together."

She studied him and the look in her blue eyes melted his heart. "I think I just fell in love with you again."

Finn arched a brow. "Isn't there some song about falling over and over again? I kind of like that idea."

"Oh, you."

He chuckled and kissed her, convinced he'd never tire of greeting each morning with her at his side. "What's on your agenda today?"

"I'm meeting with Becca." Ava rolled her eyes. "She decided where she wants her store, but can't decide on a name."

"Really? Why not?"

"She thinks she wants an alliteration," Ava tried to explain. "But every time she comes up with one, there's an issue."

"How hard is it to name a business?"

"What does Becca's Bows and Baubles say to you?" Ava asked.

"That she sells hair ribbons, wrapping paper and jewelry."

"I thought the same thing," Ava admitted. "But that's only a small part of her store's offerings. She's also considering Becca's Bargains, Becca's Bazaar, Becca's Beachside Bonnets ..."

"I see what you mean. What about Becca's Browse and Buy?" he tossed out off the top of his head, assuming Ava would laugh.

"You know," she repeated the name silently a few times. "That's not bad. I'll have to run it by her. Thank you."

"My pleasure." Finn cupped her face and kissed her, his lips teasing, molding, sipping on hers until she groaned and opened for him. It would be so easy to allow his thought processes to scatter, but before letting that happen, he slowly released her mouth.

"Where are you going?" Ava purred. "My meeting isn't for an hour."

Finn folded his hands into fists to keep from diving beneath her robe to where he knew there was nothing but soft, silky skin. "I'm supposed to meet Killian in fifteen minutes," he murmured. "And you're making it very hard—"

"I can feel that," she giggled, scrambling out of his lap. "Guess you'd better go."

"Watch it, pretty lady," he tugged her against him, "you play with fire …"

"Promises, promises." She kissed him again. "Do you think he has news?"

"I hope so."

He'd taken two steps toward the door but, with what had happened the last time she'd gone to the pier fresh in his mind, took her hand again. "Be careful today, love. I don't want …"

Ava fisted a hand in his jacket and went up on her toes to kiss him. "I'll be careful if you will."

"You know me, love," he winked and opened the door, "I'm like a cat who has nine lives."

She blew him a kiss, but as he shut the door, he thought he heard her murmur, "But how many of those have you used?"

The number five ran through his head as he made his way across the grounds of the Inn toward his car. Just as had been the case a few other times, the sense of being watched was strong. Slowly, he stopped and glanced around, but when he didn't see anyone who didn't belong continued walking. He arrived at the parking lot to find he'd unwittingly parked next to Ava's ex-husband.

"You're Peter Foster, right?" When the other man looked up, Finn was surprised to see a wary look on his face.

"I am." Peter's blue eyes met Finn's dark ones. "And you are?"

"Forgive me." Finn rounded his car and held out his hand. "I'm Finn Reade, Killian's father. I thought since our children are engaged …"

Peter's demeanor completely changed, his body relaxed and his smile grew. "I'm sorry. It's nice to meet you. Emma told me you were in town."

"For a few weeks now," Finn confirmed. "Will you be here for the holidays?"

When Peter grinned and said Emma had invited him and his wife, Finn made a mental note to talk to Ava. With any luck, they would be …. But until he could take care of the mysterious notes, his thoughts and wishes were on hold.

"It was nice meeting you. Now, I'm off to an appointment with Killian. Have a good day."

Finn waved and as he drove away from the Inn refocused on what Killian could have found. Odds were someone connected to Sutton had found out he was the Shadow Angel and was now expecting him to hand over something.

While the picture of Poppies made one think that was the prize, it made no sense. Especially since the recovery notice had appeared in the newspaper.

What about the silver?

Did Alistair know he'd been the Shadow Angel?

He couldn't answer that, but since Quinn had connected Sutton to his father, it remained a possibility.

He found Killian at his desk, on the phone, wearing a worried expression.

"I'll ask around, Sally," he was saying. "I'm sure he's alright. You know that age."

"What's going on?" Finn asked as soon as Killian hung up. "You look worried."

Several expressions crossed Killian's face. "Hayden didn't show up for work this morning."

"He's what? Twenty. Probably overslept."

"He lives above Sally's, and she checked."

"Oh," Finn shook his head. "I'm beginning to get the picture. He stayed over somewhere and ..."

"That's what I suggested," Killian admitted. "But Sally believes he would have answered his phone."

"Do you need to go look for him?"

"No." Killian took out a folder and pulled out a couple of sheets of paper. "I'm sure it's nothing. I wanted to show you this."

"Alright." Finn sat and leaned on the desk to study Killian's notes. "You talked to someone in Scotland Yard, right?"

"Aye. My Captain from the NYPD knows someone, so I called in a favor."

"And you didn't have to say why?"

Killian's brow went up. "Did I tell them I was looking into the Shadow Angel cases? No."

Finn relaxed slightly, even though he knew he could trust his son, and went back to studying the notes.

"Remy's case is still open?"

"Aye." Killian pointed to a note he'd scribbled at the bottom of a page. "Read that."

Figure caught on a security camera running from the tube station. An oversized coat and hat shielded the individual's face. About 5'6" to 5'8".

"But they never found the guy?" Finn shrugged. "How does that help?"

"I'm getting there," Killian assured him. "You found mention of Hudson connected to a Matilda Newman, right?"

"Yes. In 2015. Fall, I think. Why?"

"Because," Killian placed another page where Finn could read it, "look."

Newman's neighbor's security camera recorded a figure jumping the fence at 2:00 a.m. the night they stole a gold necklace. The individual wore black clothing and a stocking cap covered their face. It was too far to guess at their height, but from the back as the person ran away, the investigator wrote-—a woman?

"A woman?" That spark ignited inside Finn. The one that had always told him he was getting close to answers. "Did you find out why they thought it was a woman?"

"Said they thought the person was too curvy to be a male."

"Are you thinking Hudson is a woman?"

"Aye." Killian tapped a few keys on his laptop and flipped it around. "Since the most obvious answer is it's someone connected to Sutton, I've been looking into his family. Ella was from the states and moved back with the kids when she left London. I've wondered ..." Then his phone buzzed.

The photo was old, at least ten years, which meant the children had changed. But as Finn studied the photo, he noticed there was something familiar about several of the people in the picture. The eyes of one child, the mouth of another, and the smile of the wife. He'd seen them before.

"Alright, Liam. I'll check," Killian was saying. "Thanks." As soon as he hung up, he took the computer back.

"What is it, Killian?"

"Liam said the fire investigator found a print on some of the debris from one of the fires. I'm going to see if they have an identity."

"What's the possibility of that?"

"I don't ... bloody hell." He turned the computer so Finn could see who the print belonged to.

"I'm going to kill her," Finn muttered, the pieces clicking into place.

❧

The Pier
November 16
10:30 a.m.

Ava left Becca taking measurements of her new space and stepped outside to answer her phone. "Emma? Is everything alright?"

"Mom," Emma exclaimed breathlessly. "You're on the pier, right?"

Ava glanced around, assuming Emma had to be close by, but didn't see her. "I am. But how did you know?"

Emma giggled, a relaxed sound making Ava wonder if she'd put the argument with Jack out of her mind. "Swan Harbor's gossip line. There are no secrets."

I wouldn't be so sure about that, Ava wanted to say, but opted for, "I see. What's going on?"

"I need a favor."

"Sure, honey," Ava quickly agreed. "What is it?"

"I need you to rescue dad."

"What!?" Ava swallowed hard, and an uneasy feeling settled in her stomach. "Did you say I need to rescue your father?"

"Yes!" Emma exclaimed. "He still has groupies and ..."

It had been almost thirty years since Peter had last starred in a movie, and fans still chasing him hadn't been something she'd considered.

"What do you expect me to do about that?" Ava bit her tongue when she heard the sharp manner in which her question came out.

"Mom." The tone of Emma's voice told her to prepare for some tough questions. "When you told me you were worried about my seeing dad, you never mentioned how you felt about seeing him again."

Ava could admit to herself Peter's treatment of her had affected how she'd always viewed dating. It had been one reason she'd gone on only a few dates in the past ten years and had never dated the same man more than twice.

"Mom?" Emma tried again. "You told me dad's treatment of you left bruises. Have those healed?"

"I," Ava let the word hang, while she searched inside to see how she felt. A lot had happened since she'd come to Swan Harbor to check on Emma. And a lot had happened since she'd seen Peter when he'd been checking in. Finn had told her he loved her ... and she'd told him the same. Since then, they'd spent every night together.

"Of course, they've healed," she assured Emma. "What do I need to do?"

But as she turned the corner and saw a rather large group of women congregated outside Les Patisserie, she had to wonder if she was ready for this.

"Anita," Ava grabbed her friend by the elbow and separated her from the others. "Do I even want to know?"

"It's Dax Blue," Anita squealed, her voice more animated than Ava had ever seen. "We're hoping for an autograph."

Ava wanted to snark about his autograph being worthless, but she wasn't the same person she'd been before Finn.

"Ladies," Ava sighed, "I'm aware he played Dax Blue approximately thirty years ago. Today, though, he's Peter Foster, Emma's father."

Several pairs of eyes stared at her, daring her to usurp their position in front of the window.

"We saw him at Emma's clinic the other day," Anita confessed. "He was quite charming."

"Why didn't you ask for an autograph then?"

"Because," the woman Ava now knew was Heidi replied, "Emma shooed us away before we thought of it."

"She's right," Anita nodded. "We were too busy staring."

"He is pretty dreamy," Paula murmured. "Look at how that lock of hair falls across his forehead."

"How about this?" Ava posed, pulling from her years of experience in getting others to follow her directive. "Why don't I talk to him about those autographs, and then we'll see ..."

Paula gave her a disgruntled look. "Well, okay. But I'm only leaving because I have a fondness for Killian."

"Understood." Ava made a mental note to tell Killian to make an extra stop at the pastry shop.

"Now, if you ladies will excuse me?" Ava waded into the group and peered through the window. Peter was sitting at a table with his back to her. She took a deep breath and opened the door.

He was sitting on the far side of the room and for a split second, a sliver of sympathy ran through her.

Whoa, Ava, where did that come from?

When they'd been married, Peter had adored the limelight, but he was no longer in the business. And after making a special trip to Swan Harbor to see his daughter, he was hiding.

"Emma sent me to rescue you." She slid into a chair across the table from him.

Peter's blue eyes met hers and in them she saw surprise, followed by wariness. "Come again?"

"Emma asked me to rescue you," she repeated.

He glanced over his shoulder, but Ava knew the women had dispersed, temporarily at least. "I'm surprised you don't want to throw me to the wolves."

Ava chuckled. "At one time, that would have been my goal." She shrugged and settled back in her chair. "But Emma and I had a wonderful talk, and she's in a good place. As am I."

Peter grinned, and the smile reminded her of the man she'd loved when she was twenty-two. "Emma has turned into a beautiful, caring adult, no thanks to us."

"She has," Ava agreed. "And she's carving out a place in this town just like her grandparents did."

"Your mother was from Swan Harbor?"

"Yes." Ava took a breath and stepped out on a limb she'd never expected to inhabit. "My father destroyed my grandparents, just like he did you."

Peter studied her carefully, making Ava fight to sit still. "You're not the same woman you were when Leo died."

"Isn't that a good thing?"

"We've both changed," he murmured. "I was a real dick to you, Ava. I'm sorry."

"Wow," Ava retorted. "The great Peter Foster knows how to say he's sorry."

A ruddy hue dotted his high cheekbones. "There wasn't much great about that man. Except his ego. And it was great … big."

"Yes, it was," she agreed. "But the young girl who chased you with a single-minded goal had her own issues. Let's be happy we aren't those people any longer, and talk about our beautiful daughter."

He grinned. "I'd like that. And to know what you said to get rid of the women who were waiting to pounce."

"Oh, that was easy," Ava laughed. "I just promised them autographs."

"You what?" he choked out.

"Promised them autographs," Ava echoed.

Peter sent her a side-eyed glance. "You didn't?"

"I did."

"But," he sputtered. "I don't carry pictures of myself any longer."

"Oh, don't worry about it." Ava waved her hand as if it was no big deal. "I can ask Emma to print a few for you. Or you can just sign whatever they bring."

He squinted at her. "You're yanking my chain, aren't you?"

"Maybe," she chuckled. "I'm sorry. But I did promise autographs, so we'll need to figure out something. In the meantime, tell me about your new wife. What's her name?"

"Amber." Peter smiled, and his features completely transformed.

He's smitten, Ava thought. Just like she was with Finn. And suddenly, she couldn't wait to talk to Emma. She was ready for everyone to know.

Camelot Arms Apartments
November 16
11:15 a.m.

KILLIAN WAS THIRTY MINUTES BEHIND HIS FATHER, BUT HE HAD one thing Finn was missing ... the apartment number. However, the years as the Shadow Angel had given him an uncanny ability to find the right information at the most opportune time. Which was the reason he was still worried.

"Bloody hell," Killian grumbled, running up the stairs to the third floor. "I shouldn't have shown him that picture."

"True," Liam agreed. "You should have known he'd be pissed. Did you forget Ava was hurt in that fire?"

"But to threaten to kill ..." Killian shook his head, "I just ..."

"Remember when he was all up in arms about Santora being after us?" Liam asked.

Killian hummed, recalling that uncomfortable phone call. "But he didn't threaten to kill him."

"Oh yes he did," Liam corrected. "He told me 'no one messes with what's his. If they did, he'd 'have to kill them'."

"Great, just what I didn't need to hear." Killian stopped at the top of the third floor and glanced at the directory. "This way."

"What are you going to do when we get there?" Liam tossed out the question he'd been asking himself. "Arrest dad?"

"I don't know, Liam," he admitted. "I won't allow dad to kill anyone, but—"

"—You can relate to what he's feeling?"

"Aye. I'd want to kill too, if Emma had been hurt."

"And I feel the same way about Elsa," Liam pointed out. "Let's just hope it doesn't come to that."

"Agree." Killian stopped and glanced around the corner where he could see his father in front of a door. "He's still standing outside."

"That's good, right?" Liam offered. "Maybe he's having second thoughts.

"Maybe," Killian grumbled. "Except ... bloody hell!" He took off running, knowing the element of surprise had just disappeared. "Dad, stop."

Finn glanced over his shoulder. "What are you going to do, Killian? Shoot me?"

"Of course not! But you just broke into that apartment," Killian exclaimed. "I want nothing to get in the way of a clean arrest."

"Put yourself in my shoes," Finn demanded. "She started fires on the ship, hurt Ava, and is trying to destroy my life by bringing my past back. How much more am I expected to endure before I ..." He took a couple of deep breaths. "Do what you must. But I'm not leaving until it's over."

Killian watched his father storm into the apartment and exchanged looks with Liam. "What the bloody hell do I do now?"

Liam hitched the pack he was carrying a little higher on his shoulder. "He's going to do what he needs to do. I say we help him."

"I was afraid you were going to say that," Killian grumbled, pushing the door farther open. "After you."

"Why thank you," Liam quipped. "So nice of you to hold the door for me."

"Wanker." Killian shut the door behind them. And while they waited, he needed to figure out how he was going to explain everything to Dylan.

TWENTY-NINE

Camelot Arms Apartments
November 16
12:30 p.m.

Finn sat in a rocking chair facing the door of an apartment, sparsely furnished with an old sofa, a table, and two chairs. They'd found paper that matched the notes he'd received, a computer, and a printer. Killian's bedroom discoveries meant his presence wasn't actually required. But yet ... he waited.

When he'd recognized her picture, anger had rolled through him, and he'd wanted to kill her. But since arriving at her apartment, his emotions had changed. There'd been frustration she wasn't home, sorrow she'd thrown her life away, and, most of all, confusion. Which was why he hadn't left. The need to know the answers had surpassed all his other feelings.

Someone jiggled the doorknob just before the lock clicked, and then opened the door. The woman he'd been waiting for stepped inside, keys in one hand and a lunch bag from Sally's in the other.

"Wh-What are you doing in my apartment?" She shut the door behind her.

"I think you know," Finn told her, his voice coming across much lower and more dangerous sounding than he'd expected.

She sent him a look that if it could kill, he would have been dead. "Why don't you enlighten me?"

Her eyes darted toward the hall before returning to him. The almost panicked look in them told Finn all he needed to know. That one of his boys had stepped out of the bedroom and she was beginning to understand she was screwed.

"Yes," he confirmed her unspoken question. "We found your '*guests.*' And what a story those young men have to tell."

"They were foolish," she retorted, her bravado still fully in place.

"Were they?" Finn mused. "Or was it you who was the foolish one ... Peyton? Or would you rather I call you Hudson?"

"What did you call me?" Peyton dropped onto the sofa, holding the Sally's bag as a shield.

"You heard me correctly," Finn continued to push, hoping she'd give in and give him the answers he wanted. "I called you Hudson. Where did that come from, anyway?"

She sat there for several minutes, gnawing on her bottom, most likely contemplating her situation.

"Learn anything, Dad?" Killian set one of the kitchen chairs close to where he was sitting.

"No. We were just getting acquainted," Finn explained. "How are Hayden and Owen?"

"Liam said they'll be fine," Killian shared, just before returning his attention to Peyton, "but you have some explaining to do."

"Shall I tell you what I know?" Finn offered. When she didn't say anything one way or the other, he settled into his chair for story time. "Be sure and correct me if I get anything wrong."

"This should be good." Peyton crossed one leg over the other as if she were bored. "Have at it."

"You were the 'baby' Ella wanted to say goodnight to, the night the Shadow Angel took Poppies to return to the Queen," Finn began his tale. "And, for a few years anyway, everything was fine. But then, your father was being investigated for fraud, and found out the painting he had was a copy. How am I doing so far?"

"That's right," she snapped. "We were a happy family until the investigation and discovery, and then everything changed."

"Daddy wasn't so fun then?" Finn questioned.

"No! His entire focus was on finding out who took the painting. And once he heard it was the Shadow Angel, that was his focus. He wanted to destroy you."

"Of that, I have no doubt," Finn acknowledged. "And because you wanted his attention, you became his very own finder, Hudson. Where did that come from, anyway?"

She sat there for several minutes, and he wasn't sure if she was going to answer, but then she gave a noncommittal shrug. "My mom grew up close to the Hudson, so ..."

And generic enough she could hide behind. "Did he even know it was you he was corresponding with? Or did you keep your identity a secret, thinking once you found out who the Shadow Angel was, you'd tell him? But that proved to be a little more difficult than you expected, didn't it? Remy refused to give you a name, so you shot him."

The blood drained from her face, and she readjusted on the sofa. "I didn't mean to shoot him! But all he had to do was give me a name."

"And when he didn't, you put six bullets into him," Finn barked. "How is that not meaning to shoot him?"

"He just made me so mad," Peyton replied. "Then he laughed at me, and I—"

"—Pulled the trigger," Finn answered, his heart twisting at the thought that he'd been right. Remy had died protecting his identity.

She stood and out of the corner of his eye, Finn noticed Killian sat a little straighter, his hand resting on the top of his weapon.

"You need to understand," she cried, pacing back and forth in the small space. "My father was *obsessed* with finding you. But I needed him to pay attention to *me*. To care about *me*."

"And it didn't matter what you did," Finn guessed. "Sutton couldn't care less, because you were a girl. So, you became Hudson ... a male who could help daddy find his perceived nemesis."

"And it was working too," she practically gloated. "As Hudson, I could get him whatever he wanted. And as his daughter, I could talk to him about it. And then—"

"—Sutton connected with Alistair Jones. And all on his own found out who the Shadow Angel was, and about a treasure."

"Yes!" she practically spit.

"Did you regroup right then?" he asked curiously. "Or did that happen after they arrested Alistair?"

"Oh, it was before," she boasted. "Returned to the states and sent Owen to get a job with you, and I moved to sleepy Swan Harbor."

"Because of the silver?"

"No," she grumbled. "I was going to seduce Killian."

"Me?" Killian practically choked on the word.

"Yes, but you only had eyes for Emma, so—"

"—You went after Hayden?" Killian asked. "Why?"

"Because you'd taken an interest in him and—"

"—You saw him as a means to an end," Killian retorted disgustedly.

Peyton shrugged. "Whatever."

"And what about Owen?" Finn questioned, kicking himself for allowing that one to get by him.

"Oh, he didn't want to do it," Peyton admitted. "He didn't even know what the notes said."

"So, it was you who broke into my home?" Finn guessed. "What were you looking for?"

"Something to destroy you," Peyton surprised him by saying.

"You didn't know about the silver, did you?"

She dropped back down on the sofa, pulled out a sandwich from the Sally's bag, and took a bite, making him wait before answering, "Not right then."

"And Owen? He's your brother. How could you hit him over the head and keep him tied up like you did?"

"He developed a conscious," she complained. "I overheard a conversation between Professor Jones and his brother and realized who they were."

"Killian and Liam's cousins?"

Peyton looked up quickly. "What did you say?"

"You didn't know?" Finn exchanged looks with Killian. "So, you found out they were Alistair's sons?"

"Yes. A lot of good that did, as they had no clue where the silver was located."

Finn closed his hands into fists. "You set the fire, so you could search the ship?"

Peyton's eyes locked with his. "No one was supposed to be there. Why do you think I got a job at the restaurant? Jack never came to work that early, but ..."

"—That morning, Jack, Aiden, Quinn, and Ava were there. Is that when Owen developed a conscious?"

"He was on his way to tell you," she grumbled. "I had to do something."

"Well, guess what?" Finn taunted. "You didn't do your homework, as there isn't any silver."

"What?" She jumped up. "Why would Alistair tell my dad there was a treasure, if there wasn't?"

"Wishful thinking," suggested Finn.

"You'll have a lot of time to think about it where you're going," Killian added.

But Finn had been watching Peyton, and as soon as Killian stood, she was ready. Peyton threw open the door, and Finn took off after her.

He owed her for Remy, Ava, his property, and so much more.

She was fast, and on her way to her car before Finn was halfway down the stairs.

"This is Swan Harbor, Peyton," Finn cried. "Give yourself up."

"Forget it."

He heard her click the locks on her car and, just as she slammed the door, Finn dove for the handle.

"Bloody hell," he yelled when she started the car.

"Dad, watch out," Killian shouted.

Finn took his eyes off her for a split second, but it was enough for her to gun the engine and take off. He backpedaled to get out of her way and tripped, hitting his head.

"Dad!" Killian yelled. "Are you alright?"

"She got away!" Finn slowly pushed up to a sitting position.

Killian studied him with concerned eyes. "Don't worry. She won't get far."

"You're sure?"

"This is Swan Harbor, Dad. My guess is the gossip line is tracking her as we speak."

"But how—?"

"After we found Hayden and Owen, I called it in. In fact," he hesitated as two ambulances drove into the complex. "Here's their ride now. Do you need Liam to look at you?"

Finn glanced at his hands, and while they were a little skinned, with a little water, they'd be fine. It was the body aches he was already anticipating, making getting out of bed a chore.

But if Ava's beside you ....

"Thank you for coming after me, Killian." Finn ducked his head, slightly embarrassed by his behavior.

"We're family, Dad," Killian replied. "You don't need to thank me."

"Well, I appreciate it." Finn smiled. "If you need anything, just let me know."

"I'll do that. But right now, the only thing I need is for you to let Ava know you're alright."

"Gossip line?"

"Bloody hell, no," Killian grumbled. "Emma. Do you have any idea how many texts she's sent?"

"Sorry about that, I–"

"Go, dad." Killian pulled out his phone to where Finn could hear the constant pings.

"I'm going."

He climbed into the car, and on the way to the Inn begin to rehearse the words he wanted to say ...

The Lighthouse Inn
November 16
2:30 p.m.

AVA WAS OUT OF HER CHAIR AND RUNNING TO THE DOOR BEFORE IT was completely opened. When Finn stepped inside, and their eyes met, she froze. His clothes were dusty and there was a smudge of something on his forehead.

"Are you okay?" she asked him quietly, needing it to be so.

Finn hesitated, and her heart slowed, breaking a little at a time. Then, his mouth curled, his eyes glittered, and her heart took off. Finn took the steps necessary to reach her and pulled her against his warm body, and all was right with her world.

He brushed his hands ran up and down her back and buried his face in her neck. The sound of his breathing, the feel of his heart beating under her ear, and his musky smell.

She wasn't sure how long they stood there, saying nothing, surrounded only by the soft music she'd turned on earlier. He stepped back just enough to cup her face, and as she stared into his eyes, there were so many things she wanted to say. But somehow, she knew, he was reading them … just as she was reading what was in his.

It was over.

The future was theirs.

"I love you," they whispered simultaneously.

Ava's eyes pooled and spilled over, and when Finn swept the tears away with his thumbs, her heart flipped several times.

"Don't cry, love." His lips skimmed across her cheekbone. "I'm alright." He dropped a kiss on her other cheek. "It's all over." Then his lips settled on hers, and she forgot to breathe.

There were so many questions she wanted to ask, but the longer his mouth caressed hers, they ceased to matter. Her heart raced, and everywhere they touched the nerve endings sparked, and all she could do was feel.

His fingers dug into her shoulders and slid down her back, pressing her softness against his much harder body. He groaned and lifted his mouth, and the gentle puffs of his breath had her dragging her eyes open.

She needed more, and undid his coat, pushing it off his shoulders. Before it hit the floor, she'd lifted his sweater and slid her hands underneath, to rest on his smooth skin.

A little shiver went through him, and she couldn't resist leaning in for another kiss. His lips plundered, and she had no choice but to hold on and follow his lead.

"Ava," he tore his mouth away and picked her up, "I need you."

"I'm here." She carded her fingers through his hair and tugged his mouth closer.

When his lips covered hers, it made her dizzy as he carried her across the threshold into the bedroom. There was a hush in the air, surrounding them, enclosing them in their own little world.

Until … someone knocked on the door.

"Bloody hell, who's that?" Finn barked.

"Ignore it," she murmured, latching onto a soft spot beneath his ear.

"Alright." He angled his head, giving her better access.

Then the person knocked again.

Finn let go of her legs and kissed her once more, this one swift, but hot. "I'll get rid of them."

"Okay," she murmured, her lips still tingling. "Hurry."

He winked and left the room, and with him gone, it still took several heartbeats before she'd gathered her wits. She'd just grabbed the comforter when she heard him greet the newcomer.

"Emma."

Ava heard the surprise in Finn's voice, and curiosity had her stepping closer to the door to listen.

"I hope I didn't interrupt anything," Emma was saying.

"I was just going to hang up my coat and shower off my encounter with Peyton," Finn replied, reminding Ava she still needed to know what happened.

"I won't be long," Emma went on. "But I wanted to tell you, I know."

"You know?" Finn repeated, and Ava could hear the hesitation in his voice.

"About you and my mom," Emma clarified.

"What is it you know about us?"

He was protecting her, Ava realized. Because even though he'd admitted his feelings to his sons, she'd hadn't told Emma. But her thoughts, when she'd been talking to Peter, propelled her forward.

Ava stepped from the bedroom to see Finn standing next to the door holding his coat.. When their eyes met, he smiled, and the look in his eyes he kept banked when they were with family appeared. It said, *I love you, and I want the world to know.* Whenever that look showed up, it made her feel cherished.

"Mom!" Emma exclaimed. "I was just ..."

Ava smiled at her daughter. "I'm glad you're here, honey. I was hoping to talk to you."

Emma side-eyed her. "Did everything go okay with dad?"

"It was fine." Ava brushed it off. "But I sort of promised autographs to a few of his fans. Maybe you can help him with pictures."

"Okay." Emma stretched out the word. "If not dad, then what did you need me for?"

Ava glanced at Finn, and his look said, *This is your show. I'll just follow your lead.*

"I, I heard what you said. That you know about Finn and me."

He slipped his arm around her, making her fight not to sag against him. She could do this—but somehow it felt like another teen moment.

"I'm sorry I didn't tell you we were seeing each other but ..."

A smile flitted across Emma's face, and Ava couldn't decide if that was a good thing or ....

"Mom." Emma laughed, and Ava's knees almost gave out with relief. "It would have been nice to be in the loop, but I understand."

"You do?"

"Yes." Emma giggled. "But I have to say, you two have fooled no one."

Ava exchanged looks with Finn. "What do you mean?"

Emma arched a brow. "The gossip line has been busy talking about you two."

"Bloody hell." Finn stepped away from them to hang up his coat.

"Don't worry," Emma murmured. "It just means the town has accepted you."

Ava smiled, and a warm feeling bloomed inside. "I'm glad."

"Me too." Emma glanced out the window and turned to go. "I'll leave you two alone. But watch the weather. We're expecting snow."

Ava held the door and as Emma stepped out, she hugged her and whispered, "I'm glad you found your Flynn Ryder."

"Me too," Ava murmured. "Me too."

As soon as she shut the door, Finn was there waiting for her to step into his arms. "I've got you."

The happiness inside kept growing, and a part of her kept thinking it should be illegal to be so happy. "Are you ready to fill me in?"

Finn gave a long-suffering sigh. "I guess."

"Talk fast. Then we can ..." She wiggled her eyebrows comically.

"Promises, promises ...."

"Try me."

"Oh, I intend to," he warned.

Ava shivered with anticipation and tucked herself into a corner of the sofa, ready for whatever he had to say.

The Lighthouse Inn

November 16
3:30 p.m.

Finn had given Ava a rundown of everything he'd learned from Killian, as well as the parts he'd surmised, and what had happened with Peyton. But with nothing holding them back, he was nervous. Worried they weren't on the same page.

No games, remember?

"So," he began with the toughest subject. "You saw Peter today?"

"Emma asked me to *rescue* him." She rolled her eyes. "I couldn't believe these grown women were standing outside the restaurant, ogling him through the window."

"You were alright ... talking with him?"

"Peter loves his wife and," she hesitated, and her voice softened, "I love you."

"That's very good to know. In fact, hold on ..."

Finn left her on the sofa and went to get the box he'd hidden in a drawer. Once he had it, he felt like an awkward teen and not a fifty-six-year-old man.

When he returned to the living room, he found her staring out the window. "Do you think we should make a quick trip to the store?"

"That depends." Finn led her to the sofa and sat on a table in front of her.

"What does it depend on, Finn?"

He answered her with a kiss, then touched each of her charms. The mother and child, carousel, carriage, tower, and puppy. "You said this was our journey."

"It is," she dimpled. "But several things have happened since we found Paris."

"They have." He opened the box and took out a small charm. "I love you Ava King. And I know it's only been a little over two weeks since we've been together. But I want a future with you."

"I want that too."

He laid the silver charm of a groom holding his bride in his arms on her palm. "Then ... will you marry me?"

"On one condition."

"Only one?"

"I don't want a big wedding like last time."

Finn couldn't keep his smile from spreading, and his heart from racing at what he was going to ask next. "Would you be interested in stealing away with me before we get snowed in?"

"To get married?"

"I feel like I've been waiting to love you my entire life, and now that we're together, I don't want to wait. Plus," Finn clipped the charm onto her bracelet. "I don't want to take anything away from the kids' weddings."

"Will the kids be mad?"

"They'll be happy for us," he replied, knowing he was right. "But ... it's snowing, so ... I need an answer."

"Pushy, aren't you?" She launched herself into his arms, knocking them both onto the floor. "Yes! I'll marry you!"

"Really?" Finn rolled her under him and kissed the tip of her nose. "Good. Let's celebrate."

"I thought we had to go."

"We will," he promised. "Just as soon as we seal this deal with a kiss."

As his lips touched hers, it had never felt more right.

THIRTY

Ava's Cottage
Thanksgiving
10:00 a.m.

Emma stood patiently, waiting to see what Patty was going to set in front of her. She'd given Jack onions to dice, Elsa chestnuts to peel and dice, and Lilly apples to cut.

"Here you go." Patty dumped a loaf of bread on the table. "Cut these in 3/4" cubes. Got it?"

"Got it." Emma exchanged glances with Elsa, who'd had a smile on her face all day. Some of it, she was sure, had to do with her wedding day quickly approaching, but the rest had to do with Patty. Somehow the memory of how to prepare a traditional Thanksgiving Day dinner had floated to the surface, and she'd bossed anyone around who dared argue.

For Emma, the day was proving to be one of those long-ago dreams she'd never imagined could come true. But it had ....

What a difference a year made, she couldn't help but think. She was engaged, friends with both of her parents, her best friend had moved to Swan Harbor, and her family had expanded.

Jack glanced up and winked. There were tears running down his face, but whether that was from the onions or happiness, she wasn't sure.

"Today's a day of thanks," he told her quietly. "I won't bring up freeing Jonesy."

"You know my thoughts on that, Jack," Emma reminded him. "We wait until spring ... or—"

"—Find a place where the water is warm, and he can have protection from the elements," Jack repeated the very words she'd uttered to him since the discovery of the journal.

"I'm glad you've been listening."

He gave her a pointed look. "I've been listening, but I'm stubborn."

"So, that's where that trait came from," Killian quipped. "I wasn't sure."

"She gets it from both sides," Amber, her father's wife, spoke up. "Peter has his moments."

Everyone laughed, and again that feeling of contentment washed over her. That lost girl had come a long way.

"Wait!" Patty scolded her, picking up one of the bread cubes. "I said 3/4". Those aren't big enough."

"Sorry," Emma mumbled, meeting Elsa's smirk. "I'll try to do better."

"That's a good girl."

"What time are Finn and Ava arriving again?" Elsa asked.

"2:00 p.m." Emma thought back on her last conversation with her mother. "Something is going on with them."

"Well, duh," Elsa giggled. "Where are they again?"

"Supposedly New York. One of the businesses mom backed had its grand opening. Connie's Cupcakes, I believe."

"You don't think Connie's Cupcakes is having its grand opening?"

"I don't believe mom needed to be there so long," Emma retorted.

"They wanted to be alone," Elsa grinned. "I think it's romantic. You're not still worried, are you?"

"No," Emma denied. "It just seems fast."

"When their hearts spoke, they listened," Jack murmured. But instead of saying anything else, he scooped the onions he'd chopped into a bowl, and then carried them to where Patty was making the stuffing.

"And Swan Harbor has a way of making you listen to your heart," Elsa pointed out.

"Yes, it does." Emma flexed her fingers, causing the diamond in her engagement ring to flash. Which reminded her she really needed to tell Killian what date they were getting married.

"Have you told him?" Elsa read her mind.

"I was just thinking about that," Emma admitted. "If the opportunity arises, I'll tell him today."

As if he'd heard her, Killian looked up, and their eyes locked. He raised that damn brow of his, and she had to fight the need to run into his arms. That periodic unsettled feeling was back again, causing her stomach to twist.

"I love you." Killian blew her a kiss.

She forced the feeling away and focused on the conversation going on around her. It was her first holiday with a large group of family members, and she was determined to enjoy it.

Ava's Cottage
Thanksgiving
2:00 p.m.

FINN PUT THE CAR INTO PARK AND LOOKED AT HIS BRIDE. SHE WAS sitting quietly, the scarf he'd wrapped around her eyes before they'd left the hotel still firmly in place.

"Are you ready?" he asked, kissing her fingertips.

"We're here?"

"We are."

"And no hints?"

"No. Hold on." When he stepped out and saw all the cars parked in his drive, he had to blink to clear his vision. Winnie's words had been playing in his head often lately. It had taken him a while, but he couldn't help but think he'd finally found the happy beginning that had been waiting for him. And through those doors was his family.

"Watch your head."

"Hold on to me."

"Forever and always," he promised, leading her toward the door.

She tilted her head. "Where are we? Something smells delicious."

Finn kissed her and slowly removed the scarf. "Welcome home, love."

He opened the door, and when they walked inside, the joy on Ava's face was worth the extra money he'd paid to have a few of the re-decorations completed.

"You did this?"

"How could I have done it?" he whispered. "I was with you."

"Oh, you," she exclaimed, turning to greet Emma.

"Welcome back to Swan Harbor, Son." Jack shook his hand and pulled him aside. "I see you took my advice and fought for her."

"It wasn't that difficult of a decision," Finn replied. "Did I miss anything while I was gone?"

"Snow." Jack's eyes twinkled. "And the opportunity to toss a few bucks into the pool regarding your time away."

"What!?" Finn laughed. "A pool?"

"Yes." Jack nodded. "Last I checked, the squares were all taken."

"Do I want to know?"

"Probably not," Jack snickered. "I'll let you catch up with your boys."

"What was that all about?" Killian asked, when Jack walked away.

"I was going to ask you the same thing." Finn looked from Killian to Liam. "Do you know anything about a pool?"

"It wasn't my idea." Killian immediately tossed the blame. "Ask Liam."

"Bloody hell, Liam," Finn snapped. "What did you do?"

"Now, it's nothing bad," Liam defended himself. "I was just speculating one day, when I'd stopped at Sally's and well ..."

"It grew from there," Finn guessed.

"Yeah," Liam admitted. "But if I win, it will come in handy for our honeymoon."

"And if I win," Killian added. "I will go toward our new home, or our wedding."

"Do I want to see this pool?" Finn glanced between his boys.

Liam exchanged a look with Killian, and when all he got was a shrug, handed his father the piece of paper. "You don't get a vote, though. Besides, the dates have all booked."

Finn glanced across the room to where Jack was showing Ava a plate. The smile on her face had his heart rolling around in his chest, and only the matching smirks on his sons' faces had him unfolding the paper.

On the top of the page, the word Engaged was written in black ink, and

Married in blue ink. Numbered squares lined the page, starting with the sixteenth and ending with the current date. A line divided each square in half. And each had a blue name and a black name written inside.

"You're betting on whether Ava or I got engaged or married while we were gone?" Finn realized how right Emma had been when she'd said they had fooled no one.

Liam shrugged. "The pool wasn't my idea. Blame Sally for that. But you must admit, it was a good one."

Finn shook his head, his matchmaker son's abilities never ceasing to amaze him.

"So, Dad," Liam took the list back from him, "who won?"

"It would serve all you busybodies right if no one had won," Finn retorted.

"But?" Liam continued to prod.

They'd planned on waiting until everyone was seated for dinner to share the news, but Finn didn't think he wanted to wait any longer, to claim Ava as his wife.

"Stay tuned." He headed across the room to where she was still talking to Jack.

"Finn." Ava took his hand as if it were the most natural thing in the world. "Jack's been telling me the china belonged to my grandmother."

"Beautiful," he murmured, never taking his eyes off her.

"Oh, you." She bumped him playfully with her shoulder.

He laughed ... happy she was so predictable. And charmed ... she got embarrassed when he called her beautiful.

"Do you need something?"

"You." Finn kissed her hand. "I want to make our announcement. Do you mind?"

"I'd like that."

"Good." He snagged one of the crystal glasses from the table and tapped a spoon against it. "Can I have your attention, please?"

The room suddenly silenced, and Finn glanced down at Ava to see a slight wariness mixed with happiness on her face.

"Come on, Dad," Liam called. "Tell us who won."

Ava frowned. "Who won what?"

"There was a betting pool going around while we were gone," he explained. "On if we were getting engaged or married and when."

"Really?"

"Yes." Liam slipped his arm around Elsa. "My winnings will help on our honeymoon."

"While someone might win the money," Finn slipped Ava's wedding band from his pocket, "it was I who won the prize." He slid it onto her finger. "We were married on the twentieth."

Liam let out a whoop. "And, engaged?"

"The sixteenth," Finn told them.

Jack laughed. "I knew it!"

"How the bloody hell did you know that?" Killian exclaimed.

"Jonesy," Jack shrugged. "When I went to see him on the seventeenth, his feathers were fuller, and he held head a little higher. His hope was strong."

Finn glanced down at Ava's upturned face. "We told them we were married and instead of congratulating us, they're bickering over a prize."

"You said they wouldn't be upset," she pointed out.

"So, I did, Mrs. King-Reade, so I did." Finn tugged her close for a kiss, figuring if their family were busy using their mouths to argue, he'd use his for other, more enjoyable activities.

Ava's Cottage
Thanksgiving
7:00 p.m.

AVA FOLDED HER LEGS UNDER HER AND SIGHED WITH HAPPINESS. Their Thanksgiving meal had been everything she'd hoped for, and more. Lively conversation, good-natured teasing, all tied together with a sense of belonging. She'd not only been in the middle of her family but also of her home.

"You look happy, Mom." Emma handed her a cup of hot chocolate and slipped under the old quilt she'd found when she'd stepped out onto the veranda.

"Very," Ava forced out through a throat thick with emotion. "You aren't too disappointed we didn't wait to get married, are you?"

Emma sipped on her drink, and Ava found she was holding her breath, anticipating what her daughter's response was going to be.

"No, Mom," Emma alleged. "You've waited a long time to find a man to love you like you deserve to be loved. I'm thrilled for you two."

"Good." Ava relaxed farther into the wooden swing. "Finn makes me feel–"

"–Special, cherished ... loved," Emma stated, as if she knew exactly what Ava had been thinking.

"Speaking from experience?"

"Yes."

"But you still haven't told Killian when your wedding is?" Ava shook her head. "What are you waiting for?"

Emma sent her an impish grin. "I've been planning to tell him today. I'm just waiting for the right time."

"Another wedding to plan," Ava smiled. "I like that idea."

Emma sighed, and Ava couldn't help but think her daughter's level of happiness mirrored her own.

"How's Paris and family?" she asked. "Did her owners come and get her?"

"Finn didn't tell you?"

"Tell me what?" Thinking if it were bad news, she'd have to have a talk with him about trying to protect her.

"Paris was lost, because her owner had to go to a nursing home," Emma explained.

Ava's heart hurt at the thought of the sweet dog losing her owner. "What's going to happen to her ... and her puppies?"

"Finn really didn't tell you?"

"No."

"Oops," Emma giggled. "I probably just ruined the surprise."

"What did he do?"

"Adopted her," Emma admitted. "And a puppy, unless he's adopted."

"He got me a dog," Ava replied, the feelings inside impossible to label. "Do you have a new picture? I bet the puppies have grown."

"I knew you were going to say that," Emma laughed, tugging her phone out of her pocket. "I took these this morning."

Ava stared at the puppies, melting a little more at the thought that Finn understood how she'd felt about them. But as she looked at the picture, a box behind them caught her attention.

"Emma, see that box?" She pointed to what she was referring to. "Where did it come from?"

"I thought it was something Killian brought with him when he moved in," Emma told her. "But when he said no, I asked Sadie. She said you carried it inside the day you found Paris."

Ava thought back on the day Finn had pulled her into the cave, known as Lover's Cove, and had a vague recollection of it next to a pile of rocks.

"It was inside the cave," she remembered. "Paris had hidden behind it and a pile of rocks. Almost as if there'd been a cave in."

"There might have been," Emma murmured. "Remember our dynamite scare?"

"You think the box was buried and uncovered when the dynamite exploded?"

"Maybe. But why?"

There were memories trying to connect in her head, because she'd seen that box ... or at least a depiction of the box before.

"Any chance you still have the picture of the journal page?"

Emma studied her for several seconds before reaching for the phone. "Probably. I'm horrible about deleting pictures."

Ava sat on the edge of her seat while Emma searched for it, the feeling she was on to something growing stronger.

"Here." Emma handed her the phone.

A chill worked its way up Ava's spine when she looked at the drawing. "Emma, do you see what I see?" She pointed to the chest drawn by Ian Jones on the journal page. "Doesn't that look like the box I found in the cave?"

Emma slid the pictures back and forth a couple of times. "It does."

"What if Ian wasn't referring to being reunited with Hope, his ship—"

"—But with Hope's words." Emma finished her thought.

"Yes." Ava flipped the blanket off her legs. "Let's go."

Emma glanced over her shoulder into the house where Jack and Peter were arguing American football versus European soccer with the Reade and Jones men. "Shouldn't we ...?"

"Remember what grandmother Rose's letter said," Ava reminded Emma. "'Supposedly, the answer lies within the charms of this bracelet, as it's been in our family for years. But now, it's up to you and yours, my precious granddaughter, to reunite Hope with her lover. Until then, Swan Harbor is living on borrowed hope. Trust Jack. He knows.' It's up to *us*, Emma. Are you with me?"

Emma tossed the blanket aside. "Let's go."

Ava tossed the keys to Emma. "You know your way around better than I do."

Emma's laugh was carefree. "If Finn complains, I'm blaming you."

"I know how to handle him," Ava grinned.

"TMI, mom," Emma scolded.

Ava chuckled, and as they started down the hill, she couldn't help but think about what might have been lost forever, if it weren't for the Reade men... all of them.

With the streets quiet, they made it to the vet in record time. When Ava saw the chest in person, she was more convinced than ever it had belonged to Ian Jones.

"It's locked." Emma fingered the old lock. "And the ring doesn't open it."

"Grandmother Rose said something about the charms on your bracelet. Is there some sort of '*key*' on your bracelet?"

"There's more than '*some sort*' of key," Emma grinned. "I'll be right back."

Ava ran her finger over the wood, and then grabbed a paper clip to dig some of the dirt out of the lock. As she worked, she couldn't stop the little thrill that raced through her. Centuries ago, Hope had fallen in love with Ian and, for reasons unknown, their destiny hadn't been to live happily ever after. But if her happy beginning could play into helping reunite them in some little way, then everything she'd gone through had occurred for a reason.

"Okay." Emma held up a small key attached to her bracelet. "Wish me luck."

"You don't need luck." Ava slipped the key smoothly into the lock. "I know it's a match."

Time had caused the lock to stiffen, and Emma had to stop and squirt it with a lubricant. But then once she slipped the key back into the lock, it turned easily, and the lock popped.

"Help me, mom," Emma whispered, the moment affecting her as strongly as it was Ava. "Rose said it was 'you and yours'."

Ava grasped one side, both pushing the lid up to expose the treasures inside. "We did it." She lifted the book, and an attached leather pouch. "But I think—"

"—We should open it with everyone?"

"Yes. For some reason, that feels important."

"We'll have to interrupt the football argument," Emma laughed.

"Something tells me they'll be okay with that." At least Finn would, she knew, suddenly feeling an urgent need to have him close. She grabbed her phone and sent him a text.

Ava's Cottage
Thanksgiving
9:00 p.m.

WHEN HIS PHONE BUZZED, FINN ASSUMED THE TEXT WAS FROM HIS wife. The message, however, surprised him.

> Ava: On the way back from Emma's. We found Hope's journal. Her words and Ian's will finally be reunited.

"Killian, did you know Ava and Emma left?"

"No," Killian frowned. "Where did they go?"

"Your place," Finn shrugged. "But they're on their way back."

For the next fifteen minutes, he found he couldn't sit still, and as soon as he heard a car, opened the door to greet them.

"Come look." Ava kissed him and rushed inside excitedly.

"What did you find, Ava?" Jack asked softly.

"We think it's Hope's journal." She gave a quick rundown about the box and the key on Emma's bracelet. "It was in Rose's letter. Ian's family held the key to finding his journal."

"And our family held the key to finding Hope's," Jack stated.

"Yes. And just like you opened Ian's, I want you to open Hope's."

Ava handed Jack the book, and Finn was waiting for her. She wrapped her arms around his waist, and he could feel a subtle tremor run through her slender frame. When the pouch was upended and two rings fell onto the table, a tear rolled down her cheek.

"Their wedding rings," Ava murmured.

Finn kissed the top of her head and pressed it tightly against his shoulder.

"There's something written inside." Jack held the tarnished silver up to the light. "But I can't read it."

"Baking soda." Patty plucked the rings out of his hand and took them into the kitchen.

Ava sent him a panicked look, worried what the other woman might do. But when Elsa followed her mother, she relaxed against him.

While the rings were being worked on, Jack opened the book and read, "*Property of Hope Prince.*" Then rapidly flipped through the pages.

Finn frowned, watching the other man's behavior. "What is it, Jack?"

"It's Hope and Ian's story." Jack glanced at Emma and Killian. He closed the book and held it out to them. "Their happily-ever-after was cut short. When are you getting married?"

Killian looked at Emma, and Finn felt Ava tense. "I've been wondering that too, Doc. When are you going to marry me?"

Emma grinned. "I knew there was something I forgot to tell you."

"Well, Doc?" Killian tugged her into his arms. "Give me the date."

"How does Valentine's Day sound?"

As soon as Emma posed the question, Ava grinned and relaxed against him.

"Valentine's Day." Killian cupped Emma's face and kissed her softly. "Perfect."

"It *is* perfect," Jack agreed. "The very day Ian returned his ship to Swan Harbor."

"It's not great." Elsa returned with Patty, carrying the rings. "But read what's written inside."

Jack held the larger ring up to the light. "*The heart wants ... and a date 14/02/1719.*" He then read off the smaller ring. "*... What the heart wants ... and 14/02/1719.*"

"Their wedding day," Ava murmured.

"Emma and Killian bringing it full circle, even if it is over three hundred years later," Finn acknowledged.

"Another new beginning," Ava whispered with a smile.

When everyone descended on Emma and Killian, Finn took Ava's hand and led her across the room. "Tell me, love. Are you still afraid of anything?"

Ava dimpled. "All my fears stemmed from the fear of taking a chance. And since we're married, well ..." She brushed her fingers across his cheek. "You rescued me from that tower, Finn. You helped me believe I was stronger than I thought. You've given me everything I've ever wanted."

"Everything?"

"Yes." She nodded toward the room at large. "We have a home that's filled with hope, family, love ..."

"I love you," he murmured, his lips hovering over hers in anticipation of the next word.

"And kisses," she barely got out, before he melded their lips and settled in for a good long while.

EPILOGUE

Ava's Cottage
Saturday after Thanksgiving
1:00 p.m.

"Are you alright?"

The knocking on the car window penetrated the fog surrounding Aiden. "I'm fine," he opened his door and got out, "I was just ..."

"Thinking?" Captain Jack suggested kindly.

"Daydreaming, my mum would say."

Jack chuckled. "Rose used to say the same thing about me."

As they started up the driveway of Finn and Ava's home, Bandit darted in the opposite direction. Jack stumbled, almost falling, and dropped the box he'd been carrying.

"Jack!" Aiden grabbed the other man's arm. "Are you alright?"

"Damn fool dog," Jack scolded. "Sit."

"I'm sorry, Jack." Aiden tossed the books back into the box. "I should have–"

"Now don't you feel the need to say you're sorry?" Jack grinned. "It wasn't your fault Bandit saw a bird.

"Yes, well," Aiden murmured. "I should have taken the box and ..."

"No harm done." Jack patted his shoulder reassuringly and changed the subject. "Where's that brother of yours?"

"He's off on a story," Aiden explained.

"That sounds exciting." Jack's dark eyes twinkled. "But he's going to miss all the fun."

"Fun?"

"Oh yes," Jack went on. "Christmas in Swan Harbor is a treat. The Christmas Tree Lighting is the first big activity."

Aiden adjusted the box when they stepped onto the porch and knocked on the front door. "I wondered what they were doing in the square. There were several trucks being unloaded the last time I drove by."

"Oh, it's a big deal." Jack laughed. "In fact, last year ..."

His voice faded when the door opened. "Jack, Bandit, and Aiden." Ava smiled. "I'm glad you could make it."

Aiden stepped into the house behind Jack, and when he saw the room was full, started looking for a reason to hide out. Conversation was not his strong suit, especially when Quinn wasn't around to fill in any blank spaces.

"Where can I put these?" Aiden lifted the box of books, noticing the pirate's journal on the top.

"Books?" Ava echoed.

"The ones that belonged to Rose," Jack reminded her. "And Ian and Hope's journals. Emma and Killian should really read them."

Aiden's gaze met Ava's briefly before drifting to the others in the room.

"Aiden, do you know Rachel Adams, Harper Taylor, and her grandmother, Terri Patterson?"

"Ladies." Aiden smiled at the women, recognizing one from the University. "Doctor Taylor, it's nice to see you again."

"Doctor Jones," she murmured, her voice soft and melodious.

"You want the books in the study?" Jack asked Ava, relieving Aiden of the burden of asking again.

"Please."

"Follow me."

Jack took off, leaving Aiden to smile and nod goodbye, as he trailed the other man out of the room and up the stairs.

"Just set the box anywhere," Jack indicated. "Except those journals."

Aiden left the box on the desk and after moving around several books inside, located the journals. "Do you know anything about Ian's time in Swan Harbor?"

Jack glanced up. "I don't. Maybe in the archives. Why?"

Aiden wandered to the window and stared out at the Spanish galleon anchoring one end of the renovated pier in the distance.

"Since discovering there was a pirate in our family," Aiden began, "my sister, Sarah, has become obsessed. And as I'm a researcher, I thought ..."

"You'd research," Jack finished.

Aiden shrugged. "I've been thinking about writing a book and well ..."

He heard Jack cross the room to stand next to him. "I think Ian and Hope have a story that needs to be told.

"Think so? If you were writing it, where would you start?"

Jack sent him a grin. "Where every good romance begins, with the first meet."

"Have you read the journals?" Aiden flipped the book around and turned to the first page.

"I," Jack hesitated several seconds, "looked through a few pages, but then pushed them away."

"But why?" Aiden studied the other man. "You looked for them for years. Why not continue learning everything you can about the man, the woman, and the ship?"

When Jack turned back to face him, he was wearing a contemplative expression. "I don't believe Ian and Hope's story is for me to tell."

"You think it's Killian and Emma's," Aiden repeated what Jack had said on Thanksgiving evening.

"Perhaps." Jack inclined his head. "But this is Swan Harbor, Son. Something tells me, as a Jones, you'll have a part in their story as well."

"Really?" Aiden frowned. "Isn't their story over?"

"Great love stories are never over." Captain Jack winked. "If they were, there would be no happily-ever-after, now would there?"

"Like Rosalind and Orlando, Jane and Rochester, Catherine and Heathcliff, or Elizabeth and Darcy," Aiden rattled off great pairings from the literature he so dearly loved.

A proud smile spread across Jack's face, suggesting his point had gotten across. "Lovers that continue to live between the pages years later. Someday that will be Ian and Hope."

"Except their ending was more Romeo and Juliet," Aiden muttered.

"I prefer to believe they'll be reunited like Vega and Altair," Jack confessed.

"Reunited one day in the stars," Aiden replied, referring to the myth.

"But I'm hopeful they'll be together more than just one day a year." Jack smiled. "And what about you, Aiden? Is there a great love in your life?

... someone who loves me for what I am ...

"Hardly," Aiden scoffed. "Quinn was the one who always had a woman on his arm. I was more comfortable with my books."

"He's a sissy, Miriam," Alistair ranted. "Look at him. Always has his nose in a book."

"Don't you worry about Aiden," Miriam murmured. "He's a sensitive soul, and someday will meet the woman worthy of his heart."

"Your time will come," Jack went on. "You're in Swan Harbor now. Listen to your heart when it speaks. It knows."

While on one hand, as a lover of literature, Aiden could appreciate the idea there was a great love out there for everyone. But one for him, he wasn't sure.

I want someone whose weakness is his greatest strength.

"I think I smelled some of Terri's lemon crinkle cookies when we arrived," Jack broke into Aiden's thoughts. "I believe I'll go help myself."

Aiden watched him go, and while he should follow, the need to stay had him slowly going through the books in the box. *Goodnight Moon, Runaway Bunny,* and several others he'd read as a child. But nothing that pushed him to join the others. Or helped him with his other problem.

He took out his phone, opened the app, and read,

> Dear Clark,
>
> I'm looking for someone, not to follow, but to walk by my side. Someone who can see through walls that aren't impenetrable and leap the ones that are. Someone whose weakness is his greatest strength. And someone who loves me for what I am and not for what he wants me to be.
>
> I've not found him yet and don't have high hopes. But when growing up, I've been told to listen to my heart when it speaks, so I'm still waiting.
>
> Your match,

Rosalind

"Who's Clark and Rosalind?" Liam quipped, peering over his shoulder.

Aiden quickly flipped around, "Bloody hell, Liam."

"Sorry," Liam grinned. "Jack said you were here so ..."

"No, I'm sorry," Aiden apologized. "I shouldn't have raised my voice."

The intense look on Liam's face had Aiden fighting to stand still. "What's going on?"

Aiden blew out a breath, and since Quinn wasn't around, spilled, "Three departments at several Universities have combined their research. They created an app, collected several thousand single names, forced us to fill out a questionnaire, and matched us."

"And you're?"

"Clark," Aiden admitted.

"Clark?"

Aiden shrugged. "We had to come up with a fake name and, well, I've always admired Superman."

"Superman?" Liam laughed. "Why?"

"He was confident in everything he did."

"So, is that your first exchange with this Rosalind?"

"Yes." When Liam said nothing but looked at him expectantly, Aiden added, "Every month, they've shuffled the algorithms and Rosalind is my newest match. We correspond for a month, and if we think we might want to '*meet*,' we set a time and place for New Year's Eve."

"So, write her back." Liam shrugged as if it were no big deal.

"Easier said than done."

"Well, it's a good thing I'm here then." The intense look on Liam's face had Aiden backing up a step. "I'm quite good at matchmaking."

"Do I want to know the reason you believe this to be true?" Aiden studied his newly found cousin.

"Look at Ava and Finn."

"You," Aiden questioned, "paired Ava and Finn?"

"I gave them a little push."

He wasn't sure if he believed the words coming from Liam's mouth, but he could admit the other man was always comfortable in the company of others. "Alright," he opened the app, "tell me what to say."

"Listen to me, Cuz," Liam rubbed his hands together with glee, "I'll help you."

"Well, at least you didn't tell me to listen to my heart," Aiden muttered.

"Well, that's a given," Liam replied. "You're in Swan Harbor, after all."

Briefly, Aiden wondered what he was getting himself into, but he guessed he was alright listening to Liam. It was the idea of his heart speaking that had him rolling his eyes as he watched his cousin type.

Dear Rosalind ....

❧

*In **A Tree, Mistletoe & A Sunset,** Aiden's and Harper's romance is sweet and romantic. Now, the mystery - let's just say it's unique.*

❧

Quick Author's Note:

I hope you enjoyed Finn's and Ava's story and learning more about the hope story. Did anything in the book surprise you—Ava's family, the connected mysteries, or anything about the hope story?

As of May 2025, I've written 25 books, and Finn remains one of my most stubborn male characters, but one of my favorite. As an aside, Kisses, Family & Love won 2nd place in the Palm Beach Literary contest in 2021.

Ava and Finn continue to show up through the Hope & Heart few books. There's also a *gift* she orders for him from the *Rebecca's Fantasy* catalog. It has its own story.

Ava's and Finn's song is Michael Bublé's Hold On. Here's the link.

Swan Harbor's Hope Playlist.

https://sophiebartow.com/swan-harbors-hope-story-playlist/

Moving Right Along:

If you enjoyed reading *Kisses, Family & Hope* and would like another scene, sign up for my newsletter. I send my newsletters on the 5th, 15th, and 25th of each month and include tidbits. Book sales, giveaways, teasers, new releases, and early releases. I've even been known to toss in one or two of my favorite recipes or a picture of my cat or dog.

It's Ava & Finn's honeymoon, and he aims to be Ava's Flynn Ryder. There's also a piece of surprising news shared. Just click on the title to receive the link.

Ava's Flynn Ryder.
https://www.subscribepage.com/swan-harbor_bonus_scenes

Thanks for hanging with me this long.
Until next time,
Sophie
P.S.
In Book 5, **A Tree, Mistletoe & A Sunset**, Aiden Jones, Killian and Liam's cousin, is involved in a research project. Harper Taylor, one of the many Pattersons, has returned to Swan Harbor with a broken heart. You learn more about the hope story, and the mystery is totally unlike any of my other books. Get ready for a laugh.

A Tree, Mistletoe & A Sunset
https://books2read.com/ATreeMistletoeSunset

A TREE, MISTLETOE & A SUNSET BLURB
SWAN HARBOR HOPE STORY BOOK 4

Mystery
Mistletoe
One Perfect Match

Harper Taylor didn't expect to return to Swan Harbor with a bruised heart —or find herself dodging gossip and fending off holiday matchmaking. Teaching helps her regain her footing, yet it's the quiet English professor with the knowing smile and kind eyes who makes her feel again. Between her grandmother's antics, and a secret match program that's gone off-script, Harper begins to wonder if fate—and maybe Swan Harbor—had a plan all along.

Aiden Jones came to Swan Harbor looking for peace and a fresh start. He didn't expect to be manning a bra-claiming station under a Christmas tree, or fake-dating his brilliant and beautiful colleague to avoid a holiday disaster. When he begins looking for reasons to spend time with Harper Taylor—smart, strong, and a little bit scarred, things get real. He's not used to being the hero in anyone's story. But when holiday mayhem stirs up more than just town gossip, Aiden discovers he's exactly where he's meant to be.

Welcome to Swan Harbor, where the Christmas lights sparkle, the bras fly, and no one's secrets are safe for long. This year, the town square's tree lighting delivers more than cheer—leading to a mystery no one can quite solve. As Harper, Aiden, and their friends navigate tangled emotions, secret identities, and a few misplaced undergarments, the magic of the season proves that sometimes, the best love stories begin with a little mischief and a lot of heart.

This holiday season, the hearts are warm, the bras are missing, and love might just be in the air.

Read an excerpt, watch the trailer, then download a copy of
A Tree, Mistletoe & A Sunset
https://sophiebartow.com/book/a-tree-mistletoe-a-sunset/

Mystical Waters Canyon
Where hearts can be heard.

WHISPERS OF LUCK

WHISPERS OF THE PAST

October 31, 2025

WHISPERS OF A MIRACLE

December 2025

WHISPERS OF LOVE

February 2026

Hope & Hearts Series
Without hope, there would be no happy endings.

FROM DARKNESS INTO LOVE

KITTENS, PUPPIES & LOVE

BROTHERS, HOPE & HEARTS

KISSES, FAMILY & HOPE

A TREE, MISTLETOE & A SUNSET

HOPE, HEARTS & FOREVER

THE MEMORY OF LOVE

THE INNOCENCE OF LOVE

THE FORGIVENESS OF LOVE

THE POWER OF LOVE

THE CHRISTMAS LOVE SONG

THE KISS OF LOVE

THE LESSONS OF LOVE

THE HEART OF LOVE

THE JOURNEY TO LOVE

Bonus Hope & Hearts

CYGNETS & DREAMS

Hope & Hearts Historical Novellas

GUIDED BY LIGHT - 1952

GUIDED BY HEART - 1964

GUIDED BY LOVE - 1969

WELCOME TO SWAN HARBOR- 1979

FINDING HER LOST HEART- 1983/1990

GUIDED BY A KISS - 1995

ABOUT THE AUTHOR

Sophie crafts small-town mystery romances that weave intricate plots with richly developed characters. Her female leads are intelligent, resourceful, and resilient, while her male characters, often stubborn, exude sexiness, wit, and a protective nature. She delights in building slow-burn romances, savoring the tension and delaying that first kiss for as long as possible. No matter the trope, every story she writes has a happy ending.

After a fulfilling 30-plus-year career as a speech-language pathologist, working with adult post-stroke and Parkinson's patients, she is enjoying her new journey. With their four children spread out, Sophie and her husband live in South Florida. They share their home with a pampered cat named Irma.

You can find her on her website: **https://sophiebartow.com/**   *Sophiexo*

facebook.com/SmallTownAuthorSophieBartow

x.com/SophieBartow

instagram.com/sophiebartow

goodreads.com/sophiebartow

bookbub.com/profile/sophie-bartow

pinterest.com/SophieBartow